W9-DDS-572

He'd always been an upbeat, positive, cheerful guy. But that fall Sonny Leland was happier than he could ever remember. He and Dawn went to all the second-run movies at the dollar theater. They shouted and cheered together at basketball games. They visited museums and hiked in the mountains. Sonny was in love, crazy, desperately, mindlessly in love. Classes, work, even the meetings at the frat house were annoying roadblocks on his way to the pizza joint and the woman he loved.

What was even more amazing was that Dawn loved him, too.

She'd told him so. Though he would have known anyway. Her eyes lit up when he walked in. She spent every waking moment in his company when she wasn't working. She didn't give even the most cursory notice to other guys who came her way. And when he held her in his arms, they just fit perfectly. Their love was their favorite subject of conversation.

*Also by PAMELA MORSI*

SUBURBAN RENEWAL
LETTING GO
DOING GOOD

*Watch for Pamela Morsi's next novel*
*Available from MIRA Books*
*Spring 2006*

# PAMELA MORSI
## By Summer's End

MIRA®

If you purchased this book without a cover you should be aware
that this book is stolen property. It was reported as "unsold and
destroyed" to the publisher, and neither the author nor the
publisher has received any payment for this "stripped book."

MIRA®

RECYCLED PAPER · RECYCLED PAPER

ISBN 0-7783-2139-8

BY SUMMER'S END

Copyright © 2005 by Pamela Morsi.

All rights reserved. Except for use in any review, the reproduction or
utilization of this work in whole or in part in any form by any electronic,
mechanical or other means, now known or hereafter invented, including
xerography, photocopying and recording, or in any information storage or
retrieval system, is forbidden without the written permission of the publisher,
MIRA Books, 225 Duncan Mill Road, Don Mills, Ontario, Canada M3B 3K9.

All characters in this book have no existence outside the imagination of the
author and have no relation whatsoever to anyone bearing the same name
or names. They are not even distantly inspired by any individual known or
unknown to the author, and all incidents are pure invention.

MIRA and the Star Colophon are trademarks used under license and registered
in Australia, New Zealand, Philippines, United States Patent and Trademark
Office and in other countries.

www.MIRABooks.com

Printed in U.S.A.

For Sydnee Doherty,
who handed me my family history,
and showed me the city of Knoxville.

# REAL LIFE
## 1

—▶ ◀—

It began like all our moves began. There was nothing about it that stood out as unusual. I came home from school one afternoon in early May to find Mom packing our things into brown cardboard boxes.

"Sonny has left us."

Mom paused dramatically as if in anticipation of an outburst of screams, tears or grief. I glanced toward my sister. Sierra wasn't surprised, either. Based on our life so far, the world was populated by guys named Sonny. They always left. And they never left her, they left *us*.

"We can't move yet!" I complained. "There's only two weeks until the end of school!"

Mom shrugged, unconcerned. "Then you're mostly done with it. Leaving a little early won't matter."

My mother's convictions about my education centered mostly on the belief that for her girls, it didn't really matter. Sierra was so pretty, her future was set whether she memorized the dates of the American Revolution or not. And Mom seemed pretty certain that whatever my ambitions might be, I was likely to achieve them without any information that I might pick up in public school. Mom said I was the brains of the family. I wasn't really qualified, but somebody had to take up the job. Neither Mom nor Sierra was up to it.

"The rent's a week past due," Mom told us. "If we can get packed up and out of here before morning, it'll save us some bucks as well as a nasty, unpleasant encounter with the landlord."

I wanted to scream, but I just complained under my breath.

"I wish that just once, *just once*, I could finish something, do what I said I was going to do, leave a town with time to say goodbye."

My ravings were ignored. My mother and sister were positively Newtonian. When in motion they would remain in motion unless acted upon by an outside source.

I tried to take on that role.

"What about your job, Mom?" I asked her.

Mom pulled her long, heavily permed and artificially colored auburn hair up off the back of her neck and secured it there with a giant silver plastic clasp. Typically, she was dressed in skintight Daisy Duke shorts and a halter top. Bulging up from the top of Mom's cleavage, I could see the familiar tattoo on her right breast. It was a heart-shaped vine of yellow roses, in the center were the words *Always Sonny*.

She shrugged. "They sell drinks everywhere," she answered.

That was true. In my life so far, we'd already lived everywhere and Mom always had a job. She was a cocktail waitress, a good one. And being pretty didn't hurt. Mom had nice features, big blue eyes and a great figure. She loved makeup and used a lot. She was like somebody you could see in a movie. Not like the lead actress or anything, but one of the other characters. The ones that don't have names, only descriptions. Mom would have been Redneck Girlfriend or Slutty Hairdresser. She had those kind of looks.

"Please Mom, let's not go!"

She gave me a little smile and a wink, but I knew it was useless.

Sierra was already packing. "Let's head for Los Angeles," she said. "It doesn't get so dang hot out there. I don't think I could stand another summer in Texas."

"I hate L.A.," I told her. "The schools are awful and we always end up in a broken-down car stuck on some freeway."

Sierra shrugged. "Okay, well then, Vegas," she said. "Let's go to Vegas, Mom. I'm almost fifteen. I could lie about it and maybe get a job in a casino or something."

Mom gave Sierra a look of disapproval. "We're not going to Vegas," she said, adamantly. "And you're not working in a casino, ever. I want more for my girls than that."

One thing I never doubted about Mom. She loved us and she always tried to do what she thought was best. I guess I did sometimes think that her definition of *best* was questionable.

I pulled a garbage bag from the box and began to stash my things in it. Fortunately, or unfortunately, I didn't have a lot of stuff. When you move a lot, you leave things behind. Sometimes, when we were in a big hurry, we'd leave everything behind. I didn't mind too much. I thought of my lost possessions as something like Hansel and Gretel's crumbs in the forest, somehow, someday, all those lost things left behind would help me find my way back.

Back. Back to where it all began.

Well, maybe not to where it began. I can't really go back to where it began. Because it didn't begin with me. But *I* began thirteen years ago. My name is Dakota Leland. I'm the youngest daughter of Sonny and Dawn Leland. Of course, Sonny was not my dad's real name. Nobody's real name is Sonny. My dad's real name was Vernon Henry Leland, Jr. Pretty awful, huh? I guess that's why he was called Sonny.

Mom fell in love with him when she was very young. She got pregnant with Sierra when she was seventeen and they wanted to get married. It was all very romantic. Of course, his family didn't approve. So they ran off and rented a mobile home. I like to think that Romeo and Juliet, if they'd been older and smarter, might have done the same.

Sierra says that she remembers our daddy. But, of course, I know she doesn't. She's only twenty months older than me and it's a fact, literally written in stone—a headstone—that Vernon Henry Leland, Jr. died three weeks before I was born.

Nobody can remember somebody they knew before they were two. But I don't point that out to Sierra. She wants to believe that she remembers Daddy, so I let her.

It's an honest mistake, I think. There've been so many guys in Mom's life named Sonny. It must be pathological. Nobody could just, at random, fall for that many guys with the same non-name. But whatever, they sort of just blend together.

The first one I remember was Sonny Bridges. He

used to let me ride on his motorcycle. His real name was Daryl. There was Sonny Spivak. He could never remember our names and always called us "Kid." Sonny Wendt liked to cook. Sonny Cimino was Italian. Those were the ones I'd liked. There were others. Some forgettable, just around for a few days. Others were unforgettable. There was one guy who kept looking at Sierra. She told Mom that it gave her the creeps. We left town the next day. And there was one who gave Mom a black eye. She got him back good. When he fell asleep she handcuffed him to the bed. Then she woke him up by hitting him in the crotch with a yellow plastic baseball bat. Boy, did that guy holler. That was in Florida. Mom said to remind her never to go back to Florida. We left my baseball bat there, but that was okay. I didn't really want it anymore.

This last guy was Sonny Moroney. He was okay. But it wasn't like I would miss him.

"If we're not going to L.A. or Vegas, where are we going?" Sierra asked as we loaded everything into the rusting Dodge that Mom managed to keep running year after year.

"Don't worry," she said. "But it'll be nice."

She always thought it would be nice.

"I hope our next place has like a swimming pool," Sierra said. "I mean, wouldn't that be great. I could work on my tan. I need a new bikini. I saw one in Target. It's like perfect. They'll have the same suits in all the Target stores, won't they? I'm sure they will."

She continued to chatter. Neither me nor Mom responded or encouraged her. Mom's thoughts were elsewhere. And I was too upset about moving to waste any thoughts on swimming pools or bathing suits.

We swung by the library so that I could return my books. I didn't feel too bad about giving up the three I hadn't read. But the one that I was right in the middle of, sheesh, I really hated to let it go. It was titled *Understanding Chaos: An Introduction to Non-Linear Physics*. Although I was a total science geek, physics wasn't typically a middle school subject. But the idea of understanding chaos, that really appealed to me. My life seemed to be mostly chaos and it would have been great to understand it.

I could have dropped them in the night return box outside, but instead, I left Mom and Sierra in the car and I raced in to the main desk. There was only one guy behind the counter and I didn't recognize him. I pulled my library card out of my wallet.

"I need to turn this in. I'm leaving town," I told him.

The guy shrugged. "You can just keep it, you might be back," he said.

"No," I told him. "I want to turn it in. I won't be coming back and I want to turn it in."

I set the card on the counter and pushed it toward him, my fingers still on it. He reached for the card and for a moment we were both touching it as I hesitated to let it go. Then the moment was over. I released my connection and stepped back, folding my arms across my chest as if I were cold or maybe just to make sure my heart stayed inside me.

"Goodbye," I told the anonymous library clerk.

"Goodbye," he answered.

# REAL LIFE
## 2

—◆—

That night, Mom headed east on Interstate 30 as if she were being chased by state troopers. Fortunately, we were not.

When she had to buy gas, she went into the convenience store and got a giant cup of black coffee for herself as well as a huge sack of popcorn, some donuts, cupcakes, chips and a twelve pack of cold colas. She bought a couple of dozen candy bars. Chocolate had become Mom's obsession the last few months. It was practically the only thing she would eat. Sierra called it her Amazing Chocolate Diet, because she'd dropped maybe ten pounds eating that way.

It didn't work for me. My jeans were getting too tight in the thighs and my face kept breaking out.

Mom set the cruise control on about ninety. Her Toby Keith CD was blaring on the stereo. And she kept the window down as she chain-smoked.

I was seated in the back for the first part of the trip, clinging to my seat belt shoulder harness as if it were a lifeline.

Sierra always wanted to sit with Mom. She sang along with the music for a while. She read roadside signs. She chattered on endlessly about mostly nothing. Sierra was just exactly the kind of daughter that a mom would want on a car trip. She was easygoing, delightful and pleasant. That was the surprising thing about my sister. It was hard not to like her. And believe me, I tried.

Sierra was the pretty one. I guess among all sisters, one gets that designation. For Sierra it was hands down. No competition. She was blond, blue-eyed, perfect teeth, tall, long-legged and slim. Now, at fifteen, she had gotten boobs and a booty. She was like totally a *Betty*, as in Betty Rubble. My cartoon equivalent was definitely Olive Oyl.

Eventually, as the night wore on, Sierra got tired and wanted to trade places so she could sleep. That was okay with me. There was no way that I could sleep. As Mom zoomed through the night passing eighteen-wheelers trucking at top speed as if they were standing still, I watched the white lines on the roadway and braced myself for the inevitable crash and death.

The only time I could relax was when we stopped for frequent bathroom breaks. Sierra woke up for some of those; others she didn't. I was glad to just get out of the car and stand on the ground for a few minutes, grateful not to be moving.

"I'm glad we can stop whenever we want," I said to Mom when she stopped to let me go to the bathroom at a rest area just outside of Little Rock. "When it's just us girls, we can do just what we want."

Mom nodded. She knew what I meant. When we went somewhere with Sonny—whichever Sonny—stopping was always a negotiated agreement.

"Do you know why men are like horoscopes?" she asked me.

I rolled my eyes. Mom loved men jokes.

"Why?" I responded.

"Because they always tell you what to do and they're almost always wrong."

Mom laughed a little. I shook my head. I didn't think it was all that funny. Sierra would have appreciated it. Those two could swap testosterone ticklers for hours. But Sierra was asleep, so the humor was wasted on me.

We were back to driving then, silently together for a long time. I was watching the road, and Mom seemed lost in thought.

"Is your sister asleep?" Mom asked, startling me. She was glancing in the rearview mirror as if to see for herself.

I turned and looked.

"Yeah, she's snoozing away," I answered, a little bit jealous.

Mom nodded and then a couple of minutes later asked, "How much do you actually know about Sonny?"

I was stuck for a moment. The guy was not really a standout. He drank a lot of beer. He watched a lot of ball games. He liked to slap Mom on the rear and call her "woman" instead of her name. All her boyfriends were like that.

"Well," I began as I fumbled for something unique. "He loved reruns of *Walker, Texas Ranger.*"

Mom glanced at me, shocked for a moment and then she laughed and shook her head. "Not him," she said. "I was asking about your father. What have I told you about Sonny Leland?"

"Oh, him," I said and then thought for a moment.

"You said that he was a really nice guy. Smart, good-looking. And that he died in an accident at work. A tree fell on him or something."

Mom nodded, but she didn't look at me, she was staring straight ahead. I could see her profile in the dim blue light of the dashboard. She took a deep drag on her cigarette and then blew it out in the direction of the open window.

"What did he look like?" I asked her.

She thought about that for a moment. "He was tall," she said. "Six foot two and muscles. Dreamy, I would have said at the time. Sandy-blond hair, bright brown eyes that seemed able to see anything and he was always smiling." She glanced over at me. "He looked a lot like my Dakota."

"Like me? I thought you said he was good-looking."

"He was," Mom insisted. "And you are, too."

I shrugged that off as motherly prejudice.

"Did I tell you that he was the first person who ever loved me?" Mom asked.

"Yes."

Mom hadn't been loved a lot.

"Sonny Leland was the best thing that ever happened to me," she said. "He loved me effortlessly and unconditionally. It must have been the way that he'd been loved. It just came natural to him. It was so healing for me."

I had no comment. What could a kid say to that? *Way cool.* Or maybe, *Gee tough luck, him dying and all.*

"I'm sorry I didn't get to know him, Mom," I said, finally.

"Yeah, me, too," she answered.

Nothing more was said.

As we sped on into the night I began, for the very first time, to really think about Sonny Leland. I began to imagine what my life might have been like if he had lived. It had been just one tree after all. One tree in a forest of trees. What if it hadn't been chosen for cutting that day? Or they had chosen to cut it earlier or later. What if the wind had been blowing in another direction? Or the wind had not been blowing at all. It might have rained that day. He could have been late to work. Or he could have had a cold and stayed home altogether. It wouldn't have taken much to change everything. Sonny Leland might have lived. And my life would have been so different.

# SONNY DAYS
## 3

— ◀ —

Cumberland Street was near enough to campus for students to walk to and far enough away that they thought nothing that happened there would ever catch up with them.

Sonny Leland was sitting in a corner booth at Proletariat Pizza. He was drinking a beer and conversing with three of his fraternity brothers. Topics for discussion ranged from the Iran-Contra scandal to plate tectonics, the Vols current football season to Professor Dietrich's chemistry exam. And ultimately to the very attractive waitress who was serving them.

"She looks like cheerleader material to me," geeky Brian Posner said. Cheerleaders were far out of his league.

"Not a chance," Kerry Denning disagreed. "She's not athletic enough. Those are jiggle boobs. Cheerleaders carry pom-poms for a reason. She's way too curvy to pull it off."

"I wish she would pull it off," Larry Gilbert said with a guffaw. "That would really make this Friday night worth it."

There was laughter all around. But Sonny's was a mere chuckle. The bleached blonde with the big hair and broad smile had really captured his attention. He could hardly take his eyes off her.

For that reason it was especially annoying when a couple of tables over the skinny brunette waitress with stooped shoulders and a tired expression began being harassed by a couple of half-drunk jerks.

Sonny attempted to ignore their loud, unkind remarks and the blanched expression on the tired young woman's face. He hoped the waitress would just walk away and the idiots would pick up some other game. But when she tried, one of them reached out and grabbed her. He tried to pull her onto his lap, all the time complaining about her "bony ass."

With a sigh, Sonny slid out of the seat.

"Oh, geez, Sonny," Larry complained. "Let it go, it's not your fight."

"Save your breath," Kerry said. "You know it's wasted. Besides, what else do we have to do on a dateless Friday night?"

Kerry slid out beside him as Sonny approached the table.

"Cut it out guys," he said. "Leave her alone."

The short fellow was so surprised at the intervention that he let the girl go and she immediately hurried away.

His smart-mouth buddy across the table turned Sonny's words into his own joke. "I think that's why she's all shriveled up like that," he said. "I think guys have been leaving her alone for a lifetime."

The three drunken jerks snorted with laughter.

Sonny grabbed the biggest one by the collar and hoisted him outside. Kerry, Brian and Larry marched the other two right behind them. It wasn't much of a fight, really. Just a lot of pushing and cursing. The big guy threw a couple of punches at Sonny. He easily managed to deflect them and didn't even bother to hit back. Within five minutes it was over and the jerks were headed on down the street, screaming epithets in their wake.

The frat brothers congratulated each other with slaps on the back and they returned to their pizza. Both the skinny brunette and the luscious blonde were waiting.

The brunette was starry-eyed, ecstatic.

"Thank you so much," she said. "I don't know what the deal was with them. One of those guys is in my World History class. He's never even spoken to me before. I don't know why he decided to tonight, and why he had to be so mean."

Sonny shrugged. "Beer and Friday night. It makes guys do strange things."

She nodded. "I'm Sheila," she said, offering her hand. "I am so grateful for your help."

He shook it. "It was no big deal," he assured her. "We needed the exercise, right guys?"

There was a murmur of agreement behind him.

Sonny let his gaze wander to the other waitress, the one who'd so captured his attention. He'd hoped to see the same adoration that shone in Sheila's eyes. He was doomed to disappointment. She was very matter-of-fact.

"The good news," the blonde said. "The dickheads are gone. The bad news, they got out of here without paying the check."

Sonny immediately pulled out his wallet, though his conscience pricked him. He'd just cashed his

work-study paycheck. That was his pocket money for
the next month. His parents were comfortably middle-class. His dad was a physics professor. But college
was expensive for anyone and Sonny took some
pride in holding down his fifteen-hour-a-week lab assistant job. Paying for the jerks, plus his share of his
own table, would put a real dent in his back pocket.

Still he handed the money to the pretty girl and
she smiled at him. Money couldn't buy a smile like
that.

"So, Sheila," he said to the brunette as the blonde
carried his cash to the register. "What's your
friend's name?"

For an instant the brunette looked crestfallen, but
she recovered quickly.

"Her name's Dawn," she said. "Lots of guys try to
hit on her. She flirts with them all, but when it comes
to leaving here with somebody she's very particular."

Sonny took that piece of information in and ex-
amined it carefully.

"Do you think she might get particular about me?"

Sheila shrugged. "She might."

In fact, she did.

Sonny sent his frat brothers on to pub crawl the
rest of the street. He hung around the restaurant
until closing, hoping. He sat at the counter now. She
mostly ignored him. He didn't try to distract her or
cheat her boss from any time. But he just stayed
there, drinking, though he'd switched to limeade.
And when she came to wipe down the counter in
front of him, which seemed fairly often for a surface
that was completely clean, he talked to her.

"So what's your sign?" Sonny asked.

She looked at him like he was an idiot.

"Wait, wait," he said, laughing. "I take that question back. What's your favorite flower?"

That made her pause.

"My favorite flower?"

He nodded. "Everybody's got a favorite flower."

She shook her head. "I don't know," she said. "Truth is, I don't get a lot of flowers."

"Well, you might if you came up with a favorite."

"Okay," she said. "How about yellow roses."

"Ahh," Sonny said. "That's a good choice. A very good choice. A truly thoughtless answer would have been red roses or white roses. Everybody likes those. And if you picked like orchids or hyacinth it would put you out of the mainstream too far, and I wouldn't know what it meant. But yellow roses, that works."

She shook her head and walked away.

The next time she was in speaking range he tried to get more information.

"This question's multiple choice," he said.

"Multiple choice?"

"Hey, it's what we're both trained for, right?"

She didn't respond.

"Okay, which would you most prefer for a first date?" he said.

"What first date?" she asked.

"I'm not being presumptuous," he assured her. "Just posing a question. First date A, a movie, not *Full Metal Jacket,* but maybe *Moonstruck.* B, picnicking, in the mountains. Maybe we could hike up to Sharp's Ridge, a jug of wine and loaf of bread and thou. Or C, a fancy dress-up thing, maybe a Sweetheart Dance or a symphony gala."

She looked thoughtful and at the same time wary as she continued to wipe down the same spot in a circular motion in front of her.

"I guess the picnic," she said, finally. "But I like movies a lot, too."

"Whew, that's a relief," he teased. "You just saved me a tux rental."

She laughed. Sonny loved the way she laughed.

At 1:00 a.m. he was standing by the back door when she left work.

"Do you have your own car or may I walk you home?" he asked.

She hesitated.

"You don't have to walk me."

"I know I don't have to," he told her. "I want to. I hope you're not afraid of me. I know you don't know me, but I can be trusted not to try to make some move on you or something. I really just want to walk with you, talk with you."

She continued to hesitate.

"Really, it's not far," she said.

"You live off campus?" he asked, surprised.

"No, no," she insisted quickly. "I live... I live in one of the dorms. One of the close ones."

Sonny smiled at her. "I'm a Residence Hall rowdy myself. I hope to move into the frat house next year, but I'm still caught in that 'living on campus' policy. What about you? Are you a freshman, too?"

"Uh... maybe," she said. "Maybe I'm a freshman or maybe not."

Sonny raised his eyebrows.

"A woman of mystery," he said. "You must know us guys can't resist romantic intrigue."

She laughed.

They walked up Cumberland. Knoxville's busy student strip had grown mostly quiet, except for the occasional clanging of garbage cans and one lone intoxicated student singing "Born to Boogie" at the top of his lungs.

As the two conversed, Sonny couldn't decide if Dawn was outgoing or shy. While she talked and laughed and flirted with him outrageously, she revealed almost nothing about herself, her life. Even the most innocuous questions, what classes are you in? what's your major? where's your hometown? were deflected and unanswered. She wasn't even being up front about where they were headed, but she led him across the footbridge and came to a stop in front of Strong Hall.

"Is this where you live?"

She shrugged. "It might be," she said. "Or I might just be going in the front door and out the back."

Sonny laughed and shook his head. "Does this mean you're not giving me your phone number?"

"Guess so," she answered.

"So you're just not interested, huh?" he said with a sigh. "I really gave it my best shot, I thought."

Surprisingly Dawn leaned forward and planted a friendly kiss on his cheek. "I like you," she admitted. "But I'm sure you can understand my problem here. I see this heroic cool guy, he's tall, has sandy hair, beautiful eyes, quirky grin, great pecs and I say to myself, 'this guy is way too good-looking to be trusted with my fragile heart.'"

"You can trust me," he assured her.

She shook her head. "I've heard that line before."

"So you're not even going to give me a chance?"

"Better not," she said.

Sonny shrugged, fatalistically. "You're going to miss out on a great guy," he warned her.

She smiled at him and turned to go. Then inexplicably she hesitated.

"I've got the day off tomorrow," she said. "Meet me in front of the pizza place at say eleven, and we could do that picnic. If you don't show up, well, it's probably for the best."

Sonny did show up, with a backpack of bread and wine and cheese and an armful of yellow roses.

# REAL LIFE
## 4

◄━━━━◄━━━━

"You're snoring!" Sierra said, shaking me awake.

For a moment I was kind of lost, then I realized that I was still in the front seat of the Dodge, except now it was morning. Despite my nervousness at Mom's driving, exhaustion must have gotten to me. I woke to find Mom pulling off the interstate into some sort of anonymous downtown city.

"I want to trade seats with Dakota," she said to Mom.

"Later," she responded a little too abruptly.

"Where are we?" I asked.

"Knoxville," Mom answered quietly.

A sort of warning flag went off in my brain somewhere. There was something about Knoxville… Sierra's chattering kept me from pursuing it.

"We drove through Nashville two hours ago," she said. "I tried to get Mom to stop. I told her I could get a job in a music studio or something. Wouldn't that be totally cool? I'd like meet all the musicians. Maybe I could be like the person who tells them what clothes are cool and what's not."

Mom ignored Sierra. She was ignoring us both. She was tired, tired and quiet. But I knew for sure now that she had not been rushing aimlessly down the road. It was morning and she knew where she was going and nothing or no one was going to dissuade her from the direction she'd chosen.

"Knoxville?" I asked her. "Didn't you used to live in Knoxville?"

"Don't talk to me right now, I'm looking for an address."

I kept quiet and glanced back at Sierra. She looked curious, but she had none of the sense of dread and foreboding that I felt. Mom never retraced her steps. She never went back to places we'd been. And I was certain that she'd never intended to return to this place.

We drove through the neat manicured streets. She pulled over finally in front of an ordinary-looking older home. It sat on a rise above the sidewalk. Three steps up to the long walkway, then four more to the front porch. The house was a mix of brick and wood, painted different shades of green, which made the shrubs and bushes around it blend together. It felt as if the house had been there forever, grown up from the soil as naturally as the grass and trees surrounding it.

"Okay," Mom said, taking a deep breath. "What time is it anyway?"

"It's almost nine," I said.

"Pretty early, I guess," she responded. "Old people get up early."

"Who lives here?" Sierra asked from the back seat.

"Some people I used to know," Mom answered. She was deliberately vague. And she was nervous. Mom was never nervous. She checked her makeup in the rearview mirror. I looked at her face, as well. She looked tense and pale and frightened. I suddenly felt exactly the same.

"Sierra, get me a T-shirt out of that green bag," she said.

My sister unzipped the suitcase and rummaged around for a minute.

"That one's fine."

Mom pulled the one she was wearing over her head and tossed it in the back seat. The replacement was pale pink and not nearly as pretty, but it did cover her chest, completely hiding the heart of roses tattoo.

She added a smear of lipstick and then smiled at the mirror as if she needed practice.

"You girls just stay here in the car," she told us, then reaching into the back seat she squeezed Sierra's hand. "Wish me luck."

"Good luck, Mom," my sister responded.

I rolled my eyes. "Good luck with what?"

Mom didn't answer. She got out of the car, walked around the front and headed up the steps toward the house.

"Good luck with what?" I repeated the question to Sierra.

She shrugged.

I turned my attention back to Mom and the house. She was standing on the porch, waiting for somebody to answer the bell.

"Who lives here?" I asked aloud.

"Probably some club owner," Sierra answered. "Mom's first priority when we hit a new town is getting a job."

"But this is not a new town," I told her. "This is where Mom lived as a teenager. This is where she met our dad. She always said she hated this town and all the people in it. She calls them Knox Villains."

Sierra glanced up from her magazine for the first time.

"Oh yeah, right," she said, finally as curious as me.

Up on the porch, the front door had opened. Mom was talking to somebody. I leaned forward in my seat to try to see through the screen. It was impossible. It did seem like Mom was on the porch for a long time. Finally she was invited inside.

"I wonder if this is one of the houses she lived in," Sierra said. "It's a pretty cool neighborhood."

I shook my head. "No, Mom never lived here," I said with certainty.

From everything I knew about her, Mom's life in Tennessee had been a long string of bad breaks and tough times. For the first few years her alcoholic mother had passed her around from one unwilling relative to another. Great-aunts, cousins, distant whatevers twice removed. Anyone who could be pressed upon to take her had her dumped on the doorstep. At age ten she officially became a ward of Knox County. She lived in a series of foster homes and after some runaway incidents spent time in a detention center. From the stories she'd told, the places she mentioned, the kind of people she'd met, there was no question in my mind that she had never lived here. This place felt safe, secure. There was nothing like that in Mom's history.

"I'm ready to sit in the front," Sierra told me. "You know the back seat makes me car sick."

I turned to look at my sister and rolled my eyes. "You can't get car sick when we're parked," I told her, but opened my door anyway. It wasn't worth fighting over.

I stood by the car as Sierra gathered up her magazines and her makeup bag, her collection of Beanie Babies and her shoes. All had to be transferred to the front seat with her.

A movement down the sidewalk caught my attention. Some old guy with a little dog was walking in our direction. I always liked dogs. I always wished I had one, but Mom could never see us taking care of an animal. We moved around too much and she "had enough stuff to be responsible for."

The dog had longish hair, a terrier of some sort, I guess. His coat was all silver with age, but he was happy, perky. His face gave the impression that he was smiling. Of course, maybe it was just that his mouth was open and his tongue hanging out. The leash he was attached to seemed less like a restriction than a costume. He was leading the man. And letting the man believe that he was in control.

I smiled and as the dog got closer he hurried over to me, politely sniffing at my sandals.

"Cute puppy," I told the old guy.

He glanced up, surprised. He'd been lost in thought.

"He's no puppy, young lady," he told me. "This dog is almost fourteen."

I bent down to pet him.

"Be careful not to scratch him," the man said. "He's got a skin condition that makes him very vulnerable to rashes and infections."

I nodded and was careful just to pat.

"I wouldn't hurt you," I promised the dog. "What's his name?"

"Rocky," the man replied.

I nodded. "Like Balboa? He's a fighter, huh?"

"No, I think he was named for the mountains."

"Well, he's really cute," Sierra said, now standing beside me.

"Thank you," the man replied, but when he glanced at Sierra, his smile wavered.

He was looking at her and his jaw dropped open. Now I admit, my sister's had plenty of guys react that way. But there was something different about this old guy. Something that felt really strange.

"Excuse me," he said abruptly and turned away.

He was headed up the steps toward the house when he stopped and turned to look at us again. Slowly, as if every step were dangerous, he came back toward us. When he was standing two feet away he kept shifting his gaze from me to Sierra. Finally he spoke.

"Are you Sonny's girls?" he asked.

It was like the hairs stood up on the back of my neck. Or like the reruns for *Lost in Space—Danger! Will Robinson!* What if he was talking about one of the bad Sonnys? The one who leered at Sierra or just one that was pissed off when Mom left.

Sierra apparently suffered none of these fears.

"Yeah, we're Sonny's girls," she told him. "I'm Sierra and this is Dakota."

He just kept looking at us, his expression changed from question to amazement.

"How… Why…" He shook his head. "Where's Dawn?"

"She went into that house," Sierra told him.

He glanced at the front door and then back at us.

"Ahh…well…come in, come on in," he said. "Rocky, make some room for the girls to walk."

Mom told us to wait in the car, but Sierra was following the guy and the dog, like he was the Pied Piper or something. I couldn't just hang back by myself.

We walked up the sidewalk steps and past the carefully trimmed lawn and the neatly cared for beds of bright blooming flowers.

Without knocking, the man pulled open the screen and unlocked the front door. He bent down to unleash the dog. It hurried inside. Smiling, he stood once more, holding the door open to allow us to go in first. I followed Sierra.

The small tiled entryway was artificially cool, a bit dark and separated from the other rooms, but I could hear Mom's voice through the open doorway.

"Mrs. Leland, please," she said. "I'm begging you. That's what you've always wanted, isn't it? To have me beg. Well, now I am. I'm sick and scared and at the end of my rope. I'm begging for the sake of my children."

Uncertainty, like a cold fear, swept through me. I glanced toward the man. He'd heard the same words that I had. To my surprise, he grabbed me by one hand and Sierra by the other. Literally he swept us into the room.

"Phrona, look who I found on our doorstep," he said, a little too loud and too casually. "Sierra, Dakota, go give your Grandma Leland a big kiss."

We stood rooted to the spot.

I knew I was staring at the elegant, fashionably dressed woman seated across the room, but somehow I could hardly look away.

"Dawn, you look lovely," the man said.

It wasn't true. Mom's nose was red and her eyes were puffy. She'd obviously been crying. She had a crumpled tissue in her hand, but she put a deliberate smile on her face as she stood up to greet him. He gave her a peck on the cheek.

"So you've brought the girls for a visit," he said. "We are so thrilled. Aren't we, Phrona?"

My grandmother looked up at him and then at us. Her moment of hesitation said everything. Her words, when she finally spoke them, were neither welcome nor greeting.

"They've come for a summer stay with us," she said. "We'll put the girls in the garden bedroom. Dawn can have the guest suite. It has its own little sitting area."

"Thank you, Mrs. Leland," Mom told her. It was a whispered response, but I heard it.

# REAL LIFE
## 5

———◆————

There was a weird sense of unreality as Mom pulled the Dodge into the driveway and we began unloading our stuff into their house. I guess on some level I'd known that I had grandparents, but when you live your whole life without anybody ever mentioning them, you just kind of think of them as being like the parents in cartoon adventures, rarely seen and never important to the story.

But suddenly they were now front and center and who knew what to think about that?

Sierra, of course, was completely unfazed. She was cheerful and delighted, making a big deal over their house and calling them Grandma and Grandpa. I took my cue from Mom. She called them Vern and Mrs. Leland. I wasn't about to claim them as family if she didn't.

But it was hard to fault them on welcome. Vern continued to act as if our showing up uninvited was just a wonderful surprise. He helped us with our boxes, talked to us about the neighborhood, even laughed at Sierra trying to get the dog to carry stuff into the house.

Mrs. Leland emptied out a big double chest in the garden room so that Sierra and I could have a place for our clothes.

"I'll get this closet emptied, as well," she told me. "It's probably not big enough, but it will have to do."

I glanced at the storage area behind the mirrored door. It was more room than we'd had at our last place.

"This will be fine," I assured her, maybe sounding a little bit lofty. "We won't need to unpack our winter things, or school clothes and all that."

The truth was that my entire wardrobe was basically jeans and T-shirts. Sierra had more stuff, but there was easily enough space for everything she owned.

"Is this going to be my room?" Sierra said with a delightful giggle.

"You'll have to share with your sister," Mrs. Leland told her.

She continued to giggle and twirl around in the center of the room, before throwing herself on one of the twin beds.

"This is the nicest room I've ever had in my life," she announced.

I wanted to kick her. It was so disloyal to Mom. Mom always got us nice places to live. Maybe they weren't like the Lelands' house. But it wasn't like some kind of palace! It was just an old house with some nice furniture. The room was wallpapered in a pale green with bright, flowery bedspreads and there were double doors that led out to a little rock patio and garden. I mean, it was nice. But it wasn't incredible. Sierra was acting like we'd just stepped into *The Princess Diaries* and this stiff, cold stranger was our personal Julie Andrews.

Resisting an eye roll, I decided to leave the cinematic set and see if Mom needed any help.

The guest suite was at the front of the house. It

wasn't really two rooms. Just one room with a little enclosed porch. The windows were on the street side, but you didn't notice that. You were high enough to see over the neighbors and get a view of downtown Knoxville in the distance.

"It's nice, huh?" Mom said.

I shrugged.

"What are we doing here?" I asked her.

She continued unpacking, avoiding my eyes as she answered. "It's time you and Sierra got to know your grandparents," she said. "Tennessee is certainly cooler than Texas this time of year. It will be good to spend the summer here. Don't you think?"

"Not particularly," I answered.

"There's lots of things to do here," she said, her enthusiasm deliberate. "There are lakes and mountains and wonderful museums, music in the park. You're going to love it, Dakota, I'm sure of that."

"What are we doing here?" I repeated. "All I ever heard about these people, Mr. and Mrs. Leland, was that they didn't approve of you and Daddy getting married. If they didn't like us or want us, then what are we doing here?"

Mom glanced up sharply. "It never had anything to do with you," she told me. "Don't buy into that kind of nonsense, you're much too bright. The Lelands didn't approve of me. And they were angry with Sonny, but it didn't have anything to do with you girls."

"You haven't answered my question," I pointed out. "And anyway, if they didn't approve of you and were mad at their own son, why should I give them a chance?"

"Because that was a long time ago," Mom answered. "Because they had some good reasons not to approve of me and some even better ones to be mad at Sonny."

I shook my head, not willing to accept that.

"And because I said so," Mom declared. "End of discussion."

"No way," I answered.

"Way," she said, rising to her feet. She walked over and put her arms around me. I tried to resist, but I couldn't. "Dakota," she told me. "I need for you to be on your best behavior for the next few weeks. I know you may not want to, but do it anyway, just because I tell you to."

Mom didn't usually ask me that kind of thing. Ordinarily she trusted me to use my own judgment about how to treat people. The fact that now I was virtually ordered to be nice made me even less willing to be so.

"Mom!" I complained.

"Please," she countered.

"Okay," I answered, reluctantly.

"Good, let's get the rest of the stuff out of the car. How's your sister doing?"

I made an obscene sound. "You know Sierra," I said. "If she were going down with the *Titanic* she'd be all thrilled and excited about taking a nice cold swim."

Mom laughed. "I know," she said. "Sonny was like that, too. It's great, but it can really get to be annoying."

I knew, without asking, that she wasn't referring to any of the Sonnys that I knew personally. She was talking about this Sonny. The one that had belonged to the people here. He had never really been featured in our daily conversation. But now he seemed suddenly more a part of us.

The rest of the day seemed to go on forever. I had a tremendous sense of being uncomfortable. We were in the house of strangers and we were all tiptoeing around each other. For lunch we had tuna salad and tomato soup out on the Leland patio.

Vern was determined to have a pleasant conversation and apparently the safest subjects for the discussion were me and Sierra. He asked us questions about ourselves and what kind of things we liked.

Sierra piped up immediately. She talked mostly about clothes and what she'd read in the fashion mags. I'd never paid any attention when she talked about that stuff.

The Lelands showed a polite attentiveness.

Sierra presented both pros and cons for the current fashion war between chunky heels verses pointy-toed sling backs. And who knew that blue eyeshadow was making a comeback?

With everybody's attention on my sister, I was able to really get a good look at these people who were my grandparents. They were old, I guess. I guess they had to be old, but they weren't like elderly or anything. Vern was mostly bald, but what hair remained on the back of his head still had plenty of dark brown mixed with the gray. He was tall, but not particularly muscular. Pretty slim except for a thickening around the middle. He had a nice face. Strong, masculine, yet it wasn't stern or foreboding. I especially liked his eyes. Even behind the wire-rimmed glasses I could see the empathy of those eyes.

Mrs. Leland was better looking. She was tall, almost as tall as her husband. Sleek and chic, with movements so graceful I wondered if they were practiced. She seemed like a woman who would know how to serve tea or maybe play the piano. But in all her graciousness there was something less open about her. It took me several minutes to figure it out. Then I realized that she never really looked at us. She looked in our direction, she talked with us, but somehow she managed, very discreetly, to make us invisible to her.

We were down to plates of crumbs by the time Sierra began to run out of topics. Vern kept the conversation from lagging.

"And what about you, Dakota?" he asked. "What are your interests?"

"She's our family geek," Sierra answered for me. "In all the schools we've been in, wherever we go, Dakota walks in and the very first day she just wows the teachers. I tell her that her personal slogan must be All A's al-ways."

Sierra giggled at her own attempt at humor. I knew she was trying to build me up. She didn't value school much, but she knew that some people did. She always wanted to give people who liked her a reason to like me, as well. Sometimes it worked. But somehow, with the Lelands, I wasn't sure if I wanted it to. I felt cautious, secretive. I didn't want them to know too much about me.

"An all A's student?" Vern said. "That's wonderful. What's your favorite subject?"

"English," I lied. I liked English okay, but it didn't even make my top three.

"English," Vern repeated, nodding. "That's a first for us. Phrona's a history buff. It was her major in college and she's kept an active interest all these years. My passion is physics. I taught here at the university for thirty-two years. I never had anybody to talk to about it at home. Sonny's love was botany. Any kind of plant, he just found infinitely interesting. He was going to turn that into a career before…"

His sentence just sort of trailed off and we were left with a giant uncomfortable silence. *Before he died* were the words left unsaid. Vern hadn't wanted to say them, because he hadn't wanted to hear them. It was as if, for a short moment, he'd forgotten. But now the truth was back and it was big and empty and hurtful. Everybody was looking down at the plates. I wanted to say something to make the sad quiet around the table go away, but I didn't know how. My father had been dead all my life, yet somehow with these people it felt like it *had* just happened. I could feel their hurt as if it had just happened. I was desperate to do something to make the bad feeling disappear, to say something, but I didn't know what to say. The moment dragged on forever.

"Forestry," Mom said, unexpectedly.

That was the first word she'd spoken.

"What?" Mrs. Leland asked. She was looking Mom in the face for the first time since we'd sat down.

"Forestry," Mom repeated. "That was what Sonny was talking about before his death. He liked working in the woods, but he had some real issues with the timber-cutting industry. He told me he wanted to go back to school to study forestry. He thought he could really make a contribution there."

A different kind of thoughtful quiet followed that and I thought, for a minute, that Mom had made it worse. That by mentioning him again the blank spot would just get bigger. But amazingly it didn't.

Vern sort of chuckled and shook his head. Even Mrs. Leland managed a ghost of a smile.

The rest of the day both dragged and rushed by. I was torn between a strong desire to race outside, check out the neighborhood, find the library, get a bus map, all the things I'd automatically do in a new town. But another part of me felt weird, scared. This was not like any other town. This was a place from Mom's past and we'd come back here for a reason.

Mom had decided on a nap after lunch and Sierra installed herself in front of the TV to watch *General Hospital*. I said I was going to nap, too. But I can't really sleep in the daytime.

I wandered around the room a bit and then went out the glass doors to the garden. It was a beautiful afternoon with a cool breeze, bright sunshine and all the flowers in the garden were in bloom. At the far end of the yard I could see an old swing hanging from a tree limb. I made my way in that direction.

I fanned through a collection of spiderwebs to discover that the chain was rusty and the paint on the seat peeling. But it looked sturdy enough and I sat down. For a couple of minutes I just lolled there lazily listening to the rustle of the leaves and the buzz of insects. I'm not sure how long it was before I became aware of the voices. I glanced around and saw that built onto the back of the garage was a little office of some kind. The Lelands were inside and they were arguing.

I slipped out of the swing and tiptoed to the side of the garage, maybe ten feet from the door.

"I just can't stand it, Vern. I can't have her here. I don't think I can bear it."

"Phrona, she's got no other choice and neither do we," he answered. "Once she sees the doctor and we get some idea of what is going on, then we can talk it through. We can figure out what's best for everyone concerned."

"What is best for me is if I never had to see her face again as long as I live."

I didn't want to hear anymore. I hurried back to the house as quickly as I could without calling attention to myself. Mom always said that eavesdroppers never hear anything good about themselves. I guess it was true.

I slipped back through the glass doors and laid down on the bed. Staring up at the ceiling, I wondered what was going on. Why didn't Mrs. Leland like my mother? And why did she let us stay here feeling the way she did? Why was my mother going to see a doctor?

Sierra barged in.

"Is your soap over?"

She shook her head. "I just came to get my nail polish," she answered. "What's with you? You look all freaked out or something."

"I overheard Mrs. Leland say that Mom was going to see a doctor," I said.

Sierra thought about that for a moment and then nodded slowly.

"What do you think?" I asked her.

"I guess she must be pregnant," Sierra answered.

"Pregnant?" I didn't believe it. "You watch too much TV," I told her. "Mom is not pregnant."

"You know, I bet she is," my sister said, rapidly warming up to the idea. "It makes perfect sense, really. We didn't get any warning that she and Moroney were breaking up."

"So, we never get any warning," I pointed out. "Mom keeps her private life private. At least from us."

"You're the one who pointed out that we never backtrack."

"Yeah, but it's not because she's PG," I said with certainty. "Didn't you hear her tell Mrs. Leland that she's sick?"

"So. Women are always sick the first few months," Sierra said.

"No. That's not it. I'm sure that's not it."

"Okay then," she said. "But tell me, why else would she have dragged us back here?"

# SONNY DAYS
## 6

He'd always been an upbeat, positive, cheerful guy. But that fall Sonny Leland was happier than he could ever remember. He and Dawn went to all the second-run movies at the dollar theater. They shouted and cheered together at basketball games. They visited museums and hiked in the mountains. They went to concerts in World's Fair Park and on long walks along the river. Sonny was in love— crazy, desperately, mindlessly in love. He went through his days in an urgency. Classes, work, even the meetings at the frat house were annoying road-blocks on his way to the pizza joint and the woman he loved.

What was even more amazing was that Dawn loved him, too.

She'd told him so. Though he would have known anyway. Her eyes lit up when he walked in. She spent every waking moment, when she wasn't working, in his company. She didn't give even the most cursory notice to other guys who came her way. And when he held her in his arms, they just fit perfectly. Their love was their favorite subject of conversation.

"I've never felt about anyone the way I feel about you," he told her as they lay side by side on the campus grass gazing at floating clouds. "I mean, I had girl-friends before, but it was never anything like this."

"I didn't even know I could feel like this," she ad-mitted. "And nobody ever really cared about me be-fore. Nobody ever loved me."

Sonny nodded. "Me, neither, except my parents of course, and that's different."

"Oh, yeah," Dawn agreed quickly. "That's differ-ent. Look at that one over there." She pointed to a fluffy puff of cumulus in the distance. "That one looks like a pirate ship."

"A pirate ship?" Sonny leaned up on his elbows and squinted at the cloud in question. "I think it's some kind of animal with a really small head."

They started having sex just a few weeks after they met. Sonny had held back making a move. And in truth, he'd been surprised when she didn't make any attempt to stop things or even slow them down.

He'd had one other sexual partner in high school, a former steady girlfriend. But when they'd graduated, they'd gone their separate ways with only a slightly tearful goodbye. She'd been a nice person and a fun friend. Physical gratification had been wonderful. But it was nothing like what he felt now, for Dawn.

Dawn was everything. There was nothing about her that he could imagine as imperfect. She was gor-geous to look at—that went without saying. And she was funny and crazy and downright undignified at times. She was so full of life, just the sound of her voice could lighten up everybody around her. He loved the way she just let him talk and talk and talk. It was as if anything he said, no matter how pedan-tic or far-fetched, fascinated her. He'd come from class, virtually repeating what the professor had said. She always listened as if it were endlessly interesting.

The last seat at the counter was now his regular perch at the pizza place. That's where he ate all his meals and did all his studying. His frat brothers always knew where to find him. Though they complained that he never wanted to hang out or bar crawl.

Sonny didn't socialize much anymore. He rarely went out with his friends. For some reason Dawn was uncomfortable around most of his buddies and their girlfriends. And it was just more fun to be alone with her.

When he needed money he'd try to see his dad at his office on campus. Dad was always busy and visits would, of necessity, be short. Even when his father asked what was going on, why hadn't he come by or called, Sonny dissembled and had gotten away with it.

His mother was not so easily put off. She called his room before 7:00 a.m. on a Saturday morning.

"I'm roasting leg of lamb tomorrow," she told him. It was his favorite meal. Firmly she added, "I expect you to be there."

Sonny's face fell as he stared at the phone, but then an idea occurred to him. Perhaps it was time.

"I want to bring a friend," he said.

There was a slight hesitation on the other end of the line.

"Of course," his mother said, barely able to conceal her curiosity. "Is it anyone that I know?"

"I don't think so," Sonny answered. "What time? One? One-thirty?"

"One-thirty is fine."

"We'll see you then," he said and hung up quickly before she tried to drag more information out of him.

He headed for his morning shower whistling. He wasn't nervous or anxious about introducing Dawn to his family. In fact, he could hardly wait for them to meet her.

Sonny had always had a great relationship with his parents. As an only child, he knew that he'd been doted upon and probably spoiled rotten, but he had an empathic temperament. He loved his folks and he knew how proud of him they were.

"You're my life's great joy," his mother told him often.

His dad was not as verbal about it, but Sonny knew he felt the same way.

There was not even the slightest worry in Sonny's mind about introducing them to the love of his own life. He knew they would love her, too.

"Your parents?" Dawn said the word in an ominous whisper. "I can't meet your parents."

"Of course you can," Sonny told her. "You'll have to meet them sometime."

"Why?"

"Because they're my parents."

"Oh, no, Sonny, I really can't."

"Dawn?"

"No, really," she insisted. "I don't meet parents. That's not one of my things. I'll meet your friends. I'll even go to those crazy parties at your frat house, but I won't meet any parents."

She was adamant. Sonny wasted the greater part

of their Saturday night date trying to convince her. The next afternoon, disgruntled and out of sorts, he showed up at home without her.

"Is your friend going to meet you here?" his mother asked.

"No," Sonny answered. "She decided not to come."

"She?"

"Yeah," he answered. His mother was obviously very curious, but Sonny was still smarting from Dawn's rejection and held off any further questions. That is, until they were seated for dinner. The table was set with his mother's best china and the handsome leg of lamb and its accompanying vegetables looked as appetizing as they smelled.

The three of them clasped hands across the dinner table as they always had, as his father, Vern, said grace.

After the amen, his dad smiled at him.

"It's good to have you home," he said. "Dinner at this table just doesn't feel much like a family with just Phrona and me."

"Thanks Dad."

"So tell us about your girl," his father said. "You know your mother is about to expire from curiosity."

"I really wanted you to get to meet her," Sonny said. "She's...she's just wonderful. You're going to love her."

"Does that mean you love her?" his mother asked, a teasing lilt to her voice.

Sonny nodded. "She's the one."

His parents exchanged startled glances across the table and then both of them burst into excited questions. So many and so fast, Sonny had no chance of answering.

"One at a time," he said, laughing. "Mama, you can go first."

"Okay, okay," his mother said. "Start with the basics. What's her name?"

"Dawn Dixon," Sonny answered and turned to his dad.

"Where did you meet her?"

"Proletariat Pizza," he answered. "She's waiting tables there as an after-class job."

"She's a student?"

Sonny nodded. "She's a freshman, too. She lives in Strong Hall."

"What's she studying?"

Sonny drew a blank and hesitated. "You know, I don't think I ever asked," he admitted. "First year, we're all taking the same things."

His parents nodded in agreement.

"Where's she from?"

"Here in Knoxville," he said.

"Do we know any Dixons?" Phrona asked Vern.

"I think they must have moved around a lot," Sonny said. "I got the impression that she was in a lot of different schools growing up."

"What does her father do?"

Sonny shrugged. "I haven't a clue. I guess we don't talk about our folks much."

"Well, of course not," his mother said. "Young people have much better things than that to talk about."

Vern agreed with a chuckle. "And those things aren't the important things," he said. "I'm sure that

no matter who her parents are, what they do or
where they live, if you love her, Sonny, we will, too."

"Of course we will," his mother agreed.

But it hadn't worked out that way.

His mother, a genealogy hobbyist, had gotten curious about the Dixons and began researching the
family. Unfortunately, there were so many Dixon family lines in Tennessee that she just had to have more
information. She called Sonny on several occasions
asking for names, dates, places, something she could
work with. When he never came up with anything,
she took matters into her own hands. Sonny heard
about it soon enough.

"Your mother was in here today." Dawn's words
were spoken like an accusation. "I will not be inves-
tigated like some perp on *Unsolved Mysteries.*"

Sonny shook his head. "Mama's not like that," he
assured her. "She just loves family history stuff. She's
traced us back to the Pilgrims."

"She's saying I'm not good enough for you because my family doesn't go back that far."

"All families go back to someone, somewhere," he
told her. "It's not like it's a competition, it's just ancestors. Ancestors are like toes, they might be curious or ordinary, but everybody's got them and
nobody spends a lot of time thinking about them."

"My *toes* are strictly my own and I don't discuss
them with anybody," Dawn stated adamantly.

"Okay, fair enough," Sonny said. "I'll tell Mama that
from now on she should mind her own business."

"I don't think that's going to be good enough,"
Dawn said. "Why don't you just tell *Mama* that we've
broken up. That's what she wants to hear anyway."

Sonny was incredulous.

"Dawn?"

"I don't want to see you anymore," she said. "Don't come in here, don't call me. It's over. I knew it wouldn't last, and I was right. Go!"

She'd pointed to the door, but Sonny didn't leave. He sat down on his usual stool at the counter, waiting for her to cool down so they could talk again. He waited all evening.

Dawn never spoke to him again. She wouldn't even look in his direction. At closing, he waited by the back door. To his surprise, a big, hairy guy with a huge, flashy pickup showed up, as well. With barely a glance in Sonny's direction, Dawn got in the ape's truck and they drove away. He thought there were tears in her eyes, but in the dim light of the alley he couldn't be sure.

The next day, he went to see his mother.

"I'm not sure today is the best day to talk to her," Vern warned him.

"Oh?"

"Your girlfriend insulted her," his father said. "She called your mother a nosy bitch."

Sonny blanched.

"Why?" he asked.

"I don't have a clue," Vern answered. "But you know how Phrona hates coarse talk like that."

"Mama must have said something to her first," Sonny insisted. "Dawn is a sweet, lovely, happy person. She wouldn't attack for no reason."

Vern shrugged and shook his head. "Phrona sure didn't go down there with causing trouble in mind. She's been so giddy and excited all week about your new girlfriend. I told her it was probably best to let you arrange an introduction, but she just couldn't wait to meet her."

"Well, Mama must have done something," Sonny told him. "Dawn is so furious, she broke up with me over it."

"Well, that's the best news I've had all day," his mother said, coming in from the dining room doorway.

Sonny didn't like that a bit. He was suffering the worst emotional pain he'd experienced in his young, sheltered life. And he didn't know what it was about. He loved Dawn. She had become the center of his universe. She was the first thought in his mind when he awakened in the morning. And the last when he fell asleep at night. In these last months he'd rearranged all his dreams for his future to fit neatly around his dream of being with her. But his life had been inexplicably turned upside down. And he hadn't a clue as to how or why it had happened.

He'd come to his parents for help and comfort. But instead his mother was adding more heartbreak to his already wrenching disappointment.

"How can you say that, Mama?" he asked her. "I love Dawn."

Phrona shook her head. "This girl isn't who you think she is," she said. "I've been making some phone calls. Knoxville may be a city, but it's also still a small town."

"You've been scraping up gossip about my girlfriend?" Sonny was incredulous. "Did you actually think I would want to hear any of it?"

"Sonny, I've found out some things that you ought to know."

If he hadn't been so emotionally bruised. If he hadn't been caught off guard. If a meteor had hit or the house caught on fire, the next moments might have been different. But they weren't. Sonny rose to his feet, as angry at his mother as he had ever been with another human being.

"I don't want to hear one word," he declared. "I love her. I want to spend the rest of my life with her. And anything about her that I need to know, I'll hear it only from her."

"Sonny, she's been lying to you!"

"No! I'm not listening to any of this," he said. "You're my mother and I love and respect you, but I will not sit here while you spread some nasty gossip about my Dawn."

He left the house then. Deliberately not slamming the door. Slamming the door would be a kid thing. He was no longer a kid. He was a man and he was fighting for the woman he loved.

He drove directly to Proletariat Pizza. He had to talk to her. But she wasn't there.

"I thought Dawn was working today," he said to Sheila.

Sheila lowered her voice to answer, her expression full of sympathy.

"She called in this morning and just quit. No reason, no notice. The boss is furious."

Sonny walked up the street to Strong Hall. He didn't know what was going on, but he was determined to find out. He approached the hospitality desk.

"Dawn Dixon," he said to the receptionist.

She put the name into her computer. He waited.

"Could you spell that last name?"

He did.

"No, she's not living here at Strong," the woman said.

"I know she lives here," Sonny said. "I've walked her home a hundred times."

"Maybe she's moved," the woman suggested. "Let me check the entire student housing list."

Sonny waited as more computer keys clicked and clicked.

"No Dawn Dixon in any of our residence halls," she told him. "Why don't you check with the bursar's office. If she lives off campus, they may be able to help you with an address."

He spent the next hour in the administration building, listening, waiting, arguing.

"There is no Dawn Dixon currently on any UT campus and none listed among our former students."

The inevitability of that fact had been weighing on Sonny, but having it voiced aloud was like a kick in the stomach.

# REAL LIFE
## 7

➤ ◆

It was that next morning when I noticed the photographs. They were sitting in plain sight on the little mantel in the dining room. I must have walked past them a dozen times and never noticed.

My mind was elsewhere. Sierra had slept in, as usual, but I got up and made myself at home with toast and jelly. Two minutes after I got there, Mrs. Leland walked in. She was obviously startled to see me, but instead of saying so, she gave me a sort of fake half smile and asked me if I'd found everything I wanted. I was polite, but I basically ignored her. She made coffee and pretended to be busy over by the sink. I knew she had to be pretending because there was nothing that could possibly be done. Hers was the cleanest kitchen I'd ever been in. The counters were all gleaming. There wasn't a smudge on the tile, a crumb on the floor or a even an empty *Pop-Tarts* wrapper hanging out of the garbage. It was almost creepy. Sierra and I took turns doing dish duty, but neither of us ever got so into it. Mrs. Leland was definitely one of those women on the TV commercials, ecstatic over some antibacterial liquid or paper towel.

More reason to dislike her. I ate my toast and brooded.

When Mom entered the kitchen, she was already showered and dressed. She greeted us both with a cheery smile, but I knew it wasn't genuine. She was wearing what I called her *fake-it* getup. The gray suit was kind of tweedy, very conservative. It had hung in Mom's closet always and was worn only for occasions like contesting a speeding ticket, attending a parent-teacher conference or going to a funeral.

"May I get you some coffee?" Mrs. Leland asked her.

"Yeah, great," Mom answered.

"Cream and sugar?"

"All I need is some artificial sweetener," she answered.

"I'm afraid I don't have any of that."

Mom nodded. "Sugar's fine then."

She stirred her coffee and Mrs. Leland hovered at her sink for a few minutes before grabbing up a watering can and heading out the back door inferring that she was going to tend her flowers.

"Where are you off to?" I asked Mom.

She smiled, but she didn't look me in the eye. "Oh, just some personal business," she said, evasively.

"I heard something about a doctor," I admitted.

She didn't seem surprised that I'd wormed out that info. Mom looked at me directly then.

"It's probably just some gynecological thing," she said with a wink. "I know how you hate talking about that stuff."

That was true. I'd started having my period the winter before and it still seemed like the yuckiest, most uncomfortable and inconvenient thing imaginable. Sierra thought I should be grateful, finally maturing up, later than a lot of my classmates. But to me it was just a nuisance. I couldn't, however, let my aversion to discussion of the female world be used to sidetrack me from finding out what was going on.

"Sierra says that you're probably pregnant," I told her, being deliberately nonchalant.

Mom's jaw dropped open. Her expression was incredulous and then she actually laughed.

"I'm underestimating your sister's creativity and imagination," she said. "Or maybe she's just watching too much TV."

"So if you're not pregnant," I said, "why are you going to the doctor?"

"There are lots of reasons to see a doctor," Mom answered. "I don't really have an appointment at this clinic, so I'd better get over there so I can pressure them to try to work me into the schedule."

She drank down her coffee and got up to leave.

"Mom!" I whined.

She reached over and flicked my nose, playfully. "When I have anything certain to tell you and Sierra, I will."

It wasn't much of an answer, but she wouldn't be budged from it.

"At least stay and have breakfast with me."

"You're finished already," she answered. "Tomorrow. We'll make it a date. Breakfast tomorrow."

She winked at me again and then she was gone. A few minutes later I heard the loud muffler on the Dodge as the car started up.

I sat there in the big, superclean kitchen alone.

I got up and carried the dishes to the sink. Normally I would have rinsed them off and put them in the dishwasher. But I figured if Mrs. Leland liked cleaning so much, then she could do it.

I glanced through the little storage room between the kitchen and the back door. Through the window I could see Mrs. Leland. She set the watering can on the edge of the patio and walked back to the office behind the garage. I took the opportunity to snoop through a few cabinets. I wasn't really looking for anything, just looking.

It was all basic stuff, detergent and spray cleaners, paper products and canned goods.

In the bottom cabinet near the door, I noticed the dog food and wondered where Rocky had gotten to. I'd never had a dog before and I'd always kind of wanted one. It seemed like such a neat, ordinary thing. A kid and a dog. That was like a regular childhood. I walked through the house, whistling and calling for him, but he didn't come.

The place was pretty much empty. Mom's little suite was messy and chaotic already. She'd apparently tried on lots of outfits before deciding on the gray funeral suit.

I peeked into the Lelands' bedroom. Nobody was there, so I tiptoed in. It was decorated in pale tones of yellow and gold. The bed was made, the dresser uncluttered. Vern's house shoes were sitting precisely parallel just under the edge of the bedspread fringe. The closet doors were closed. From inside the master bath I could see the dim glow of a night-light. It felt weird being there. I sniffed the air, testing the rumor that old people smell bad. But it was all candle scent, faint with gardenia.

Obviously, the dog was not there, but I took the

opportunity to stand a few feet inside the door and survey the area. It was a guilty pleasure, invading their privacy. I lolled in it for several minutes before tiptoeing out.

I expected Vern's study to be a dark, cavelike, mannish sort of place. But the old scarred, knotty pine was surprisingly cheerful, the worn—almost ragged—leather lounge chair was inviting and there were more books than I'd ever seen outside the public library. I walked along the bookshelf, fingering the titles. If there was an order to it, it wasn't obvious to me. A history of the Teapot Dome scandal sat next to a Steinbeck novel.

Near to the window there was a little table with a chess board set up. A game was obviously in progress. There was an old-fashioned turntable nearby and a stack of those big black plastic records. I picked one up, expecting Elvis or something equally sixties. There was a picture of some guy who looked like he ought to be on money. The title was *Haydn's Surprise, Symphony No. 94 in G.* I'd never heard of Haydn, so I shrugged and put it back.

Vern was not as neat as his wife, that was clear. The desk was piled with folders, papers and notebooks, and yellow sticky notes were tacked up everywhere. Especially on the area around the computer monitor. It was mostly math stuff, equations and formulas. I was pretty good at math, but this was very tough and there were symbols I wasn't familiar with. All in all, I liked Vern's room. I thought I could hang there. But not in the morning. It was definitely a doldrums-of-afternoon kind of place.

I kept exploring, checking out the front hallway

and the living room. It was in the dining room that
I saw the photos. At first my eye passed right over
the frames as if they were just more knickknacks in
a house loaded with them. Then inexplicably, like a
tingle up the spine, I sensed they were more. Set out
on the top of the buffet I saw a small framed toddler
next to a somber Eagle Scout, a gap-toothed Little
Leaguer beside a grinning kid in a wet swimsuit, a
serious boy in a white choir robe, a young man in a
mortarboard.

"Dad."

The name slipped from my lips involuntarily.

This was him. This was Sonny Leland. This was
the man who'd really loved my mother, who'd given
me life, whose existence had brought me to this
place. This was Sonny Leland. He was more than a
tattoo on my mother's breast. Here was a whole life
in a dozen framed photos.

Hesitantly, I reached up and touched one. He was
in his soccer uniform, burgundy and gold with
striped socks. He'd been about my age, I guess. He
was lanky like me. He didn't look like me, not exactly. But I could see familiar things about him, about
me. This was really my father. I was really part of
him.

I heard the front door open.

Inexplicably I grabbed up the soccer picture and
stashed it inside my shirt.

There was the scratch of scurrying dog paws on
the entryway tile.

"Where are you going?" Vern called out.

Rocky didn't answer, but a minute later he was at
my side.

"Hey, puppy," I said. "I've been looking for you."

Eagerly, happily, he stretched up, resting his front feet on my knee so that I could pet him. He had a great smile. The white hair around his snout gave him the appearance of a little old man with a gray beard. His little pink tongue hung out of one side of his mouth. His enthusiasm belied his age.

"You've been looking at the photographs?" Vern said from the doorway.

I was defensive.

"I was only looking."

"Sure, look at them all you want," he said. "I'm sure there's some you haven't seen."

"I haven't seen any of them," I said. "I've never seen a picture of my dad."

That statement made him pause. His brow furrowed.

"There's more," he said. "Lots and lots more."

He gestured for me to follow him. In the hallway he turned on the overhead light and opened a glass-fronted bookshelf. Inside were rows of photo albums.

"We took a lot of pictures of that boy," Vern told me. "He was our only child. We took snapshots all the time. We had a Brownie when we got married. Then we wore out a couple of Instamatics and a Disc before we graduated to 35mm."

I didn't say anything, but I guess I must have looked as clueless as I felt.

"Those are cameras," he explained. "We always had a camera. And we took pictures of Sonny all the time."

"That's nice," I said.

He nodded and sighed a little sadly, I thought.

"Your grandmother is very orderly," he said. "She could never stand having loose photos lying around. She spent untold hours getting them into albums."

He handed me one. I held it tightly in my arms, not so much to savor it as to ensure that the framed photo tucked inside my shirt didn't spill out.

"You can look at these anytime," Vern said. "I'm sure that's what Sonny would have wanted."

"Yeah," I agreed, still uneasy.

Sierra came out of her room. Unlike me, she didn't wash up or dress before breakfast. She was in her Radiohead T-shirt, bare feet and wild hair.

"What's going on?" she asked.

"I was just showing your sister where we keep the photo albums of Sonny."

"There are photo albums? Cool."

Vern handed her one of the thick, heavy books and she began a conversation with him as she carried it into the kitchen with her.

Grateful for the distraction, I hurried to the room and shut the door behind me. For added security, I jerked the drapes shut. Then I pulled my suitcase out from under the bed. It still contained all my extra clothes and special possessions, those I wasn't willing to put on display.

I pulled the soccer photo out of my shirt, wrapped it in an old sweater and hid it deep in the bottom of the scarred piece of luggage.

These people had hundreds of photos of my dad. I didn't even have one. When we left this place, I had no intention of leaving it behind.

# SONNY DAYS
## 8

It had taken Sonny almost a week to find her. It was a miracle at that. He was amazed at how little he actually knew about her. She had no friends he could consult. No history that she'd related. He remembered her mentioning Central High. But he couldn't find any record of her graduating from there or any other local school. He was beginning to wonder is she'd given him a fake name.

Reluctantly, because he felt he had no other choice, he went to talk to his mother. Not to have her share gossip about the woman he loved, but to find out if there was anything she knew that could help him.

He found Phrona in her new little makeshift office that had been added onto the back of garage. For most of his life, his mother's *vocation* had been mothering him. A former Knoxville debutante and a Fulbright scholar, she'd put her pursuit of history on the back burner to pursue the world of drool and dirty diapers. Being Sonny's mom had become her entire world for eighteen years. And she had been excellent at it. Endlessly patient with him. Determined to make even the most routine task a learning experience. She devoted herself to his happiness and development. It was a wonderful childhood. Sonny's home was always clean. His meals were nutritious and tasty. His friends were always welcome. And he knew every moment of every day that he was loved.

When he'd chosen to move into the dorm at college, his mother didn't even voice a complaint. Though he knew it must have been hard. *Empty nesting* was what the pop psychologists were calling it. Watching your life's purpose walk out the front door and wave goodbye required quite an adjustment. With her husband only ten years from retirement, it felt silly to start a career. Then, at a summer picnic with visiting relatives, she'd discovered genealogy. It was the perfect blending of two things she loved, family and history. And she'd taken it up with a passion.

Her office was lined with books. On one wall she'd taped up nine generations of her direct line back to her Puritan roots in the south of England.

Sonny seated himself in the comfortable armchair wedged between the corner of two bookshelves. His mother had swiveled hers around to face him.

"This girl is not for you, Sonny," she said. "I understand that you have strong feelings for her, but she's not right for you."

Sonny tightened his jaw. He wasn't angry, but he intended to be firm. "Tell me what you *know*, Mama," he said. "When it comes to Dawn, I'm not interested in what you *think*, only what you *know*."

"I know that she's been lying to you."

"Not revealing personal stuff is not the same as lying," he defended, though in honesty he did feel she had lied.

"I'm not splitting hairs with you," his mother said.

"I was prepared to like the girl. But I certainly wasn't prepared to be publicly insulted by her."

"I'm sure she regrets that," Sonny said, hoping it was true. "But surely you can see her side of it. She thought you were prying into her life."

"She only thought I was prying because she had something to hide," Phrona pointed out.

"Everybody has a right to their privacy," Sonny said.

"But nobody has a right to talk to me as if I were some loathsome worm. And nobody has the right to lie to my son."

"Mother, I don't need your protection."

"Maybe you think that you don't," Phrona answered. "But this girl has obviously hurt you. She'll continue to do that. People become what they are meant to be. Whether it's their genetics or their upbringing, this girl will never be capable of love or family."

Sonny felt both anger and confusion. "What a terrible thing to say!"

"What a terrible truth to live with," his mother countered. "The girl's family is so worthless they wouldn't even bother with her. And she's been unable to bond with any foster family in Knox County."

"What?"

"That's the word I got from Jane Wickham's daughter-in-law's sister, you know, the one who works for child welfare."

Sonny didn't remember any of the women mentioned, but he nodded nonetheless.

"This girl's branch of the Dixon family are unmitigated trash and busy hooking up with the same," Phrona said. "They are worthless drunks, petty thieves and career criminals. Her father's been in and out of prison a dozen times. Her mother left town when Dawn was just a baby and dumped her with an old aunt, who neglected the child. She was passed around until nobody would take her and the state intervened. Her own flesh and blood gave her over and said good riddance."

Sonny swallowed hard. It was difficult to connect this history with the happy, carefree young woman that he knew.

"She was a runaway from a half-dozen foster homes before the system declared her incorrigible and locked her into juvenile detention," Phrona said. "That's a juvenile prison, Sonny. She spent her formative years with girls who were thieves and prostitutes and murderers."

"But she was just a runaway," Sonny pointed out.

His mother sighed and shook her head.

"I know you believe that you love her, Sonny. But a woman like this will never be able to love you in return. She'll never be able to share a stable home and family."

Sonny shook his head. He didn't doubt that his mother was telling him the facts, but he refused to believe the conclusion that they led her to.

"I love Dawn," he said. "I love her and I need her. If she's never been loved, then being loved by me will be good for her. And letting her go would be a tragedy for both of us."

He left his parents' home more determined than ever to find the woman he'd lost. He sought out her former caseworkers and the court services people who'd helped her become an emancipated minor.

He talked to former employers and even a couple of members of the Dixon family who cheerfully declared that they wouldn't know her if they saw her on the street.

It was Sheila who flagged him down one afternoon as he once again searched every hangout on Cumberland.

"I saw Dawn's paycheck in the outgoing mail," she told him as she handed him a scribbled lunch ticket. "This is where she had it sent."

The address led Sonny to an area of older homes very near the UT campus. For want of a better name the run-down neighborhood was known as the Student Slum. The huge white house was neglected and faded. On the porch a half-dozen black mailboxes hinted at the chopped-up nature of the residences behind its front door.

Sonny hesitated on the sidewalk. The afternoon was hot and the smell of a freshly mown lawn was in the air. A very skinny old man sat on the front porch steps. He was holding an empty green bean can into which he was spitting tobacco.

"Hi," Sonny called out as approached.

The man looked up at him without speaking.

Sonny stopped at the steps and glanced down the line of mailboxes. Some had names haphazardly taped to them, most did not.

"I'm looking for Dawn Dixon. Does she live here?"

The old man's eyes narrowed and he perused Sonny up and down.

"Are you one of them social workers?"

Sonny was momentarily puzzled at the question. "No, I'm her boyfriend."

The man's expression immediately changed. He actually smiled, revealing a mouthful of very brown-stained teeth.

"Hers is the garage apartment, around the back," he said. "She just got home a few minutes ago. Her roommate ain't come from work yet. She'll probably be here in another half hour or so. You'd better take your chance to be alone."

The old guy winked at Sonny.

He thanked him and walked around the house and down the driveway. The garage doors were open and displayed not cars, but a dozen dented and smelly garbage cans, junk appliances and rolls of old carpeting. The stairs to the apartment were on the far side. There was a small landing halfway up where a mismatched selection of women's underwear hung on an improvised clothesline. He stepped past it feeling as if he were intruding someplace where he was not welcome.

He stood in front of the threshold and knocked on the door.

"It's open!" a voice called back.

Sonny hesitated.

Uncertain, he turned the doorknob and peeked inside. From somewhere inside he could hear the water running.

"Hello!" he called out.

"Come on in!" He recognized the voice as Dawn's. "I'm in the shower. I'll be right out."

Sonny let himself in. The apartment was really just two rooms. Sparse with furniture but overrun with clothes that seemed to be draped everywhere on everything. He thought about seating himself, but the couch and all the chairs were covered. So he just walked around. Though it was more like pacing than wandering the apartment.

The kitchen consisted of one wall that had a sink, refrigerator, stove and a couple of cabinets. There was no giant mess or pile of dishes. It was surprisingly neat and tidy, especially when compared to the draping clothes disaster in the rest of the house. The table, however, was piled with mail and tiny shampoo bottles, cartons of cigarettes and magazines. He was just walking away, when he saw his name.

The corner of a lined-paper tablet was visible beneath a handful of little soaps from the Holiday Inn. He saw *Vernon Henry Leland*. He pulled it out of the stack. It actually read in fancy girlish script, *Mr. and Mrs. Vernon Henry Leland*. His parents? That was even more curious. Then as he looked at the rest of the page he saw *Mrs. Dawn Leland and Dawn and Sonny Leland* in various writing styles.

He smiled. It felt like the first time he'd smiled in a week.

She was practicing her signature. She'd said that she was done with him, but she was still dreaming of a future together.

He was going to make sure that happened.

In the other room the sound of water stopped. Guilty, Sonny stepped away from the table to stand in the middle of the room. He could hear her movements.

"We're getting low on toilet paper again," Dawn called out. "What they have at the cafeteria is so cheap it's hardly worth taking. Do you think you could get some from the arena?"

Sonny knew the question wasn't for him, but he answered it anyway.

"No, but I could pick some up at the convenience store on the corner," he replied.

There was an instant of complete stillness. Then Dawn stood in the bedroom doorway clad only in two towels, one around her body and the other twisted on her hair. She didn't look happy.

"What are you doing in here?"

"You invited me in."

"I thought you were Teresa's boyfriend."

"I don't even know Teresa," he answered. "But I'm your boyfriend."

She shook her head. "Sonny, no…" she began.

"I've heard your whole story," he interrupted. "I know that you've been lying to me. And I know how you operate. When things get tough, you just run away. But you can't run away from how much I love you, Dawn. Those kinds of feelings always catch up to you."

"Oh, Sonny," she said. "You should have just cut your losses and moved on."

"You and me together, there's no loss in that. It's all win-win."

She shook her head. "With me, Sonny, it's more often lose-lose."

"Not anymore," he said. "That's all behind you."

"It is me," she insisted. "I can never settle down, never be happy. Can never have anyone long-term or let them have me."

"I refuse to believe that," he told her. "You've loved me for months. I know you want to be with me, not just now, but forever. Without you, I just feel like the best part of me is missing."

Her expression was tender, almost tearful.

"Sonny, that is the sweetest thing anyone has ever said," she told him. "But it just won't work."

"Why not?"

"Your mother hates me."

He didn't deny it, but he shrugged. "From what I hear, you're not crazy about her, either."

"I was really nasty to her," Dawn admitted.

"You both love me," he said. "Eventually that will have to bring you together."

"I don't think life works that way," she said.

"It does, Dawn," he promised. "I know that eventually it does."

"I don't think we have that much time," she said.

"We have our whole lives."

She sighed heavily and shook her head.

"I'm pregnant," Dawn stated flatly.

Sonny felt his jaw drop open, but no words came out.

In a perfect world, Sonny thought, he would have continued to date Dawn as he finished college. His parents would have had more time to get to know her, to become accustomed to her, to realize that their impressions of her might be wrong. But Dawn and Sonny didn't live in a perfect world.

"I guess that's why I got so mad at your mother," Dawn continued. "I was already terrified of losing you. In my whole life I've never loved anybody as much as I do you. But I'd made so much stuff up, I'd told so many lies. I knew it would be impossible to convince you I hadn't gotten pregnant on purpose."

"I would never have thought that."

She shrugged. "Well, it doesn't matter," she said.

"I've already decided that I'm not going to expect anything from you. I'm keeping the baby, but you don't need to be a part of it. I'm leaving town as soon as I can get a little money together. You won't ever even hear from me again."

She turned and walked back into the bedroom.

Sonny hesitated only a minute before following her.

Dawn was perched in front of the vanity on a swivel stool. She'd removed the towel from her wet hair. It lay along her shoulders, a mass of twists and tangles. She grabbed up a comb and began a determined, almost angry attack on the snagged mass.

He walked up and stood behind her, watching her face in the mirror. His mother was not right about her. She *could* care for another person, she *could* form a loving bond. But very ordinary hope, that most of the people in the world took for granted, was not something she'd experienced. She expected rejection, to be unloved, to be alone.

Sonny took the comb out of her hand and began easing it through the mess of curls.

"You're not a blonde anymore," he said.

Dawn nodded. "I thought I'd try brunette for a while, hoping no one would recognize me," she said. "Sometimes I think that the only thing I can change about my life is my hair color."

He continued to comb. Sonny had caressed her many times, but he never touched her as he did now, with such casual intimacy and purpose. Slowly, gently, with deliberate intent to cause not a pain or pull, he sorted out the mess of knots and snarls and laid the smoothed tresses on her bare shoulders.

For a while she watched him. Then she closed her eyes. He didn't know if she was trying to blot out the sight or memorize it for a lifetime.

"Your world is about to change a lot," he said.

Dawn looked up at him and acknowledged that truth with a careless shrug.

"It'll be great," she insisted. "I'll go to a new town, maybe even a new state. Nobody will know me. I can start all over."

Sonny nodded.

"Okay, if that's what you want," he said. "I'd better get packing."

"Packing?"

"I'm coming with you," he said. "If you're leaving town, then *we're* leaving town."

Dawn shook her head.

"No, Sonny," she said. "You don't have to do that."

"I know I don't have to do it," he said. "I *want* to do it."

"You have a life here," Dawn insisted. "You have family here and a future here."

Sonny spun the stool around and squatted down beside her. He laid his hand on her breast. "Dawn, this is my life, my future, my family. In your heart is the only place I want to be. And I want to be there always."

"Oh, Sonny," she said, her eyes glistening with tears. "I could never forget you."

He took a deep breath. He went for the brass ring. Everything he wanted in life seemed to be hanging on it.

"Marry me, Dawn," he said. "Marry me and live your life with me. We can stay or we can go. I just

want to be with you. I don't care if it's here in Knoxville or in Kuala Lumpur."

"Kuala where? Is that the place with the little
bears?"

"No, the koala bears are in Australia. Kuala Lumpur
is somewhere else. Dawn, please say yes," he pleaded.

He could see her hesitating.

He knew she was afraid. It was so hard for her to
trust. But that afternoon, that moment, she took a
leap of faith.

"Okay."

Dawn and Sonny Leland were married in the
Knox County Courthouse with only the judge's clerical assistants as witnesses. Despite what anyone else
may have thought or imagined, both were very
happy.

# REAL LIFE
## 9
### →◄

"What are you staring at, geek head?"

Sierra's question jerked me out of my faraway fantasy.

"Nothing," I replied.

"What are you doing out here?"

I was sitting in the cushioned metal glider on the front porch.

"I'm watching for Mom," I answered.

"She's still not back from the doctor, huh?" Sierra said, as if she'd just noticed.

"No."

"How long can it take to pee in a cup?"

I rolled my eyes and sighed. "She's not pregnant."

"I bet she is."

"I asked her and she said no."

"She's in denial."

"You don't know anything."

"Oh, yeah, right," Sierra scoffed. "*I* don't know anything. Unlike Baby Kota, who knows it all."

"Don't call me Kota!" I insisted angrily.

"Kota. Kota. Kota," she snottily repeated my most despised nickname.

One of the Sonnys had given me that name. He was the freckled guy with the big monster truck. I liked him and I thought Kota sounded cute, so I encouraged everybody to call me that. Until one of my nine-year-old classmates transformed it to Kota-X and ultimately to *Kotex*. I tried to shut that twerp up, but couldn't. Everybody in school caught on. I lived miserably as a sanitary napkin for almost all of fourth grade. When we moved, I threatened Sierra on pain of death never to refer to me as Kota again.

I raised my fist with the intention of socking her right in the shin. Unfortunately, I was distracted by the sound of a car slowing in front of the house. I stopped in midmotion and turned, expecting Mom.

One of those cool little hybrid sedans pulled into the driveway next door. A man got out. He was an ordinary guy, a business kind of guy, wearing tan slacks, a white shirt and tie. Glancing up at us, he gave a friendly wave as if he knew us.

I was so surprised, I didn't respond. Sierra, however, waved back with enthusiasm.

"All right!" she said to me. "Great-looking hunk living next door. This town is improving."

I gazed up at my sister in stupefaction. "He's just some old guy," I pointed out.

"So is Matthew McConaughey," Sierra pointed out. "But with the right clothes and haircut, he's straight up dishy."

I honestly didn't see it, but I kept looking anyway.

He opened the back door of the car and a minute later a kid emerged. The boy was blond, skinny, wearing jean shorts and a Wesley Center Day Camp T-shirt. He looked up at us, too.

What a dork! I thought. He was nearly as tall as me, but he still sat in the back seat with child locks.

"Bummer!" Sierra said behind me with a sigh. "You'd know the cute ones are already taken. And in this town, how many cute ones can there be?"

She was obviously still talking about the kid's father. Having lost interest, Sierra went back inside the house. I watched as the two conversed on the driveway. The boy shot a couple of surreptitious looks in my direction, shaking his head. His father apparently overruled him and he followed reluctantly as they headed in my direction.

Immediately I sat up straighter wondering what I'd done or why they were coming my way.

"Hi, there!" the man called out still halfway across the lawn.

"Hi." My reply was a little less enthusiastic.

He came right up to the edge of the porch.

"I'm Del Tegge," he said. He looked like he wanted to offer his hand, but with me not moving one inch in his direction, he shoved them into his pockets, trying to be casual.

"This is my son, Spencer."

"Hi," I repeated.

There was a moment of uncomfortable hesitation. Sierra was right, the guy was nice looking in a parent kind of way. His hair was thinning in the front, but it was neatly parted and still looked good. His eyes were bright and inquisitive, as if the whole world were fascinating. He was wearing Dockers and a neatly pressed button-down sport shirt. This was definitely not a tattoos and beer-belly kind of guy. This was someone's dad. For that alone, I immediately liked him.

"So, you're a friend of Vern and Phrona?" he asked.

A yes seemed the obvious answer since I was sitting on their porch steps, but then again I could have been a cat burglar casing the joint.

"They're…they're my grandparents."

It felt strange to say that, strange to hear it out loud. And it sure looked as if it came as strange news to the Del Tegge guy. His mouth dropped open so far, he would have lost his teeth if they hadn't been attached.

"I…I didn't know they had children," he said.

"My dad died before I was born," I told him.

"Oh, I'm sorry," he responded automatically, as if it had something to do with him.

I shrugged and turned my attention to the kid. He was as resistible close up as he'd been at a distance. His features were delicate, almost feminine. His mouth was bulging with a latticework of shiny gray metal. He couldn't meet my eyes. He knew he was a dork. He also knew that his dad was about to humiliate him and there was nothing he could do to stop it.

"You're here for a summer visit?" Del asked.

"Yeah, I guess we'll be here awhile," I answered.

"That's great! Spence is here with me for the summer," he said, clapping his son on the shoulder in a camaraderie fashion. "He hasn't met very many people, so he has nobody to play with here in the neighborhood."

Humiliation complete. He'd not only branded Spence as friendless, but the suggestion that anyone of his age would "play" was proclaiming lameness extraordinaire.

I almost felt sorry for him. Almost.

"How old are you?" the man asked me.

"Thirteen."

"Spence is eleven," he told me. "But he's tall for his age and very bright. He was the youngest entrant to make it to the city-wide science fair."

"Science guy, huh?" I said, taking pity on the poor schmuck. "Sure, we can *play* together some time. We'll play science, that's always fun."

The kid knew I was blowing. He nodded. It was a weird kind of nod, head down, fatalistic, nothing positive about it.

But the father smiled, really pleased.

He had a nice smile. I was glad that I had bothered, even if it was a lie.

"Great! Great," he said. "I was hoping Spence would find a friend. I never expected it to be the girl next door."

He laughed, like it was a little joke. I managed a warm grin.

"Yeah, sure," I continued, more genuinely. "I don't have any friends here, either. I just have my sister. Maybe she can hang with us, too."

The kid's head was still down, but he was looking up at me.

"I can't do it today though," I told them. "My mom had to go out and she expects me to be waiting here for her when she gets back. But soon, maybe tomorrow or some other time."

"Sure, that's great," the man said.

A little clumsily they said goodbye.

"Bye Del," I said. "See ya around, Spencer."

I watched them walk to their own house and go inside. Spence never looked back. That was good.

The kid knew the score. The dad didn't have a clue. But that was all right. What dads didn't know couldn't hurt them. The kid was a real loser. Science geeks usually are, and I can speak from experience on that. As long as the dad didn't know, then he could be cool with the kid. He could be proud.

I continued to sit there for a few more minutes. I was wishing that I could finish my book, wondering if there was a library. I still didn't know where there was a bus line, but all that had taken a back seat to wondering about Mom, out there in Knoxville somewhere in her funeral suit.

As time stretched on, my imagination was beginning to run wild with speculation.... Somebody'd run a red light and she was lying in the street injured.... The doctor had mistaken her for someone else and she'd be rushed into surgery to amputate a healthy leg.... She'd dumped us here, she was never coming back....

When the Dodge came cruising up the street, I jumped to my feet. Mom was driving a little too fast and when she turned into the driveway, she jumped the curb. I'd seen some of her boyfriends do worse, but Mom was always very careful with the car. We always needed it for our getaways.

She came to a stop at the side of the house, just out of my line of vision. I waited, expecting to hear the car door slam followed by the sound of her heels on the driveway heading in my direction. Nothing. I stood up and leaned forward to see if she'd driven around to the back, maybe to go in through the kitchen. No, the car was just sitting there in the driveway.

Curious, I approached.

Mom was sitting in the driver's seat, her arms across the steering wheel, her head down resting on them. I walked around the car to the open window next to her. Inside me a scared, sinking feeling began to take hold. It was hot outside, but I began to tremble as if I were cold, my teeth were chattering.

"Mom?"

She jerked upright. I'd startled her. Her eyes were red and swollen and awash with tears.

I froze at the sight. It wasn't as if I'd never seen Mom cry. She often cried during breakups with boyfriends and occasionally she'd boo-hoo at a sappy movie. But this was different. I don't know how I knew that, but I knew it.

"What are you doing here?"

She said it as if it were some accusation.

"I'm waiting for you."

She wiped her eyes on the back of her hand, opened the door and grabbed her purse. She'd given up on the gray jacket in the heat of the afternoon, but she still looked very un-Mom-like in the plain gray skirt and a white shell blouse.

"What did the doctor say?"

We were walking along the driveway. Ignoring my question, she wrapped her arm around my shoulder and kissed me on the top of my head.

"What have you been up to today?" she asked.

"Mostly just waiting for you," I told her. "I met the neighbors, played with the dog. But mostly I just waited for you."

Together we walked around the car and across the lawn toward the front door.

"Where's your sister?" she asked.

I shrugged.

"*General Hospital, People's Court,* some serious, unhappy place out there in TV land," I answered.

Mom laughed a little. I hoped she would.

"Sierra does love her daytime drama," she said. "But TV on a day like this. That's just an absolute waste."

"Yeah, I guess so."

"You girls need to get out and explore the city," Mom said. "Would you like that? Knoxville is a really nice place to be a kid."

"I thought you hated this town," I said.

"Where'd you get an idea like that?" she asked.

"Uh...well maybe it was something about the term *Knox Villains.*"

"Ouch," Mom said, as if the truth pinched her. "Okay, so maybe I exaggerated a bit."

"Sometimes that happens."

"Would you like to go to the library?" she asked.

"Yes!" I agreed, excitedly.

"I thought that might perk you up," she said.

"You knew it would," I told her. "And we'll make Sierra come along for her own good. She won't read anything, but maybe just being around the books, some kind of knowledge will seep in."

"I doubt that," Mom said. "But I guess we can try. I'll get Vern to take you."

I stopped in my tracks. "Vern?"

She nodded.

"I want you to take us, Mom."

"I can't," she said. "I've got some things to do."

"What things?"

"Personal things," she answered. "Besides I just got home. I'm tired. It'll be better to go with Vern. He lives here and actually knows where the library is."

"You used to live here," I pointed out.

She shook her head. "That was a lot of years ago," she said. "And I didn't spend any time in the library."

"Not at all?"

"I don't remember even visiting the place," she said. "I was like Sierra. No, actually I was worse. She reads fashion magazines. I didn't read anything but exit signs."

"Exit signs?" I asked, curiously.

She tweaked my nose.

"I was always on the lookout for a way to escape," she said.

# REAL LIFE
## 10

━◆━

There was something going on. I knew it. Sierra knew it. I suppose even Vern knew it, but nobody was saying anything. Mom had a brief, whispered conversation with the man who was my dad's father, and he started rousting us out of the house.

Mom moved her car to the far side of the driveway, underneath an old basketball net, so that Vern could back out his older but very shiny and well-kept Saab.

Sierra was so taken with the car that she completely forgot about how annoyed she was from being dragged from the television.

I watched Mom standing on the patio. She was smiling, waving. But there was something bittersweet about her expression. As if we were going off on some exciting new adventure and she could not come with us. Just before we were out of sight, I saw her turn and head toward the little office behind the garage. She was going to speak with Mrs. Leland.

Vern's lightheartedness seemed deliberate. I didn't want to be drawn into it. For Sierra, though, it was welcome. A trip to the library was no thrill, but somehow Vern's eagerness to show her the city and his enthusiasm for it attracted her.

"This is the Old City," he told her, pointing out an

area of dark brick buildings on the far side of a huge web of railroad tracks. "It used to be a pretty run-down area, but they've been restoring it. There are nice restaurants now. And nightspots."

"Do teenagers hang out there?"

"I don't know, maybe," he said.

Sierra craned her neck forward trying to look. I wouldn't even glance in that direction.

When we stopped at a red light, she pointed to an area near the river. It had flags flying and fountains with water shooting high in the sky. In the center was a huge golden dome.

"What's that over there?" she asked.

"That's the Sunsphere," Vern answered. "It's the centerpiece of World's Fair Park." He glanced back at me. "Did you know Knoxville was once the site of the World's Fair?"

My response was a shrug, being deliberately negative.

"Did you go there?" Sierra asked.

"Sure, we went nearly every week," he answered. "Sonny was about your age, I guess. He'd always liked science, but the exhibits sparked his interest and his friends', as well. They'd come down here after school to just hang around. Sonny loved all the noise and people from all over the globe and the sheer excitement of it." Vern paused thoughtfully for a moment as if savoring the memory. "They have wonderful concerts down there now."

"Oh! I love concerts," Sierra told him eagerly. "I went to see BlastOBrees when we were in Seattle. It knocked me out completely."

"I think he means concerts like Mozart and Beethoven," I interrupted. "Classical stuff."

"Oh." Sierra's comment was short and deflated.

"It's a venue for popular music, too," Vern assured her. "I saw in the paper that KC and the Sunshine Band are going to perform there."

Sierra sneaking a look back at me and mouthed KC and the Sunshine Band in the form of a question. I shook my head, not knowing any more than she.

The library was right in the downtown. Vern pulled into the parking garage and we took an elevator up.

"We met your neighbors today," Sierra said to him, simply making conversation.

"Oh?"

"What were the names?" Sierra asked me. She hadn't actually met anyone.

"Del Tegge," I answered. "And his kid, Spencer."

Vern nodded. "Good man," he said. He made that sound like a high compliment. "Del and I have a game of chess going most of the time."

"He's hoping that Dakota and his son can be friends," Sierra said.

I wanted to strangle her for mentioning it, but I had only myself to blame for telling her in the first place.

Vern turned to me and nodded approvingly. "That would be a real nice thing, honey," he told me. "Del and Cassandra just got through a miserable divorce. I suspect Spence could really use a friend."

I suppose I should have been honest and told him that I had no intention of ever spending one more minute with Spencer Tegge. But with him looking down at me that way, as if he liked me and respected me, I just suddenly had a hard time being the person that I truly am.

"I guess it wouldn't hurt to show the kid a little attention," I said.

Vern smiled at me. I recognized that smile. It was my father's smile in the photograph under my bed. It was Daddy's smile exactly.

"I think the teen section is here on the second floor," Vern told us, as the elevator doors opened.

Neither Sierra and I were particularly interested in the "teen section." She would only care about the magazines. And I had graduated from young adult books in the fifth grade. Still we got off the elevator and followed him through the media area to the comfortable zone known by the staff as the Hangout.

It was not a totally uncool place. Several comfortable chairs and a couch looked out a big plate glass window onto the street. On the walls were posters of rock stars and sports celebs urging us to read. One really hot pop diva was holding her book in such a weird fashion it was obvious that she'd never read anything in her life. I didn't say anything because Sierra admired her a lot for her cool clothes and the guys she dated.

"So what do you think?" Vern asked.

"It's a nice library," I answered honestly. And I had been in enough of them to make comparisons.

"Okay then, you girls make yourselves at home," he said. "If you need me, I'll be browsing around in nonfiction."

"Sure," we both agreed.

We located the current magazines and Sierra

made herself comfortable with a stack of them. She loved the glossy pictures and she wasn't particular. She would be as content with high fashion or entertainment or gossip rags. Just as long as it was slick and colorful with more photos than text she'd be happy.

I was less easily appeased. My plan was to go downstairs to wander through the shelves of adult fiction. I was headed in the direction of the circular stairs when I spotted Vern at one of the computer terminals. He was looking up a specific title or subject. As he picked up his notes and headed to the stacks, I was suddenly reminded of the book that I'd left behind in Grand Prairie. The one about chaos theory. What a great idea, to see if this library had a copy.

I hurried over to the terminal. I sat down on the stool, ready to input my title, when I caught sight of the list of books displayed on the screen Vern had left behind.

*Raising the Babies of Your Babies*
*Frontline Grandparenting*
*When Your Children Give You Their Children*
*Grandma, Where Has Mommy Gone?*

I stared at the titles, my heart in my throat. At first I couldn't quite get my mind around what it meant. But when I got it, it hit me like a ton of bricks.

I'd been right. I'd been completely right. All this weird change in Mom's MO was disastrous news. Mom was dumping us. She was dumping us here with these strangers. After all these years of dragging us from town to town, from Sonny to Sonny, she was finally leaving us behind with the only people who might conceivably take us.

I just couldn't believe it. I just wouldn't believe it. I couldn't let it happen.

I ran to the magazine section. Sierra had moved from the spot I'd left her. She was standing with a tall, young guy who had a skateboard in a sling draped over his shoulder.

"Sierra," I interrupted. "I need to talk to you."

She glanced toward me, her expression annoyed.

"Not now," she said.

"Now," I insisted. "It's important."

"What could be that important?"

"This is."

She looked at the guy and rolled her eyes.

"It's my kid sister," she told him.

He nodded, giving me a skeptical look and her a big grin.

"Go ahead, take a minute," he told Sierra. "I'm not going anywhere."

Sierra gave him a wink and moved away at a very unhurried pace. We stepped out of earshot. She was still smiling when she groused at me through clenched teeth.

"Can't you see I'm kind of busy here?" she said.

"Sierra, I think Mom's dumping us," I told her.

"What?"

"Vern's looking up books on how to raise kids that get dumped on you," I explained. "Mom must be dumping us here."

"Don't be stupid," she said. "Mom's never going to dump us. She loves us. She'd never leave us."

"She's acting really weird, you know something is going on, and now he's looking up these books. It has to mean that. What else could it mean?"

"Look, everything is going to be fine," she insisted, glancing back to make sure that guy was still waiting for her. "You've like been turning into a basket case ever since we got here. Mom's cool. Knoxville is great. You're in the library, your favorite place. Why don't you just chill and have a good time? Don't bother me anymore. I'm busy talking to Seth."

She walked away, unwilling to listen anymore. That's the very big downside reality of being the youngest. Even when you're smarter, your big sister will never take you seriously.

I was genuinely scared. For all I knew, Mom was, at that very moment, packing up the car and heading out of town. Just disappearing would make sense to her, I was sure. Get us out of the way and get gone without any tears or explanations. I'd seen her leave a lot of Sonnys just that way.

I hurried down to the circulation desk.

"I need to borrow your telephone," I told the young woman at the desk.

"It's not our policy to allow public use of this phone," she answered without even glancing up. "There's a pay phone down the street in front of the courthouse."

"I don't have money for a pay phone," I admitted, my voice rising with every word. "And this is an emergency."

She looked up at me then. I guess I must have appeared as desperate as I felt. Surprisingly, she opened the little half door on the end of the counter and motioned to a phone on an empty desk.

I sat down and picked up the receiver immediately. I just held it in my hand for a moment before putting it down. The library clerk was waiting on a patron at the desk.

"Do you have a phone directory?"

Her expression turned long-suffering but she motioned to the desk.

"Third drawer on your right."

I frantically searched through the book, running my finger down a long list of names until I spotted it. Leland, Vernon H. I quickly punched in the number. It rang twice.

"Hello."

"Mrs. Leland, I need to speak to my mother."

"Sierra?"

"No, this is Dakota. I need to speak to my mother."

"Just a minute."

The wait was a miserable lifetime as I imagined Mom, clothes and bags and boxes stacked in the back seat, pulling out of the Leland driveway forever.

"Hello?"

"Mom, you're still there?"

"Of course I'm here," she answered. "What's wrong, Dakota?"

"You can't leave us," I said. "You can't dump us here. We've been with you too long. You need us, Mom. I know we're lots of trouble, but you need us."

There was a long hesitation on the line.

"I don't know what you're talking about," she said finally.

"I'm talking about why we're here," I said. "Why'd you bring us to the Lelands? You never go back to places you've been. You never meet up with people you knew. You're dumping us here with these strangers, aren't you?"

"No, of course I'm not," she said. "Nothing in the world could make me leave you, if I had a choice."

I'd just began to relax during the first part of that statement, before the second part kicked in.

"What does that mean?"

Again she hesitated.

"I wanted to wait until I have everything sorted in my mind," she said. "I guess when you get home, we can sit down, the three of us, and have a little talk."

"I can't wait, Mom," I told her. "You have to tell me what's going on before I go completely nuts."

"Oh, Dakota," she said with a huge sigh. "This is not the kind of news that you tell over the phone."

"You've got to tell me."

"Sweetie, I'm sick," she said simply.

"Sick? What kind of sick?"

"Very sick," she answered. "I have cancer."

# SONNY DAYS
## 11

— ◆ —

It became quickly evident to Sonny that it was his mother's fervent hope that his marriage fail. Or maybe she was just hoping it wouldn't succeed. The news about the baby was received with all the joy and fanfare of the arrival of a plague. His determination to "make things right" with a hasty wedding was not a solution that particularly pleased his parents.

"There is no such thing as a shotgun wedding these days," his father pointed out. "Lots of children are born out of wedlock. There's no real shame in that anymore."

"Dawn and I wanted to get married," Sonny explained. "Sure, we would have liked to have waited, but there's no need. I want to be a part of my child's life."

He and Vern were alone together in the study of his parents' house. Seated opposite each other at the chess table, they took turns moving the pieces but neither was paying attention to the game.

Sonny moved the black pawn to e5 and took the white pawn at d4.

The women in their lives were notably absent. His mother had offered Dawn only the coldest of invitations. Dawn declined, insisting she had no intention of "ever darkening that harpy's door."

His dad looked unhappy, but at least he wasn't

angry. He moved his bishop to take the black pawn at d4.

"I don't know Dawn," Vern said. "Therefore I am in no position to make judgments about her."

Sonny nodded gratefully.

"I do know you," his father continued. "I know that you are smart and responsible. But you can be hasty and rash. I believe this marriage is both those things."

Sonny raised his chin. "It's my choice," he said. "My life and my decision."

Black knight took the white bishop at d4.

Vern nodded acceptance. "That's true," he admitted. "Your mother and I don't agree with your decision, but then we don't have to. We only have to continue to love you and wish you well."

The words sounded good, but there was something ominous about them.

White rook took the black knight at d4.

"We won't be offering any further financial support," Vern said. "As a married man, you'll be expected to support your family yourself."

"That's my first priority, to get a better job with longer hours," Sonny said. "Maybe something in the evenings. We won't be able to afford much of a place. But we can get by on very little. I think I can make up the difference from what it has been costing you to support me to what it will be costing to support us. You and Mama could pay my tuition and the same money you would have provided for the dorm and books. Your expenses won't actually go up."

He moved the black rook to f8.

"No, Sonny," Vern said quietly. "We won't be doing that. One of the unspoken understandings about accepting financial support from other people is that those people then have a say in your life. Clearly you don't want that. You've made a lifelong commitment to a woman and a child without even bothering to consult us, without even hearing our opinions or considering our council. You do have the right to do that. But we don't have any obligation to pay for it."

Sonny felt he'd been kicked in the stomach.

"I know that you are not obliged to pay anything," he said. "I understand that you are angry. I'm sure you're right that we should have talked this over. But with the...bad blood...between Mama and Dawn, I didn't feel as if a rational discussion between adults would be possible."

Vern moved the white pawn to e5.

"Your wedding wasn't the only hasty, ill-considered decision you've made here," he said. "I believe we can assume that this child coming into the world was unplanned. That was reckless on your part."

"Accidents happen, Dad," Sonny replied. "There is no one hundred percent fail-safe contraceptive."

Sonny moved the black knight to h7.

His father raised an eyebrow. "There is abstinence," Vern said.

There was no way to argue that.

Vern's white pawn took the black pawn at d6.

"Please listen, Dad," Sonny pleaded. "I know that you and Mama are angry and disappointed in me. I'm really sorry about that. I can't change what's already happened. But if you punish me by not helping me, there's a very good chance that I won't be able to finish school."

Vern nodded. "I'm probably more aware of that than you are," he said.

"Then you have to help."

Sonny moved the black pawn to c5.

His father shook his head. "I'm not doing this to punish you," he told Sonny. "Your mother, she's really mad, she's probably in this to punish you or manipulate you, but that's not my thinking."

"What are you thinking?" Sonny asked.

"I'm thinking that you've have a very nice, middle-class upbringing," Vern said. "That you've never had to struggle or worry or face adversity. We made it easy for you. The world was handed to you on a platter. That's not always best for people. You're going to have to figure out your own way now, and it's going to be tough. But I have confidence in you. You'll make it on your own and you'll have cause to be proud of yourself. And you and your little wife will not have to be beholden to us ever at all. That can be a good thing."

Vern moved the white queen to a8.

"Checkmate," he said.

In the weeks following, Sonny continued to feel hurt and disappointed at his parents' rejection. Dawn was delighted.

"We don't need them," she told him. "Just blow 'em off and forget they ever existed. That's what I did with my relatives and I highly recommend it."

Sonny wasn't ready to do that. But with his mother's obvious resentment and his increased obligations, he saw them less and less. If he was going to ever be able to afford college again, he wouldn't be able to take a minimum-wage job. He tried to find something that paid more. Without education and in a tough job market, it wasn't easy. Ultimately, he joined up with a logging crew. It was hard, dangerous, outside work. But it paid well.

"Just stick close to me," Lonnie Beale, a veteran tree feller in his midforties, told him the first day. "I've been managing to come home every day for twenty-two years. You do like I do and you'll do all right."

It was a time in Sonny's life when things were tough and complicated. He'd always been close to his father, always been able to talk things over with him. That relationship was now strained. On the daily grind, Lonnie became a surrogate father to him.

"Dawn says she happier than she's ever been in her life. But anything and everything that goes wrong and she just bursts into tears."

Lonnie chuckled. "That's just baby carrying," he reassured him. "My late wife, God rest her soul, gave me six before her heart give out. Each and every one come different. Some she was crazy as a hatter for nine months. Others she's sweet. Some she's crying. Another she's mad enough to kill me. Hormones don't have no sense, so don't waste your time trying to make sense of 'em."

Sonny laughed.

"Just keep loving her," Lonnie advised. "Say 'yes, dear' and 'no, dear' and wait it out. She'll be the gal you thought you married soon enough."

The afternoon Dawn went into labor, the hospital called the supervisor on the radio. The cell phone reception was terrible on the mountain where they were cutting. He got a lift into town in the cab of a log truck. He was antsy, nervous, the ride seemed interminable.

When he finally arrived at the hospital, he was surprised to see his parents there.

"Did Dawn call you?"

"The hospital notified us as the emergency contact," Vern said. "They weren't sure you'd get the message. And naturally we want to be here for the birth of our first grandchild."

His mother didn't look all that pleased. But they were here and Sonny was grateful. Though he didn't really have time to say so. The baby was crowning, they told him. He had to hurry to the birthing room if he was going to see his child come into the world.

He should have felt a little foolish dressed as he was in blue scrubs and a paper hair net, but for Sonny that was nothing when compared to the overwhelming experience of fatherhood. Dawn held his hand, moaning and sweating as she pushed their baby into the world.

"It's a girl," the physician announced.

"A girl?"

Somehow that was even more unbelievable. This was a little girl, a real human being that hadn't existed before but was now here on earth and was his responsibility.

The doctor let him cut the cord. His hands were shaking.

Sonny was laughing and crying and talking to his young wife all at the same time.

"She's beautiful! Dawn, she's absolutely beautiful."

"Is she all right? Does she have all her fingers and toes?"

He reassured her. "She's perfect, perfect."

While the nurses washed and weighed the baby and wrapped her in a little pink blanket, Sonny leaned over Dawn and kissed her.

"Are you sorry it's not a boy?" she asked him.

The question surprised him. "A boy? Yuk. I'm a boy, and they're not all they're cracked up to be," he answered. "They're messy and dirty. They're like lava lamps, fun to look at but not too bright. I love girls. A girl suits me perfectly."

Dawn gave him a serious look. "You're sure," she said.

Sonny nodded. "I'm the luckiest guy in the world to have two wonderful girls. I have my Dawn and now I have this little sweetie."

The nurse brought the baby over and laid her at her mother's breast. The child opened her eyes for a moment then gave a big yawn. They both oohed and aahed as if she'd done something wonderful.

"What are we going to call her?" Dawn asked.

Sonny looked thoughtful. "I don't know. Did you have something in mind?"

She looked at me closely. "Well, I was thinking of something like Emily or Sarah," she told him.

"Those are pretty names, I guess," he said. "But pretty ordinary and this little girl is definitely extraordinary. I think we need to give her a name that fits that."

"Like what?"

"Well, she's beautiful and majestic and she's from the mountains of Tennessee. Maybe we should give her a mountain name."

Dawn lowered her head and eyed him skeptically. "You're going to call my daughter Rocky Top?"

He laughed.

"Let's name her after mountains, beautiful mountains," he said.

"I don't know any mountains," Dawn admitted.

"Well, there's Yosemite," Sonny said. "But that would be a lot for a little girl to spell. Guess she could call herself Sam for short. She might grow up to have red hair, but the handlebar moustache would be tough."

"Shut up!" Dawn scolded playfully and feigned a punch at him for being silly. The cartoon character Yosemite Sam did not in the least resemble their beautiful daughter.

"Well, I do think it has to be mountains," Sonny said. "You know how much I love the mountains."

Dawn was thoughtful. "Appalachia? Himalaya?"

"She's kind of small for those big places," Sonny said. "We ought to go with a smaller range. We'll call her Sierra," Sonny said. "Do you like that?"

Dawn sighed. "That's a perfect name for our perfect little girl."

His parents were less thrilled.

"What kind of name is that?" his mother asked.

"It's a pretty name," he answered.

Phrona puffed out a little sigh of disgust. From her purse she retrieved a hefty printout.

"Sonny, you have a venerable heritage to draw upon. I've compiled family names back through the Massachusetts ancestors and to Combe St. Nicholas and Northover," she said. "You don't just give a child a name. It's important to tie future generations to the past." She tore off the back pages of the stack. "Here are the girls."

Randomly Sonny glanced through the list.

"Mehitable? Zinithia?" He shook his head. "Come on, Mama."

She was adamant. "It's a long list. There are plenty of Sarahs and Chloes and Hannahs."

"No," he told her, firmly. "Dawn and I are naming our daughter Sierra. Get to like it."

# REAL LIFE
## 12

——▶ ◀——

Mom made me promise not to say anything to Sierra. She wanted to talk to us both, alone. When we got home from the library she called us into her room. We sat down on her bed, while she paced. After a couple of moments of her walking silently back and forth, she suggested we move to the porch. That wasn't any better. Mom tried to sit in a chair across from the glider, but she couldn't be still.

"Let's walk," she said.

We headed along the sidewalk, Mom and Sierra side by side, me following behind. The late afternoon was overcast and muggy, with all the uncomfortable heat of summer and none of the pleasure of sunshine.

My sister, giddy and self-involved as always, took this opportunity to tell Mom about the guy she'd met at the library. No one would ever accuse Sierra of being secretive. She gave Mom what sounded like a word-for-word replay of her conversation with Seth. She told it as if the information revealed about the sport of skateboarding was fascinating.

I wanted to kick her. With all the stuff Mom had on her mind, the last thing I thought she needed was an up-close-and-personal view of Sierra's love life.

Mom, however, seemed to relax as Sierra talked.

She began smiling and even laughed once at some truly inane comment my sister made.

By the time we reached the edge of the neighborhood, Mom was more like herself, bolstered somehow by Sierra's self-absorption.

In the shade of the giant cement interstate overpass, a small, well-kept playground had sprouted. There was a large wooden fort with turrets and a bridge that could be accessed directly by stairs or, for the more adventurous, rope ladders were available. Mom led us through the open gate and toward an empty area where there was a merry-go-round. She and Sierra sat down and urged me to push them.

I ran around the edge to get them going and then jumped on as we spun round and round like little kids.

As we slowed, Mom held her feet straight out, careful not to drag the ground. She was making it last as long as possible. Only when we were at a complete stop did she turn and lay a hand on Sierra's arm with only a quick glance in my direction.

"There's no way to say this, except just to say it," she began. "I have cancer."

I expected Sierra to react like I had. Shock and fear and a thousand questions. Surprisingly, she seemed very calm. She let Mom talk. And despite the secrecy that had surrounded our move to Knoxville, Mom seemed to welcome the opportunity to tell what she knew. She talked and talked and talked to us. She talked about how good the hospital was, how nice the doctors were, how much safer treatments had become.

She never once talked about dying. That was all I could think about.

"So this surgery you're going to have," Sierra

asked. "It's like they take out the cancer and then you're done with it?"

"No, the lymphomas are not like that," Mom answered. "They don't really settle in an organ. The lymph glands go all over the body, like the veins and arteries. So you may get a mass in one place or the other, but the cancer is sort of everywhere all at once."

"And so they take out the tumors as you get them?"

"No, that's not what they do with this kind of cancer. They're taking this tumor out to get a really good look at it," she answered. "They will send it off to a lab and get it analyzed so they can say with certainty what stage it is at and how best to treat it."

"Maybe they'll find out it's really not a cancer at all," Sierra suggested.

Mom shook her head. "It's definitely non-Hodgkin's lymphoma. They've even got a more specific name for it. But the doctors here have ordered more tests and they want to confirm for themselves the type and stage. If it turns out to be exactly what they think it is now, well, it's what they call an aggressive cancer. I'll have to start getting treatment right away."

"So what is the treatment like?" Sierra asked.

"It's…it's medicine," she said. "They just give me medicine. They call it chemotherapy, but I know that word sounds very scary, probably scarier than it ought to sound. It's really just medicine."

"Are you going to lose your hair?" Sierra asked.

I wanted to kick her; she was totally missing the point.

Mom shrugged. "Maybe," she said. "With chemo, that's pretty common."

Sierra nodded. "That anchorwoman on TV who had breast cancer said that her hair came back in a slightly lighter color and naturally curly. Wouldn't that be cool, to start off again with all new hair?"

I rolled my eyes. My sister was a certifiable smush brain! But Mom laughed.

"Yeah," she agreed with Sierra. "That might be cool."

The attitude of the two of them so cheerful and casual just made me crazy. They played on the swings and teased each other, like nothing really real was even happening.

While Sierra was being a doofus on the monkey bars, Mom turned her attention to me.

"It's all going to be fine," she told me.

I wasn't reassured.

"You knew you had cancer before we came to Tennessee." My tone sounded accusing, but that's exactly how I felt.

"Of course I knew," she admitted. "This knot came up in my groin. I ignored it for months, but it didn't go away. Finally, I went to the doctor. I got the preliminary results the day that we left."

"So Sonny Moroney didn't leave us," I said. "You made that up."

Mom shook her head. "He did leave," she said. "We both knew that he would. We'd talked about my options. But his option was to walk away and he did that."

"So you told him," I accused. "You told some nobody boyfriend who just walks in and out of your life, but you didn't tell us. You didn't tell me."

"I'm telling you now," Mom said.

"Why didn't you say anything to us?" I asked her. "You just ripped us up and dragged us across the country to live with strangers without any explanation. Why did you have to be so secretive?"

Mom hesitated for a long moment. "Because I'm the mother," she answered. "I had to figure out what is best for us. I know you think our family is a democracy, but it's not. I'm the adult. The decisions are mine."

"It's not what's best for *us*. It's what's best for you," I complained louder. "You brought us here so that you could dump us with Vern and Mrs. Leland."

She shook her head. "I told you, that's crazy, Dakota. I'd never leave you girls."

"If you die you'll leave, permanently. And it's pretty convenient to die with us living in their house."

"I didn't say anything about dying," Mom answered. "And don't you breathe even a word about it around your sister."

"But that's what all this is about," I said. "I'm not an idiot, Mom. I can figure things out."

"It's my backup," she said. "If, and I said *if*, something were to happen to me, I have to have some backup. I grew up in foster care. If we'd stayed in Texas, foster care would have been my backup. I would go anywhere, do anything, get along with anyone to keep my daughters from having to do the same."

"You could just stay alive then," I snarled.

I was angry. I was really angry. I knew it was stupid to feel that way, but that's exactly how I felt.

"Dakota, I'm going to do everything I can to keep

living," she told me softly. "And I'm doing that for you girls. If it was just me, I'd run again. I'd head down to the Keys or maybe even Mexico. I'd hang out on the beach and drink to sunrises, have a few laughs with what time I have left. If I was alone in the world, that's what I'd do. But, I'm not alone in the world. I have you and Sierra and I'm going to do everything that the doctors tell me."

"So you'll be all right then?"

I didn't get my question answered. Sierra ran up then to join us. I would never have said anything around my sister.

As we walked back to the Leland's house, it was the two of them together again and me on the sidewalk behind. I had never felt so left out in my life. I was totally scared. And they were acting as if they were just setting off on another goofy road trip.

It was even worse for me as the evening went on. During dinner Mom and Sierra kept yukking it up. Vern seemed inclined to follow their lead. So the only serious-looking people at the table were me and Mrs. Leland. I was not at all pleased to be on her team.

At least she waited for dessert to go over the details that we all knew.

"So this 'second look' biopsy will be day after tomorrow?" she said.

"Yes," Mom answered.

"How long will you be in the hospital? A couple of days?"

"Maybe not even overnight," Mom answered. "If everything goes well, they ought to let me come home as soon as I'm out of recovery."

"Then you'll probably require some care after you get home," Mrs. Leland said.

"Not much, I'm sure. And the girls are very good at that sort of thing," Mom said. "We've always taken care of each other."

"That's a tremendous responsibility for children," Mrs. Leland said.

"My girls are very mature for their age," Mom said.

"I'm sure they've had to be," she said.

I knew that was meant as a deliberate jab at Mom. She punched right back.

"Yes, my girls have never had the chance to get spoiled and lazy like middle-class children," Mom said. "I hope the kids in this neighborhood don't turn out to be a bad influence on them."

That ticked her off.

Mrs. Leland glanced first at Sierra and then at me. "I have concerns of my own," she said. "We've lived in Old North Knoxville for thirty-seven years. We know everyone and they all know us. You'll need to impress upon your daughters the need for them to be on their best behavior."

Mom went silent. I could tell by her eyes that she was mad enough to reach across the table and choke Mrs. Leland. Instead, she retaliated with dark humor.

"Oh, of course," she told her and turned to us. "Girls, you can only stay out drinking and gambling on the weekends. And please remember, it's polite to step out to the porch when you light up your crack pipes."

Mrs. Leland looked like a deer in headlights.

Vern laughed, a little too deliberately.

"Don't worry about a thing, Dawn," he said. "Sierra and Dakota will be fine. Two bright, enthusiastic young girls, I'm sure they'll be no trouble and a big help to all of us. We had a lovely time at the library. I gave them a little minitour of downtown. Not much to see, I suppose when you've lived so many places. But there is a lot here to explore. It will be wonderful. We'll do hiking trips and go swimming. The summer is a magic time in Tennessee. I know you both will just love it here."

Mrs. Leland didn't comment, she went back to eating.

"My neighbor, Del, takes his boy to a day camp thing at the church," Vern said. "Would you girls be interested in doing something like that? You could meet a lot of nice kids."

Sierra smiled at him, a little too sweetly. "I'm probably too old for that," she said and then looked at me, her eyes sparkling, devious. "But I'm sure Dakota would like to go."

My sister should have known not to try to match wits with me.

"Yeah, that would be great," I said. "Spence told me that lots of cool guys hang out there. They actually have skateboarding as one of their special activities."

One of the big advantages of having a sister with the brain function of a pea pod is that you can really put stuff over on her. Sierra's eyes got big, her mouth opened, but she didn't know what to say. She knew I might be lying, but she couldn't be sure.

Unfortunately, Mom is not so easily fooled.

"I don't think either of the girls really needs to be

in camp," she said. "They're used to being on their own while I'm working. I'm sure they'll do fine while I'm in treatment."

"Okay," Vern agreed, nodding. "They'll meet most everybody in church anyway."

There was a long silent pause before Mrs. Leland spoke up.

"Yes, I suppose we will have to take them to Sunday services," she said, almost sighing. "I don't suppose they've had much exposure to religious life."

Mom took the bait again.

"No, unless you count those animal sacrifices under the light of the full moon."

"That is not funny." Mrs. Leland was miffed. "Knoxville is a very conservative community."

"You say the word *conservative* as if it were a virtue instead of a mind-set."

"What would you know about virtue?" Mrs. Leland said under her breath, just loud enough for everyone to hear it.

"Phrona!" Vern's voice was harsh.

Both women immediately became silent.

He gave his wife a stern look and then one almost equally as censuring to my mother. "We're not going to have this kind of bickering among the family."

"It's my fault," Mom said, startling Sierra and me. Her tone was unexpectedly conciliatory. "I really want the girls to get on here," she told the Lelands. "I want Knoxville to be a good experience for them."

"Of course it will be," Vern said.

I don't think anybody else was as certain.

# REAL LIFE
## 13

—▶ ◀—

They cut the bad lymph node out. It was what the doctors in Texas had thought it was, what the doctors in Tennessee hoped that it wasn't. It was Mom who told us.

"It's what they call a high-grade large cell lymphoma," she told us. "It's considered very aggressive. So we have to be aggressive, too."

She was to start chemotherapy the very next week. She'd go to the clinic once a week, where they would give her IVs. At home she would wear a pump that would give her another medicine. And she would take pills every day. She'd do this for three weeks and then she'd get a week off. Mom said that like it was some kind of vacation. Then the next week the chemo would start up again.

"How long does this go on?" I asked her.

"Only six or eight cycles," she said.

I wasn't sure what she meant. "How long is a cycle?"

"Well, it's the whole month," she answered. "Three weeks of chemo and a week off."

"You're talking like six to eight months?"

"Well, for sure I'm going to be hanging around

with you girls, living off the Lelands, like a big old slug all summer," she said.

Sierra laughed. "A summer of slugs. I can go for that."

Mom talked like it was no big deal. Medicine was medicine, she said. But I knew this stuff was no aspirin or cold pill. It was like taking poison.

To be reassuring, Mom took us to the hospital to show us around.

"I just want you to see the place, so you'll know where I'll be all the time," she told us.

I think she was trying to make us feel better about everything. The Cancer Center at the University of Tennessee was brand-new. It was clean and bright, the walls were adorned with beautiful artwork and the floor-to-ceiling windows looked out on views of south Knoxville and the river. I guess she thought we'd see what a nice place this was and we'd be more confident that everything was going to be all right.

The staff all seemed young and friendly, laughing and joking around, a lot different than the patients. The place was filled with thin, frail-looking people with off-color complexions and hollow eyes.

It was Mom's appearance that was the most reassuring. She'd thrown off the dowdy wardrobe that had been her basic uniform since arriving at the Lelands. She was wearing a spaghetti-strap knit top that clearly showed off her nipples and was cut low enough in front that the entire heart-shaped vine of roses tattoo was visible. Her favorite jeans were low-riding and tight fitting. The rhinestones along the hem drew attention to the five-inch glam high heels that made her look tall and sexy.

It was Mom at her most ultimate Mom-ness. This is the person I knew her to be. And it felt a lot better somehow looking at her like that than the way she'd been these last few days.

She was flirty and sexy with all the guys. Doctors and janitors alike were given her brightest smile and teasing attention. That allowed me to sort of shine in the glow of the attention around us. It's hard not to enjoy that.

I got stuck sitting in the waiting room. She had Sierra go back to a treatment room with her while they put in the catheter port.

"Your sister has a better stomach for this kind of thing," she told me.

I didn't think that was true. But it was clear that Sierra was more fun to be around. It was all I could do not to mope and whine. I needed Mom and I was scared.

Sierra either didn't have my worries or she hid it better. She was a kind of G-rated version of Mom's frothy, sparkling personality. The two of them together could warm up a steel girder. Nobody in this place was nearly that cold.

Even the nursing staff, which was mostly female, seem to get a kick out of them. Mom never suffered a lot from other women's jealousy. Somehow her exuberance was so infectious it was hard to work up any competitive feeling. And having cancer gave her even more leeway than usual.

I sat there on the narrow mauve chair, trying not to look at the other patients. Trying not to imagine my mom looking so sick and old.

There was a rack of pamphlets on one wall. I wandered over and checked out the titles. Lots of different kinds of cancer were represented. I didn't see anything on the kind Mom had. There were leaflets about chemo and other therapies. Some about diet and exercise during cancer treatment. A couple on psychological aspects. Then one caught my eye. *Helping Your Children Cope with Your Cancer.* I picked it up casually. Somehow I didn't want anybody looking at me.

I carried it back to my chair and read it. I caught myself hoping that it was going to tell me something, something that would make me feel better and safer and all right with this. I read nothing like that.

Mom and Sierra finally came out. Mom was pale but she seemed all right. She'd buttoned her sleeves back down so I couldn't see what they had done.

Sierra couldn't talk enough about it. She was fascinated.

"And they put like a metal wire into the tube and took an X ray so that they could see that it was going right into the heart."

The folks in the waiting room, in general, were not interested in my sister's chatter. I thought we ought to get out of there before we were likely to wear out our welcome.

"I'm getting hungry," I told Mom. "Can we go get something to eat now?"

Mom happily agreed.

I think she assumed that she'd succeeded in calming my fears.

As we headed toward the parking garage, Sierra was chattering about being a nurse.

"You know it might be really fun," she said. "Except for those baggy pants uniform things are totally gross. Do you think there might be other clothes that a nurse could wear? I'd really want to look better than that."

Mom was nodding and listening. I had to speak up.

"There's more to nursing than the clothes you wear," I pointed out.

Sierra waved away my concern.

"Oh, I know there's blood and stuff," she said. "I think I could stick one of those tubes up someone's heart. Well, maybe not the first time, but eventually."

"I wouldn't want you practicing on me," I said.

"Not all of them do that kind of thing," she said. "Maybe I could be one of those nurses that just walks around with the doctor and cheers people up."

"Nursing, the cheering profession?" I questioned sarcastically. "You're confusing it with another vocation that involves megaphones and pom-poms."

I didn't get to say anything more as along a long sunlit corridor that separated the Cancer Center from the parking garage we unexpectedly met up with a couple of familiar faces.

"Well, hello!" the guy said. "Look, Spence, it's the girls next door."

Del Tegge was looking really good in Dockers and a button-down shirt. Not good like hot. But good like good. It was as if he had a sign around his neck that said Hey, This is a Really Nice Guy.

Just like our last encounter, he brought out the best in me.

"Hi, Mr. Tegge, hi, Spencer," I said, politely. "This is my mom, Dawn Leland, and my sister, Sierra."

The guy was all smiles and friendly. He allowed

his gaze to drift downward for just one quick glance at Mom's tattoo, then he kept his gaze focused very deliberately on her eyes.

"Mrs. Leland, Sierra, it's so nice to meet you both," he said.

Mom laughed and feigned a horrified expression. "Dawn, call me Dawn," she told him. "When you said *Mrs. Leland,* I had to look over my shoulder to make sure Sophrona wasn't standing behind me."

"Dawn," he agreed, nodding. The way he spoke the name it sounded almost lyrical. "And you have to call me Del. We're your neighbors in Old North Knoxville."

"Well, how lucky is that for us!" Mom said, a little bit over the top. "And you're Spencer?"

Mom bent over to ruffle the kid's hair and get down to his eye level. He didn't have his dad's basic decency. He was staring in openmouthed awe at her breasts. Of course, with her bent forward like that, she was practically shoving them in his face.

The same behavior that had given me such hope inside the Cancer Center was now hopelessly embarrassing me. Why did she have to be like this? How come she couldn't see how un-Mom-like she was behaving?

I couldn't lash out at my mother, so I went after Spence.

"So what are you doing out of kiddie camp?" I asked him, snidely. "Time off for good behavior?"

"It's Saturday," he answered, defensively.

"Spence is meeting his mother and stepdad for lunch," Del clarified.

"They're here?" Mom asked.

"His stepfather is Wiktor Bodnarchuk."

He said the name like we would know it. We didn't.

"He's Chief of Oncology," Del said. "If you do your treatment here, I'm sure you'll meet him."

There was an uncomfortable moment of silence. I wasn't sure just why, until Del stammered into apologetic explanation.

"I'm…I'm a close friend of Vern," he said. "I asked about your visit and…he…mentioned your illness."

Mom shrugged. "It's not some big secret," she said.

I think she was offended, but Del came across as so sincere, it would be hard to be angry at the guy.

"Listen," he said. "While you're in the hospital or whenever, we'd be delighted for the girls to hang at our house. Wouldn't we, Spence?"

The kid didn't answer, he was still partially mesmerized by my mother's chest.

Mom managed a polite, noncommittal response and we said goodbye.

I had no intention of going over to hang out with Spencer. But the truth was, when the next day came, Mom had Vern drive her to the hospital, Sierra parked herself in front of the TV and Mrs. Leland went out to her garage office, and I was pretty bored. And being bored gave me too much time to worry about what was happening. I just didn't want to think about it. I tried to believe it was as simple as Mom said. *Chemotherapy* was just a fancy name for *medicine*. Mom would take her medicine, she'd get better and we'd move on. That was how it had to be.

The fear that it might be something else drove me next door. I rang the doorbell.

Spence opened it up. He looked as surprised to see me as I was to be there.

"Hi."

"Hi," I answered. "I've got nothing to do. I thought I'd come over here."

He nodded, a little uncertain.

"Who is it, Spence?" his dad called from another room.

"It's Dakota Leland."

"Hey, Dakota, come on in," Del Tegge called out. I could hear him before I saw him.

Spence directed me toward the dining room. The table was covered with papers spread out all over it and more boxes all around.

"What are you doing?"

"Preparing for a public meeting," Tegge answered. "I've got to get all my ducks in a row if I have any hope of getting them going in the right direction."

"My dad's an environmental activist," Spence said.

"Oh."

Del smiled at me. "I bet you're a friend to the environment," he said.

I shrugged. "I'm not an enemy of it, I don't guess."

He laughed.

"Kids like you and Spence, that's what activism is all about," he said. "Adults like me are creating a mess that you'll have to spend your lives cleaning up. I'm just trying to get a little head start for you."

I nodded. "So you're like saving species and stuff like that."

"Sometimes," he said. "That's a big thing, a dramatic thing. But a lot of the work that we need to do is small. Just tiny little steps that can make a difference. Tonight is a public meeting on a landfill site. It's my job to try to anticipate all the possible impacts to groundwater, air quality, vegetation and wildlife. Wading through all the science and speculation is like working out a really complex mathematical problem. And then being able to explain it so that everybody can understand it is like starting with molecules of hydrogen and oxygen to make iced tea."

I didn't really understand what he meant, but I acted like I did. We watched him for a few minutes. He sorted papers and made notes. Finally he suggested that Spence show me his room.

"Sure, come on," he said.

We went upstairs and toward the back of the house. The room was pretty big, and not particularly uncool. He had a dormer off the back that led to a small balcony with a telescope pointed up toward the sky. The walls of his room were decorated with space posters and vivid Hubble photos. A very cool and expensive laptop computer sat open on his desk. The screen saver was a slide show of the constellations.

"So you're like into astronomy and that stuff," I said, voicing the obvious.

"Yeah," he told me. "I'm geeky and I'm a science guy. You should really keep your distance. Don't want anything to rub off."

I couldn't really pretend I didn't know what he was talking about. I hadn't been too nice to him. I guessed I was going to have to try.

"Honestly, I kind of like science myself," I told him as an apology. "Sorry I've been so snotty."

"It's okay," he said.

I figured he got that nice stuff from his dad.

"I guess it hasn't been such a great time for you, with your mom sick and all."

"I don't want to talk about my mom," I told him as I plopped down on the bed. It had a navy-blue comforter with tiny stars and four big star-shaped pillows.

"This is pretty cool," I told him.

Spence shrugged. "My mom picked it out," he said. "My other bedroom is decorated in music."

"Like rock stars?"

He shook his head. "Like sheet music. I play the piano. But I don't have a piano here."

"So you have two bedrooms."

"Yeah," Spence said, slumping down to sit cross-legged on the floor. "Two stereos, two computers, two TVs, two of everything. That way I can go back and forth without carrying a suitcase. So neither parent feels like I'm visiting."

"That seems good," I said.

"It's good for them."

"I can't imagine having two bedrooms of your own. I've never even had my own bedroom yet," I admitted. "I always have to share with my sister."

Spence nodded. "I'm getting a brother in October," he said. "My mom is pregnant."

"That's got to be great," I said.

"Yeah, I think it's going to be okay," he said. "She and my stepdad are really excited. He has three daughters that are grown up and married and Mom has me. So this will be their first kid together."

"The baby won't be sharing your room, will he?"

"Not likely," he said. "Mom and Wiktor have a big house in Sequoyah Hills. Six bedrooms. And Mom's redoing the downstairs this summer to add a nursery onto the master bedroom suite."

"Wow! They must be rich."

Spence nodded. "My mom is really into money," he said. "That's why she divorced my dad."

"Your dad doesn't have money?"

"Not enough."

"I guess divorce is pretty tough," I said. "Your dad seems really nice," I said.

"My mom is great, too," he assured me. "And my stepfather is not like Mr. Bad, either. Everything is really okay. Mostly I feel fine about it. But I guess sometimes I just don't."

I nodded like I understood, but of course, I didn't.

"Did your folks fight a lot?" I asked. "I mean before the divorce."

He shrugged. "They argued a lot. But they always argued. It didn't seem like fighting. I mean they weren't screaming at each other. It was just the same arguments over and over."

"About money?"

"Yeah. And Dad's job," he answered.

"She doesn't like his job."

"He didn't do what she'd planned," Spence explained. "They got married when they graduated college. Dad was a biology major and he was supposed to go to medical school. That summer, before he started, he got interested in ecology and decided to pursue a Ph.D. in environmental science."

"And she didn't like that."

Spence shook his head. "She married him thinking he was going to be a doctor. She wanted to be married to a doctor. Now she is."

I nodded. There was nothing else to say about it.

"So I guess your father is dead, right?"

"Yeah, I didn't know him. He died before I was born."

"We didn't even know the Lelands had a son," he told me. "It's weird they never mentioned him."

"They've got pictures in the house," I said. "Tons and tons of pictures. I guess they have so many so they won't have to talk about him."

"What happened? Did he have some disease or something?"

I got up from the bed and began checking out all the stuff Spence had on the shelves along the wall. There were some books, board games, a disc player and some weird puzzles. There was a big blue geode that he used as a paperweight.

"My dad was killed in a logging accident," I answered. "I don't know much about it. My mom never says much and I just met my grandparents."

"You could ask them," Spence pointed out.

"I think everybody gets sad when he's mentioned," I told him. "I don't want everybody being sad."

"But you'd still like to know."

"Yeah," I admitted with a sigh. "I'd still like to know."

Spence was nodding, sympathetic. But I knew that just like I couldn't understand his parents' divorce, he couldn't understand having a dad who'd died before you were born.

"What's this thing?" I asked him, holding up a weird toy that looked like a space-wars gun with an open umbrella on the front. "Is this how E.T. phones home?"

Spence grinned. "Not exactly," he said. "It's called a Nature Sounds Receiver. Dad got it for me. He thinks it's really cool to sit around and listen to birds and frogs and stuff. But look…"

Spence took the thing out of my hands and headed out to his telescope balcony, motioning me to follow.

"Put the earphones on and just point it," he said. "You can always pick up something."

I adjusted the little black foam pieces on my head and pointed it toward the backyard. I could hear some unidentifiable scratching noise. I didn't know if it was a squirrel or some kind of digging animal or what.

"Point it toward a house," Spence said.

I moved the gun toward the left, past the garage at the Leland house. I was startled at the clarity of Mrs. Leland's voice.

"What's become more obvious to me," she was saying, "is the followers of Reverend White didn't have all that much to do with the congregation of Governor Winthrop."

She hesitated. I realized she must be on the telephone.

"Yes, certainly," she continued. "But all those meetings are carefully documented. You just have to take the time to search through the NEHS."

Another pause.

"Well, of course I'll help you," she said. "But right

now things here are in a bit of an uproar. My daughter-in-law is taking cancer treatment and her children
are going to be underfoot for a while."

A moment passed.

"Well, I'm just praying for a full recovery," Mrs.
Leland said. "The last thing in the world I'd want is
to have these two girls living with us permanently."

"It's wild, isn't it?" Spence said, beside me. "You
can pick up whole conversations word for word."

# SONNY DAYS
## 14

━━ ◆ ━━

By the time they brought Sierra home from the hospital, it became obvious to Sonny that even if he did save enough money to pay tuition, returning to college was not going to be easy. The baby had a sunny disposition and slept well. She had no health problems, not even colic. Still, keeping up with her was a lot of effort and Dawn was exhausted by the time he got home from work.

He was tired, too. But it was different. His bones ached and his arms felt like Jell-O. But she'd been talking baby talk all day and up to her ears in poopy diapers. He liked the time he spent with his daughter. And he felt it was important that Dawn got a break. The idea of jumping up to head for an evening class got pushed further and further into the future.

They rented a place in a nice mobile home park near the offices of the logging company. It was wooded and kid friendly. There were several young mothers who stayed home there all day. Most, like Dawn, had husbands up in the timber. Sonny was hopeful that she would make some friends. That didn't seem to happen. Dawn was outgoing and friendly when they met people. But when anybody began to get close, she backed away.

"They're not like me, Sonny," she said.

"What does that mean?"

"If they knew me, they wouldn't like me," she said.

"Give 'em a chance," he implored her.

Dawn shook her head. "Give them a chance to walk all over me? Not likely. I've got you. I've got the baby. I don't need anyone else."

That attitude bothered him, but he figured time would change it. And he had enough other worries going on that her lack of friends seemed unimportant by comparison.

The company Sonny worked for was acquired by a larger, more profitable timber concern. Things were changing on the job and it didn't seem to be for the better. Instead of harvesting trees for hardwood flooring, they were now clear-cutting entire stands for the chip mills. The high-capacity automated plants would grind down trees for making paper, pressboard and rayon.

The feel of what they were doing, the atmosphere on the job, changed significantly. It was as if one day they were following in the footsteps of their forefathers in utilizing a resource. And the next day they were all drudging in an outdoor sweatshop.

Sonny asked Lonnie about it.

"It's because we're not working in the timber business anymore," he said.

"The chip mills are part of the timber business," Sonny pointed out.

Lonnie nodded. "I didn't mean to suggest they weren't," he said. "What I'm saying is that we used to work for a company that was set up to make lumber. Now we're in a corporation that's been set up to make money. Wood, coal, hemorrhoid creams, it's all the same to them. Just methods for making money."

Sonny was afraid he was right.

"What worries me," Lonnie continued, "is the way we're showing a profit. We follow the rules, but to the letter only."

Sonny had seen that himself. They'd clear-cut an area with oaks, poplars, hickories and walnuts. They would fulfill their requirement to replant the stand, but they'd replace it with cheaper, faster growing pines, slowly but surely depleting the hardwoods of the area.

The new company treated the limbing and bucking sites with the same level of barely adequate adherence. They located the skid trails with more thought to the convenience of loading than the prevention of soil damage. And the patchy grasses they left for cover seemed insufficient to prevent erosion.

It was a different timber industry. Among the workers, nobody liked it. But when paychecks got fatter, Sonny, like everybody else, tried harder to keep his mouth shut. He put the extra pay into the savings account. If clear-cutting would pay college tuition, then it couldn't be all that bad.

In truth, the changes he saw in the mountains sparked his interest in the industry. He was inexplicably drawn to learning more about it. He began to drop by the library to read logging industry magazines. He checked out every book they had on wood harvesting and timber.

"I think when I go back to school, I may change my major to forestry management," he told Dawn one night.

She'd been quiet all evening. And when he spoke to her, she didn't respond.

He assumed she was just tired and not paying attention. Sierra had started walking, which was good news. But mostly she ran instead of walked and Dawn spent most of her days chasing her.

"I'm thinking about changing my major when I return to school," he repeated.

"I heard you," she said, still not looking in his direction.

The silence lingered.

"Is there something wrong?" he asked.

"I went to see the doctor today."

Sonny was immediately alert. "Has Sierra been sick? It's not time for another checkup."

"I didn't take the baby to the doctor, I went myself."

"Yeah?"

"I'm pregnant again."

Sonny tried to keep his jaw from dropping on the floor as the bottom fell out of his world. Nausea churned at the back of his throat. And he felt light-headed enough to faint.

"I'm sorry," Dawn said. She bit her lip, but couldn't keep the tears from seeping out of the side of her eyes. "The doctor said there is no perfect method. This happens sometimes. I'm so sorry."

"I…I'm not," Sonny said bravely. "I…I'm delighted. I…ah…well, as an only child myself, I always wanted Sierra to have a sibling. This is great. I'm so happy. I'm so very, very happy," he lied.

Sonny pulled Dawn into his arms and held her as the sobs broke through. He held her and the trickle of tears ran to a flood and she sobbed and shuddered as if the world had come to an end.

"There's no reason to be brokenhearted about this," he told her.

"I want you to get to go to college," she told him.

"I will go," he assured her, though he felt it was a lie even as he said it. "I'll start back next year, or the year after. I have lots of time, Dawn. I have lots of time."

For the next seven months as they awaited the birth of their second child, Sonny deliberately put all thoughts of returning to the university behind him. He took his saved tuition money and bought a used car. A four-door 1989 Dodge.

"A family needs a family car," he told Dawn, who teased him about buying such a stodgy, grown-up vehicle.

And one of their first family trips in the family car was to the pound. The barking of the dogs bothered Sierra. But when Sonny handed her the little black ball of fur to pet, she giggled.

"I think this is the one," Sonny told Dawn.

"I can't believe you want to get a dog," she said. "It's so much trouble."

Sonny nodded. "That's what makes it worth it," he said. "A dog keeps a family grounded. And they can be your closest friend."

Dawn seemed uncertain.

"What are we going to call him?"

"I think we should stick with this mountain theme we've got going," he said. "Let's call him Rocky."

Dawn agreed, but with a reluctant sigh. She'd never been around animals and didn't know how she felt about them. Still, the puppy rode home inside the warmth of her jacket.

On the job, Sonny concentrated on learning everything he could. If he was going to live out his life as a logger, he decided that he'd be a really hardworking, exemplary one, like Lonnie.

Lonnie was the lead man on the eight-man crew and operated the feller machine. Sonny and Mitch were the fellers. They cut down the trees with chain saws or, occasionally, axes. Lloyd was the bucker. He trimmed off the tops and branches and cut the resulting logs into specified lengths. Hodge and Caney fastened chokes around the logs and used a tractor to skid them down to the deck area where Rob Pearson ran the loading equipment. Though this team exclusively cut timber together, they weren't the only guys on the sites. Log sorters, graders and scalers, chasers and riggers worked interchangeably among the crews. Of course, there were the regular visits from the company office. And occasional oversight inspections from state and federal agencies.

Sonny didn't mind the work. The day went fast. The pay was good. He tried to ignore the things that bothered him. The guys on the crew were all hard workers and easy to get along with. Most of them were struggling to support young families, just like himself.

It was a gray, October morning, nearly ten-thirty, when Sonny stood in the limbing and bucking yard, waiting for his next tree. Two crews had been working the hillside for several weeks. That morning they were almost down and working very close to each other. It made everyone a little jittery. There was too much going on at once, too many people working, so it was impossible to keep an eye on everyone and everything. Which is what safe timber cutting is all about.

Finally Lonnie had told his crew just to wait. They'd limb and buck what they had while the other crew did their felling. And then they could fell while the other team limbed and bucked. It might mean an extra long day for all of them. But it felt safer.

Now they were just waiting, passing time. This late in the morning all the coffee thermoses were empty. Smoking was not allowed this close to the cutting. And no one was comfortable enough to sit down. So they were just standing. Standing around waiting their turn.

"How's your wife doing?" Lonnie asked.

"One more month to the due date," Sonny answered. "But the doctor said she could come anytime now. Sierra was a little early."

"Do you know what it's going be yet?"

"Another girl," Sonny said.

"You disappointed?"

Sonny shook his head. "Just so she's healthy," he said.

Lonnie nodded agreement. "I like girls myself," he admitted. "At least when you bring them into the world, you're pretty sure they won't end up eating sawdust all their days."

"There's more women in the crews all the time."

"Don't bother me none," Lonnie said. "But I sure want better for my own girls."

"Me, too," Sonny agreed.

"I want all my children to go to college," Lonnie said.

"Yeah, I want that, too," Sonny admitted.

It wasn't a big surprise that he felt that way. It was what his parents had done. It had been what he'd wanted for himself. Strange that for the first time in all this time, he realized he felt exactly the way his own father might have felt.

He missed his dad. He missed their chess games and the holiday dinners. Truthfully, he missed both his parents. He wanted to see them, talk to them, share his life with them. And he wanted them to know Sierra and the new baby. He wanted the children to know them and love them, as well.

"College is too damned expensive," Lonnie said beside him. "I ain't sure that one man by himself can do it. I don't know if even New York's Donnie Trump could afford to send six."

"It's a lot of money."

"I'm going to try," Lonnie said. "I don't know if I'll manage it, but I'm going to try."

Sonny nodded, acknowledging the challenge.

"My two oldest girls will make it for sure," Lonnie said. "I've got some money saved for them and they're already looking into grants and scholarships."

"That's good," Sonny said.

"The girls remind me of their mama. Smart, they are, and pretty to boot," Lonnie bragged.

Sonny gave him a teasing smile. "You know, in a few more weeks, I think I'll be able to say exactly the same thing about my two."

Lonnie laughed out loud. "I'll just bet you will," he admitted.

At that moment there was a crack of timber. Sonny wasn't sure what was unique about the sound, but he knew immediately, unerringly, that it sounded wrong, very wrong.

"Damned thing's falling into our stand," Lloyd complained from nearby.

Sonny looked up. A nearby feller had cut the top out of a tree. It should have landed on the far side in the area where the other team had been working. Instead it was headed for uncut trees just up the mountain from them.

"Holy shit!" Lonnie cursed. "Clear out of here. Everybody clear out!"

It happened so fast, yet in Sonny's mind every instant was indelibly fixed. The falling tree fragment hit a standing tree, snapping a huge limb that kicked back in their direction. It came down and down and down. Smashing into other limbs on other trees as it came down toward them. Its destination the ground on which they stood.

There was yelling. There was running. He heard screaming. Lots of screaming. It didn't sound like pain. It sounded like fear.

# REAL LIFE
## 15

———◆—◆———

Mom's chemo began. The world didn't stop. The sun came out every day and there was no pact of silence. The first week wasn't really so bad. It was as if she was going to be the same as always. She laughed and joked and said things that got on Mrs. Leland's nerves. I began to relax. Maybe it was just medicine.

But by the second week she was pale and nauseated. She carried a plastic trash can with her everywhere. She didn't know from one minute to the next if she was going to throw up.

She was exhausted, but claimed that she couldn't sleep. She refused to stay in bed.

"It's only going to get worse," she told us. "If I start lying around now, I might as well give up."

The pump—which hung from her shoulders on a blue nylon strap for forty-eight hours at a time—beeped whenever her arm was crooked or she was lying the wrong direction. Just about any time she drifted off, it would beep her awake.

It was the drug in the pump that put the lie to the whole "it's just medicine" story. Sierra was the one who helped her with it. Changing the dressing, swabbing the sutures and flushing the line with heparin.

Mom warned her. "Don't get any of this stuff on

you," she said. "If it spills, I don't want you cleaning it up. It's very toxic, a deadly poison, and it could soak into your skin."

"You're worried that it might soak into Sierra's skin, but you're having it pumped directly into your heart," I pointed out.

Mom gave me that look that I got sometimes that was meant to say, *Don't upset your sister. Just because you know things, you don't have to share them.*

I was no longer sure that Sierra didn't understand perfectly. She was the one who was there for Mom. She was the one who seemed to know the right things to say, the right things to do. She was the one who was really a help. Maybe nursing was the cheering profession.

Sierra insisted that not only must Mom get up and get dressed, she had to put on her makeup, as well.

"Nothing can perk up the day like a cute pair of shorts and some candy-colored lipstick," my sister told her.

Mom smiled at Sierra and cupped one side of my sister's face with her hand. It was a tender gesture. A long way from Mom's usual quick-witted sarcasm.

Sierra helped her dress and invited her to watch soaps. But when Vern suggested it was a great morning to sit outside, Mom took him up on it.

At first Mom tried the front porch glider, but the motion made her queasy. Eventually she ended up lying on a patio chaise. Sierra gave her a magazine, but she didn't even pretend to look at it. She just lay in the sunshine like a lazy cat, Rocky curled up on the cushion beside her feet.

Sierra and I took turns sitting out there with her.

We were a good tag team. Sierra liked to talk and she could entertain Mom for a while. Then we'd trade off. I didn't have much to say, so Mom could drift off in the silence as I kept my thoughts to myself.

At midday Mrs. Leland fixed her some food on a tray. It was very fancy with the soup and the little half sandwich on matching luncheon dishes and a strawberry sliced to look like a flower.

"I think she's still sick to her stomach," I told her. "So she's probably not hungry."

"Why don't you take it out to her anyway," she told me. "It's important that she continue to eat."

I didn't quite believe that Mrs. Leland cared. But then I figured it was important to her to keep Mom alive so she wouldn't end up stuck with us. I wanted to tell her not to bother. Sierra and I would take care of Mom. And if something terrible happened, we would never stay here.

Of course, nothing was going to happen to Mom. I reminded myself. It just couldn't. We needed Mom to take care of us. And we would always take care of her.

I carried the food out there and set it beside her.

"Oh, this is so sweet," Mom said.

I shrugged. "Mrs. Leland did it."

"That was really nice of her," Mom said. "She's really trying to be nice to us. We need to be nice back."

"Of course," Sierra said, as if there were no reasons not to.

I nodded to Mom, but my heart wasn't in it.

I sat there with them. Mom was picking at the food as Sierra got her up to date on the romance of Ben and J.Lo and the latest supermodel to wed into European royalty.

My mind had already begun to wander when Vern called out to me from the kitchen door.

"Dakota, you've got a telephone call."

Sierra looked up, puzzled. "Who would call you?"

I shrugged and then decided to tease. "Maybe one of those skateboarders I gave my number to."

"You didn't!" Sierra looked genuinely horrified.

Mom chuckled. It was the first laugh we'd heard from her all day and it was very much worth it.

"Of course she didn't," Mom told Sierra.

I went into the house and picked up the phone that was in the little hallway cubby.

"Hello."

"Dakota, it's me, Spence."

"Oh, hi."

"I found out how your dad died," he said.

"What?"

"I found out how your dad died. I'm printing it now."

"Printing what?"

"The facts about the accident, how he died."

For a minute it was like my brain couldn't function right. Then I realized what he was saying and my heart began pounding like a drum.

"I'll be right there."

I raced through the house and out to the patio.

"I'm going next door."

If Mom and Sierra were surprised, if they said "okay" or "no way" or anything at all, I didn't take time to notice. I ran out the back gate and across the driveway. Spence was waiting for me on his porch.

As I hurried inside the door, he called out toward the back of the house.

"It's Dakota, Dad, we're going upstairs."

"Hi, Dakota."

"Hi, Mr. Tegge," I called out as we rushed up to the second floor and down the hallway to Spence's room.

It looked very much like it had the last time I was there, except now the laptop was attached to the printer and there were stacks of papers all over.

"Okay, I'm here. Tell me what this is all about," I said as soon as the door closed behind us.

"Well, you did say you wanted to know what happened to your dad."

"Yeah, right."

"So I went on the Internet."

"The Internet? My father is on the Internet?"

"Well, not him exactly," Spence said. "But I got to thinking that there might be some newspaper articles about the accident or an obituary or something."

"Was there?"

"I couldn't find anything about the accident, but there was an obituary."

"An obituary? About my dad?"

"It didn't say much," Spence told me, shrugging it off. "But it did give me the death date and tell me what company he'd been working for. So I looked up the company. They got conglomerated into another company a long time ago. But I was able to track down the fact that they had a fatality investigation by OSHA in the early nineties."

Spence was grinning from ear to ear.

"Once I knew who it was and when it was, it was a piece of cake to pull up the report on it," he said. "Look it's all here. It's got to be him. The death date matches the obit."

He held out the paper to me. My hands were shaking as I took it from him. The page was divided in little blocks. At the top it read "Region IV" and at the sides "TN." The title of the block was "Description of Fatal Incident and Standards-Citations Related to the Event."

It was as if my eyes couldn't focus. These words printed on this ordinary piece of paper had changed my life so completely, so irrevocably. I couldn't just see them, I had to hear them. I read the short paragraph aloud.

"'At approximately 10:30 a.m. on October 15, 1991, a twenty-one-year-old male employee of the Hetta Cove Logging Company was fatally injured when struck by a tree limb. A nearby crew was topping a forty-eight-foot pine that kicked back, falling into a standing tree adjacent to a bucking area. A break-off limb from the standing tree impaled the victim causing multiple abdominal and chest injuries.'"

I paused trying to understand the words, trying to picture the scene. Neither was clear.

"'Total number of citations issued: One. Number of citations issued related to the event: One: Work areas not separated by safe distance.'"

"That's a real low number," Spence told me. "Most of these reports have lots of them." He was shuffling through other papers. "One of these has twenty-six citations. Man, if they give twenty-six citations, you know that it was really somebody's fault. If there's just one, then, I guess it was just bad luck."

"Bad luck," I repeated. "Bad luck." I'd thought I

would feel better knowing something. That all the uncertainty and speculation was what made it feel bad. I didn't know Sonny Leland. I never met him. I never heard the sound of his voice. How could his death mean anything to me? But the sadness that welled up in me was huge. And it was worse, far worse, to know that something that could mean so much could happen so stupidly and with no one to blame.

I wanted to scream, to hit, to throw something. I saw the blue geode that Spence was using as a paperweight. I grabbed it up and slung it across the room. It hit the TV with a horrible crash of breaking glass. It felt as if it had broken right through my heart.

I dropped to my knees, sobbing. My insides had been ripped out. There was this huge part of me that was just empty, wholly, painfully empty.

I heard Spencer's dad come storming in.

"What the devil is going on?"

I tried to get a hold on myself. I tried to stop crying. I covered my mouth with both hands but I couldn't prevent the sound from coming out.

"Just a little accident," Spence said loudly over my noisy grieving.

"Why is she crying?"

"She broke the TV."

"Delbert Spencer Tegge!" His voice was commanding, demanding. "Tell it to me straight and immediately!"

"She wanted to know how her dad died," I heard Spence explaining. "Nobody talks about it and she wanted to know. I found the accident report on the Internet. I didn't know she'd get upset like this."

The man knelt down beside me.

*I'm sorry,* I tried to say, but I was still muffling my sobs and the words couldn't come out. *I'm sorry.*

He was reading the paper I'd dropped beside me on the floor, then he let it slip through his fingers and he wrapped his arms around me and pulled me against his chest. I don't think a man had ever held me in his arms. It felt safe. It felt good. Mr. Tegge pried my hands away from my mouth.

"Let it out, honey," he said. "It's okay. You're among friends. Just let it out."

I did.

He held me and rocked me and I cried and cried. Spence was there, on the other side of me. He had an arm around me, too.

I should have felt embarrassed, humiliated, stupid. But I didn't. I was sad and scared and mourning the loss of my dad. And these people, these neighbors that I hardly knew, they were mourning him with me.

# REAL LIFE
## 16

—▶ ◀—

I put the papers that Spence had found for me, the *Logging Fatalities Report* and the obituary from the *Knoxville Sentinel*, under my bed with the soccer picture. I worried a lot about paying for Spence's broken TV. But I didn't dwell on my minibreakdown. When I'd finally got myself together, Mr. Tegge and Spence and I talked it over. I'd never really had an opportunity to grieve for my father. And now, when I was in a new place, living with people I hardly knew and worried about my mom, it was expected that the specifics of the tragedy might hit me hard.

Del Tegge made it all sound so logical, acceptable. I'm pretty sure that Sierra would have called my behavior freaky. And more than likely all of the Sonnys in Mom's recent past would have suggested the psych ward.

Spence was really lucky to have such a great dad.

In the next couple of weeks I found myself more and more in the company of the Tegges. Some of it was my own choosing. I began to hang out with Spencer. But Old North Knoxville was a small enough neighborhood that we ran into them frequently.

We saw them in church. The Lelands, I discovered, were regular Sunday morning worshipers. But they didn't attend any of the churches in their area. The first Sunday after Mom's chemo, the five of us crowded into the Saab and headed downtown. I was really shocked that Mom decided to go. She'd dropped us off at Sunday schools from time to time. And she never discouraged us from going with our friends. But in my memory, weddings and funerals were the only times she'd ever darken the door. But she'd come in to breakfast Sunday morning wearing her gray suit.

"This church is a part of our family heritage," Vern explained to us as we drove up the hill on Henley Street.

Sierra was all perked up and interested. She shot a quick smile to Mrs. Leland. The woman responded with a nod. The two had gone on a shopping expedition. Probably because the old harpy didn't approve of my sister's clothes. But Sierra was in seventh heaven in her new designer suit. She could have easily passed for twenty-five. And she was willing to try to please anybody who had the money and willingness to buy for her.

"Tell them the story, Phrona," Vern urged. "The place will mean more to them if they know the background."

Mrs. Leland shot him a look across the front seat, but she didn't argue.

"When the building of this church was proposed," she said, "my family was among a group of very prominent and wealthy parishioners who pledged funds for its construction."

It was curious how she could talk to us directly

from the front seat and be both holding her nose in the air and looking down on us at the same time.

"That wouldn't have been much of a hardship, of course, in 1928," she said. "But after the market crash everyone was virtually penniless."

She hesitated momentarily and then turned to glance at each of us separately, making sure everyone, including Mom, was paying attention.

"Our family honors their obligations," she declared. "That dark time was no exception. My grandfather sold all of our furniture and the silverware from our dining table to pay what he had pledged. And he wasn't alone. Every family managed to come up with the funds that they'd promised. This beautiful building went up during a time when no one in the city had a dime to spare. So every time you girls see that gothic spire on the skyline, you can remember it as a standing memorial to the faithful, steadfast sacrifices of Knoxville families."

Sierra gazed at the church on the hill in awe. Mom rolled her eyes.

Inside we followed Vern up to a pew near the front. They always sat in the same place it seemed and all the people around them knew them, greeted them and were curious and eager to meet their daughter-in-law and grandchildren. The church was very cathedrallike with beamed ceilings distant overhead and lots of dark woods and stained glass.

The service was described by Vern as High Methodist, which I guess accounted for all the robes and candles. The singing was nice and the minister was interesting and brief. When the communion began, Sierra marched right up to the rail beside Mrs. Leland

and Vern. Mom stayed in her place, so I stayed in mine.

In the end, it was not so bad and I was glad that we had come. Maybe some prayers would help Mom. Or help me help Mom. Or both.

As we filed out onto the walkway in front of the building, a familiar face came up behind me with a customary middle school greeting.

"Hey, girl."

I turned to see Spence and his dad. They both had on suits and ties. Spence just looked kind of nerdy in his, but Del Tegge was very handsome.

"Hi," I said to them both.

"How are you doing this morning, Dakota?" Del asked me.

"Fine."

He nodded. "If you're interested in coming to Sunday school," he said, "you're welcome to ride with us. We're here early every week."

"Every week? Spence doesn't like to miss, huh?" I teased.

The kid made a face at me, but we'd become close enough friends that we were able to joke with each other.

"I teach one of the high school classes," Del said. "So I have to be here. But we both like it. It's a good way to spend a Sunday."

"Yeah, I guess," I admitted.

Del's eyes slid past me to smile at my mom and offer his hand.

"You're looking very lovely today, Dawn," he said.

Mom glanced down at the gray suit and then back

up at Del. "Maybe you need to get out more," she said.

He smiled at her little jab.

"How do you like our church?" he asked.

Mom shrugged. She didn't seem that impressed by either Del's good looks or his compliments.

"I've been here before," she answered. "This is where they had my husband's funeral. Of course, the place looks different without a casket in the middle."

It was as if she were throwing his friendliness back in his teeth. I couldn't imagine why she was doing that. He was only trying to be nice to her. Maybe it was the Lelands.

He greeted them, too. Mrs. Leland clasped his hand in her own and told him how much she'd missed having him around the house. Vern suggested he come over for a game of chess and he promised to do so very soon.

I, of course, didn't have to wait for a visit. As soon as we'd gotten home and finished lunch, I hurried over to their door. It was much better lolling around their place. Though I often spent time on Spence's balcony with the Nature Sounds Receiver finding out what was really going on in the Leland house.

That Sunday we spent almost an hour laughing our heads off as we eavesdropped on Sierra and her skateboard crush, Seth. He'd come rolling up the street and jumped up the curb, just to show that he could. She walked down to the privacy of the sidewalk steps to talk to him.

Spence and I lay flat on our bellies on the balcony, he with one earphone and me with the other.

"It must be hard to skateboard in this neighborhood," she said. "With all the hills and everything."

"Not for me," he assured her. "I'm like an athlete. I mean, skateboarding is a sport and all."

"Yeah, I've seen those competitions on TV," Sierra said. "Where they go up and down those ramp things and twirl the board around."

"Well, yeah, those competitions are interesting," he said. "But they're really kind of setups. I'm into street skating. Ramping, that's really like ancient history nearly."

I was honestly surprised at how well Sierra was able to talk to him. It was my experience that her topics of conversation were limited to soaps, celebs and clothes. But she asked him question after question about skateboarding and he talked and talked about it.

Finally he got around to the purpose of his visit.

"I thought maybe we could like catch a ride out to the cineplex and take in a movie," he said.

"Yeah, sure. I guess we could catch a ride. Most of the guys I date have cars," Sierra told him.

I knew for a fact that she'd never had a car date in her life.

"I'm getting a car next year," Seth bragged. "As soon as I get my license. But for now, these four wheels get me pretty much wherever I want to go." His bravado wilted somewhat. "Except for the cineplex. I always have to catch a ride to get there."

Sierra giggled. "And I don't think a skateboard is really made for two."

He laughed, as well. "We could try."

Seth jumped up and offered her a hand up. He put

the skateboard on the sidewalk and began laughing as they both tried to stand on it.

"Your feet are just way too big," she complained.

"Well, stand on top of them," he said.

They continued to try to maneuver. It was easy to see that the real purpose of this was for Seth to have a perfectly good reason to put his arms around her waist. It was why they kept up the clumsy, silly attempts.

"Spence!"

We heard Mr. Tegge calling out from downstairs.

"Spence, your mother's on the phone."

He pulled his headphone out of his ear and handed it to me. "I'll be right back," he said.

I watched Sierra and Seth for another minute. Then I caught sight of Vern heading out to Mrs. Leland's garage office. I turned the little umbrella in that direction, pointing straight into the doorway.

"Busy?" he asked her and he walked in.

"Just sorting through some tombstone photos from that cousin in Scituate," she answered.

"I think church went very well," Vern said.

"You don't expect much, do you?" Mrs. Leland scoffed. "She went only because we insisted and she was minimally polite. She couldn't even manage a smile for Del. That woman is never going to fit in here. She never has and she never will."

"Phrona," he said, his tone pleading. "I'm not letting those girls go a second time. You ran Dawn off thirteen years ago. I'm not going to let that happen again."

"There is nothing that I can do if she is not going to try," Mrs. Leland said.

"You can try," Vern said.

"I'm not sure it's worth it," she said.

"It's worth it to me."

There was a long silence. I adjusted the receiver, worried that I wasn't picking up what was happening. Then Vern spoke again.

"You have to admit, the girls are wonderful," he said.

Mrs. Leland sniffed. "Well, the older girl is certainly biddable enough and pretty," she said. "The younger one doesn't cause any problems. And she seems to have made friends with little Spencer."

"They have names, Phrona," Vern told her. "Dakota has Sonny's looks and Sierra has his disposition."

"And they both have their mother's low-class, trashy ways," she said.

"I'm ashamed of you," Vern said, sharply. "Does a background really matter that much to you?"

"It's not a background," she answered. "It's never been that. Not the day I met her, not today. The woman is incapable of forming a bond. She's been living like a gypsy her whole life and as soon as she's better, if she gets better, she'll be off on the road one more time. And her daughters will grow up to be just like her. Bubba chasing butterflies, flitting from truck stop to truck stop as time marches on."

"Face facts, Phrona! These girls are our family," he insisted. "The only family we've got that exists in more ways than a name on a genealogy tree."

"You're the one who needs to face facts, Vernon. Our son was our family. He's dead and that's the end of it," she said. "All of this heritage, from the Puritans, the Revolution, a new nation and the taming of a continent, our family's history is the history of America. But it all came down to one gray day in the forest thirteen years ago and it ended."

"My son is dead. I know that," Vern said. "But I'm not dead and neither are my granddaughters. If you're determined not to have a life, nobody can stop you."

Suddenly Spence plopped down beside me. "I'm back."

I jerked the earphones out and turned the receiver back toward the street, pretending that I was still listening to Sierra and Seth.

# SONNY DAYS
## 17

——▶ ◀——

It had happened so fast, yet in memory every moment was distinct, clear, vivid. The broken piece of limb was coming right at him. The jagged edge as dangerous and deadly as any spear that had ever been thrown. In that instant, Sonny believed that he was taking the last breath of his life. It was all over. He would never see Dawn or Sierra again. He would never know the face of his daughter, yet unborn. This was the end of his life. A stupid, tragic accident on a gray, October morning.

Then, inexplicably, a broad-shouldered back, clad in a flannel shirt and bright-orange safety vest, blocked his sight. The impact of the limb knocked him backward. Then he was staring up into leaves and branches with a heavy weight upon his chest.

His first feelings were of confusion. He was amazed that he was still alive. He was light-headed, dazed. But through his personal fog he could hear the sounds of orders being shouted and the scrambling of people around the area.

"If we get a choke chain on it we can drag it off with a tractor," he heard someone say distinctly.

"That could injure them worse. Let's do it by hand. Cut these back and we'll heave it off."

The branches above him began to move and something cut deep into his chest.

"I'm here!" he screamed. "I'm alive."

There was jerking and shaking of the leaves all around him as the branches were broken away.

"Oh, hell, no," he heard someone say. It sounded like Lloyd.

Then he saw Caney's face above, his brow was furrowed and his complexion sallow.

"We're going to get him off of you," he said.

"Him? Who?"

"Lonnie," he answered as he grabbed Sonny under the armpits. Somebody counted to three and Caney pulled.

Sonny glanced down toward his boots and saw the top of Lonnie's bald head and the shoulders that had stepped in front of him. He realized that the weight on his chest had not been just the tree, it had been Lonnie, as well.

"Is he all right?"

Caney didn't answer that. He dragged Sonny some distance from the fallen tree.

"Just lay here quietlike," he told him. "We don't know how bad you're injured. By now they've got an ambulance on the way and the paramedics will come up and get you."

Sonny watched as Caney headed back up to the accident. He stopped by the side of the trail and threw up. There could be no more implicit indication that the circumstances were bad.

Nobody said anything to him about Lonnie. Not the guys on the crew, not the ambulance attendants, not the people in the emergency room. But they didn't have to. Sonny saw the accident again and again in his mind. He saw the jagged, killer limb coming toward him. He saw his friend step in front, taking the brunt of the force.

"Lonnie saved my life," he told Dawn later in the hospital. "He stepped in front of me on purpose, killing himself and saving my life."

She didn't dispute his claim. How could she? His chest had a shallow, three-foot-long gash in it where the limb had pierced his body. It had gone completely through Lonnie to get there. Sonny's leg was badly broken and required surgery and a set of metal screws. He was a mass of small cuts and bruises. But he was alive. Lonnie was not.

Sonny's parents came to the hospital the next day. He was so glad to see them. He had missed them, though he hadn't until that moment realized how much. After they tearfully, anxiously assured themselves that Sonny was all right they both relaxed.

"We tried to come see you last night," his mother said. "Your *wife* wouldn't let us in."

Vern shushed her with a warning look. Sonny actually smiled.

"Mama, she's scared and she's alone," he said. "You're right about her. She doesn't know how to have a family. We're just going to have to teach her."

His mother was momentarily speechless.

"She's home with Sierra this morning," he said. "She didn't have anyone to baby-sit for her. Last night she left her with a neighbor, but she can't just do that with people she hardly knows."

"No, certainly not," Phrona said, haughtily.

"That's what I mean about not understanding family," he told her. "She should know that you and Dad would gladly keep Sierra for us. Especially in an emergency like this."

His mother, obviously, didn't know what to say. But his father did.

"Of course we would. And we will," he said. "I'll go give her a phone call. We'll go by and pick up our granddaughter on the way home. That way Dawn can spend the entire afternoon and evening with you."

They kept Sonny in the hospital for five days, though they let him out on furlough the morning of Lonnie's funeral, which he insisted upon attending.

They all went, his parents, his wife, his daughter. Vern rented a minivan, which was easier for Sonny to get in and out of. They traveled together, through gray misty weather and the gloom of low clouds. Lonnie's family lived in Strawberry Plains. The sanctuary at Assembly of God was packed to capacity.

Perhaps because it was known that Sonny had been in the accident, or maybe just because it was convenient, the Lelands were directed toward the front of the church. They were seated right behind the Beale family, with Sonny in his wheelchair in the aisle.

He would have known Lonnie's children anywhere, Sonny thought. The two older girls were pretty, just as he'd said. And the boys all looked like younger versions of the man himself.

The preacher talked about Lonnie's love for his late wife, his devotion to his children, his kindness among those in his community. Sonny was drowning in guilt. When he looked at Lonnie's family, he felt terrible. But when he looked at Sierra all sweet and smiling and Dawn, nearly big enough to burst with the new baby, he was so grateful to be alive.

They filed past the open casket. Lonnie, barbered and wearing a suit and tie, looked only vaguely reminiscent of the man that Sonny knew.

After the graveside service he had Dawn wheel him over to talk to the family. The oldest daughter's name was Tonya.

"I wanted you to know that your father saved my life," he told her.

The story came out of him exactly as he remembered. It felt good to tell it, to share the obligation of remembering it. Sonny opened his shirt and showed the still red and angry scar from the limb that had passed through Lonnie's body.

Sonny's recitation was such a relief. But Lonnie's teenage daughter didn't look as if she were comforted.

"Do you think he did it on purpose?" she asked.

"Yes," Sonny told her. "Of course he did. He was very brave and noble."

"But we needed him," Tonya said, her eyes welling with tears. She gestured toward her brothers and sisters in and around the green awning that sheltered their father's grave. "How will I keep our family together without him?"

Sonny had no answer for her.

With Sierra to care for, Sonny on a walker and Dawn poised to give birth any moment, Vern suggested that Sonny and his family temporarily move in with them. Both Dawn and Phrona were horrified with the suggestion, but Sonny accepted so quickly that neither had time to make an open protest. Not that complaints were not made to their respective husbands.

Dawn declared adamantly that she "would never set foot in that woman's house."

Sonny could tell from Vern's haggard expression that his mother's objections were relentless. But on the day of his release from the hospital, Sonny, Dawn and Sierra moved into the Leland house. The two women coped by having as little interaction as humanly possible and not passing one word between them. The atmosphere was tense, occasionally hostile. But it didn't seem to bother Sierra, who blossomed under the constant attention.

Rocky loved the big backyard. And although Phrona complained about having an animal in the house, she fixed him a bed in the laundry room and made sure he always had food and water.

Sonny's boyhood room was on the back of the house with its own doorway to the garden. But the front bedroom with a wide bathroom attached was the most convenient for convalescing. It was a small area for three people, but Vern immediately conceived the idea of enclosing the adjacent porch to add nursery space.

The renovation work was relatively minor and Vern paid a bonus to get it done quickly. It was all but finished the day Dawn went into labor.

She had seen the doctor the previous day. He'd pronounced her healthy and stable, and that she was at least another week away from delivery. So, Vern and Sonny felt perfectly safe when they headed out to an appointment with the orthopedist.

The two sat in the waiting room for quite a while. Just talking, waiting. It was almost strange—what a golden time it was for them. To simply chat as father and son was a luxury both had missed.

"I don't think Mama and Dawn are ever going to like each other," Sonny told his father.

Vern nodded. "It's amazing how much bad blood they've managed to conjure up between them in such a short time. But I wouldn't worry too much. You know that no woman, not Madame Curie or Mother Teresa would be good enough for her son. Keep that in mind."

"I considered asking them out," Sonny joked. "But I worried that Ms. Curie was a bit old for me and Mother Teresa really had her heart set on being a nun."

The two laughed together.

"Dawn does have her problems," Sonny said more seriously. "Sometimes I think she's like a wounded bird. But she's my wife and the mother of my kids. I love her. She's smart and funny and full of energy. She has potential to create a happy, full life for herself."

"If she loves you and the children," Vern said, "then I think that wounded bird has everything she'll need to fly again."

"Thanks, Dad," Sonny said.

Vern wrapped an arm around his son's shoulder.

"When I think about the accident," Sonny told him, "I think about not being here for her. I just really worry."

Vern nodded. "That's part of it," he said. "When you take on the responsibilities of a wife and kids, worrying about them just comes with the territory."

Sonny agreed. "But if something did happen to me," he said, "I know I could count on you and Mama to help Dawn. She'd have a hard time raising those kids alone."

"Of course we'd be there for her," Vern assured him. "Just like I know that when I'm gone, as long as your mother is still living, you'll take care of her."

"Well, of course," Sonny said. "That's what family is all about."

"Yes."

The doctor took X rays of Sonny's leg and was pleased at how well the bone was healing around the metal screws.

"You can start putting a light weight on that leg," he told him. "But take it easy."

Sonny exchanged the walker for crutches and felt considerably lighter. The mood on the way home was jovial and carefree. When they pulled up in the driveway, they were surprised that Sonny's car wasn't parked there.

His brow furrowed. "I don't think Dawn ought to be driving," he said.

"I hope she and Phrona didn't have some kind of falling out." Vern worried. He pulled up closer to the garage.

Sonny immediately opened the door and began the slow, careful process necessary to get out of the car.

"Wait!" his father said. "There's a note on the back door."

Sonny stayed where he was, craning his neck to see what was happening. Vern hurried to the back step, pulled the note off the door, read it quickly and rushed back to the car.

"Dawn went into labor, they're at the hospital," he said.

Sonny shut the passenger side door and reattached his seat belt. His father was already backing out of the driveway.

The afternoon traffic was already picking up and it was slow going as they got closer to the hospital. They were stopped at a traffic light when the showcase from a shop window caught Sonny's eye.

"Pull in here," he said.

"What?"

"Pull in here."

Vern did as he was told.

"You want me to get something?" he asked Sonny.

"No," his son said. "I want to do this myself."

Sonny managed to get out and hobble into the flower shop. In only a couple of moments he was headed back to the car with a huge bouquet of yellow roses tucked under his arm.

Vern helped him into his seat. The fast-paced exertion was tough on him, but he looked happy.

Cutting through on side streets, Vern managed to make up some time and they were at the E.R. entrance to the hospital in no time.

"Get out and go find your wife," Vern told him. "I'll park the car."

With directions from an orderly he passed in the hall, Sonny found his way to the birthing center.

"My wife, Dawn Leland, is here somewhere," he said.

"Number four," the nurse at the desk told him, pointing up the hallway. "Is she all right?" Sonny asked. "Has she had the baby?"

"I think you're here in plenty of time," she said. "Her mother is with her."

"Her mother?"

"Or maybe it's your mother," the woman said.

Sonny slowly made his way to the room she indicated. He heard his wife's groaning and panting before he saw her.

Standing in the doorway, the sight before him was almost unfathomable. Dawn was in the bed, covered with sweat and straining in midcontraction. His mother was right beside her, holding her hand and talking to her softly, gently, encouragingly.

Sierra was sitting on the floor scribbling on pieces of a magazine that she'd torn to bits. When she glanced up and saw him her eyes lit up and she raised her arms.

"Da!" she called out her name for him.

The two women turned to look at him.

"Sonny, you've made it!" his wife and mother called out almost simultaneously.

With his crutches, he couldn't pick up Sierra, so he patted her on the head and then hobbled over to the bedside.

"How are you doing?" he asked Dawn. "Has Mama been taking good care of you?"

"She's been wonderful," Dawn admitted, though she couldn't look her mother-in-law in the eye. "She's got a cool head in a crisis and she's very supportive."

Phrona shrugged off the compliment, unable to meet anyone's gaze, either.

"Driving a woman to the hospital and holding her hand through a few labor pains is not so much to ask," his mother said. She was trying to maintain the haughty, superior attitude that had become her typical behavior around Dawn. She couldn't quite manage it.

"The right help at the right time is very important to give," Sonny told her. He held the flowers in her direction. "Maybe these should go to you."

Phrona gave him a frown of disapproval. "Don't be silly. I'd drive a total stranger to the hospital. And I'd hold her hand until her husband turned up. These baby girls are my grandchildren."

Sonny nodded.

"They are the Leland legacy going forward into the future," she said. "That means a lot to me."

"I know," he said, quietly.

Phrona glanced at the flowers he carried and tutted in disapproval. "Yellow roses, for heaven's sake," she said. "Don't you know that red is the color that you're supposed to bring to your wife."

Sonny chuckled. "That's an ordinary wife, Mama," he said. "My Dawn is never ordinary."

He handed the flowers to her.

"They are beautiful, Sonny," she told him. Then her brow furrowed and she handed them back. "Here comes another contraction."

Their second beautiful, healthy daughter was born less than an hour later. The delivery was not as difficult as Sonny remembered from the last time. It helped to have both his parents running in and out of the birthing room, keeping Sierra busy and Dawn distracted.

Sonny had wondered about his ability to love a new child as much as he loved Sierra, but when he held his second daughter in his arms, he knew immediately that there was more than enough heart inside him to give each of the girls an abundance.

"She's beautiful, perfect, wonderful," Dawn said.

Sonny agreed, but said only, "Thank you."

They brought in his parents, who held her and cooed and bragged on her as if she were a spectacular new species. Even Sierra wanted to pet the baby, whom she called "puppy."

When Sonny and Dawn were alone again, he tentatively broached a potentially prickly subject. Having known the baby was to be another girl, they'd already picked out the name Dakota, but Sonny made a suggestion.

"I think it would mean a lot to my mother and her Leland legacy stuff if maybe we could give the baby a family name for the middle name," he said. "There are lots of Annes and Elizabeths, we wouldn't have to pick Hester or Prudence. And she could always just use the initial if she doesn't like it."

His throat went dry as she hesitated. Maybe it was too much to ask. Dawn had never had much in life that was her own. Now he was asking her to share a part of one special something that was truly, indisputably hers, her child.

His wife gazed down at the baby in her arms and finally nodded. "I guess it would be nice to give her some tie to the family," she said. "I remember always wanting to feel a part of someone. It might be great to feel connected to hundreds of years of someones. But, if we're going to do it, let's not be halfhearted. Dakota Sophrona. It's a mouthful, but at least it sort of rhymes."

# REAL LIFE
## 18

The next Wednesday after supper, Del and Spence came over to the Leland house. After a couple of moments of social chitchat Del and Vern shut themselves up in his office to play chess. Spence was there to hang out with me. Mrs. Leland didn't seem to get that. She thought that he was a guest in the house and that she should be involved in entertaining him.

She suggested we play cards together; I almost rolled my eyes. None of us was that keen on it. And I feared she'd try either canasta or Go Fish. She taught us Nertz, which was very fast and exciting. It was like a grown-up game, without being old-ladylike.

Spence and I were neck and neck for the top score. Mrs. Leland was next with Sierra trailing badly. Surprisingly we were all having fun and it didn't seem all that weird to have this adult with us. What really knocked me out was when Mom came in and took a seat next to Spence.

She was wearing tight white shorts and a midriff top that didn't quite hide the top of the heart of roses tattoo.

Spence's scores immediately went down the tube. He couldn't keep his eyes on the cards. His points minus his Nertz was coming up with negative numbers hand after hand. Mom smiled at him, as if she approved of his distraction. That just made it worse.

Mom watched us play for a while then, surprisingly, Mrs. Leland gave her a deck of cards and she joined in. Mom was good at the game and within a few minutes we were all laughing and enjoying ourselves.

Spence relaxed as he got more used to her and then he started playing better. Mom talked to him like she would to us. That pretty much untied his tongue.

We'd been at the game for about a half hour when Vern and Del came out of the study.

"We couldn't keep our minds on the board," Del told us. "It sounded like all the action was in here. You are having entirely too much fun for us to ignore."

They sat down, too, and Mrs. Leland searched through the drawers of the sideboard for more decks. Two more people made for a lot in the dining room and there were huge piles of cards in the center of the table.

I began to have this strange feeling, warm feeling. There was so much laughing, so much camaraderie. Even Mrs. Leland seemed exuberant and happy. It was like some *Cosby Show, Eight Is Enough, Seventh Heaven* TV moment. All of us together around a table. It felt like what other people thought family might be. It felt like what I'd always wished my family could be. I tried not to look at it too closely, certain it would evaporate before my eyes. It was just a pleasant moment in time. I didn't want to get too accustomed to it.

Surprisingly Mom was the first to get two hundred points, especially since she missed out of the first few hands. I came in second. Then Mrs. Leland, Spence, Sierra and Vern. Del came in dead last, but he was really funny about it.

"I thought it was like golf," he said, pretending to be surprised at losing. "You mean lowest score doesn't win? Aww rats, I would have played differently."

Everybody laughed at him and acted like it was all our fault for not explaining the game. It was all silliness, but nice. It made the outcome seem not as important as the fun of playing.

Mrs. Leland served us milk and cookies. The adults got decaf coffee, except for Mom, who fixed herself a cup of tea.

Afterward Sierra and I were helping Vern sort out the card decks. Spence tugged at my arm.

I glanced up at him and he made a weird head gesture, like "let's get out of here."

He headed toward the kitchen and motioned for me to follow.

"Mrs. Leland, I gotta show Dakota something in my house," he called out as he was rushing me out the back door.

"What's going on?"

"You tell me," he said. "Didn't you see it?"

"See what?"

"Your mom and my dad walked out on the front porch together."

"So?"

"So, don't you want to find out what they're saying?"

I did want to know. I was suddenly terrified that
Del would tell Mom about my breakdown over the
report about my dad's death. Parents always shared
that kind of thing. I didn't want Mom to know about
that. That was just one more thing for her to worry
about. I didn't want her to worry about me. She
would probably feel guilty at not having told me
more. And it would bring up all her own sad feelings
about Sonny's death.

"Don't let him tell," I murmured a prayer as we
slipped into the Tegges' back door and ran up to
Spence's room in total darkness.

"If we turn on a light, Dad would obviously notice and might come over and check it out," Spence
said.

That didn't sound bad to me. But he didn't want
them to move until we could hear what they were
saying.

Spence grabbed up the receiver, but stopped me
as I opened the door to the balcony.

"Sound waves don't bend," he told me. "We'll
have to get to my front yard to get a clear shot."

He said it as if speaking from experience. I
wouldn't have been surprised to hear that he'd already spied on me or Sierra or both on that front porch.

We went down the stairs and tiptoed out the back
door. We snuck around the far side of the house, not
wanting to draw attention to ourselves. With great
stealth we made our way across the lawn. Spence
went down on his belly behind a clump of rhododen-
drons. I was right beside him. He eased the dish
through the bottom of the leaves and limbs until he
had a bead on the glider of the Lelands' front porch.

He flipped on the switch.

"Got 'em," he whispered.

He handed me an earphone. The first sound that I heard was my mother's laugh. It was a full-of-life belly laugh, the kind she got when she'd had one beer too many. I felt momentarily confused. He obviously had not told her about what I'd done. But I didn't like the two of them getting too chummy. If she started drinking and flirting with Del Tegge, treating him in that way that she always treated guys I would...I would... I didn't know what I would do. I wanted to race out of the bushes and interrupt them. Somehow I couldn't bear for Del to think of her like that. To treat her in that familiar way that men treated her.

I needn't have worried.

"That's the worst joke I ever heard," my mom said when she finally got her composure. "Where did you ever hear such a lousy joke?"

"Spence brings them home from day camp," he said. "He's my only social contact with the outside world. Consider yourself fortunate that it wasn't about boogers or flatulence."

"I'm grateful, believe me, I'm grateful," Mom said. "I've been through those preteen years already. Girls are not as bad, maybe, but definitely *gross* is the byword of the age."

"Yeah, it's my impression," he told her, "that for acquiring an icky vision of the universe, nothing beats talking with middle schoolers."

"Who would have thought that you could be funny?" my mom said, sounding genuinely surprised.

"A single dad in Knoxville," Del answered. "I'd

better be funny. It's the only way I keep from wallowing in self-pity."

"You don't seem like the self-pity type to me," Mom told him.

"Only because it looks so unattractive and it really hurts my job prospects," he said.

That made her laugh again.

"All parents whine about their lives from time to time," he explained. "It's just that if you're married, you do it with your spouse and nobody knows. If you're single you have to vent to friends and coworkers. Is that why everybody is suddenly busy the minute I show up at the coffee machine?"

Mom was amused at that, too.

"So, what happened with your marriage?" she asked him.

There was a moment of hesitation. "And you're very direct, aren't you?"

"I think that's the cancer," she told him. "It provokes some kind of low bullshit, low evasion reaction."

"I dunno," Del answered. "You impress me as having been a low bullshit type for a very long time."

"I think you've got me figured out," she said. "So are you telling or evading?"

"There's not much to tell," Del said. "Our marriage was pretty much dead on arrival."

"You just weren't right for each other," Mom said.

"On the contrary, we were perfect for each other," he said. "We both grew up here in Knoxville. Our parents are friends. We went to the same schools and day camps and church picnics. She was my high school prom date and the only girl I even dated in college. She knew everything about my childhood and I knew everything about hers."

"That sounds like a good match," Mom said.

"It sure sounded that way to us and everyone who knew us," Del said. "We were on our honeymoon when we first realized that when it came down to what we wanted for our future, we didn't have one thing in common."

"Oh, wow," Dawn responded.

"We stayed together for a few years," he continued. "Trying to reconcile all those irreconcilable differences. I'm not sorry for that. We had Spencer and that is, certainly, the best thing that ever happened to me. But the truth is the day we parted company I think we were both humming the *Hallelujah* chorus under our breath."

"No hard feelings?" Mom asked him. "Your ex *is* married to Dr. Sexy-Accent Moneybags."

"Oh, you've met Wiktor," he said.

"Yeah, he came by to shake my hand," she said. "I think handshake is all he does on the charity cases."

"Right," Del said.

"So, no hard feelings?" she said.

"No," Del answered. "She got what she wanted and I...I guess what I wanted just wasn't her. What about you? Did you have a marriage made in heaven?"

"Pretty much," Dawn answered. I could almost hear a sigh in her voice. "Then he died and I've been in relationship hell ever since."

"How come?"

"He and I were not at all alike," she said. "Guys

like him never give me the time of day. I don't know
what he saw in me, but against all smart reasoning
he loved me. When I lost him, well, I went back to
the kind of guys that live my kind of life."

"Why would you do that?" he asked.

"It was more familiar, I guess. And mostly you get
about as much as you give," she said. "I didn't have
all that much left to give."

"Or maybe you just wanted to keep it to yourself,"
Del said.

She hesitated. "Maybe," she said.

"At least you shared it with the kids," he said.
"Your girls are great."

"Thank you," she said. "They are pretty amazing.
I don't know how that happened. I didn't have a
clue how to raise kids. Not even the bad example of
my own parents. I just made it up as I went along."

"My theory," Del told her, "is that we never make
the same mistakes our parents made. We make different mistakes."

"Well, my parents made *every* mistake," Mom
said.

"Then maybe that's why you got it all right," he
said.

She laughed again, but it wasn't so much humor
as appreciation.

"I guess I'd better round up Spencer and head for
home," Del said. "I've really enjoyed talking with
you, Dawn. I'd like to do it again sometime."

Mom hesitated. "I…I don't know, I… Really with
the girls and the cancer thing and living here with the
Lelands I'm not sure I want to…to get involved."

"I'm not asking for a live-in, Dawn," he said. "Just

some occasional small talk. We're about the same age. We live on the same street. We both have kids. That's enough in common for some ordinary chit-chat. Some days I'm so starved for adult conversation I start spilling my guts to the telemarketers."

Mom laughed at that.

"Yeah, you know you must have become a boring guy when those people hang up on you," he said.

"Okay," she said. "Sure, we can talk. I'd enjoy that."

"Me, too," he said. His voice was low and soft. "Bye."

We heard the sound of the front door. Peering through the darkness I could see Mom sitting alone on the swing.

Later that night I related our spying adventure to Sierra.

My sister was clawing me for details, but ultimately was disappointed.

"Darn it all!" she said. "I was so hoping Del would kiss her."

I sat up in bed to peer at her through the darkness of the bedroom.

"Kiss her? Are you crazy?"

"I told you Del is an amazing hottie," Sierra said. "I know Mom must have such a crush. But he's so nerdy. He'll never be able to make a move on her."

"And he shouldn't," I told him. "Del is great, but he's just not Mom's type."

"Mom's type is whoever she's interested in," Sierra said. "Right now, Del is the only game in town. Mom can't help but be interested. Pursuing him would give her something positive to occupy her time."

"You're crazy," I said. "Your brain has been totally warped from too much daytime TV. Del is completely cool and I'm sure Mom likes him. But it's not like that. And them getting together would be just way wrong. There is nothing about him that would work for her. And vice versa."

"You're still such a kid," Sierra said, with an accusing dismissal. "Mom and Del need each other. By his own admission, Del spends way too much time alone. And you know Mom. She's not going to be anywhere long without having some guy on the string."

"That's when things are normal," I said. "They're not normal now. Mom is sick. She doesn't need to be chasing after boyfriends, she needs to be getting well."

"Right," Sierra agreed. "And that's why we should be doing everything we can to encourage that romance. Love is the glue that keeps life together."

I rolled my eyes. "That's just crap," I told my sister. But a part of me continued to wonder about it.

# REAL LIFE
## 19

◆━━◆

It was the first day after her second cycle of chemo that Mom's hair came out.

Vern had decided to take us all on a day trip to Norris Lake. We were getting dressed and packing up our swimsuits when she came into the room and got us.

"I need you with me," she said.

At first I thought she only meant Sierra, but she motioned for me to come, as well. We went into her bathroom. She sat down on the stool in front of the mirror and pointed to her hairbrush. A huge wad of hair clung to it.

"There was scads of the stuff on my pillow this morning," Mom said. "Sierra, brush it out. Let's see what we've got left."

I took a seat on the vanity, and Sierra stood behind Mom. It was weird to see it just come out. It wasn't as if it was hurting Mom. Or that it was being pulled out by the brush. It was like it wasn't attached at all. Like it had been lying on her head by force of habit.

About three-fourths of her hair came out. She was left with a couple of completely bald patches and a visible scalp covered by a few long, reddish-blond wisps.

We were all staring in the mirror together. Silently, solemnly staring at the reflection.

Mom suddenly chuckled and shook her head.

"Sierra, can you see your own expression?" she asked. "Sweetie, you look like you just had to sit through an *Ultimate Fear Factor* marathon. It's just hair."

Sierra nodded, but she still looked concerned.

"I'm not sure how we should fix it," she said.

Mom gazed in the mirror. "Get the razor I shave my legs with out of the bathtub," she said. "I think a bowling ball would be preferable." We lathered Mom's head, but Sierra was still hesitant to do the deed.

Mom handed the razor to me and I shaved a section right down the middle.

"Now we really have to do it," she said. "Come on, Sierra. We're making progress here."

Sierra took the razor from me and finished the job. Mom looked over her efforts like a new do from the salon, even using the hand mirror to get a view of the back.

"Well, now I know what my head looks like," she said. "I've been alive for thirty-four years and this is the first unobstructed view I've ever had of it."

"Yeah, I guess so," I said.

"The scalp is very white," Sierra pointed out. "But I think it keeps you from looking quite so pale."

Mom shot her a look and nodded.

"Very good, Sierra," she said. "You girls are really getting the hang of this support thing. Try to see this as a lesson. Don't place too much value on your looks, because they can desert you on very short notice."

"Your looks haven't deserted you!" Sierra insisted.

"No, Mom," I agreed. "It's only your hair that's gone."

"We can get you a wig, Mom," Sierra said. "I think that's what most women do."

Mom nodded. "I can't have a wig today. Maybe I can tie a scarf around my head or something."

In the end, Mom settled on a red bandana covered with a baseball cap. Mrs. Leland noticed, but didn't make any comment. Vern gave her an upbeat grin.

"Nice hat," he said.

We stowed all our gear in the trunk and squeezed into the back seat of the Saab, with me in the middle. Rocky sat in Sierra's lap, his snout hanging out the open window.

The state park lake was about an hour's drive. It was rustic and a little run-down. But in the middle of the week, it was clean and fairly quiet, not over-crowded.

"We haven't been out here in twenty years," Vern told us. "The Tennessee Valley Authority built this place in the 1930s to show people who'd never seen nature controlled that a big damn project could be both practical and beautiful. It's hard to argue with the outcome."

The lake, with its deep cove beach and clear blue water, was surrounded by high forested ridges, that somehow made the big lake seem private and secluded.

There were sun worshipers laid out on towels, little kids with shovels and buckets, volleyball players facing off across a net and a couple of kite flyers gazing skyward.

We stripped down to our bathing suits and imme-

diately went for a splash in the shallows of the cove.
Rocky was running, jumping, swimming, barking
like he was a puppy. Vern joined in as we kicked
around in the water, playfully getting each other wet.

Mom was wearing her red vinyl bikini. I remembered it from the previous year, when it was still in
fashion. It was very revealing, but what it revealed
was a little scary. Standing next to Sierra, Mom
looked as if she'd lost a tremendous amount of
weight. She and Sierra had the same body style,
curvy, hourglass. Now, Mom's ribs were visible and
the prominence of her pelvic bone at the side of her
hip drew more attention than the skimpy suit she
was wearing.

We decided to swim out to the platform. Mom declined.

"You go on," she told us. "Rocky and I will hang
here next to the shore."

"I'll stay here with your mother," Vern said, sitting
down in about a foot of water. "Keep her and the dog
safe from drowning."

Mom sat down next to him, laughing.

Sierra and I swam out. The platform, a twelve-foot
square with diving boards on two sides and ladders
on the other, was the hangout for teenagers. A few
younger kids were trying to enjoy themselves. But
mostly it was kids our age. Some were wild and
crazy, having fun. Some were acting cool.

We didn't know anybody, of course. But we
didn't have to. From the moment my sister stepped
up on the deck, she was the center of everything, the
focus of everyone. Guys of every stripe—geeks,
jocks, poets—clamored for her attention. At least

Sierra wasn't one of those prissy types afraid to get her hair wet. She didn't accept her natural charisma as a license to play queen. She genuinely liked people and wanted to have fun. And when she did, the kids around her did, as well. Almost instantly she had every guy on the platform wanting to hang with her. And most of the girls simultaneously wishing she'd be their best friend or drop from the face of the earth.

Sierra's popularity didn't bother me. For one thing, I was used to it. In my lime-green tank suit— flat in front, flat in back, but with big thighs—nobody noticed me. And with everyone concentrating on her, I was always free to do whatever I wanted without the annoyance that anybody might be watching me. I dived and leaped and tried to perfect my clumsy backflip without any unwanted attention. It was fun and I didn't need anybody else. Though a friend would have been nice. I momentarily wished that Spence had come with us. But his dad was working and he was in day camp.

I took a break to catch my breath. Finding a seat on a corner of the platform, facing the beach, I dangled my feet in the water and gazed out at the shore.

Mom and Vern were still sitting together, both of them were looking in my direction, keeping an eye on us at the platform. And they were talking. I wondered what they had to say to each other. Maybe it was just ordinary stuff like how warm the day happened to be and the likelihood that there would be rain next week. But it might be more. Mom could be telling him about how it felt to have cancer. Was she saying how sad it was to lose her hair? Or were they talking about twenty years ago, when Vern last came here, probably with my dad.

That thought went over me with goose bumps.

Maybe Sonny Leland once sat right where I was sitting. Maybe he had practiced his backflip, just like me. I glanced back at Sierra, who was joking with a couple of boys. Mrs. Leland said my dad had Sierra's disposition. Maybe he was the popular guy. He probably wouldn't have noticed me, either.

No, I was sure I would have been special to him. If he'd known me, he would have liked me.

Beyond Mom and Vern up on the shore, Mrs. Leland had a picnic table laid out. I was far away, so I really couldn't see clearly, but it looked as if the table was full of food and drinks and a trickle of smoke rose from the nearby barbeque grill. Mrs. Leland was sitting alone. I couldn't see her expression, of course. But there was something about the scene, something about her all by herself, that was just sad. I didn't even like the woman, but somehow it just looked so sad.

I glanced back at Sierra. She was in the middle of a gaggle of guys. They were sharing diving secrets. Other girls were hanging around the edges, trying to worm themselves into the conversation. There was no place for me. Mrs. Leland was alone all by herself. I was alone in a crowd. I pushed off into the water and swam toward shore. When I got to the shallows, I stood up and walked leisurely past Mom and Vern.

"Hey, sweetie," Mom said. "Did Sierra forget you exist again?"

I shrugged. "No big deal," I assured her. "I'm just going up to get something to eat. You want something?"

"I'm fine," she said. "I'll stay here and keep an eye on your sister."

"Vern? You want a soda or something?"

He shook his head. "Not right now," he said.

I walked up the rise to our picnic site. Mrs. Leland was sitting on the concrete bench on the near side of the table. She was facing the lake, looking out at the action on the platform. But I knew somehow that, unlike Mom and Vern, she wasn't watching out for Sierra.

"Hi."

She glanced in my direction, though not quite at me and offered that tight smile that was about all she could ever manage.

"There are soft drinks in the cooler," she said. "And if you're hungry, you can fix yourself a plate."

My stomach was rumbling a little, so I looked at what was available to eat. It was astounding. It looked like she'd picked up one of those lifestyle magazines with a glossy color photo and a caption reading "Elegant Lake Luncheon." There were no hot dogs on buns with mustard and potato chips. There was a lattice-topped quiche, a salad with beets and pine nuts, a huge bowl of fruit and melons and a plate of cheeses.

"What are you going to grill?" I asked her, pointing to the charcoal.

"Chicken satay," she answered, pulling the cover off a dish filled with meat on sticks. "Would you like some?"

"Maybe later," I told her, thinking to myself that it was a stupid, showy, pretentious kind of picnic.

I grabbed up a piece of bread and bent it around

some cheese before taking a seat beside her. All of the sad, loneliness that had struck me as so obvious from the distance of the diving platform was overridden up close by Mrs. Leland's deliberate dislike and disapproval. We had that in common. She didn't like me and I didn't like her. But she knew things. Things that maybe it might hurt to ask. I didn't care if she hurt.

"You used to come out here with my dad."

It was a statement not a question.

At first I didn't think she was going to respond. She continued to look out over the water. Finally she spoke.

"We came out in the summertime from when he was just a toddler until he was old enough to drive himself," she said. "Some days he'd swim. Some days he'd hike. He loved it out here." There was a long hesitation. "I didn't think I would ever come back."

"It's a nice place," I said. "That's reason enough to come on your own."

"It's a family place," she said.

"Yeah, I guess so," I said. "But that's not everybody here. There are couples. And see that old lady down there **near** Mom and Vern? She's all by herself."

Mrs. Leland glanced down at the woman. About thirty yards across from them she sat in a webbed lawn chair, a huge beach bag at her side. She was curiously watching everything. Occasionally trying to strike up a conversation with passing children.

"Pathetic," Mrs. Leland declared.

"Why?"

"She's sitting there in the middle of today and remembering her own children and times long gone," Mrs. Leland said. "She should be dealing with the realities and getting on with her life. It's pathetic to cling to the past."

I thought about Mom losing her hair.

"Maybe the present is too miserable and the future looks too scary," I said.

Mrs. Leland shrugged. "Perhaps," she said and looked away as if the subject no longer interested her.

Mom and Vern were headed our way. Vern was talking. He had his right arm bent and Mom had her hand on his bicep, leaning on him for support.

Mrs. Leland was watching them, too. I didn't know what she was thinking, but she didn't look all that happy.

When they reached the picnic table, Mom sat down beside me.

She gave me a wink and a tired smile.

"I don't know what you two were thinking, sitting out on the beach for so long," Mrs. Leland said. "They were very clear in that pamphlet on lymphoma that you should be limiting your exposure to UV rays."

"We were watching Sierra," Vern said.

"You could have watched her," his wife said. "And allowed Dawn to get out of the sun. The chemotherapy makes her skin a lot more sensitive. Or did you know that?"

"I knew it," Mom said quietly. She turned to me. "What are you up to?" she asked me.

I suppose my typical answer to that question would have been "nothing." But at that moment, I knew Mom needed more from me. I felt that she needed me to talk. She needed me to distract attention from her, to take on Mrs. Leland when she didn't have the strength to do so. She needed me to do something, so I did.

"Isn't this lunch spectacular?" I said. "Real plates instead of paper. And every food you ever wanted to try. There's crackers with fancy stuff on them. I bet it's yummy."

"Goose liver pate," Vern said, smiling at me. "That's one of my favorites."

"I've never eaten any," I told him. "I hope it's better than regular liver."

"Infinitely," he said.

"And Mom, there're some shish kebab things that go on the grill," I said.

"Satay," Mrs. Leland corrected me. "Chicken satay. With peanut sauce for dipping."

"We really want to try that, don't we, Mom?" I said.

Mom nodded. She gave me a little secret smile to let me know that she understood what I was doing and why I was talking. I was taking care of her.

"I'll get this on the grill," Mrs. Leland said as she picked up the container with the meat on sticks.

I hurried over next to her.

"Let me help you, Mrs. Leland," I said, putting on my best Helpful-Hannah demeanor.

The woman startled slightly and looked at me, really looked at me, eye to eye for maybe the first time ever.

"Please, Dakota, you may call me…"

She hesitated, not sure how to finish her sentence.

What was she thinking? Grandma? Phrona? I knew she wouldn't be able to bear hearing me use either one.

"Well, you needn't call me Mrs. Leland," she said finally.

# SONNY DAYS
## 20

———➤ ◄———

They brought the baby home from the hospital. Not to the crowded, run-down mobile home, but to the Leland house in Old North Knoxville. It was a magic time. Sonny thought, more than once, that they should have named the little girl Peace instead of Dakota. She was the shred of common concern that now seemed capable of weaving his family back together.

It appeared to Sonny that his mother had been impressed by Dawn's grit. His mother wasn't one of those women who could quickly change her mind, but it was as if she had at last found something to admire in her daughter-in-law. And she was beginning to accept her granddaughters as a part of herself. She allowed Sierra to follow her around like a puppy all day long. And she was willing and eager to hold the baby anytime she was asked.

Sonny worried that Dawn might feel threatened by Phrona's help. And he was pretty sure it would have been true if the baby was their first. The advantage now of having two in diapers, an active toddler and a newborn, was that Dawn was too busy, too tired, too frazzled, to peer closely at family dynamics. When a helping hand was offered, she had no time to examine it for agendas or speculate on ulterior motives.

Of course, nothing was perfect.

"Your mother is going to spoil Sierra," Dawn told him. "She dresses her like a princess. And she lets her watch too much TV."

Phrona voiced her own concerns. "The new baby is neither as pretty nor as cheerful as Sierra. Despite the breast-feeding, I don't think Dawn is bonding with her appropriately."

Sonny patiently listened and reassured them both. They were the two women he loved most in the world and helping them get along was a role that he welcomed.

Two families living in one house was guaranteed to create a certain amount of friction. He knew that Dawn was eager to have a place to call her own again. And he was sure that his parents would be happy to get their lives back to normal, as well.

It was an outside source that brought the subject up for discussion.

Sonny received a call from a representative from the company. He wanted to stop by to see him in the afternoon. He had some papers to be signed.

Vern was home with the sniffles. He'd spent the entire day dozing in his chair in front of the TV hugging a tissue box. By chance, when the company man, Mr. Webb, arrived, both Sierra and the baby were napping. A rare occasion for both to be down simultaneously. So when Sonny, who had graduated from crutches to a cane, welcomed the guest and invited him into the living room, everyone was there.

There were a few moments of idle chitchat with polite as well as official inquiries about the condition of Sonny's leg.

"Workmen's compensation should be taking care of the medical bills," Mr. Webb told him.

Sonny nodded. "I haven't noticed any problems so far."

"Has the doctor given you any indication of when you'll be cleared to go back to the job?"

"He said light duty in a couple of weeks and then if my leg continues to heal at the rate it's been going, I could be back in the trees in another month."

Mr. Webb nodded. "That sounds about right." The man was writing Sonny's response into his notes.

"Well, we're certainly looking forward to getting you back to work," Mr. Webb said. "From everything I've seen and read about you, you are an exemplary employee. Just the kind of young man who has a real future with this company."

"Thank you."

"And," he continued, "I think we can even give you something here that will tangibly demonstrate our appreciation and support."

From his briefcase he pulled out a stack of papers held together with a clip.

"We have a check here for four thousand dollars," Mr. Webb said. "We'd like to offer it to you as a settlement for your injury."

"Oh?" Sonny was surprised. He shot a look to his father, who appeared to be taken off guard, as well.

"It's the company's way of covering any lost pay or extra expenses that you might incur," he said.

"That's really great," Sonny said.

"We only need you to sign this agreement, accepting the money and pledging not to hold us responsible for the accident or be a participant in any legal proceeding stemming from the accident."

He pulled the check off the top of the stack and handed the rest of the papers to Sonny.

"That is nice," he said, though he felt strangely cautious as if something about this was not quite what it appeared to be.

He began perusing the documents. He didn't get very far. The language of the legal world was difficult, hard to grasp. Mr. Webb leaned closer, he was smiling.

"Basically it's a standard release of liability," he said. "Lawyers? Whew, who can understand them?" He gave a little chuckle.

Sonny tried to smile, but in truth, he didn't like the sound of it.

"Why don't you just leave this here with me and I can look it over, study it a little before I sign," he said.

"Of course, I can do that," Mr. Webb replied. "But then I can't leave you the check today. I'm sure you have a lot of bills and things you need to buy for your wife, your children. But I won't be able to leave the check today."

"That's fine," Sonny said.

"You wouldn't want my son to sign papers he hadn't read and understood," Vern said.

"I'd be happy to go over them with you now," Mr. Webb suggested.

"No," Sonny said. "Leave them and leave your card. I'll look them over and give you a call."

Mr. Webb was hesitant, but Sonny finally did manage to get him out the front door.

"Wow! Four thousand dollars is a lot of money," Dawn said.

Phrona agreed. "It seems like a very generous offer."

"Maybe it is," Sonny said. "I don't know."

"You weren't thinking of suing them, were you?" Phrona asked.

Sonny shook his head. "No, I don't think I'd need to. My medical bills are covered and I'm expecting a full recovery and a normal life ahead of me."

Vern nodded. "I agree with Sonny, there's no reason to sue, but I don't know. Something doesn't sound quite on the up-and-up with this."

"Maybe it's just a generous company," Phrona said.

"No, not at all," Sonny told her. "They are skinflints and corner cutters. Unless they've really turned over a new leaf, I can't imagine them being charitable."

"These people don't know you," Dawn said. "Maybe they think you might take them to court and they just want to make sure it doesn't happen."

Sonny was reading over the papers.

"Dad, this thing about not being a participant in any legal action, what do you think that means?"

"I'm not sure."

"Do you think that it means I couldn't be a witness?" Sonny asked. "I might not be the victim or the court case they're worried about."

Vern nodded slowly. "I wonder what they offered the Beale family," he said.

Sonny was curious, as well. "Those poor kids," he said. "I hope, between the company and the state, they're being taken care of."

"Maybe you can check up on them when you go back to work," Dawn suggested.

Vern cleared his throat meaningfully. Then there was a strangely quiet moment in the room.

"Sonny, I..." Vern began abruptly, shooting a look at Phrona. "Your mother and I meant to discuss this with you earlier." He paused to wipe his nose and his wife continued.

"We don't really want you out there cutting timber again," Phrona said. "It's too hard. It's too dangerous. It's not what we want for our son. And this... this close call has convinced us that we have to speak up."

Sonny gave her a loving smile and when he answered, his tone was soft and dutiful.

"It's hard and dangerous for everybody, Mama," he said. "And nobody wants their children to do it. But somebody has to. It's a very good job and I have a family to support."

Vern interjected his own thoughts.

"We were hoping," he said, "that we could talk you into returning to college."

Sonny felt a momentary stab of longing, but he resisted it. That was not his life these days. And he was lucky to have the life he had.

"Dad, I appreciate it," he said. "But I'm not a happy-go-lucky frat boy anymore. I've got a wife and two children. I have to make a living."

"Phrona and I have talked about taking a second mortgage on the house," Vern said. "If you went to school full-time, maybe you could complete your studies in three years. You'd be welcome to live here with us. I think we could swing it."

Sonny was stunned. He glanced at Dawn. She looked wary.

"It would involve sacrifice on your part," Phrona said. "We can pay your expenses and keep food on the table, but you wouldn't be able to have your own place. You'd have to live crowded in here with us until you graduate."

Sonny knew that his wife wouldn't be interested in that. What woman would? To live in your mother-in-law's house, under her scrutiny 24/7 for three years. No young mother would want to do that. And Dawn, who'd been running from unfavorable situations all her life, had finally made a place for herself, and would be less able than most to give up a home of her own.

"It's really kind..." he began.

"It *is* really kind," Dawn piped in. "Too kind. And if we were in any position to refuse it, we would. But I don't know how Sonny will ever complete his education without your help. It is something that he really wants."

She glanced toward Sonny and Vern and then met her mother-in-law eye to eye. "I will do whatever I can to get along here and make this easier on everybody. I want my girls to have a stable, happy home. I don't really know how to give them that, because I never had it myself. You've given Sonny a wonderful childhood and now you're offering a great start for Sierra and Dakota. I am very grateful, Mrs. Leland. I may not always show it, but I am very grateful."

"Please, dear, call me..." she hesitated.

"Mama," Vern stated firmly. "It won't confuse the kids if Dawn and Sonny both just call you Mama."

For an instant Dawn's eyes bugged out like an insect's and Phrona appeared likely to gag on the suggestion. But both women managed to choke out a response.

"If you would like that?" Dawn asked.

"That…that would be fine," Phrona said.

"So great, that's settled," Vern said. "The kids will move in here semipermanently, Sonny starts back to school next semester. And I guess that means when he sees Mr. Webb about signing the papers to get his money, he can resign at the same time."

It seemed like a very good plan.

Sonny continued to think about Lonnie's children and the papers he was going to sign. He waited until Saturday and asked Vern to drive out to Strawberry Plains. It was a dark, rainy, ugly day—not really a great time for being out on the highway. But he didn't know for sure where the children were living. And he was certain that he couldn't visit during the week, because he assumed the children would all be in school.

Tonya was not. They found her working at a convenience store on the highway. She'd already lost that look of hopeful young teenager poised for university. After only a couple of months she'd already metamorphosed into the tough, real-life, working-class woman that the world expected her to be.

"I've got to keep the family together," she told them. "I can't do that if I'm going to high school."

"Don't you have any other relatives?" Sonny asked. "Uncles, aunts, somebody."

"Of course we do," she said. "But there's nobody that can take all of us. I don't want us to be split up."

"Maybe you could get some help from welfare or

something," Vern said. "So you'd be able to stay together and still pay your bills."

"Don't breathe a word about us to the county," Tonya said, horrified. "If they find out we're trying to make it on our own, they'll have us all farmed out in no time. We'll be fine as long as we're together. We've lost our parents. If we lose each other…"

Her words faded off into uncertainty.

"Did a man from the logging company come by and offer you money?" Sonny asked her.

"Yeah," she said. "He had a check for five thousand dollars! That would sure keep the bills paid up for a while."

"So you signed for it."

Tonya shook her head. "I was afraid to," she admitted. "I'm not legal age. I don't think I can sign anything. I thought maybe we could stall him until after my birthday in August. I don't know what I'd do with a big check like that anyway. Who would I get to cash it?"

"You could deposit it in the bank," he said.

"I haven't been to the bank," Tonya told him. "I'm afraid to talk to them. Dad's got money saved that I know is ours. But I'm afraid they might not give it to me. They could call the county on us."

The young woman's fear of social services seemed overblown. But Sonny and Vern weren't any more familiar with "the county" and what they might or might not do than Tonya. It occurred to Sonny that he knew someone who was.

He called Dawn at home.

"I know about Knox County," she told him. "They live in Jefferson. But I'm sure the rules are probably the same."

"What should she do?"

"She needs to get herself appointed guardian of the younger children," Dawn said.

"She's afraid to contact anyone," Sonny told her. "She won't even go to the bank for her father's money. She's afraid the welfare department will grab everybody up and throw them in foster care."

"Like they want another half-dozen kids to worry about," Dawn said with a cynical chuckle. "Let me call the woman here in town who helped me. I can keep Tonya's name out of it and ask who she should talk to and how to get it done."

Within the next few days, Dawn had the name of a lawyer in Dandridge, Melissa Curtis, who was not that much older than Tonya herself and very sympathetic. She easily got Tonya declared an adult. And the judge was perfectly willing to give her custody of the younger children with only minimum oversight by social workers. The lawyer also probated Lonnie's will, giving Tonya financial discretion for the savings that their father had left them.

A few days later, they were surprised when Melissa called and asked to meet with Sonny and Dawn. Vern and Phrona baby-sat as they talked with her in the living room.

"I believe that the company was negligent in following safety standards for the cutting that day," she said. "Could you tell me what you remember about the accident?"

Sonny related the details as clearly as he could remember.

"So there was concern about two felling crews working so close to each other," she said.

Sonny nodded. "That's why Lonnie had us stop cutting. We'd take our turn so there would be less chance of something going wrong."

"But something went wrong anyway," she said.

He nodded.

She wrote some things down in her notes as they waited.

"I understand that the company has offered you a settlement," she said.

"Yeah," Sonny told her. "They're going to give us four thousand dollars. That's generous considering I'm expecting a complete recovery. I haven't accepted it yet. I wanted to be sure of what I was signing."

"Good idea," she said.

"It's strange that they didn't offer much more to the Beale family," Sonny said.

She nodded. "I think they expected that the kids, being kids, would just jump at it."

"Yeah, I guess so," he said. "And they probably would have if they'd known that it wouldn't bring trouble down on them."

"I'm going to see if I can get them more," Melissa said. "They've been deprived of not only their father's love and care but his income, as well. I think the company can do better by them."

Sonny thought about that for a moment and then nodded. "I think they should pay more," he said. "Not just because the kids deserve it, but because I do believe they were at fault. And the only language the company understands is money. The cost of working in risky situations has got to be higher than it is profitable. If not, more people are likely to be killed."

"I agree," Melissa said. "And I think most of the guys that were there that day agree. But they all have families to support and jobs to keep. There aren't many who are willing to testify to what happened."

Sonny was surprised at that. "It's not like it's a secret," he said. "Everybody there knew what went wrong. We even talked about it at Lonnie's funeral."

"Talking about it and testifying about it are two different things," Melissa pointed out. "As I said, they have jobs with the company. And you, well, I'm sure that agreement they want you to sign will preclude your opportunity of making any statements under oath."

Dawn and Sonny turned to glance at each other. They could almost see their plans for that money going up in smoke before their eyes. But there was no hesitation or dispute in their response.

"I'll testify," Sonny said. "Lonnie saved my life. I am grateful just to be here to tell what happened."

"Even if it means getting no money at all?" Melissa asked.

Sonny nodded affirmatively.

Dawn shrugged and clasped his hand in her own. "I guess that's just four thousand dollars that my husband and I won't need," she said.

# REAL LIFE
## 21

➤ ◄

My mom was in a really tough place in her life. She was broke and sick and living among strangers. I finally began to get it that the only way I could really help her was to distract Mrs. Leland.

Sierra was doing a better job than me. She liked clothes and she liked to shop. Mrs. Leland enjoyed that. So the two of them spent some amount of time on that. But even my sister can't shop every moment. And Sierra was getting deeper into her crush with Seth every day. The sound of his Spitfires on the sidewalk in front of the house became more and more familiar. So much so that Spence and I lost interest in the boring things they said to each other. They went out together to the movies. Vern took them. According to Sierra, he was very good at being right there and yet maintained invisibility. She thought him highly preferable over Seth's parents, who she thought didn't like her all that much.

So Sierra's social life was going great, but that got in the way of her ability to keep Mom and Mrs. Leland separated. I needed to get the woman to like me, be interested in me. I couldn't imagine any way to do that. So I went to somebody I thought might know.

"How do you get someone to like you?" I asked

Del Tegge one hot afternoon as he sat on his back-porch steps. He was dirty and sweaty from lawn mowing. His hair was all stuck down to head and his muscle shirt was all wet and plastered against his chest.

He raised a skeptical eyebrow at me. "You mean, like a boy?" he asked.

"Yuk, no," I assured him. "I leave the boys to Sierra. I mean like, well, a regular person. I mean, you like me. I can tell that. What makes it okay to hang out with me? How can I make, say, another grown-up be interested?"

He didn't shrug off my question. I knew he wouldn't. And he didn't just spout some canned answer like teachers do. He actually thought about it for a minute or two.

"I do like you," he said. "And I think it's for the same reason I like all my friends," he said. "You're smart and funny. I find you entertaining to talk to. You respect my interests and you're willing to listen to me talk about them, sometimes more than you want. That's what being a friend is."

"Just listening while somebody talks about stuff?"

"Like Spence and his stargazing," he said. "I know that's not really your thing. But you let him talk about it. And you don't get all mush-faced and say, 'bor-ring,' even though we both know that sometimes he is."

I nodded slowly. "Yeah, okay," I said. "It's like Sierra listening to all that talk about skateboarding."

Del chuckled. "Yes, I think that's it exactly."

"And that works on everybody?"

He thought about that a moment before nodding. "I think that's true about everybody," he agreed.

"The trick, maybe, is figuring out what a person's interests might be. It's not always like Seth, where they just blurt it out. Some people are much more subtle."

"I guess so."

"Like your mother," Del said. "Dawn will talk about her kids. She'll tell jokes and funny stories. And she'll also just gut you with that rapier cynicism of hers. But she's not very revealing about what's going on inside. What it is that she wants in life."

"She wants a guy named Sonny," I told him. "That's all she ever wants."

Del smiled. "Yeah, I've seen the tattoo," he said.

"You have?" I was surprised. "I've never caught you looking."

"A gentleman never gets caught looking," he told me, laughing. "I'm working on that with Spence."

"Lost cause," I told him. "So, if I want to make some person like me," I said, "I need to figure out what that person is interested in and just let them talk about that."

"I think that will work," he said.

"Okay, great," I said and got up to go.

"Wait!" he said. "Aren't you going to give me any hints about your mom? Besides the name thing?"

"You really want to be friends with my mom?" I asked him. "You are *so* not her type."

He shrugged. "She's not really my type, either," he admitted. "Maybe that's what intrigues me about her."

"Weird," I told him.

"The guys she dates, what do they talk about?"

"Themselves mostly," I said.

"Does she talk about herself?"

"No way, never," I said. "She doesn't like the past. She likes to keep moving on."

Del nodded. He was thinking about her. Speculating about her. I wanted to ask him not to. I remembered what Sierra had said. The crap about the two needing each other. I didn't think it was true and I didn't figure that would be good. Mom could get involved with some guy and that would be okay. But a guy like Del, he'd be hard to leave. And leaving was all part of Mom's thing. I didn't think I could make him understand that. I didn't understand it myself. So I did the next best thing. I sabotaged him.

"Ask Mom about growing up in foster care," I told him as I hurried out of the gate. Lying was not my top skill. I didn't want any questions and I didn't want him to read anything on my face.

If Del even mentioned foster care to Mom, it would be the last conversation they'd ever share. Better for both of them that things went sour now, before either of them really cared.

I was grateful for Del's advice. And I watched Mrs. Leland, trying to figure out her particular star-gazing-skateboard interest. I could sit up on Spence's balcony with the Nature Sounds Receiver and hear everything that went on in her office. But nothing much went on. Just the tapping of computer keys and the occasional one-sided phone conversation.

I decided to talk to Vern about it. He was in his office working at his computer.

"May I interrupt you?" I asked from the doorway.

He glanced up and smiled, motioning me in. "You're always welcome to come in here," he said.

"That's one of the many advantages of being retired. I can always break for granddaughters."

I smiled at him, but I was curious, too. "Do you really think of us as your granddaughters?"

"Of course," he said. "That's who you are."

"I know," I said. "But we were never around here. You never really knew us."

Vern nodded, but it didn't change his opinion. "All the time you were gone, I knew you were out there," he said. "I knew that you were somewhere and that Dawn would keep you safe."

"And you missed us?"

"Yes," he said, very softly. "I missed seeing you grow up. But I'm glad you're here now."

I felt sad for him, wanting us, losing us. I knew from the argument that I'd listened in to that he blamed Mrs. Leland. That he believed that his wife had run my mother off. That wasn't true.

"Mom always runs," I said.

"What?"

"Mom runs. When things get bad or scary or just complicated, Mom just gets in the car and goes. I know you blame Mrs. Leland for Mom leaving, but she would have left anyway."

"Maybe so," he said. "But then again, the slightest change can make all the difference."

His words tugged at me strangely. That was exactly what I'd thought about my dad. If just one thing had been different that day, he might not have died. I wanted to think that, but it bothered me, too.

"Is that really true?" I asked him. "Can a small change really make a big difference?"

"Well, that's a very good question," he said. "Have you ever heard of the chaos theory?"

That coincidence made me sit up straighter.

"Yeah," I said. "I checked out a book about it, but I never got to read it. Do you know about the chaos theory?"

He nodded and turned to his computer. "Let's see what I can find here," he said.

He clicked through a couple of programs and pulled up a really neat picture, sort of a swirling shell in a bright vivid pink.

"Wow, what is that?" I asked him.

"It's a fractal," he said.

"It's really cool looking," I told him.

Vern agreed. Along with the picture was a long string of numbers in a complicated math problem.

"This picture is the physical representation of this equation," he said.

"Cool."

"It seems very stable doesn't it?"

"Yeah, I guess so."

"Okay, why don't you alter just one number," he said.

"Which one?"

"Your choice," he said. "Just change one number."

I looked it over. "This fourteen," I pointed out. "I'll change it to thirteen, my age."

Vern nodded and entered in the change.

"Okay, let's see the fractal." He pulled up the display.

I gasped. I expected to see a difference. I thought part of the picture would be changed. Maybe some of the edges would look different. But it was a totally different picture. It was no longer bright pink, it was dark purple. And it didn't look like a swirling shell, but more like an asteroid floating through a starlit space.

"How does this happen?"

"It's chaos theory," he said. "Randomness is very sensitive to even the smallest changes. You've heard about how the flapping of a butterfly's wing in Hong Kong could change tornado patterns in Texas."

"That's some kind of urban legend or something," I said.

"Actually, the butterfly effect is a classic example in the premise of chaos theory," he said. "No matter how small the change in initial conditions, the outcome can be radically different. Try some on your own."

I pulled a chair up beside him and began working with the numbers.

The fractals were really fun to do. It was sort of a mixture of math and paint-by-number. The software that Vern had made it easy to display even the simplest equations in a beautiful three-dimensional image.

I tried to get the math formula so similar that the picture would be almost the same. But no matter how slight I made the initial difference, even down to thousandth fractions, the tiny changes would grow at an enormous rate until the sets were unrecognizable as being mathematically similar.

"That's why we call it chaos," Vern explained. "Because it takes so very little to transform the outcome so completely. The premise turns Newton's determinism model totally on its head."

"So this is like new science?" I asked.

"Relatively new," Vern answered. "There were some hints about its possibility in the nineteenth century. But it wasn't recognizable until the last four decades."

"Why not?" I asked. "In school it sounds like science already knows like all the laws of nature and stuff."

"We know just enough to reveal how much we don't know," he told me.

"Why don't we know? Couldn't somebody like Einstein just figure it out?"

"Of course he could have," Vern answered. "But sometimes even the smartest physicists and mathematicians and biologists have to wait for the breakthrough. Copernicus was the father of astronomy. But even he couldn't help us really understand space and the solar system until Galileo invented the telescope. That helped human eyes to see the vast distances for the first time."

"What breakthrough did we have to wait for to understand chaos?"

"Computers are the tool that we needed to help us with that," he said. "It wasn't that our eyes were too weak so much as our brains were not powerful enough."

Vern and I hung out together all afternoon doing fractals, altering them, making them positive or negative, adding and subtracting X factors. We printed some of the coolest ones on the color printer. I thought the space-ish ones would look better in Spence's room among the Hubble posters.

I learned more than just some cool math stuff. I

learned that Del had been right. Taking an interest in someone else's interest really does bring people together. I felt like I could talk with Vern, joke with him, be straight with him, like he was a friend. I could even ask him serious questions.

"What happened to make my mom leave Knox-ville?" I asked him as we sat, sipping sodas among the best of the fractals we'd printed.

He hesitated. Vern was a thoughtful guy. Most of the men I'd known in my life—i.e. the guys my mom dated—were not. I liked that about him.

"When there's a crisis in the family," he told me carefully, "sometimes it doesn't bring out the best in people."

"Yeah?"

I waited patiently, as he chose his words.

"Dawn and your grandmother had words," he said.

"It was Mrs. Leland's fault," I said quickly, hoping that it was true.

Vern nodded, but he wasn't completely in agreement.

"They were both to blame," he said. "They were both harsh and they were both cruel. And it was for the same reason. Sonny, whom they loved so much, was lost to us forever. That hurt a lot. I don't know if you can understand this, but sometimes when people are hurting, they lash out at other people."

I nodded. "Yeah, Mom does that sometimes," I told him. "I just always know she doesn't mean it."

"Your grandmother doesn't mean it, either," Vern said. "But she and Dawn aren't close enough to know that about each other."

I didn't figure they would ever get to be.

"What did they say to each other?" I asked him.

Vern gave me a long look, like he was trying to decide whether to trust me with the information. I guess he realized that he could.

"They blamed each other for Sonny's death," Vern said.

"Each other?" I was puzzled. "It was an accident in the woods. How could Mom or Mrs. Leland be to blame?"

"Because of *why* he was out there in the woods," Vern said. His voice sounded really sad. As if maybe he blamed himself a little, too. "Your grandmother believed that if he hadn't married Dawn and needed to support his family, he would have never taken such a job. And Dawn believed that if your grandmother hadn't been punishing him for marrying her, we would have supported him and he'd have been in school."

"Neither of those things are really true, right?"

"Both of them are true," Vern said. "That's what's so hard. Things could have, would have, should have been different. But they weren't."

Vern said the words so quietly. I wanted to throw my arms around him and hug him, to tell him how sorry I was and that everything would be all right. But of course, everything was not going to be right. And I was as sorry not to have my dad as he was not to have his son.

"It's like these fractals," he said. "One slight change in the equation and the outcome would have been totally different."

I glanced down at the pictures we had made. They

were different, but none of them were awful or ugly. Could the changed outcome turn out to be just as beautiful as the original equation?

# REAL LIFE
## 22

It was great spending time with Vern, but that didn't get me very far with Mrs. Leland. I quizzed him some about what she liked. He suggested history and genealogy. History was not my best subject. And I didn't really know how to ask questions about it. "What year did Columbus discover America?" prompted an answer, but not much of a discussion.

Genealogy was just as bad. Who was my great-great-grandfather? sparked her to show me how to read a family tree diagram. But it didn't go much further.

"What was he like? What kind of man was he?" I asked.

"He died before I was born," she said. "There are some photos of him in one of the albums."

Dutifully, I went and looked through the ones she indicated. And politely peered at page after page of black-and-white photos adhered to albums with little glued-on corners.

Mrs. Leland didn't seem to care if I was interested in the family or not. But I knew there had to be something I could talk to her about. Something that she wouldn't just brush off.

As I put the album back in its place in the glass-fronted cabinets, I glanced for a moment at all the albums of Dad. There were entire shelves of snapshotted moments of the life and times of Sonny Leland.

Randomly I pulled one out. The photos were of a little guy about nine, I guess. He still had his little-boy face, but big grown-up teeth that looked so supersize, I had to laugh.

I began turning pages, following him through Halloween costumes and Santa Claus photos. There was a photo of him onstage. He was dressed up like a cowboy with a hat and bandanna. His mouth was open like he was singing.

Could my dad sing?

The question provoked me in an unusual way. I had never heard my father's voice. Never heard one word that he'd ever spoken. Suddenly the idea of him singing, what he sang, how he sounded, seemed really important to know.

I hurried into Mom's room to ask her.

She was asleep on the chair, her feet propped up on the ottoman. Her face was slightly swollen and rounded from her daily dose of prednisone. The cath-port pump was quietly pushing Adriamycin into her veins. Rocky, lying on the floor beside her, raised his head inquisitively and then seeing me, knowing I wouldn't disturb Mom, settled back down for a nap.

I could have waited until she woke up to ask her, but I realized she wouldn't know the answer. She didn't meet Sonny Leland until he was in college. She'd probably never looked through the photo albums and wouldn't have any idea what he'd been doing in a cowboy getup in front of a microphone.

I walked back into the dining room. The open album sat staring up at me. I grabbed it up and headed through the kitchen and out the back door to Mrs. Leland's office behind the garage.

She was sitting at her desk, but she was staring off into space, lost in contemplation. I didn't give a moment's thought to having disturbed her.

"What's this picture?" I asked, plopping the photo album into her lap.

She was surprised, but she covered it well.

She fumbled on the desk for her glasses and once they were perched on her nose, she peered down at the glossy colored image.

"This is a play," she said. "Sonny was in a school play."

"He looks like he's singing," I said.

She nodded. "He was. Sonny was a wonderful soprano until his voice changed. His baritone was less spectacular, but he always liked to sing."

"My mom sings sometimes," I said. "Especially when we're in the car moving someplace new. She always sings then."

"Yes, well…I haven't heard your mother sing, I suppose," she said.

"I never heard my father sing," I told her. "I never even heard his voice. I was looking at these pictures and wondering what he might have sounded like."

She was looking up at me. Then she glanced down at the album in her lap. She ran a finger along the side of the face in the photo.

"His voice was a lot like Vern's," she said. "Though not as deep. Maybe it would have gotten so with age. Every once in a while, when he called home from school, I'd think he was his father."

I nodded to her, making a mental note to try to listen to Vern more closely, to try to memorize the sound of his voice.

"I'm sorry you didn't get to know your father," Mrs. Leland said. "I'm very sorry about that."

"Yeah, but I guess I'm lucky that I got to know you and Vern," I said. "Because you're the people who always knew him. Being here, seeing you guys and living where he lived. It kind of makes him more real to me."

She frowned in a strange way, as if for an instant she didn't quite understand what I meant. Then slowly she nodded.

"Yes," she agreed. "I suppose your mother never told you much about him."

"She talks about him sometimes," I hastily defended. "But I guess it's like your great-great grandfather. If someone dies before you're born, it's really hard to know anything about him."

Mrs. Leland just stared a me for a long moment. Then it was as if a lightbulb went on.

"You're right," she said. "I do wish that I'd listened to more family stories. That I'd learned more about my parents' parents and grandparents from family members who knew them. But I didn't think to ask. I didn't even get interested in family history until most all of them were gone. You're a very smart girl to ask questions so young."

"Thanks," I said.

"Anything you want to know," she said. "Just feel free to ask me about it."

"Okay," I said.

Immediately, I decided to test the truth of that statement. I leaned forward and turned back a couple of pages in the album.

"Why are all these guys dressed the same for Halloween?" I asked.

"It's not Halloween," she said. "They were all going to a punk rock concert, so they dressed up as members of the band."

"Eww, that's weird," I said.

Mrs. Leland laughed. "I thought exactly the same thing," she said. "I told them that if they expected to be mistakenly allowed onstage, they should really try to look taller."

I giggled, too. She was right.

I dragged up a chair beside her and we began leafing through the album. She remembered all the photos, what was happening, who the other kids were, all the circumstances and funny stories attached. She seemed to enjoy looking at them as much as I did learning about them.

It was only after we'd finished and I'd taken the photo album back to the hallway and she was puttering around the kitchen starting dinner, that I realized that I'd finally found out Mrs. Leland's interest. It was her son.

I vowed then and there to spend as much time possible getting her to talk about Sonny Leland. We had dozens of photo albums to go through and a million questions I'd never had anybody to ask. It was the perfect solution to distracting her from Dawn. And it was something that I really wanted, as well.

As the days passed, I saw that it was working pretty well. I was pleased with myself and the good I was doing. I was learning all kinds of cool stuff about my dad and keeping Mrs. Leland distracted at the same time. I felt totally virtuous about that.

At least I did until Del Tegge showed up to visit Mom.

Usually he'd come over to talk to her when she was sitting on the front porch or in the shade of the back patio. But as the weather turned hotter and more humid, she hadn't been sitting out much. The outside temperature was miserable. But inside with the air-conditioning made her cold. Mostly she wandered around in a baseball cap and a bulky sweater. She'd begun to vegetate in front of the TV with Sierra.

When Del showed up at the front door, I was, at first glance, grateful that she had someone to talk to. Then I remembered what I'd told him and I worried. She was very tired. Maybe even too tired for a fight. But getting mad might not be all that good for her. What if she used up all her available energy telling the curious neighbor where to go. She could just collapse like a house of cards.

She offered him a cup of tea and they went into the kitchen together. I really felt like I couldn't leave them alone. I needed to follow them into the kitchen, but I couldn't think of any reason to be in there. I knew it would look stupid if I just walked in and sat down with them.

I did it anyway.

They both looked at me curiously, but neither

were unwelcoming. In fact, I was sort of the center of the conversation.

"I guess you're looking forward to the new school year, making friends and all that," Del said.

Mom looked at me and smiled. "Sierra's the one who's keen on the social life," she said. "My Dakota is happy with a good book."

Del nodded. "The more cerebral type, she is," he agreed. "But everybody wants to make friends."

I knew he was thinking about my conversation with him. I didn't want him to be remembering that. I didn't want him to start doing what I'd told him. I wanted to divert him.

"Vern and I have been making fractals," I said.

Mom looked puzzled. "Is that some math thing?" she asked. "Some kind of fractions?"

"No, not exactly," I told her. "It's partly math and partly physics. It's called chaos theory. It's like how small changes just magnify and magnify until the outcomes are totally different."

"Oh," Mom said, though she didn't seem to really get it.

Del was nodding. "We use it in studying environmental systems a lot," he said.

He began talking about his work. That was good. I knew he could go on and on about air and water and nature stuff while hardly taking a breath. He seemed to know as much about chaos as Vern and though he wasn't as good a teacher, Mom seemed to pick up the thread of his explanation easily enough.

"So we really postulate that chaos explains a lot in nature," he said.

"That's really interesting," Mom told him.

"It is," Del agreed. "These days a lot of behavioral scientists are looking at it, too. I don't know all that much. My understanding of human response and adaptation is only about ankle deep. But I hear that they're beginning to study things like war, political unrest and family or community dysfunction in the framework of chaotic systems."

"Really?" Mom said.

"Yeah, and it makes a lot of sense just in speculating about shoring up unstable situations," Del said. "I think we tend to look at huge problems like world peace or the AIDS epidemic and we think, 'oh, this is so big there is nothing I can do.' And what the concept of chaos suggests is that anything and everything affects the outcome, even doing nothing."

Mom gave him a long look. There was a teasing glint in her eye.

"I hate to break this news to you, Del," she said. "But the truth is, I don't spend a lot of my time thinking about how I'm going to affect world peace."

He laughed.

"Fair enough," he told her. "It doesn't hit my worry agenda as much as it should, either. But I know you must have your own issues."

"I guess my kids are my issue," Mom said. "Right now, my kids and my cancer, that's about all I have time to worry about."

Del nodded. "That's a full plate," he admitted. "But I've heard it said that getting involved, giving back, that can stretch your focus. It puts your own problems, serious as they are, into perspective."

"Getting involved? Giving back? What are you talking about?"

"I just think there are a lot of young people in this town who are struggling," he said. "I was thinking that you might—"

"Let's make popcorn!" I interrupted loudly.

Mom and Del both looked at me, startled.

"I'm starving," I told them. "Let's make some popcorn. Aren't you hungry?"

"No, I'm fine," Mom said.

"You need to eat," I insisted. "That's what the doctors say, Mom. They say that you need to eat."

"I don't think they were talking about popcorn," she replied with a chuckle.

"Popcorn's good for you," I assured her. "What about you, Del, you want popcorn?"

"Ah...sure," he said. "If you pop it, I'll eat it."

I stood up and then hesitated.

"Aren't you guys going to help me?"

"Help you what?"

"Help me make popcorn."

Mom looked at me as if I'd lost my mind. "I don't think you're going to need much help to put a bag in the microwave," she said.

I was stuck. I'd managed to stop the conversation, but now I was going to have to get up and walk across the room. I thought about saying I'd changed my mind, but that would have looked way too suspicious. I decided my best option was to just keep talking, so I did.

"Where is that microwave stuff?" I said, heading deliberately to a cabinet where I knew only dishware was kept.

"It's on the far side of the sink," Mom said. "Second cabinet, probably the second shelf." She turned back to Del. "What were you saying?"

"I can't find it," I declared.

Mom turned again. "The second cabinet," she repeated.

I opened it up. The box was at eye level right in front of me. "I don't see it," I said.

"Good grief," Mom said with a shake of her head and a good-natured sigh of exasperation. She got up and walked across the room, pulled the box out of the cabinet and handed it to me.

"Thanks," I said and then handed the box back to her as I walked over to the microwave.

I thought if I forced her to be busy, then there was no way that she could talk with Del. I hadn't counted on him getting up and coming over to help, as well.

"Who knew it took three people to make microwave popcorn," Mom said facetiously as she ripped open the little cellophane package.

Del shrugged. "Hey, food just tastes better when there are lots of people involved."

"Are you sure of that?"

He shrugged. "Maybe that's why there are fast-food restaurants," he joked.

"No, I think that's so those of us who didn't go to college can have job prospects," Mom replied.

He chuckled.

The corn began to pop and the bag was expanding. Mom got out a big bowl and set it next to me. I was secretly congratulating myself on having successfully changed the subject.

Mom turned to Del curiously.

"Now what were you saying about young people?" she asked him.

"I was thinking that you might want to get involved in some community activity," he said. "I know you're used to working, so you've got more time than usual on your hands."

"Well," Mom said. "I'm getting to spend a lot of quality time with my girls for a while."

"That's good," Del agreed. "But they are going back to school in a few weeks. You'll need something of your own to do."

Mom chuckled humorlessly.

"Non-Hodgkin's lymphoma keeps me pretty busy," she said.

The popping in the microwave reached a crescendo and then abruptly dropped off to an occasional flurry.

Del shook his head. "Hanging around here, just you and the cancer, that can't be good for your mental health."

Mom agreed. "I'm sure that it's not," she told him. "But I can't really hold down a job because of my chemo."

I took the popcorn out and began pouring it into the bowl.

Del nodded. "You've got your appointments at the clinic," he said. "And I know that some days you feel pretty crappy. But on the days you don't, I was thinking that maybe you might want to do something for somebody else."

"Like who?"

He pulled a card out of his shirt pocket and handed it to her.

"'CAVA of Knox County,'" Mom read aloud and then looked up at Del questioningly.

"Court Appointed Volunteer Advocates," he said. "I know somebody who participates in the program. It's for kids in foster care."

"Mom, here, have some popcorn," I said, anxiously pushing the bowl in her direction.

She ignored me.

"CAVA's mission is to have an advocate for every child," Del explained to her. "Someone to make sure that child doesn't get lost in the system. I'm sure there's something that you could do that wouldn't take a full-time commitment."

Mom tried to hand him back the card. "I'm not interested," she said.

"My friend says there are five hundred children placed in foster care in this county every year," Del said. "They need someone to speak for them."

"Not me," Mom said. "I'm not the right person."

"Of course you are," he told her. "Foster care was part of your life."

"A part I've put behind me," Mom said.

"You're needed," Del said. "Your experience is needed."

"My experience? All my experience was bad."

"And yet you've managed to make a success of life for yourself," he said.

Mom made a scoffing sound. "My life is successful?" Her tone was heavy with sarcasm.

Del didn't see the joke.

"You work hard, support your children, pay your taxes. Isn't that the definition of successful?"

"We're not staying here," Mom told him. "We're

leaving this town as soon as I get my strength back."
She continued to hold out the card to him, trying to
get Del to take it back.

Instead he reached for the bowl of popcorn.

# SONNY DAYS
## 23

——◆—◆——

Sonny never had to testify. As soon as the company heard that he was willing to do so, they had an immediate crisis of conscience and wanted to do the right thing for Lonnie's orphans. They managed to come up with a modest but helpful cash settlement that wouldn't set any unmanageable precedents, as well as a scholarship fund so that all the Beale children would be able to attend college.

Sonny was pleased about that. He felt good about his part in it. But his attention, by necessity, was focused on a new semester and a tough schedule of classes. When he wasn't studying he was being a dad to his two little girls and exercising to regain full use of his leg.

"I wish I knew how Tonya and her family were doing," he said to Dawn in bed one night as he rubbed the scar on his chest. "I've got to make some time to go out and check on her and the kids."

"Do you want me to do it?" Dawn asked.

Sonny was incredulous. "You've got as much to do as I have," he pointed out.

"The girls would love an outing," she told him. "I could just get them all tucked in their car seats and drive over to Strawberry Plains. It would be good to get us out of the house for a while. And fun for me to talk to anyone who has a vocabulary of more than sixteen words and isn't my mother-in-law."

Sonny laughed.

"Thanks, Dawn," he said. "I am not officially turning over my job of worrying about the Beales to you. You'll let me know if it gets to be too much, right?"

She agreed.

The young Leland family settled into life with Sonny's parents for a busy, productive and happy time. His interest was captured by his studies in a way that hadn't been possible before his venture out into the real world. The safety and security of a roof over her head and good healthy meals seemed to enhance in Dawn a grace and strength that had previously gone unnoticed. The little daughters were practically princesses, with so many loving eyes upon them every day.

Of course, no situation is perfect. Dawn and Phrona were never going to be close friends. Vern adored having the children around, but the constant noise and activity made it hard for him to work at home. And just the mere lack of privacy was hard on both couples.

So it was with great pride of accomplishment as well as a tremendous sense of relief when three years later Sonny stood in Vols stadium, wearing cap and gown, and was officially granted a Bachelor of Science.

Up in the bleachers, his lovely wife, two pretty preschoolers and his parents cheered him on.

It was a pinnacle moment and Sonny felt fantastic. He already had a good job lined up with a multinational corporation doing forestry assessment and planning. It was going to mean good money and at last being able to provide for his family.

After commencement they all went to dinner at Sonny's favorite restaurant, Chesapeake's. The lighting was low, the atmosphere subdued and linen tablecloths and the crystal glassware didn't exactly give the impression of being a child-proof sort of place. But Sierra and Dakota, neat and pretty in their new dresses, were on their best behavior.

He ordered both the crab cakes and the grouper. The little girls shared pasta and Dawn tasted lobster for the first time in her life.

His father had brought in a bottle of wine and when it was served Vern stood and held up his glass.

"I'd like to make a toast to my son, to his lovely wife and beautiful family," he said. "Phrona and I are so proud of you. So grateful to have you as our son. And so glad that you brought Dawn and these children into our lives."

It was a tearful moment all around. Sonny got up to offer his own salute.

"Dad, Mama, I don't know how to begin to thank you," he said. "And I don't mean just because you've supported me and my family, paid my tuition and let us live with you. Those are all very big things and we are grateful. But what I want to thank you for is bigger than all that."

He took a deep breath and gathered his thoughts.

"I don't think I understood this until I became a father myself," he said. "But now I think I do know, at least to some degree, what it must have felt for you to want only the best for me and to see me disregard your counsel, defy your wishes and throw your advice back into your face. It must have been disappointing, scary, frustrating, even insulting. I really hope that if or when that time comes in the life of my children I'll behave with the same kind of grace, forgiveness and understanding that you've shown me."

His little girls applauded him. His parents tried to modestly disavow any laudable behavior on their part.

"I know that I am a lucky man," Sonny said. Unconsciously, he ran a hand across his scarred chest, as had become his habit. "Not only has my wife given me a happy home and two beautiful children, she's stood by me, helped me, encouraged me to go after what I want in the world, including a college education. She's done this even though it's meant giving up a lot of the things she's wanted. I acknowledge the sacrifices she's made and vow to try to make it up to her for the rest of my life."

He leaned forward and gave Dawn a kiss, then they clinked glasses all around.

"Us, Daddy," Sierra begged. "Drink something to us."

He laughed. "She inherited that attention thing from you," Sonny said teasingly to Dawn.

She feigned surprise. "I thought she got it from Phrona," she said.

The older woman was momentarily caught off guard, then laughed with everyone else.

Sonny started his new job the very next week. And he gave to Dawn the task of finding someplace for them to live. He knew she was excited about the prospect of their own place. He also knew he could trust her to make a good deal, to consider the neighborhood school and stay within their budget.

"Whatever, wherever," he told her. "If you want to live there, then the kids and I want to live there with you."

He expected to come home the first week and find his things already packed and a new key for his pocket. That didn't happen. Day after day, Dawn went out looking at properties and found nothing she really liked. It had been over three weeks and nothing quite suited her.

"Is the budget too tight?" Sonny asked. "Can we not find what we need in our price range?"

Dawn shook her head. "I don't think that's it," she told him. "The truth is, some of these places are very nice. And all of them have more space than we've been used to. It's just…I don't know. They are not quite the home that I want for the girls."

"It isn't like we're going to live there all our lives," Sonny said. "We just need a little starter place."

"I know," Dawn said. "And I'll know the right place when I see it."

It was only a few nights later when his mother decided to put in her three cents' worth.

"The McManns are moving," she announced over dinner.

"Really?" Vern sounded surprised. "Finally decided to do it, did they? They've been talking about it for years."

"The McManns?" Dawn said. "That old couple next door? They did say they were looking at those retirement communities."

Sonny nodded. "Yeah, but have always been too scared to take the plunge."

"They still are," Phrona said. "I told them, 'You

don't have to dive, just go and stick your toe in the water. That's what's been holding them back. They're afraid that if they sell their house and then don't like the place, there's no going back."

His mother hesitated, took a deep breath and gave Sonny and Dawn a broad smile.

"I told them, 'Don't sell now,'" she continued. "I said, 'Find a nice couple that you can trust to rent your place for a couple of years, then when you're sure, you can sell.'"

His mother looked down at her plate, no longer willing to meet anyone's eye.

Sonny glanced over at Dawn. She was as surprised as he was.

"Phrona," Vern said. "I'm sure the kids were thinking about getting a little farther away than next door."

She shrugged as if that were no concern. "They'd have their own place," she said. "Next door or the next county it would still be their own place. And it will be easier for me to help Dawn with the children if I'm right next door."

Dawn wasn't saying anything. Sonny felt like he had to.

"Mama, it's very nice of you to do this for us," he said. "And we appreciate all the help with the kids, but…well, I just hope you haven't promised the Mc-Manns anything…."

"I've promised nothing," she said. "Now don't go and reject the place before you've even seen it."

He shot another glance toward Dawn.

"We'll look at it, Phrona," she said. "That's all I'll commit to, we'll look at it."

Sonny was thinking they'd set up a visit on the weekend, but his mother got on the phone and a half hour later, the McManns were at the front door.

"We'll just leave the key with you, Sonny," the old man said. "We'll walk down to the bingo game at the church. Take your time, look it over."

"Excuse the mess," Mrs. McMann told Dawn.

There wasn't any mess, of course. Sonny and Dawn let themselves into the immaculately kept house. The walls needed new paint and the decor was shabby without the chic, but there was a warmth about the place, some intangible something that said this was a home.

"It's like something out of another era," Sonny said. "I honestly expect to see Betty, Bud and Kitten come running down the stairs."

Dawn nodded.

Mrs. McMann's furniture was vintage, complete with little crocheted doilies on the backs of the chairs. The hardwood floors were dust free and polished, but showed evidence of wear and the scarring of generations of kids and grandkids. The dining room had a built-in corner cabinet for china. The three bedrooms upstairs were not overly spacious, but the master had its own bathroom and the bedroom in the back had a little balcony overlooking the yard. The kitchen was the room most out-of-date. The countertops were covered in a wood grain laminate and the appliances were harvest gold. The worn linoleum on the floor was yellowed from waxing. And as they stood there silently, it was impossible not to notice the drip, drip, drip of a leaky faucet.

"This is it," Dawn said.

"What?"

"I knew it the moment I walked in the door," Dawn said. "This is it. It's the home I've been waiting for."

Sonny was skeptical. "Are you sure?"

"Don't you like it?" she asked.

"Yeah, I like it a lot," Sonny told her. "It needs some work, but I don't mind that. I'd think it was close to perfect except, Dawn, it's next door to my parents."

His wife shrugged.

"They say to keep your friends close and your enemies closer," she told him.

Sonny opened his mouth to comment but she stayed him with a hand.

"Phrona and I understand each other," Dawn said. "We're never going to be friends, but we both love you and we both love the girls. That's enough in common for us to manage a relationship together. And it will be easier having her right next door. She can see what I'm doing and be a part of their lives every day, without being visiting constantly."

"Are you really sure?" Sonny asked again.

"I wasn't until I walked into this house," she said. "This is a home, Sonny. It's the kind of place I imagined for myself all my life. It's the kind of childhood I want for my little girls."

And so it was decided. Over the next few weeks, the McManns moved out and the younger Lelands moved in. Phrona helped Dawn with painting and cleaning. Dawn took her mother-in-law's advice on updating the look without decreasing the charm.

The Lelands' friends and neighbors began showing up with wonderful things for the couple and the house.

"We were never able to give you kids any wedding presents," Mildred Snyder explained to Dawn when she delivered a wicker bedroom set with twin beds for the girls."Now everyone in town is scouring their attics coming up with something perfect for your home."

"I know it must feel strange to have your house filled with other people's secondhand things," Carlene Ramsey told Sonny."But recycling is all the rage, isn't it? And with two little ones in the house, it will be better not to be tearing up the nice things you've spent hard-earned money for."

In fact, the gently used furniture that graced their new home was tasteful, nice and in very good condition. A flowered couch that Susan Gillette brought over was deemed "totally wrong" by Susan herself with concurrence from Phrona and Mildred. It was quickly donated to the Goodwill and a much better one set in its place.

The term *secondhand* took on a completely new meaning when Phrona toted her grandmother's Spode dinnerware into Dawn's dining room.

"You'll need something to put in that china cabinet," Phrona said.

Dawn seemed shocked, off balance, and she shot a wordless glance to her husband.

"Are you sure you want to leave those dishes with us?" he asked.

His mother wagged a finger at him."Sonny Leland, one does not refer to hundred-year-old English bone china as *dishes,*" she scolded.

"But with the girls in the house…" he said."You know kids, something could happen to this."

"I raised you with these in my house," she said. "You only broke the one piece. I always thought you were worth the price. Besides, the girls need to grow up around fine things. It's part of their heritage and one day this china will belong to one of them."

It was a breakthrough moment for Dawn. He could see it in her face. She confirmed it later that evening as they walked hand in hand along the sidewalk. The girls, with Vern and Phrona, were locked in an intense game of Candy Land. Taking full advantage of their opportunity for grown-up conversation, Sonny and Dawn went up and down the streets of their neighborhood. He talked about his new job, the people he was working with, the successes he was making, the challenges he'd not expected. Finally he turned the conversation in Dawn's direction.

"Things going well with the house? The girls?" he asked.

"Everything is great," she told him.

"How is it with my mother? I know she can drive you crazy."

Dawn nodded. "She definitely has that capability," she said. "But she doesn't intrude on our space without calling. And it is great having a baby-sitter right next door."

He nodded.

"She and Vern are good for our girls," Dawn said. "I can put up with anybody who's good for the girls."

Sonny smiled at her. "I'm really glad," he admitted. "I felt like you were okay with all this and had made peace with my mother, but today when she brought you the dishes, I saw something strange in your expression."

Dawn shrugged. "I guess it was just a realization," she said.

"Of what?"

"I can't run away anymore."

"What?"

"Always, in the past, I kept open the option that if things went wrong I could run away," she said. "Anytime we had an argument or I had a bad day, anytime your parents got on my nerves, anytime I just felt too pressured or overwhelmed, I'd imagine that I could just put the girls in the car and run. I'd drive somewhere that nobody knew us and I'd start all over."

"You'd leave me?" Sonny asked.

"I always told myself that you'd be better off without me," Dawn said. "You'd get remarried, this time to someone who was much more suited to you. You'd have other kids with her and forget all about me and the girls."

"That's not possible."

"I know," Dawn said. "It was always just a fantasy. Today I realized that."

"So you're not going to run anymore?"

"Who can run carrying hundred-year-old English bone china?" she asked.

They laughed together.

"I love you, Dawn," Sonny told her. "I want you here with me always."

"I will be," she assured him. "This is the place I've been trying to get to. I love you, too, Sonny. That by itself is all I've needed to make me stay."

# REAL LIFE
## 24

━━▶ ◀━━

As the heat of August grew more oppressive, my mom seemed to rally. She finished her second course of the chemo and rarely even mentioned her illness. All her clothes had gotten too big and she still had days when she was too nauseated to eat. She never bothered to get a wig, assuring everyone who suggested it that her hair would grow back in no time. She did have little tufts of peach fuzz in the front. She wore her ballcap from time to time. Sierra, who now used Vern's computer to search for fashion hints on the Web, had downloaded a bunch of scarf-tying techniques. And she kept wrapping them around Mom's head in really cool ways. But mostly in the heat, she just went bareheaded and we got used to seeing her that way.

Sierra began talking about school. Of course, I knew what this was all about. Seth and Sierra were now a bona fide item. They saw each other nearly every day. Seth attended a private arts academy near downtown. They both knew that if Sierra were to go to the same school, she had to apply.

When this subject came up, I couldn't even look in anybody's direction. I remembered what Mom had said to Del and I knew that she would never have planned for us to be here that long. The deal she'd made with Mrs. Leland was to stay for the summer. The summer was nearly over, even if her chemotherapy wasn't, and we should be back on the road very soon. My school clothes were still in the suitcase under my bed, packed and ready to go, along with the soccer photo of my dad. Mom was getting better and we were getting out. I knew it.

Sierra had no gleaming of understanding. We were sitting in the little sunporch area of Mom's room. All the windows were open, the early morning breeze was seeping in, but it was already warm enough that anyone but Mom would have turned on the air-conditioning. She was cold, of course, sitting in her chair wrapped in a blanket, Rocky in his favorite spot on her lap.

"It's like an art school," Sierra said. "I could like be an artist and do paintings or something and people would buy them for like museums and stuff."

"Sierra," Mom pointed out, "you don't know how to paint."

"Well, isn't that more reason why I should be going to that school?"

"They don't let people in for free," Mom explained. "And you haven't shown enough talent to have any chance at a scholarship."

"Mom, *duh*," she said, incredulously. "The Lelands have plenty of money."

"Vern is retired," she said. "They're living on a fixed income, which I'm sure is not nearly as much as you think. And that money is theirs, not yours." Mom's tone was firm.

"I'm their granddaughter," Sierra said. "If they want to spend money on me, I think we should let them. After all, they don't have anyone else. Dakota and I will get everything when they die."

"They're not dead yet," Mom said. "And I'm thinking, Miss Sierra Leland, to encourage them to leave everything to charity."

My sister turned to me for help. I had none to offer.

"We're leaving soon," I told her.

Mom glanced up, surprised.

I continued. "As soon as Mom is stronger, we're getting out of here."

"No!" Sierra was genuinely miffed.

"Maybe we'll go out to Vegas," I suggested to my sister. "The weather out there would be good for the winter. And you know how you love the place."

Sierra was shaking her head.

"I'm not going," she said. "I'm not leaving Knoxville."

"Knoxville's too little and too boring," I insisted.

"I'm staying here," she said. "This is where I want to be. If you and Mom want to leave, then go ahead without me."

Sierra flounced out of the room in a huff. Rocky raised his head up to follow her retreat curiously.

I looked over at Mom. She was snuggled deeper in her blanket and staring out the window at nothing in particular.

"She won't be mad for long," I told her.

"I know," Mom said. "Staying mad at people is just way too much trouble for your sister."

"And she doesn't mean what she said," I insisted.

Mom sighed heavily. "I think she does," she answered. "I'm getting trapped here. I'm sick and I'm trapped."

"No, you're not, Mom," I assured her. "We can get out of here. We can just jump in the car anytime and go. You're between treatments now, we could go somewhere else, anywhere else. They give chemo everywhere."

Mom reached over and patted my hand. "You're the one who's always fighting to stay put," she reminded me.

I shrugged. "Vern can take my books back to the library. I wouldn't even need to say goodbye to Spence. I could send him a postcard."

She wove her fingers in with mine and gave my hand a little squeeze. "I always thought you would be the one to tie me down."

"I just want you to be happy, Mom," I told her.

She smiled at me. "Thanks." She loosened my hand and opened the blanket wrapped around her. Her T-shirt was round-necked and low cut. She pulled down the neckline to totally reveal her tattoo. "You know why I have this?" she asked me.

"To remember my dad," I said.

She shook her head. "Not exactly," she told me. "Sonny Leland was the most important person in my life, besides you girls. I'm not any more likely to forget him than I would be to forget you. Nothing could make that happen."

"Then why the tattoo?"

"It's there to remind me that I do have it in me to be happy," she said.

"Well, of course you do!" I thought it was a very strange thing for her to say.

She laughed. "I love that about you, Dakota," she said. "I love that you are so determined to make the world work. Sierra finds it easy to be happy, her personality is just like that. But you, you're a lot like me. You have to work at it. I look at you sometimes and I think, yes, that's what I might have been like if life had just been a little more kind. I want life to be kind to you."

"It is, Mom," I assured her. "And it can be kind to you, too."

She raised her eyebrows skeptically and went back to staring off into the distance. I knew she was thinking about the cancer. I knew she was feeling trapped. I knew she wanted to be on the road. I tried to think what it was that kept us in places. There were places we stayed for months and months. For much longer than we'd been in Knoxville. Why had we stayed? What had kept us there?

Guys. I realized that we'd only stayed for guys.

"Del Tegge likes you," I blurted out.

"What?"

"Del Tegge," I said. "He likes you."

She shook her head. "He's just a nice guy," Mom told me. "He's not interested in me that way."

"He is, he is," I insisted. "Sierra thinks he is and she knows about these kinds of things. And Del asked me himself what…what he could do to make you like him."

Mom laughed out loud at that.

"Dakota," she said. "I sure hope you've really misinterpreted the guy. It's either that or he has some kind of pervy thing for bald women."

"Mom!"

She ran a hand across the top of her head. "There's nothing here but the hope of hair," she said.

"You don't need hair to be pretty," I said. "You tell Sierra all the time that beauty starts on the inside."

"Well, my insides are even sadder looking than my outside these days," Mom said. "My CAT scans even make the oncology nurses cringe."

"No, Mom, I think you're beautiful inside and out," I told her.

"Thank you," she said.

"You're welcome."

"But, Dakota," she cautioned. "Don't go getting ideas about Del and me. Guys don't fall for women who have cancer. He's just a nice man, trying to be a friend. I know you don't have a lot of experience with that kind of guy, but that's what he is. Anyway," she said, pointing to her tattoo again, "the guy is really not my type."

I'd said the same thing myself.

I hadn't wanted Mom to get involved with anyone, but now I could see that involvement might be the very best thing for her. Unfortunately, I'd already screwed up things between her and Del with the foster care thing.

There had to be something else, some other way to make a connection with a place that didn't involve men or disease. Nobody could keep running forever. Eventually there had to be some reason to just stay put.

In midafternoon, like most every day, I made my way to Mrs. Leland's behind-the-garage office. That day, surprisingly, Rocky trotted at my heels.

"Am I bothering you?" I asked from the doorway.

She motioned me in.

"Rocky, too?" I asked, as the dog hesitated on the step.

"Of course," she said. "I haven't seen much of that creature for the past few weeks."

"He hangs with my mom, a lot," I told her. "I don't know why he likes her, she's never liked animals much. We could never have a pet or anything."

"I've never been overly fond of them, either," Mrs. Leland said as Rocky sat at her feet and allowed her to stroke him.

"Why'd you get Rocky?" I asked.

"Oh, we didn't," she told me. "Sonny got Rocky for you girls. He picked him up at the pound one day and brought him home."

"For us?" I was really surprised. "Well, for Sierra, I guess."

"I think he just wanted a pet for his children, both his children," Mrs. Leland said.

I knew she was just trying to be nice to me. But I liked it anyway.

An image on her computer screen caught my attention. It was a hazy black-and-white photo of a man in a military uniform.

"Who's that?" I asked her.

She glanced over at the screen herself. "That's one of your great-uncles, Lemuel Clafford Leland," she said. "I've been searching records for him this afternoon, pondering his fate."

"He was a soldier?"

"He fought in the Civil War," she said. "But I don't think the military was his natural calling."

"He was like drafted or something?"

"No, he joined up," she said. "He was an educated man, probably could have gotten a commission, certainly he would have in the Confederate Army, but he joined the Union as a private."

"And what happened to him?"

"We don't know," she said. "He never returned from the war."

I nodded. "So you're trying to figure out where he was killed?"

She shook her head. "I'm not sure that he was," she said. "His name doesn't show up anywhere among the Union dead."

"They could have just missed him," I said. "Like those MIA people they have the flags and T-shirts for."

"That's possible," Mrs. Leland said. "But there is one other strange little piece of information that I have."

"What is it?"

"Well, before he left for the army he was involved with a married woman, Essie Milbank, Essie Medford Milbank, to be exact," she said, pursing her lips to express disapproval. "It was quite a scandal here in Knoxville. I'm sure it played a big part in his leaving for the army. Toward the end of the war, Essie just disappeared. Her husband was known to beat her and everyone suspected that he'd killed her, but her body was never found."

"So you don't think she was killed?"

"I did," Mrs. Leland said. "Until just recently, I assumed that neither of them survived the war, so many did not. But I was thinking about your mother and the way she is. If this woman had been Dawn, she would have just packed up her things and headed into the sunset. That's a solution for her. Other people might have done the same."

"Maybe they met up somewhere," I said.

Mrs. Leland was nodding. "That's what I was thinking," she said. "I was looking through old records to see if their names ever resurfaced later in some other state."

"They could have gone anywhere," I said, hopelessly.

"I think they would have headed west," Mrs. Leland said with certainty.

"Why would you think that?"

"The south is all knitted together with relatives of relatives," she said. "They had to get away from people who might recognize them. The only way to do that was to go farther west."

Mrs. Leland pulled up a Web site for the 1880 federal census.

"If they survived the war and went off together," she said, "I'm sure after fifteen years, they'd feel safe enough to answer some questions, maybe even use their real names. Or some version of their real names."

"That makes sense."

We started with Texas and began the slow, painstaking process of looking for people who fit those names in the mostly indexed, handwritten documents.

"So how exactly are these people related to me?" I asked her again, after squinting at the screen for way too long.

Mrs. Leland chuckled. "Uncle Lemuel is your great-great-grandfather's brother, there were six boys and three girls."

"Wow," I said. "I always wondered what it would be like to have a big family."

"You're like your father in that," she said. "Sonny once asked me why he had to be an only child. I didn't have an answer, but I started getting interested in genealogy."

"You wanted to give him a family," I said.

She nodded. "Yes, I guess I did," she said. "But he managed to get one for himself."

"Yeah, I guess so," I said quietly, sadly.

There was a moment of silence between us.

"I remember the day you were born," she said.

I'm sure my jaw fell open.

"Were you there the day I was born?"

She nodded. "Your grandfather and I rushed up to the hospital as soon as we heard," she said. "I didn't try to go in to see your mother. She and I…we weren't getting along that well. So Vern went in to see her and I stayed out by the window at the nursery."

"Really?"

"Yes." She smiled at me. It changed the whole look of her face. "You were such a tiny little thing, a couple of weeks early," she said. "And just howling as if you were mad at the world."

"Maybe I was."

"Maybe so."

"I didn't know you ever saw me as a baby," I told her. "I thought my mom left town as soon as I was born."

"No," Mrs. Leland said. "She didn't leave right away."

"What made her go?"

"A lot of things," Mrs. Leland said. "She wanted to get away from bad memories."

"And she wanted to get away from you." The words had just slipped out of my mouth. I hadn't intended to say that.

"Did your mother tell you that?" she asked. Her tone was very formal once more and she was back to that way of looking at me without looking at me.

"No," I assured her. "She never said anything like that. She never said anything. Just that she had to get away."

Mrs. Leland mellowed somewhat. "Well, I suppose there is a grain of truth to that. But I didn't run her off. I wanted her to stay. I wanted to keep you girls right here with us. But as soon as she got that money, she was already gone."

"What money?"

Mrs. Leland's lips came together in one thin line of disapproval. "The logging company," she said. "The one responsible for Sonny's death, offered her five thousand dollars. That's it. A young, promising life just wiped out. I don't know if the company had been negligent or if they'd been greedy. I wanted to know, but we could never find out. They bought off everybody who might have known. And they bought off your mother so cheaply. She took the money. Without any hesitation she took their blood money and left town."

"She felt trapped," I lamely tried to explain.

Mrs. Leland shook her head. "The life she ran to, the life she's brought you up in, that's the trap, not here with the people she left behind."

# REAL LIFE
## 25

Spence and I were hanging out at his house. The thermometer was hovering near one hundred, so it was one of those days to stay inside with the air-conditioning. We were playing video games on the TV in the living room. Del sat in a big lounge chair reading a book.

From the corner of my eye, I caught movement and glanced out the window.

"Here comes my mom," I said.

I was surprised and curious. She had never been over to the Tegges' house. And she didn't look happy. I knew I hadn't done anything and I wondered who had.

Del was on his feet before the doorbell rang and opening it up the instant after.

Mom didn't bother with hello. "You gave these people my number!" she accused.

"Yes, I did," Del answered. "Won't you come in?"

"Are you out of your mind? Why would you give out my phone number to strangers?"

"I gave them Vern's number," he said. "And 'these people' are not strangers, it's my friend Marcy. Now are you going to stand on the porch letting out all the cool air or are you coming inside?"

With a sigh of frustration, Mom stepped inside and Del shut the door behind her.

Mom looked around. There was a strange look on her face.

"What is this place?" she asked. "Geez, I expect Beaver Cleaver to be doing his homework at the dining room table."

"No homework today," Del said. "Just a couple of slackers playing video games."

"Hiyya, Dawn!" Spence said excitedly.

"I think that's supposed to be Mrs. Leland," Del corrected.

"No, please, I told him he could call me Dawn."

"Well, then," Del said, hesitating. "Ms. Dawn would be better."

"Gawd, you are a prig," she told him with a laugh. "Don't you know that sending a kid to middle school with those kind of manners can be dangerous to his health?"

"As if your Dakota is not just as well behaved and well spoken," he said.

Mom waved that away. "My girls just raise themselves," she insisted. "They do a better job at it than me anyway."

That wasn't true, of course, and I could see from Del's expression that he didn't believe it, either.

"But if I *was* teaching decorum, I would, for sure, cover giving out other people's phone numbers without permission."

Del nodded. "Why don't you have a seat, I'll fix you a nice cool drink and you can go over the rules for me."

"Yeah, you're thinking that you'll ply me with liquor and make me forget how pissed I am at you," she said.

"I don't actually have any liquor," he said. "But I've got some fruitless powdered fruit drink. The sugar in that is the biggest buzz in the house."

My mom shrugged. "Then fruit drink it is," she said.

Del headed for the kitchen.

"You want to play?" Spence asked her. "I'd let you have a turn."

Mom laughed and gave him a skeptical look. "I'm not so good at these games as you kids. My reflexes aren't that fast."

"You don't need reflexes for this one," I told her.

"Yeah, you get to create a whole world from cave dwellers to space and try to expand your land and influence without getting overrun by other civilizations."

"You can do all that in a video game?" She grinned at him. "Who knew?"

"I'm Caesar," Spence told her. "Dakota is Elizabeth I. You could be…ah…" He was quickly looking through the leaders of all the different groups. "You could be Joan of Arc."

"Joan of Arc?" Mom laughed.

"Don't get stuck in gender roles," I scolded Spence. "You can be Abraham Lincoln, Mom," I told her. "American history is probably your best anyway."

He showed Mom how to play, but she was content just to watch us.

Del returned with soft drinks and pretzels.

"Don't you kids know that video games are supposed to involve wrecking cars or decapitating people?" Mom said. "Where are the guns? Where are the hos and pimps?"

"You are *too* funny, Dawn," Spence said. "My mom is not nearly so cool."

"Thank God!" Mom told him, reaching over to tousle his hair. "And I bet she's not bald, either."

"I like the do," Spence assured her. "It's very hip and now. Maybe you should think about a head tattoo."

"I like this kid," Mom told Del.

"'He's a rebel and he'll never be any good,'" Del responded in song.

Mom laughed.

Spence and I didn't get the joke.

"Do you two want to go upstairs and play that in Spence's room?" Del suggested.

"The TV's broken, remember?" Spence said.

I shot Del a look, wondering if he'd ever mentioned my destructive accident to my mother. He gave me a quick reassuring wink. I knew he'd kept my secret.

"I guess this living room is big enough for all of us," Del said. "I won't tell you and Dakota how to conquer the world if you won't interrupt me as I impress Miss Dawn with my brilliant wit and humor."

"Forget your brilliant wit and humor," Mom said. "Don't think for a minute that you can distract me from how mad I am at you."

"I wouldn't dream of it," Del told her.

The adults retreated to the couch. I continued to focus my eyes on the game, but my mind was on their conversation. I could tell that Spence was doing the same.

"This really is a neat old house," Mom said.

"It has a real family feeling about it," he agreed.

"It's more than that," Mom said. "It's as if nothing bad could ever happen here."

"Ah...well, tell that to my water pipes in the winter," he joked.

"Plumbing problems aside," she said. "It's a nice house."

"I think so," Del told her. "I was really lucky to get in here. When I left Clarissa I moved into this really dinky, depressing apartment."

Mom nodded.

"I wanted my share of Spence's time," Del said. "But I hated to make him spend his weekends in the place. Then one day I was here in the neighborhood to speak to a conservation group. I had a few minutes so I was just taking a walk, looking at the old houses. I was standing in front of this one, admiring it, when Mr. McMann, the old fellow who lived here, keeled over with a stroke."

"You're kidding."

"I'm not," he said. "One minute he was tending the begonias and the next he was on the ground. I called 911 on my cell, got his wife out of the house and stayed with him until the ambulance came."

"Was he all right?"

"I don't think he was ever the same," Del said. "But he got better. The couple had been toying with the idea of moving to a retirement community for years. His stroke was what made them decide to go into assisted living. They needed to sell the house and I'd fallen in love with it. They carried the financing for me and threw in a lot of their old furniture as a gift. It was a great deal."

"You're very lucky," she said.

"That's what I think," Del told her. "I even thought that at the time, though most people were still feeling sorry for me because of my divorce."

"Oh, yeah?"

He nodded. "Being with the wrong person is much worse than being alone," he said.

Mom laughed. "I can testify to that," she said. "But I keep dragging them back to my place anyway."

Del didn't seem to think that was as funny as she did.

"So you talked to Marcy?" he asked.

"Not for long," Mom answered. "As soon as I figured out who she was and what she wanted, I cut her off as quick as I could."

"Why would you do that?"

"I told you, I'm not interested in foster care," she said. "It's something in my past. Something I don't discuss, something I don't think about anymore. It has nothing to do with me."

"Really?"

"Yes, really," she said. "Are you going to get all moral and tell me that it's my civic duty to care?"

"No," he answered. "I just got the impression that keeping your girls from any possibility of a close-up acquaintance with foster care was what drove you back to Knoxville this summer."

There was a moment of complete silence. I realized that I was just staring at the computer screen. Spence was doing the same.

"Is it my turn?" I asked him.

"Uh…yeah."

"I don't have to discuss my reasoning with you," Mom told Del.

He agreed. "No, you don't," he said. "But I'd like to discuss mine with you. You've had some hard choices to make, that's obvious. But there are plenty of parents out there without your options. They don't have any leftover in-laws. If something goes wrong for them, their kids are going to land in foster care."

"I'm sorry for that," Mom said. "But I can't change it."

"Who else can?" he said. "You know a lot. You have firsthand experience and you have the time. These kids need you."

She made a sound that facetiously dismissed his words. "Maybe they'll do all right," she said. "Lots of kids come through unscathed."

"Do they?"

"Sure. They come up with a strategy that works for them. Some idealize their parents, some demonize them. Some are sweet and helpful and friendly. Some are rebels of any cause. Some do crazy things to get attention, others try to blend in with the woodwork. My plan was to run. That worked for me."

"That's what I'm talking about," Del said. "You understand where they are and what they're doing. Some well-meaning socialite from the Junior League is not going to get that."

"I said I'm a runner," Mom told him. "Runners never go back to where they came from."

"You're back in Knoxville," he said. "I'd say that's starting a new trend."

"I'm here because I have to be," Mom said. "But I don't have time or energy to do any kind of volunteer work."

"Why not?"

"Earth to Del Tegge," she announced in a condescending voice. "I have cancer."

"That's not a full-time vocation."

"It can be."

"Until it is, it might be better to focus on something besides yourself."

Mom's shocked response was an incredulous indrawn breath.

Del lowered his voice. Spence and I kept our eyes glued to the computer, but continued to listen.

"It takes everybody to change the world," Del said. "Young people, old people, well people, sick people. There are so many things that need to be done, nobody gets a pass. This is something that you know about, somewhere that you can make a difference. If you choose to ignore it, to be too busy, to let it go on the way it always has, then you are doing to all those innocent, anonymous children exactly what was done to you."

"You're a real piece of…of crap." She lowered her voice. "Is this why your wife left you?"

"Probably," he answered.

The argument continued on and off all afternoon. Mom was adamant in her refusal. But Del just never gave up. His nagging was positively relentless. I expected any minute for Mom to just storm out of the house. Amazingly, she did not. In fact, it was as if she was enjoying the argument. She was rising to whatever challenge he came up with and every minute of it gave her energy. Bickering with Del worked better than Procrit for perking Mom up. I would have never thought of that. I was blown away with how Del could have known.

When he invited us to stay for dinner, Mom accepted.

Del called over to the Lelands' to invite Sierra. When my sister told him that Seth was coming over, her guy friend got included, as well.

It was no elaborate meal. He fired up some charcoal on the backyard grill and we ate hot dogs and hamburgers with salad and sodas.

Seth was a little standoffish at first, but Mom apparently assumed it was shyness rather than being stuck-up that made him that way. She was able to draw him in and before the food was all gone, he was relaxed and joking along with everyone else.

Surprisingly, Mom asked him a lot of questions about the art school, why he went there and what he liked about it.

"In a lot of places," he told her, "skateboarders are out of the mainstream. We have to live with all the stupid expectations that the jocks get, but nobody really respects us as like real athletes."

Mom nodded as if she understood.

"At the art school, there aren't any jocks and everybody is just a little bit out of the ordinary. I'm not saying we don't have cliques. We do. But I guess we sort of respect each other more than in regular high school."

Sierra kept looking at Mom hopefully as if she expected her to suddenly announce that Sierra would be attending. That, of course, did not happen.

But what did happen was that Mom and I both got a better idea of what Seth was about. I liked him more and thought Mom maybe felt the same.

After the sun went down and it was cooler, we played a weird game of glow-in-the-dark soccer, girls against the guys. We got trampled. Sierra was the only one on our team who was any good at all. Mom had to sit down after a few minutes and Del joined her on the deck, where he served as referee. But mostly he just seemed to be talking to Mom.

There was something truly wonderful about that night. There was lots of fun, we'd had lots of good food. All of us kids got along and Mom and Del were obviously enjoying each other's company. I thought that if I just squinted a very little bit, I could almost see what it might be like to live in a normal family. With just an ordinary middle-class mom, dad and kids. I could imagine what our life might have been like if my dad had lived, if that one little change in our chaos equation had just never come to pass.

I have to admit, I liked the vision.

It was late when we finally said our goodbyes.

Seth left first, with Sierra walking him to the end of the block. I figured they were sneaking a kiss or something.

Spence got a phone call from his mother and closeted himself up to take it.

I was gathering up all my stuff. It seemed to have an incredible ability to multiply geometrically. I'd bring one thing over and find I had ten things to bring home.

Del and my mom were standing by the door together.

"Promise me that you'll at least think about calling Marcy," he said.

"Why is this so important to you?" she asked him.

He shook his head. "I don't know exactly," he said. "But it feels right to me. Just like being with you feels right to me."

Mom shot a glance in my direction. I pretended I didn't hear and nonchalantly went around the corner. Then immediately backed up against the wall so I could stay close to the doorway and hear them.

"You've been hinting about that all evening," she said.

"Thank God you finally noticed," he said. "I was beginning to think I was going to have to make some grand declaration or something."

"I'm not ready to have any kind of relationship," she said. "I'm fighting for my life here. I've got to concentrate on getting well."

"Why not give your life something to fight for?" he said. "There's no reason why we can't date."

"Date? Are you blind or crazy? Nobody dates when they have cancer."

"I don't think there's any rule about that," he said. "And maybe if they don't, they should. It might be a whole new direction for treatment. I can talk to Wiktor about it."

"There is nothing to joke about here," Mom said. "I am sick. I am bald. My mouth is full of sores. My throat hurts so much I can hardly bear to swallow. I throw up virtually every day of my life. And I'm so tired it's a struggle just to make it from morning doze to afternoon nap. The grim reaper is double-parked in front of the curb, and you want to date?"

"Yeah. How about tomorrow night? I'll pick you up about seven," he said. "And call Marcy, so I won't have to spend the entire evening talking about that."

Mom was, for once in her life, completely speechless.

# SONNY DAYS
## 26

The first grown-up dinner party that was held in Sonny and Dawn's new home was to set up Tonya Beale with one of the guys who worked in Sonny's office.

The menu included braised beef with horseradish sauce, asparagus spears, mixed potatoes, salad and a nice red wine served in long-stemmed crystal.

Sonny wasn't sure how the setup between the two single people was going, but with the children enjoying the novelty of an overnight with the grandparents, the talk around the table was totally grownup and he was enjoying himself.

"Dawn and Sonny are like family to us,"Tonya told Paul, a tall, well-spoken engineer with a receding hairline."I don't know how our family would have gotten through the last few years without them."

Tonya and her brothers and sisters had become a personal mission for Dawn.The two older girls were both enrolled at UT and commuting into the city. Their brother was in his freshman year at the Air Force Academy. The younger children, all now in high school, were responsible hardworking kids, coping with the tragedy of losing their parents.

Dawn made sure that while the older girls were

on campus, the younger Beale children were in class and supervised after school. Because of her own experience of having only herself to count on, she wanted these kids to always feel they could count on her.

"Tonya's father was a good friend," Sonny explained, running his hand along his chest. "And he saved my life."

Sonny rarely talked about the accident and didn't wish to now. But he felt as if he had to voice that truth from time to time so that no one, including himself, would forget the circumstances.

The talk moved to Paul and his life in Charlotte before attending the university. Then the three of them swapped crazy college stories as Dawn served the dessert.

As the evening wound down, Sonny felt the satisfaction of being a happy man. He had a nice home, two wonderful kids, a promising career, good friends and a wife who was both beautiful to look at as well as generous and kind. And she was turning into a very accomplished hostess.

When they said their goodbyes at the front door, he turned to Dawn and told her so.

"Go to hell!" she said, catching him completely off guard. She stormed out into the kitchen. After a moment, he followed her.

She was angrily clattering the English bone china that she normally treated as if it were spun sugar.

"What's wrong?"

"What do you think is wrong?" she asked, turning to glare at him.

"I don't have any idea."

"No, you wouldn't."

"Dawn, tell me what is wrong."

"You all think you're too frigging good for me!" she declared. "You and Paul, just a couple of golden boys. But Tonya would be a waitress now if I hadn't helped her!"

"Yes," he agreed. "Tonya might well be a waitress and she is so grateful to you. She loves you. I love you. And I'm pretty sure Paul likes you. He raved about the dinner all evening. What is this all about? Nobody thinks they are too good for you. Did somebody say something?"

His wife stopped, took a breath and then gently set down the stack of plates that she would have slammed on the counter a moment earlier.

"No," she told him. "Nobody said anything."

"Then what is all this about."

"Nothing," she said.

Sonny took her hands in his own and drew her nearer. "It's obviously not *nothing*," he said.

He led her away from the kitchen and to the living room couch where they sat down, his arm around her shoulder.

"Tell me," he insisted.

She resisted, unwilling to voice the bitterness that she was feeling. Finally he dragged it out of her.

"You're all sitting around talking about college," she said. "That's what you talked about all night. The dorms you lived in, the classes you went to, the professors you had."

Sonny nodded. "It's the only thing I knew those two had in common," he told her. "I certainly never meant to exclude you, darling. I'm sorry that you felt like I did."

"I guess I'm just having a self-esteem crisis," she said. "It's like all our friends, everyone we know, they've all gone to college or they're working exciting jobs and I'm still the trashy, unwanted girl that nobody can believe you married."

"Dawn!"

"Oh, I know that's not true," she said. "Intellectually, I know it's not true, but I still feel it. Even after all these years, sometimes I still feel it."

"What can I do to make it go away?" he asked.

She shook her head. "You can't do anything," she told him. "It's me. It's inside of me and I'm the only one who can fix it."

"Would you like to go to college?" he asked her. "I think the girls could spare you for a few classes."

"They wouldn't let me in college," she said, aghast.

"They who?"

"The people who run the place," she said. "I dropped out of high school and have a GED. I'd never get accepted."

"I'm not so sure about that," he said. "And if they don't let you in right away, you can take courses at community college until they do."

"I don't know."

"Dawn, if it will help you feel better about yourself, then you should do it," Sonny said. "And it's not as if anything you learn is ever time wasted."

She took a couple more days to be convinced, but ultimately, Dawn Leland decided she was ready to try higher education. The university had a special program for adults returning to school. Dawn signed up for it. And after the very nerve-racking experience of sitting down with a thousand seventeen year olds to take the SAT, Dawn was officially admitted to the University of Tennessee.

Sonny was proud of her. But within weeks of classes starting, Sonny realized his part in her degree program was going to involve more than cheerleading. Dawn took her studies very seriously. And except for the girls, her schoolwork took precedence over everything else. Sonny now came home after a hard day at work to find dirty dishes piled in the sink and no food in the refrigerator.

Clean socks, a pressed shirt, a towel that at least had nothing visible on it became valued commodities. The girls were given a lot more daddy time and Sonny desperately tried to multitask with suggestions like, "Who wants Daddy to give her a ride on the vacuum cleaner?"

The first year went well. Dawn was delighted with college. Sonny and the girls were getting accustomed to the new priorities. They kept thinking that once Dakota started kindergarten, it would all be a lot easier. And for a short time, it was. Then Sonny was promoted to a regional management position.

After the initial cheers of celebration, the couple began to ponder their new set of circumstances.

"I'm going to cut my schedule to one class a semester," Dawn told him.

"One class?" Sonny was incredulous. "No way. You don't want to be one of those old ladies who get their mortarboard at age 102."

They'd built a deck onto the back of the house and were sitting out there supervising the girls playing on their swing set.

"Okay, two classes then," she said. "But don't push

me for more. You're going to have all these new responsibilities and you'll be traveling."

"Dawn, I see how important your education is to you. And it's important to me," he said. "I don't think of it as some kind of froufrou girl time for a stay-at-home mom. It's an investment in our future."

"I know. And I'm not giving it up," she assured him. "But I think I'll try a light coursework semester. We don't know what it's going to be like yet. Once we figure that out, we'll know how to manage my classes."

Dawn's plan turned out to be a very good one. Sonny's new job had him on the road more than he was at home. In his former position, he evaluated forestland and estimated logging costs and profits. Now he was actually in the loop to recommend particular sites and harvesting plans.

Sonny had known, of course, that top management did not always go with the projects that looked best on paper. They had discretion to choose whatever they thought best. He knew that other factors went into their decisions. With the new job, he discovered the unpleasantness of some of those other factors.

He complained about it to Dawn.

"It's a business," he told her. "I know that and I know that businesses are about money. But, I just didn't think that it would be quite as…I don't know…quite as without conscience as it is."

"It's a job, Sonny, not a crusade," Dawn told him. "Do what you're required to do. Keep your head down and let the decision makers make the decisions. When you become one of the decision makers, then you'll have a chance to really make a difference."

His wife's words sounded like really good advice and he tried to follow it. He put in long hours, turned in quality work and didn't ask a lot of questions. Some of the plans that were implemented made him proud. He would come home with a kiss for Dawn, enthusiasm for the kids and a mood of contented satisfaction. Other times he privately just shook his head and shared the disappointing details only with his wife.

Sonny had been in his new job not quite a year when a particular incident caught his attention.

A wealthy and influential former politician pushed the company to do a clear-cut in an area not far from his estate. Sonny was mystified as to why that wood and why now. No one would answer his questions directly, but off the record one of his colleagues wised him up.

The TVA was going to put in high-voltage power lines to run near there, actually cutting across the corner of the politician's land. He didn't want that, so he was encouraging this clear-cut on the other side of the mountain. That would make it cheaper for the power company to put their lines in there, altering their plan to claim right-of-way through the politician's property.

Sonny felt a little less than enthusiastic about the company's compliance in such a personal selfish scheme. But he was truly distressed when he learned that the newly proposed power line route would run right through an impoverished section of a small mill town, putting the modest homes of over two thousand residents literally in the shadow of the giant towers.

"This is not only ridiculous," Sonny told his boss, "it's ridiculously unfair. That hillside doesn't merit a clear-cut. And the TVA's original plan would spare a lot more trees and affect a lot fewer people. The towers wouldn't even be in sight of this rich guy's home."

The supervisor shook his head. "This may not be good forestry, but it's good business," he said. "We may need a favor from this fellow sometime. He's just the type that a company wants to have on their side. Besides, if he doesn't get us to do it, some other logging firm will."

"What about all those people in that little town?" Sonny asked. "Wouldn't it be good to have them on our side?"

The man shrugged. "You don't have to worry about them," he said. "Most of them will never make the connection between our clear-cut this spring and the power lines in their backyard ten years from now."

That night at home he raved to Dawn.

"It's just crazy," he said. "It's like, if there's not much chance we'll be caught, then it's not wrong. I can't agree with that. I can't even go along."

"I think you'll have to, unless you want to get another job," she told him.

Sonny started looking the next day. There weren't a lot of firms that were hiring. The industry was in a slump and middle-management executives were being let go. If he was going to move he'd probably have to take a step down the ladder, and find a technical job. He got a couple of interviews, but it was difficult to explain why he wanted to leave the position he had without being disloyal to the company he worked for. He chose to say nothing, which left him open to speculation. He didn't get any offers.

Over the next year, Sonny continued to do his job. But with a skeptical reluctance that was uncomfortable. Finally, he went to talk to his dad about it. Vern heard him out before voicing his own opinion.

"You've got to do what's right," his father said. "In the long run, and life is always the long run, behaving ethically is far superior to being successful."

"But I want to be both," he said.

Vern shook his head. "Sometimes you can and sometimes you can't," he said. "You'll know, Sonny. I trust you completely to know."

And he did. The time came and he knew undeniably.

The project was a typical hardwoods harvesting in an area immediately adjacent to one they'd already commenced.

"We can't do this cut," he announced to the conference room full of managers, all more senior than himself.

"What do you mean?" his immediate supervisor asked him.

"I mean we can't do it now," he said. "We can do it three months from now or six months from now or next year, but we can't do it now."

"Now is the best time to do it," one of the other men suggested. "If we wait we might lose our opportunity."

"We might," Sonny agreed. "But we might not and it's a chance we have to take."

"We can't afford to take a chance like that."

Sonny disagreed. "We can't afford to try to be out there now," he said. "We've got another job going on out there. We can't start up that close."

"We're within legal distance from the other crew," the venture's proponent said. "And they're using rigging, we'll be mechanized. It's not that dangerous."

"Yes, it is," Sonny said. "I've been out there in those logging crews. I know what it's like to have to work too close. I lost a friend in a stupid accident on a site just like this one. We can't do this."

The argument continued. At first there were a few people on Sonny's side, but as the acrimony increased and lines were drawn they quietly, one by one, withdrew their support. Finally it was just Sonny, standing alone, sure of his conviction and unwilling to back down.

"I think we'll just have to turn that decision over to top management," his supervisor said.

Sonny was hopeful that he would get to make his case. He did not. When he was called into the office of the VP for Operations, the discussion was already over.

"I know that you have personal experience with this," the man said.

"Yes, I worked in a situation very much like this one," he said. "I lost a close friend in an accident that never should have happened."

The man set his elbows on the desk and wove his fingers together thoughtfully. "Sometimes," he said, "when we have a strong emotional reaction to a particular aspect of the business, it clouds our ability to make good, viable, profit-making decisions."

Two hours later, Sonny stepped across the threshold of his house in Old North Knoxville.

"What are you doing home so early?" Dawn asked him.

"I'm not sure," he said. "I can't remember if I was fired or I quit."

# REAL LIFE
## 27

— ◆ —

Vern and I went to the movies with Sierra and Seth. Of course, we didn't go to the same movie. As soon as we parked at the cineplex, the crush couple exited, making it look and feel like they were out alone. They went into some spooky love movie. Vern and I opted for a gross comedy where we laughed our heads off. We got out before they did and made ourselves comfortable on a bench just outside the doors.

"I saw that you were on the computer for a long time today," he said. "Were you doing some more fractals?"

I shook my head. "No, I've been looking through old census records on the Internet for some of my lost ancestors."

"Really?" Vern looked at me, genuinely surprised. "Well, it sounds as if you and Phrona are getting along better these days."

I shrugged. "I don't want her peeved at us," I explained. "I think it makes things harder for Mom if she worries about how we're getting along."

"You're right," he said. "Your mother has more than enough to deal with now without worrying that you girls are fighting with your grandmother."

It still felt weird to hear Mrs. Leland described as my grandmother. I still wasn't quite comfortable with it and I sure didn't want to give Vern any wrong ideas about where my loyalties might lie.

"Mrs. Leland is okay," I told him. "And she's entitled to her opinion about Mom. She just better keep it to herself while I'm around."

Vern grinned at me and then threw an arm around my neck and gave me a quick hug.

"If it makes you feel any better to know it," he said, "I think Dawn has turned out to be very brave and very wise. It wasn't easy to come back here."

"Because she and Mrs. Leland had words," I said.

He nodded. "Angry, threatening words," he said. "And your mother won. She won and she walked away."

"And now she's back," I said. "I guess that's why Mrs. Leland hates us. She thought she'd never have to mess with us again. And now we're back here."

Vern frowned. "Phrona doesn't hate you. She loves you. She wants you here with us. That's the brave part of Dawn's behavior. She realized that you girls might need us, so she had to take the risk of bringing you here."

"What risk?"

"The risk of losing," he said. "The risk of Phrona getting her way at last."

"I don't get it," I admitted.

Vern hesitated. "When your father died, your grandmother began legal proceedings to have her declared unfit and to get custody of you and your sister."

"What?"

My voice was very loud and people nearby turned to look at us. I lowered my tone. "Mrs. Leland tried to take us away from Mom?"

He nodded.

"I thought they'd just cussed each other out," I told him. "I never... Why would she do that?"

"She was trying to do what she thought best," he said.

"Best? To take us from Mom?"

"It's hard to explain to you what it was like," Vern said. "Here was your mother, just a kid herself, she was numb with grief, she had no money, no job, and she had two little babies to care for. We tried to help her. We tried to give her money. We offered her a place to stay in our house. She turned her nose up at everything we wanted to do for her. When she went into the hospital to have you, she left Sierra with some woman she hardly knew. I wouldn't have trusted that woman to take care of the dog. Which, by the way, she didn't. Rocky was just running wild in the yard. If she hadn't mentioned him to us we would have thought he was a stray and left him there. Dawn wouldn't let us help her. She wouldn't let us do anything for you girls."

"I don't get it," I admitted. "Was Mrs. Leland trying to get custody of us just to get back at Mom?"

Vern's expression was incredulous. "No, no, of course not," Vern insisted. "Phrona was worried about you. You girls are part of Sonny, the only part we had left. And, at the time, taking care of you seemed like a reasonable thing to do," he said. "It wasn't my idea, but I went along with it. She didn't want you kids to be neglected or farmed out to the state. And she honestly worried that might happen."

"Mom loves us," I said. "She would never do that!"

"You're absolutely right," Vern said. "If she's accomplished nothing else over the last thirteen years, she's proved that she will take care of you girls. But she was very young and she didn't know anything about raising children and she was so broken up, we weren't even sure that she was capable of taking care of herself."

"But she did."

Vern nodded. "She did," he agreed. "And she's done a great job with you and your sister. Even Phrona admits that."

"What did Mom say?" I asked. "How did she react when you tried to take us?"

"She was furious," he said. "She wished us everything but well. But the truth is, I think it kind of snapped her out of her stupor. With Phrona to hate and fear, she was energized. And we found out that all those years she'd been a ward of the state hadn't been for nothing. She knew exactly who to talk to and what she needed to document. She used the system that had served her so poorly to protect her rights to her children. It was amazing. Our lawyer told us that he was impressed about how much she understood and how well she handled herself among the bureaucracy and professionals that aligned against her."

"So she won," I said.

He nodded. "We dropped our claim. The lawyer said that we'd have a better chance going after visitation with you. And…and it was very important to us to be allowed to be a part of your lives."

"But that didn't work, either," I said.

"Actually, the judge granted us one weekend a month," Vern said.

My jaw fell open. "We never came to visit you."

"Once," he said. "You came once. It was a Saturday. Dawn dropped you off and we spent the whole day with you. We fed you and played with you. Well, I guess we mostly played with Sierra. But I remember changing your diapers and trying to teach you peekaboo. We were exhausted, but we had a wonderful time."

He was smiling and he reminisced about the day. Then his expression got somber.

"When your mother came to pick you up, she'd been out. That's what young people do, I suppose. They go out. Even young people who have husbands that are only weeks in the grave. She'd had a beer, maybe two. Phrona didn't approve and she said so. The two of them got into a shouting match. Dawn was so angry when she stormed out of the house, she forgot to take the dog."

Vern sighed heavily, gazed out the window for a moment and then turned his attention back to me. He grabbed my hand and squeezed it.

"That was the last time I saw you girls before you showed up at our door," he said. "Maybe I shouldn't have told you that. But I just couldn't have you think that Phrona and I didn't want you. Everybody wanted you."

I felt tears well up in my eyes and I wasn't sure why. I didn't know how I felt. It was too much information to take in. And it tilted my view of the world.

"How did Mom keep from bringing us back to see you?" I asked.

"Once she got that money from the logging company, she was gone," he said. "For a while we tried to track her down. But she moved so much, we just gave up."

I wanted to ask how long they looked and where but I saw Sierra and Seth coming across the room toward us. They were still trying to look as if they were alone. But when Vern suggested we stop for ice cream on the way home, they were all for it.

The little place was crowded and we had to stand in line to get our cones. But while Vern was paying, Sierra managed to snag a round, pink table next to the front window.

Seth and Sierra had decided that this was a great opportunity to talk with an adult about the art academy. Maybe he wasn't going to be in on the decision, but if they could get Vern on their side, then so much the better.

"It sounds like a good school," he admitted.

"Mom thinks I don't have a lot of art experience," Sierra correctly pointed out. "But fashion is kind of like art. And I love fashion."

Surprisingly Vern agreed. "I think a lot of people in that industry have art as a background," he said.

Sierra sharply drew in a breath, like he'd said something really amazing and exciting.

Neither Vern nor I could stifle our chuckle. After a second even Seth joined us. She was so easily pleased and so obviously delighted.

"You have to tell that to Mom," Sierra told Vern. "If she hears it from me, she'll think it's just made up. But she knows you'd never lie to her."

"I thought you'd decided that you wanted to be a nurse," I told her. "What happened to that?"

"They don't have a high school for being a nurse,"

she pointed out. "And besides, maybe I could combine the careers. I could, like, come up with designer nurse uniforms. Those ugly scrub things are just not that flattering to most body types."

"Yeah," Seth agreed enthusiastically.

I rolled my eyes. "Come on," I said. "That would never work."

Vern gave me a look and made a tut-tut sound. "Never try to talk anyone out of her dream," he said. "If it won't work, the person always figures it out soon enough. And we need all those extravagant dreamers to try those things the rest of us would never take a chance on."

There was nothing scolding about his tone. I liked that about Vern. He could tell you that you were wrong without making you feel bad about it. Maybe that was part of being a teacher or something.

His words absolutely inspired Sierra. She was off and running with a thousand ideas for uniforms and fancy bed linens to replace utilitarian white.

My sister was in one of her best moods. She was funny and upbeat and her enthusiasm seem to spill out on the rest of us. It wasn't all that strange when Vern commented on it.

"You remind me so much of your father," he told her. "He was always so full of ideas and he had the gift of making people believe in them."

Sierra stopped in midgiggle and stared at Vern for a moment.

"So I'm like my dad?" she asked.

He nodded. "You are," he said. "You both are. Seeing you here, living with you. I remember so many things."

Vern's expression was faraway, but there was a smile on his face.

Sierra's brow had furrowed. "My mom always says that Sonny was very smart and very kind," she said. "So I just figured I was more like Dawn."

Vern laughed out loud at that.

"Sonny was smart and kind," Vern said. "But he was like you in his excitement about the world around him. He was also able to see the potential in things. That's what he saw in your mother. Not the person she was or even who she pretended to be, but the person she might have been if she'd had plenty of love."

"I don't think she got that much love," I admitted. "None of her boyfriends were… Well, I don't think they really loved her."

"Some of them were nice," Sierra defended.

I agreed. "I liked a lot of them. And they liked Mom, but I don't think anyone really loved her."

"But you girls loved her," Vern said. "I would say that's been all that she's needed, the love of you two wonderful girls."

"That's not the same," Sierra said. She shot a glance at Seth and gave him a blushing smile. "I love you and Phrona and Dakota and Mom. But I think it's different when you, like, are in love with a guy."

Seth was blushing now, too.

"Of course it's different," Vern said. "It would have been nice if your mother could have found a life partner after Sonny died. But not everybody does. It was very lucky that she had you two. You've been the tail on her kite."

Sierra grinned ear to ear. "I think I'll tell her that next time she gets all rare about something."

We all laughed.

"Well, it's true," Vern said. "And you may quote me if you like."

"Still, it would be nice if Mom could like fall in love or meet somebody," Sierra said.

Vern nodded.

"What about Del?" she asked, glancing in my direction. "I think he's really sweet on her."

I shook my head. "She says Del's all wrong for her," I said. "And even if he wasn't, she thinks this is like absolutely the wrong time to be getting interested in some guy. She's got to get through the rest of this chemo stuff and get well."

"There might never be a better time," Vern said. "Life is short at best. Sometimes people should just go after what they want and not wait for the right time."

"Yeah," Sierra agreed.

"Are you sure?" I asked Vern. "I mean, hasty choices can be wrong choices."

He nodded. "Or they can be the only choices," he said. "Think about your father."

"What do you mean?"

"That his apparently hasty choice was truly his only choice," he said. "If your father had waited until he was finished with school and working in a job, the way we wanted him to, then he would never have married Dawn and you girls would never have been born."

"Yeah," I said. "But he would have married someone else. He would have had other kids. Remember the chaos theory."

"Sure I remember," Vern said. "A little change in

the equation has a dramatic change in the outcome.
But maybe his time here was not part of the equation.
If he hadn't married her and had you, he might not
have had time to make a family at all. Then there
would be nothing of him left but Phrona and me."

"That would have been sad," Sierra said.

Vern nodded. "It would have been very sad for
me," he said. "It already was very sad before you
girls came back to Knoxville."

"So you think Mom should date Del?"

Vern shrugged. "If she wants to, she should," he
said. "I don't know what she wants, or if being with
Del could make her happy. But she can't allow something as ugly as cancer keep her from living a life that
she might want to live, a life that might not be as long
as we hope."

"Do you think my mom is going to die?" I asked.

Vern put an arm around my shoulder and gave
me a comforting squeeze.

"We're all going to die, honey," he said. "You, me,
your mother, all of us. But we try to put it off as long
as we can and make the most of the life that we
have."

I relaxed and let go of the breath I was holding.

Sierra was smiling brightly, like she'd just come
up with some brilliant idea.

"So life is like moving into a new place to live,"
she said. "You put stuff up on the walls like you plan
to be there forever. But you keep your suitcase under
the bed, just in case."

# REAL LIFE
## 28

— ◆ ◀ —

I never knew if Mom called that Marcy person from the CAVA. Somehow I got the impression that she didn't. The woman showed up at the Lelands' front door anyway. She was a tiny, thin lady about Mrs. Leland's age, I suppose, but a lot more wrinkly.

"Her hair is like really in style," Sierra pointed out.

I decided she must have worn it that way for the past thirty years and now it was back in at last.

"It's the only thing fashionable about her," my sister said.

I don't know fashion but, even if I did, I wouldn't have been able to argue. Her suit, while very neat and clean, obviously dated from another era. It had huge shoulder pads which accentuated the woman's very narrow frame and shapeless body. I had more curves than she did, an incidence that didn't come up that frequently.

Mom was not having a particularly good day. She wasn't throwing up or anything like that, but she was just really pale and exhausted. She glared at Marcy through slitted eyes.

"I'm really not interested," she said simply.

Marcy nodded. "I used to feel that way, too," she said. "But I've been so lucky. I've seen these children. I've seen their lives get changed for the better. That can really hold my interest."

She laughed as if what she said was funny.

Sierra laughed, too. But Mom didn't.

"What we do at CAVA is to speak for children who can't speak for themselves," Marcy said.

"So like babies," Sierra said.

"Some are babies," Marcy told her. "But our volunteers work with children of every age. Whenever the court is considering a termination proceeding for abuse or neglect, we are there to represent what the child wants and needs."

"I know a lot about unwanted kids," Mom said. "I know a lot about the courts. But I've never heard a word about any court-appointed advocates."

"The program isn't that new," Marcy said. "It began in 1990, but I suppose it might have been after your association with foster care."

Mom stiffened. "So Del told you I'd grew up in foster care."

Marcy's eyes widened. "No, he didn't," she said. "He told me that you'd had some introduction to it in the past. I presumed you'd done some kind of internship in college or some such."

Mom laughed a little, but there was no humor in it.

"I've never been to college," she told Marcy. "My 'introduction' to foster care was being dumped in it by my family. It took me years to get away. And I've never looked back."

Marcy smiled, delighted.

"Oh, you would be such an inspiration to our children," she said. "It's so hard for them to get a glimpse of their future."

Mom gave a sort of huff with a shake of her head. "That's because they don't have any," she said.

Marcy frowned, puzzled. "Every child has a future," she said. "Some better, some worse, but *future* is the definition of *childhood*, isn't it?"

Mom shrugged.

Marcy was not deterred. "If it's not, then it should be," she said, cheerfully. "I think that's what we try to do. We try to see that every child has an opportunity to make something of her life, like you have."

"Me?" Mom scoffed. "I haven't made anything of my life. I'm a cocktail waitress, currently unemployed."

"You seem to be a self-reliant, hardworking mother of two happy and well-adjusted daughters," Marcy said. "I'd say that counts as an outstanding success in any reasonable person's mind."

Mom was obviously a little surprised at the woman's words. But she could hardly disagree with them. Instead, she changed the subject.

"I'm not interested in courts," she told Marcy. "I've spent so much time in them, I developed an allergy. Even a judge's chambers can give me hives."

Marcy chuckled. "The children are not usually that fond of it, either," she said. "Of course, a lot of what we do isn't done in court. Volunteer advocates want to make sure that every child also gets all the professional care that they need. Sometimes this means medical services, more often it's counseling or therapy."

"Social workers are supposed to take care of that," Mom said.

Marcy nodded. "As I'm sure you know," she said.

"The caseload the Child Protective Services faces is tremendous. And the turnover in the field is high. Over a child's lifetime, she might have a dozen or more professionals in charge of her case. We, as volunteers, stay connected with that child through her entire association with the bureaucracy. We try to be one point of continuity."

"That sounds like a good thing," Mom admitted. "I could have used somebody like you back when I was trapped in the system. A lot of people tried to help me, I guess. But most didn't have the time or the energy to figure out what I needed. And I'd already figured out running was my favorite alternative."

Marcy nodded. "We've got some young girls who think just the way you did," she said. "They could really benefit from what you've learned."

Mom chuckled humorlessly. "I haven't really learned all that much," she told the woman. "I still consider running as a viable option. Truth is, as soon as I'm finished with chemo and well enough to travel, I'm out of this town one more time."

Marcy took in that statement without any comment. She turned the conversation to Sierra and I.

"Are you looking forward to school?" Marcy asked us.

I shrugged, careful not to give any opinion at all. But Sierra was way too shallow-brained to even realize when she might be being disloyal.

"I am," Sierra said. "I'm really hoping to get into the art academy downtown."

"Oh, you like art?"

"I don't know that much about it," Sierra said. "But my boyfriend likes it and I like him."

Marcy laughed at that.

"I'm really interested in fashion," Sierra said. "And a lot of people in fashion actually go to art school, so it seems I should go. I mean, I really want to go. Mom hasn't decided yet, so it's still up in the air."

"One of our clients is in school there," Marcy said. "They really do get a quality education."

Mom didn't answer, instead she changed the subject.

"These volunteers in CAVA, they're like you, they're social workers and lawyers and like that, right?"

Marcy seemed surprised. "I'm not a social worker," she said. "I used to be a journalist. I wrote features for the Lifestyle section of the paper. But I haven't done that for years."

"You're one of those happy retirees, devoted to good works, huh?" Mom said.

Marcy laughed. "I guess you could say that. I didn't really intend to get involved with this, but one day, I just did."

"Got bored, huh?" Mom said.

Marcy nodded. "Incredibly bored, phenomenally bored. I was afraid I was going to literally die of boredom. That is, if breast cancer didn't get me first."

"Breast cancer?"

Marcy patted her chest almost proudly. "Double mastectomy," she said. "I did chemo and radiation. I spent hours on the Internet chasing down new protocols. I wore pink ribbons every day and did walks for the cure."

"I didn't know," Mom said softly.

"That's all good work," Marcy said. "It's all important work. But the truth is, my heart wasn't in it. My breasts maybe, but not my heart." She laughed. "I decided that I just couldn't think of cancer anymore. Thinking about it was driving me crazy. Then one morning I began to think of something else. I began to think of someone else."

"What happened?"

"I opened up the paper and there was a story about a little boy named Jeremy," she said. "He was only two years old and he'd lived just a few miles from my house. He'd starved to death."

"Oh, that's so sad," Sierra said.

"Sadder than you think," Marcy told us. "He starved to death while living in a nice warm home with two parents and his grandmother."

"What?" Mom's question was incredulous.

Marcy nodded. "There was food in the house," she said. "And the child showed no evidence of beatings or bruising. The family was all on drugs and, apparently, they all assumed someone else was feeding him. Nobody noticed anything was wrong until he was dead."

"My God! How can something like that happen?"

Marcy shook her head. "No one knows. I was so angry. I finished reading the paper and I paced through my house screaming at the stupid, selfish, undeserving family who'd thought only of themselves."

Mom nodded agreement.

"That's when I realized that I was just like them," she said. "The whole world was full of children who needed me and I was too busy worrying about myself and what was good for me to even notice they were hungry."

Marcy reached over and patted Mom's hand.

"That's just me," she said. "Not everybody is like me. I just understood that I couldn't do anything to cure my cancer. But I could do a lot to make the life of an unwanted child a lot better. That was fifteen years ago. I got involved in the early days of our local CAVA and I've seen our organization make life better for hundreds of children."

Marcy smiled then.

"I think of Jeremy a lot," she said. "I don't know if I can explain this exactly as I feel it. But in a small way I've made his little short life count for something. Somehow all of the wrong and sadness of that little life spurred me and others to get out in the world and try to make a difference."

Mom nodded. "At least it did that," she agreed.

"It's made me realize that no experience should be wasted," Marcy said. "If we don't take what happens in our world and try to turn it into some purpose then it just remains all downside forever."

Mom was looking at her now. I couldn't read the expression on her face.

"I don't know what happened to you in the foster care system," Marcy said. "But whatever it was, if you don't find a way to make something good come from that experience, then it's just wasted. Your suffering should never be disrespected, especially not by yourself."

"I've made myself strong by not thinking about it," Mom said.

"Maybe," Marcy said. "Maybe that's true. Or maybe you're still running away."

Her words were serious, but immediately followed by that cheery, winning smile.

"I've got to go," she said. "And I don't want to wear you out. I'm sure your strength comes in spurts these days."

Mom nodded.

"We're getting ready to start a class," Marcy told her. "It's thirty hours of training. We do our best to get our volunteers prepared for what they need to accomplish. We need you, Dawn. These kids need you." She smiled at me and Sierra. "Your own daughters are so lucky."

"Yes," Mom admitted, glancing over at us. "They are so much luckier than I was."

"They have a mom who loves them and grandparents, too," Marcy said.

Mom walked her to the door, which was a surprise. I liked her. I thought even Mom liked her. But when she waved goodbye to us, I figured that was the last we'd ever see of her.

It wasn't. She stopped by again about two days later. I wouldn't have known she was there if I hadn't seen her car from the window over at Spence's.

The last part of the summer was getting to be a little boring. Both of our rooms were covered in fractals. We'd played video games until our fingers were callused. We'd been to the pool so much we were waterlogged. And we'd listened in on so many other people's conversations with the Nature Sounds Receiver, that it no longer even held any appeal.

We were just waiting now. Waiting for school to

start. Waiting for our lives to begin again. I thought about Spence's mother expecting a baby. He hardly ever talked about it. I didn't know how much he thought about it. But I thought about it. I thought about how she could see that her life was changing right before her eyes. But she couldn't change it, she couldn't stop it and she couldn't hurry it up. That's how I felt about the rest of summer.

A movement in the Lelands' front yard caught my eye. Marcy was leaving already. Laughing and talking to someone on the front porch as she made her way to her car.

"That woman is some friend of your dad's," I told Spence, pointing toward the window.

"Yeah?"

He got up and glanced out. We watched as she got into her car, buckled up and pulled away from the curb.

"I don't recognize her," Spence said. "But Dad knows a lot of people."

"She's trying to get my mom to do some volunteer thing," I said. "To help kids who are in foster care."

"That's a good thing," Spence said.

"She shouldn't do it," I told him. "She's sick, she needs to be taking care of herself."

"Like my mom," Spence said.

"Your mom?" I turned and gave him that you're-an-idiot look. "Your mom isn't sick, she's pregnant."

"I don't think she knows the difference," Spence said. "She's talking like I'm not going back there when school starts. She thinks she isn't up to taking care of me."

"Really?"

"I've told her that I'll take care of myself," he said. "But she doesn't listen to me."

"That's tough," I commiserated. "But don't give up. You've just got to keep talking to her. Eventually, she has to listen."

Spence nodded. "I know," he said. "I'm going to see them this weekend. It's not my regular time with them, but Dad asked them if I could sleep over there on Saturday night."

"So you can talk to her then," I said. "I'm sure you can convince her."

"Yeah," he said, his confidence rising. "Yeah, you're right. If I keep at it, I can convince her."

Spence paused.

"Don't you want to know why I'm staying with my mom on Saturday?" he asked.

I glanced up. He was grinning like he had a big secret.

"Why?" I asked.

"'Cause Dad's got a big date," he said.

He just kept grinning. It was all I could do not to kick him.

"Yeah? So what?

"Your question shouldn't be *what*," Spence said. "It should be *who*."

"Then who?"

"Your mom."

"What?"

"That's what he told me. Dad said he has a date with Dawn."

"You're crazy," I said.

Spence shrugged. "I'm just telling you what he told me."

"Mom will never go out with him," I said with certainty.

"Done deal. She's already agreed," he said.

"No."

"It's true."

"My mom is really not Del's type," I said. "I keep trying to explain that to everyone, but no one believes me."

"Maybe because you never give any reasons," Spence said.

"There are reasons, lots of them," I said.

"Okay, give me one."

I hesitated for a minute, thinking. "My mom has a tattoo," I said finally.

"No big deal. Tell me something I don't know," Spence said. "I've seen the tattoo. It's hard to miss it. I'm sure my dad has seen it, too."

"Mom didn't go to college," I said. "And when she's working, she's not a secretary or a salesclerk or even a cleaning lady. She's a cocktail waitress."

"So?"

"So your dad is a Sunday school teacher. Sunday school teachers don't date cocktail waitresses."

"Dad already wants to date her," Spence said. "He already thinks she's his type or he wouldn't have asked her out. You're supposed to be coming up with reasons that he's not her type."

"My mom only dates guys named Sonny."

"What?"

"She only dates guys named Sonny," I repeated. I knew it sounded stupid. I even knew it was stupid. That's why I hated to mention it. But it was the truth.

"My father's name was Sonny," I explained. "All

my life all the guys she's dated, they were all named Sonny."

"Sonny?"

"Yeah, it's like a nickname for somebody who is a Junior," I explained. "My father's name was Henry Vernon Leland, Jr. So people called him Sonny. All the men my mom dates are always called Sonny, too."

"It's just a nickname," Spence said.

"Yeah, well, it's a nickname that means something."

Spence jumped up and hurried over to his bookshelves. He was obviously looking for something as he hurried rummaged through a couple of drawers.

"What are you doing?" I asked.

"Wait a minute," he said. "Wait a minute. Wait, here it is."

He tossed a piece of plastic onto the floor next to me.

"What is it?" I asked as I picked it up.

"It's my ID from the Boys Club," he said.

"What do you need that for?"

"Read it," he said.

I did. "Delbert Spencer Tegge, III."

"That's me," he said. "I'm *the third* and that makes my dad…"

"Sonny," I said in a disbelieving whisper.

# SONNY DAYS
## 29

The church in Strawberry Plains looked very different for Tonya's wedding than it had for her father's funeral. There was a white linen runner down the center aisle, bows on all the sides of the pews and stands of lit candles decorating the chancel.

The four Beale sisters were wearing identical floor-length gowns in soft mint green. The girls had sewn them all at home. With Dawn's guidance, the wedding plans were formulated with the same careful methodology of any other project. Cecilia, the youngest sister, had taken a dressmaking course at the vo-tech school. She passed on what she'd learned to her sisters. They began sewing the bridesmaid dresses, improving their skills on each one. By the time they made the first cut of Tonya's white organza, they had the confidence of veteran seamstresses.

Sonny sat on the bride's side of the aisle with Dawn and the girls, but he would have been comfortable as a friend of the groom, as well.

Paul was still with the logging company. He'd had the good sense not to throw himself on Sonny's pyre. And he was keeping his ear to the ground for opportunities that Sonny might look into.

Unemployment didn't sit well with Sonny or his

family. His former experience with financial difficulties had been overcome by good pay for dangerous work as a logger. Somehow he'd thought that a college degree would shelter him from the plight of joblessness.

And his past success worked against him now. When prospective employers looked at his resume, and saw that he got a great job out of college and nice promotions, followed by an abrupt and unexplained termination, there were always questions.

Tonya came down the aisle. As Sonny looked at her he could understand how magazines and greeting cards described brides as a vision of loveliness. She was beautiful. Warmth, excitement, joy formed a glow around her and touched everyone who gazed upon it.

He thought of Lonnie.

Lonnie should have been here. Her brother, in his Air Force Mess Dress, was at her side, but it should have been Lonnie.

Sonny tried to imagine seeing his own daughters get married. Would it be like this? Would they look so happy? He hoped so. And he hoped that, unlike Lonnie, he would be there to see it.

"Who gives this woman to be married?" the preacher asked.

"My sisters and I do."

It should have been Lonnie.

Tonya and Paul clasped hands, made vows, exchanged rings. As Sonny listened he took Dawn's hand in his own. She glanced over and smiled at him. It amazed him that after all that had happened lately, she could still smile.

The unemployment thing had caught her off guard. With both girls in school all day, Dawn was taking a full course load at the university.

"I'll drop out of school and get a job," she decided immediately.

"No, you won't have to do that," Sonny told her.

She shook her head. "I don't mind, really I don't. I can wait tables or what I should really be is a cocktail waitress. That makes perfect sense. I'll be working mostly when the girls have gone to bed. All I have to do is carry a few drinks. And the money's real good."

Sonny didn't like that idea.

"Don't worry about the money," he assured her. "I'll get something else very soon."

He didn't, of course. It had been five months and he still had nothing lined up. Dawn began to insist that she needed to find work. She even began applying at bars, knowing her husband didn't want her there.

It was Phrona who eventually butted in with a solution.

"I'm not any fonder of the idea of you working in some whiskey lounge than Sonny is," she told Dawn. "But not just because I don't think it's any kind of life for my grandchildren's mother. I just think that it doesn't teach you anything or get you anywhere. Shouldn't you be using the talents that you have and the knowledge that you've acquired to do something that might really appeal to you as a life's work?"

Dawn was momentarily dumbfounded.

"I never thought of myself as having a life's work," she said. "Except for raising the girls."

Phrona nodded. "Raising Sierra and Dakota should be your first priority, but as an empty nester myself, I can tell you that you'll be a better mother if you also go after some dreams of your own."

Dawn thought about that, but couldn't come to any conclusions.

"I don't think I have any dreams," she told Sonny. "When I look at my life with you, it's wonderful. But when I look out into the world, the world that I've always known, the world I grew up in… To me, that's just a nightmare."

Phrona showed up with an answer for her, as well as a name and a number.

Dawn looked down at it and read, "Leslie Jochem, Department of Children's Services."

"She's Jane Wickham's daughter-in-law's sister," Phrona explained. "Jane says she's always looking for hardworking, responsible people to hire."

Dawn frowned. "I'm no social worker," she pointed out.

"There are lots of clerical jobs and paperwork jobs," Phrona said with a wave. "They either have something you might be interested in or they don't. You'll never know if you don't give them a call."

Dawn had. She'd also gone in for an interview. She thought that she would have nothing to say, but surprisingly they were very interested in her. "Leslie said, 'A person who has been inside the system has a perspective that the rest of us will never be able to get,'" she told Sonny later.

"And what did you say?" Sonny asked.

"I guess I was a little defensive," she admitted. "I said that when I left, I put all that behind me."

He nodded.

"But then she pointed out that I hadn't really, that what I'd been doing to help the Beales…that kind of care and oversight is exactly what a lot of the job of DCS is."

"So what do you think?" Sonny asked her.

She shrugged. "I'm still a little unsure," she said. "I worry that I'll just become part of the problem."

Sonny shook his head with certainty. "That will never happen," he said.

"How can you know that?"

"I see how you are with Sierra and Dakota," he told her. "I saw how you were with Tonya and her family. You're not going to be any different with any other kid. They will be lucky to have you."

In the end, she did accept a job. It was a paperwork job, a case assistant for a homes inspector. She didn't actually even see any children, but somehow they weren't just names to her on the paper. They were every kid she'd ever met, every home she'd ever lived in, every situation she'd ever run from. She took the job very personally.

Sonny was delighted. It was a state job. It didn't pay as much as cocktail waitressing and she was away from Sierra and Dakota for much more of the day. But he could tell that she loved the work. And that it was healing her. It was forcing her to confront the past that she'd left behind and reevaluate it for the positive things it had given her. Sitting beside her in the little country church, Sonny watched his wife. Even given their current poor financial circumstances, Dawn was happier than she'd been in a long time.

The minister pronounced Paul and Tonya as man and wife. Paul kissed his bride and then the two, blushing and happy, turned to face the congregation as they were introduced as Mr. and Mrs. for the very first time.

Beside him, Dawn was smiling through eyes full of tears.

The reception was held in the church basement. It wasn't the kind that would have impressed the apogee of Knoxville society, or rated a photo spread in some bridal magazine. There was a three-layer homemade cake, fruit punch, mints and nuts. The guest favors were only little bags of birdseed in squares of colored net.

There was no dancing allowed, but a grizzled old man was scratching out romantic tunes on an ancient fiddle. Well-wishers sat around in metal folding chairs exchanging stories and reminiscing about weddings past.

Sonny wondered what the groom's parents must think. They were an affluent couple from Charlotte. But if they found the wedding low budget, they obviously thought their new daughter-in-law to be a very precious jewel.

Sonny found a seat next to Rob Pearson, a logger he knew from his days on the crew. They caught up on each other's news. One of his sons was on the football team. His wife was now selling makeup on the side.

"So how's the fancy desk job going?" Rob asked.

Sonny was sheepish. "I don't have it anymore," he said.

The man raised an eyebrow. "What's that about?"

"Well, I sort of quit when it seemed like I wasn't going to get another choice."

"Dang, I hadn't heard that, I'm sorry," Rob told him.

"Thanks," Sonny said. "I'm sure I'll find something soon."

"Where have you been looking?"

Sonny named most of the companies that operated in the area.

"I've even applied with OSHA and the forestry service, but it takes time," he said.

"You know," the man said, lowering his voice slightly. "I heard the Brotherhood of Timber Workers is looking for a man for this area."

"Union? In east Tennessee?" Sonny was skeptical. "This is a Right to Work state."

Rob shrugged. "Guess that's why they've still got the job open."

They both laughed.

A minute later one of the bridesmaids came by to hand them cake. Rob teased her about catching the bouquet. She blushed, but managed to dissemble with admirable grace. Sonny couldn't help smiling. Lonnie's girls had turned out fine. He knew their father would have been proud.

Out in the churchyard, someone had started a game of Drop-the-Handkerchief. It was new to most of the kids who were trying to play it, including Sierra and Dakota. He watched them racing around the circle in their matching dresses. Sierra still managed to look like a photograph. Dakota's hair bow was hanging precariously from one side and the knee area of her long skirt was grass-stained.

He saw Dawn standing in a group of women. Sonny winked at her and she rolled her eyes. But a couple of minutes later she extricated herself and made her way to his side.

"It's a nice wedding," he told her.

She agreed. "It's sweet and old-fashioned," she said. "The memories will be beautiful."

"We should have had a wedding," Sonny said.

"Duh!" Dawn said facetiously. "We did."

"I don't think fifteen minutes in the judge's chambers is considered a wedding," he said.

She grinned at him. "Well, Sonny, you're just as married."

"True," he admitted. "But it would have been nice to have all our friends and family there, celebrating with us and wishing us well."

"That's because nobody felt like celebrating and nobody wished us well," she said.

He nodded. "It could have been different," he said. "I think we could have made my mother come around. She certainly likes you now."

"I don't think I would ever have been her first choice for you," Dawn said. "But she and I get along well enough. I think I've proved myself to her."

"And she's proved herself to you," Sonny said.

Dawn glanced up at him, questioning.

"She and Dad have proved that people can care about you. Not just be in love with you, like I am, but just care about you, human to human."

She thought about that for a long moment and then nodded. "You're right," she said. "I guess I believed that you cared about me, loved me, because you are unique. I don't think I believed that anyone else, anyone less extraordinary, could ever look beyond who I've been to who I might actually be."

He kissed her.

"Hey, that stuff is for the newlyweds," an old logger called out to Sonny. "You two are old married folks."

"It's a wedding," Sonny called back. "A guy can forget who he is around all these frills and bows."

A burst of good-natured laughter and nods of agreement trickled through the crowd.

Sonny and Dawn didn't get a word with the bride and groom until late in the evening. While his wife listened with delight at Tonya's exuberance over the day, he shook hands with Paul, told him what a lucky guy he was.

"I won't tell you to take good care of her," Sonny said. "Because I know that you're smart enough to recognize the value of a woman who is smart, beautiful *and* willing to put up with you."

Paul laughed and Sonny slapped him companionably on the back.

"Thank you so much for…for everything," Tonya told him. She went up on her tiptoes to hug his neck. "You and Dawn have been so good to us, to me. You've just been great, how you've helped us and cared about us."

"It isn't that hard to care about kids like you," Sonny said. "And I never forget that your dad saved my life."

She nodded. "But somehow it never feels like you're being kind to us out of some obligation you feel," Tonya said. "It's always like you really care."

"Because I do," Sonny admitted. "I guess I've just

been thinking about Lonnie a lot today. I've been really wishing that he could have been here. And I know you've really been wishing it, too."

Her pretty brown eyes brightened with tears.

"Actually, I feel that he was," she said.

Later that night as they drove back to Knoxville, the kids sound asleep in the car seats, Sonny related the story.

Dawn sighed.

"It's so sweet," she said. "And so sad."

"Sometimes when I think about it…" Sonny said. "When I think about him stepping in front of me like that. I just can't imagine why he would do that. I mean, he knew me, but he hardly knew me. And those children needed him. How could he decide in that split second to leave those kids of his behind?"

Sonny took a deep breath and shuddered as if a ghost had walked over his grave.

"I can't even imagine what could have motivated him," he told Dawn. "I know that I could never have made such a sacrifice."

"I don't know," Dawn admitted. "In my psychology class they told us that heroism and self-sacrifice can be based in the need to take control. You can't change what is happening, but you can make a response to it."

"I don't know if I agree with that," Sonny said. "Somehow I don't think that he just reacted like Pavlov's dog. I think he knew what he was doing. I think he intentionally gave up his life for mine. I just don't know why he did it."

"I am just so glad that he did," Dawn said.

"I guess…" Sonny hesitated. "I guess sometimes I

feel that Lonnie must have saved me for some reason. That I've got to fulfill some sort of important purpose. I just wish I knew what it was."

"Being a devoted husband and father is a pretty important purpose," Dawn pointed out. "The girls adore their daddy and they need you with them. And I love you, Sonny. My life wouldn't be nearly this good without you."

Sonny smiled at her, then deliberately steered the discussion away from the serious side of things.

"Yeah, you're life is pretty darn good," he said facetiously in a voice that closely mimicked his own mother's. "There's nothing quite like being married to a guy who's out of work. Having to go out and get a job yourself and wondering if you're going to be able to pay that mortgage."

"We'll manage," Dawn assured him. "I know that somehow we'll manage."

"Of course we will," he agreed. "Hey, I even got a lead on a job at the wedding."

"Really?"

"The Brotherhood of Timber Workers is looking for somebody."

"What kind of job is it?" Dawn asked.

"It doesn't matter," Sonny answered. "If I go to work in any capacity as a union organizer, I'll never get another company job in my lifetime."

"They would do that?" She sounded shocked.

"In a skinny minute," Sonny said. "Collective bargaining costs companies money. They don't want any part of it."

"But if the workers want it..."

"Local loggers have learned to keep their distance," Sonny said. "They're afraid that if they join up, someone else will get their job."

"And unions are corrupt, right?" Dawn asked. "That's what people say, that they are not really for the workers, the leaders are just out for themselves."

Sonny chuckled. "That's certainly what companies say," he admitted. "I'm sure some unions are corrupt, but most aren't and none of them have to be. The concept of laborers banding together to offset the power of big business is important to democracy. But things are hardly ever really that cut and dried. Companies are attracted to states like Tennessee because we have non-union labor. If corporations don't locate here, then all the unions in the world can't create jobs that don't exist."

"Yeah, I guess that's true for manufacturing," Dawn said. "But logging would be here because forests are here. And wouldn't loggers get paid more if they were in the union?"

"Not necessarily," Sonny told her. "Around here, logging is already highly paid labor."

"So there's no reason to join the union," Dawn said.

"That's what most people think."

"What do you think?" she asked him.

Sonny hesitated, considering.

"I think that there are other issues than just pay," he said. "There's retirement and disability. A union could make sure that companies would never pull what they tried with the Beales, a five thousand dollar payoff to compensate six orphans. And then there's safety. If the union had more local membership the best interests of the workers would carry a lot more weight. It would be a great tempering mechanism in those instances when greed gets the better of company management."

"Then you're thinking about taking the job."

Sonny shook his head. "I can't. It would kill my career. I'm sure of that."

Dawn nodded. "Or it would give you a career very different from the one that you thought you were going to have."

# REAL LIFE
## 30

———•◄———

It was hard to believe that my mother was having an actual real-life date with Del Tegge. It was one of those things that if you'd seen it on reality TV you would have said, "Aw come on, no way."

But it was really happening. And in the worst possible way. Sierra was so excited and giggly, the two of them had spent all afternoon working up to the big moment. The way they were talking, planning, speculating, it was like she was off to the prom, not a simple dinner.

The whole thing just made me totally nervous.

He was not at all her type. Still, he could have been a Sonny. Just another Sonny looking for whatever it was that Sonnys wanted from my mom.

I didn't tell her what I'd learned about his name. It was too spooky and I was afraid for her. She was sick and she was vulnerable. If he turned out to be like all the other Sonnys in her world, it wouldn't be good. Should I warn her that he might be like the rest of them? Or would she then be more determined to actually try to make the thing work?

I wasn't sure. And the more I thought about it, the scarier it got. Meanwhile, Mom tried on dresses and modeled them for me and Sierra.

My sister offered great tips and actually loaned pieces of her own wardrobe, including a very expensive well-made suit that Mrs. Leland had bought for Sierra to wear to church. It looked good on Mom. She looked like one of those nice ladies that attend functions of the PTA and served us punch and cookies.

"That looks great, Mom," I told her.

Sierra agreed. "This is totally you," she said. "Not too wild, not too boring. It says, I know who I am and you can take me anywhere."

"You think so?" Mom asked.

Sierra nodded. "Look, we've even got this scarf that works with it. I'll tie a turban around your head. You'll look more than good, you'll be downright chic."

They laughed. Mom was pleased. Sierra was pleased. Even I was beginning to loosen up some. Maybe Mom could just go out with this guy, have a nice evening and that would be enough. I liked the guy. But he didn't have to be our latest Sonny. He could just be the guy who bought Mom dinner.

I was sitting in the dining room looking through the photo albums when the doorbell rang. I was just getting up when Mom walked into the room.

"I'll get it," she told me.

I glanced over at her. I know my mouth must have dropped open like a broken hatch.

Mom had ditched the attractive Sunday suit and was wearing her shortest shirt, her highest heels and a tight low-cut top that gave a perfect look at the rose heart tattoo. A leather newsboy hat had replaced the chic turban and her makeup was heavy almost to the point of garish.

"Mom?" I asked. "What are you doing? What happened to Sierra's suit?"

"It's Sierra's," she answered calmly. "This is what I wear on dates. I decided that pretending something else is just stupid. This is who I am. This time I'm not pretending to be anyone else."

"What do you mean 'this time'?" I asked.

She shook her head. "Nothing," she said.

Sierra was as disheartened as I was. "Mom, what if he takes you someplace…someplace nice?"

I was pretty sure that Del Tegge was the kind of guy that would take a woman someplace nice.

"If he's slumming," Mom said, "then I don't expect we'll be headed anyplace but a noisy bar or a crowded dance hall."

"What if he's not slumming?" I asked. "What if he really likes you and wants to be with you?"

"Well, then we'll find that out, won't we?"

My dismay must have shown on my face.

"Hey, what's this?" she asked me, laughing and clucking me under the chin. "You're the one who's kept reminding me that he's not my type."

I should have told her he was a Sonny. I should have given her his name. But I hadn't. I'd held it back and now, now it was too late.

"Wish me luck," she said as she headed to the front door.

My heart was in my throat.

A minute later I heard the front door open. Sierra and I both sat not moving a muscle, listening.

"Whoa!" I heard him say to her. "You surprised me."

"What do you mean?" Mom asked him.

"I expected you to make me cool my heels at least ten minutes chatting with Vern and Phrona," he told her. "It's nice to have you answer the door. Are you ready?"

Then they were gone.

I turned to Sierra.

"He's a Sonny," I said.

"Huh?"

"Del, his name is Delbert Tegge, Jr.," I explained. "He could have been called Sonny."

She rolled her eyes.

"Yeah, well, he wasn't," she said.

"But don't you see he could be her type?" I said.

"Type? Type only works in soap operas," Sierra told me with a smug smile. "The people there never change who they are no matter what. If they are bad or gullible or jealous it doesn't matter what happens to them, they will be like that. Even if they get amnesia, they continue to be like that. Real life is different. When things happen in real life, it changes people."

"But Mom only dates guys named Sonny."

Sierra shrugged. "Maybe it was easier than remembering a lot of names," she said. "That way you know that in the middle of the night, you're not going to accidently call out the wrong one."

She thought her explanation was funny. I wasn't so sure.

Sierra had her own date that Saturday night and Seth showed up just a few minutes after Del.

I had to let him in. As soon as the doorbell rang, she hurried back to the bedroom for one final check.

"Hey kid," he said, by way of conversation.

I didn't have much to say to him, either. I'd decided that he was okay. As far as a boyfriend for Sierra was concerned, he'd do fine. I just didn't personally have anything I could say to him. So we just sat there in the living room, not saying anything until finally my sister showed up.

"Here I am," she announced as she walked in.

"Has your mom said anything about school?" Seth asked first thing, without even acknowledging how good Sierra looked and how much time she'd spent getting that way.

"No," she said, shaking her head. "Mom hasn't said anything yet and I tried not to really bug her too much about it today."

Seth rolled his eyes, obviously frustrated. "Enrollment ends on Tuesday," he said. "If she doesn't agree by then, we'll spend the whole year in separate schools."

Spence was at his mother's house for the weekend. So it was just me.

I thought about making some new fractals, though I already had dozens of them. You never really knew what you'd get. I looked in on Vern. He was sleeping in his chair, a copy of *New Scientist* lay open on his lap.

Rocky, on the floor at his feet, got up and trotted over to me. I petted him and he followed me as I wandered through the house. In the dining room, I closed the photo albums I'd been looking at and glanced over at the top of the mantel. The area had been cleaned a dozen times since I'd stolen the soccer photo, but apparently nobody had noticed. It still looked glaringly missing to me. But I figured it was my own guilt exaggerating its importance. It was just one photo and the Lelands had hundreds.

I had no friends to call.

I turned on the TV. I flipped through the channels. The silly sitcoms didn't interest me. And the reality shows now all seemed the same. I caught a quick glimpse of a newscast. They were talking about getting back to school. They showed shoppers out buying clothes and backpacks and supplies. School was still more than a week off. I knew from experience not to start counting on being here by the time classes began. The summer had been long and tough. But Mom seemed better now. She might be keen on hitting the road any day now.

Just the uncertainty of that had me on my feet. I paced a couple of minutes in the living room and then went to the bedroom I shared with Sierra. I would miss this place if we moved. I would miss these people. Mom had probably been right to always keep going. The longer you stay in a place, the harder it was when you have to run away.

From the back garden glass doors I saw the light from Mrs. Leland's office. After only a moment's hesitation, Rocky and I decided to make our way in that direction.

She was sitting sort of primly, as always, on a stool by the filing cabinet, sorting papers. She glanced up immediately and smiled at me.

"Did Dawn and Sierra get off all right?" she asked.

"Yeah"

"What's your grandfather up to?"

"He's sleeping in his study," I said.

She nodded. "So I suppose you have a little time on your hands," she said.

"Yeah, I thought I might look for Lemuel and Essie," I told her. "I've still got a lot of states to go."

She nodded. "Well, don't be discouraged if you don't find them," she told me. "They may have changed their names or died between the end of the war and the 1880 census. The census takers might have missed them. Or, of course, Lemuel could have been killed in battle and our whole premise of the two of them getting together may have been wrong."

"I'd hate for that to be true," I told her.

She nodded. "The most likely result is the one that we've got already," she said. "We don't know what happened and never will."

"That one is the toughest," I told her.

Mrs. Leland agreed.

I sat down at the computer and pulled out my list of states and territories from the drawer. She'd given me my own folder, so that I could keep up with where I'd looked and anything that I'd found. Most of the west I'd already looked through. We'd thought they would have headed that way. But I was down to checking Ohio and Michigan. There were Lelands everywhere. But no body matched their names or even their dates of birth.

All the records were available on the Internet, but each state and territory had to be queried separately. And many of the states were indexed by county, which could really add up to a lot of search time.

The list of last names could be located, but I'd have to look through photos of the handwritten record pages, trying to find details that matched up among the questions they asked, like age, occupation, state where you were born, state where your parents were born. We had to assume that they would stick close to the truth, even if they fudged on their names. It was our only chance to find them.

I thought it would be a boring thing to do, but it was actually exciting. It was like a mystery with lots of clues and red herrings. But it was real and it was people whose DNA was very close to my own.

It was amazing, really, how easily Mrs. Leland had accepted me as a genealogist. Much quicker than as a granddaughter, which I thought might still be a little hard for either of us to really get our minds around.

At first I'd decided to try to get close to her only to distract her from Mom. But amazingly, that didn't seem necessary anymore. For one thing, Mom was doing better. She didn't require as much defense. And then, Mrs. Leland wasn't so much on her case these days. It was almost as if she'd accepted us into her life. Or at least she'd resigned herself to it. Anyway, we were here and she was apparently making the best of it.

"What do you think of my mom dating Del Tegge?" I asked her.

She hesitated.

"Dawn is a grown woman, she may date whomever she likes."

There was something about the way she said the words that made me curious.

I glanced over at her. "Are you happy about it or not?"

"It's just a date, Dakota," she pointed out.

"Yeah, I know," I told her. "But that doesn't mean you can't have an opinion."

She smiled at me. "When you're like that, so politely determined, you remind me a great deal of your father."

"Thanks."

She turned back to her papers.

"That doesn't get you out of answering the question."

Mrs. Leland shook her head and sat thoughtfully for a moment, choosing her words.

"I like Del," she said. "I think he's a nice man, smart, interesting, a good father. I'm very sorry that his marriage didn't work out. His ex-wife is a lovely young woman from a fine family. She's very active in the community social whirl. I think Dawn is a diversion from that."

"So you think he's slumming? Mom thinks that, too."

"Oh, my goodness, no," Mrs. Leland said. "I didn't mean anything so…well, so unpleasant. I only meant that Dawn is quite different from Spence's mother. That marriage obviously didn't work, so perhaps Del finds himself drawn to the antithesis of that relationship."

"Is that good?"

Mrs. Leland shrugged. "They do say that opposites attract," she said. "Whether they can maintain a relationship over time is still open to question."

I thought about that as I squinted at the screen, deciphering handwriting over a hundred years old.

"Do you think my mom and Sonny Leland would have been able to stay together if my dad had lived?"

"There is no way to know something like that."

I glanced over at her, about to repeat my "you have an opinion" comment, but it wasn't necessary, she took the hint.

"When they married," Mrs. Leland said, "I didn't think that they would be able to stay together. I didn't think that your mother would be capable of forming long-term, stable relationships."

I nodded. "Yeah," I said. "I guess you were right about that."

Mrs. Leland crooked her head slightly and gave a strange little smile. "Actually, Dakota," she responded, "I was just going to say that I've decided that I might just have been wrong about that."

# REAL LIFE
## 31

At the last possible moment Mom decided that Sierra could go to Seth's art school. My sister's nagging had become incessant. I groaned every time the subject came up. But Mom didn't even appear to notice it. She never responded to it. She never discussed it.

Then it was like she woke the very last morning of school enrollment and decided that we were staying for a while and a private art academy was exactly what Sierra needed.

Vern and Mrs. Leland gave each other a surprised glance when Sierra told them, but he stepped up immediately to offer assistance.

"I don't know how much this is going to cost," he said to Mom. "It may be quite expensive. Phrona and I have a little money tucked away…."

Mom waved him off.

"I couldn't let you help me," she said. "You've done more than we can ever repay already. Sierra and I are going down there to enroll her this morning. We're going to throw ourselves on their mercy and see if we can get some kind of break on tuition."

I don't think the Lelands actually believed in that possibility, but Mom seemed infused with confidence.

"What kind of school would turn down a deserving young girl just because she is economically disadvantaged?" she asked rhetorically.

Most of them, I thought to myself, but managed not to comment aloud.

Mom put on her gray funeral suit and Sierra looked stylish, but modest, in a new skirt and blouse that Mrs. Leland had bought her.

"I'm so excited!" Sierra said, though her constant giggling had already suggested that. "And Seth is just over the moon with it. I mean it's total ups."

"I'll run you down there," Vern said. One of Mom's antinausea medications made her drowsy and the doctor said she shouldn't drive.

"No need," Mom assured him. "I'm a licensed driver, Sierra has her permit. I'll just have her drive me."

My sister screamed and began jumping up and down like some crazy contestant on *The Price Is Right*.

"I've got to call Seth and tell him," she said, racing out of the room.

"She ought to call the highway patrol and get them to clear the streets," I said.

Mom laughed. "Your day will come," she told me. "And after facing cancer, I figure that I'm up to risking my life with one of my daughters at the wheel."

I stood on the front porch as my sister backed out of the driveway in a slow, careful creep.

Mom rolled down her window and hollered at me. "If we're not back in two weeks, send help!"

It was a good joke and I laughed, but there was still that uncertainty in me. Today we were staying, otherwise she wouldn't be bothering to enroll Sierra in a new school. But things could change so quickly.

I couldn't let myself get attached. I had to be careful. I had to be ready. Mom was feeling so much better. If she was better, she might not finish the chemo. Even if she finished, we had only three months of treatment left. That wasn't even a whole semester. We might be on the road by Halloween.

I spent the morning looking through my clothes and thinking about school. Sierra was headed exactly where she wanted, but I didn't know anything about Whittle Springs Middle School, or as Spence called it, Whittle Middle. I was going through my school clothes, wondering what would still fit and whether I would be too dopey to ever make friends. But then, what was the use in making friends? I was in my third year of middle school and this was going to be my third school. I'd left the last one without so much as a word of goodbye. It was easier, really, if you didn't let anyone get close.

From its hiding place inside my suitcase, the soccer photo of my dad fell out and landed on the floor. I picked it up and smoothed the now familiar, smiling face with my fingers. I'd seen so many photos of him now. When I'd seen this one, I thought he looked like me. But now, it only looked like him. I carefully rewrapped it in a blouse that I could no longer wear and hid it away once more.

I heard the doorbell and was grateful to have the interruption. When I opened the door, I was surprised to see Marcy. I wanted to roll my eyes. I couldn't believe she was back. Couldn't the woman take no for an answer? Actually I liked her. She was funny and bubbly and grandmotherish. But, I didn't want to help Mom dodge her or be forced to make up excuses for why she couldn't come in. Fortunately today, I could be completely honest.

"My mom's not here," I said.

"Oh, rats, I'm sorry I missed her," Marcy said. "But it's nice to see you. You're Dakota, right? The younger one?"

"Yes, ma'am."

"I'm sorry I missed your mother," she said. "Is she at the clinic?"

Was this woman going to try to track her down?

"No, she's enrolling my sister in school," I said.

She nodded. "Did your sister decide to go to Fulton?" she said. "It's a good school."

"Actually, Sierra's going to the art academy downtown," I admitted.

"That's wonderful. I'm so happy for her," Marcy said. "That will be a really fine place for your sister. There's lot of individual attention and a real appreciation for the nontypical child."

"Yeah, well Sierra is that," I told her.

She chuckled. "Do I detect a little sibling rivalry?" she asked. "You are certainly far from ordinary yourself. Just in a different way, I think."

I shrugged. "She's the beauty, I'm the brains."

"My goodness, who told you something silly like that?" she asked. "I think your sister seems very smart in her own way. And you are very pretty."

"Oh, thanks."

"Your mother told me that you look like your father and Sierra acts like your father," Marcy said. "And I believe she mentioned that he was both smart and handsome."

"Yeah, I guess so," I said. "But Sierra looks like Mom and I...I guess I act like Mom."

Marcy smiled at me and reached out to touch my cheek. I was surprised by the gesture. People didn't touch me. Affection was never all that readily available outside of home.

"You are like your mom, I think," Marcy said. "You're the young girl she might have been if her own mother had loved her as much as she loves you."

That was a weird idea. I was uncomfortable with it. I guess Marcy could see that; she changed the subject.

"So Dawn and Sierra went downtown," she said. "When do you register for your school?"

"In public school you just show up," I explained from vast experience. "If you live in the district, they have to take you. They'll send for your records and all that stuff afterward. But for private school, you've got to get accepted. Sierra really wants to go. And this is the last day to get in."

"Today's the last day to register?" Marcy laughed. "I would have suspected that your mom would be the type to leave things to the last minute."

It sounded like that might be a criticism, but Marcy said it so nicely, smiling at the same time, that I could hardly imagine that she meant anything bad.

"I don't know when they'll be back," I said.

"It doesn't matter," Marcy said. "You can give these forms to her for me, can't you?"

"Sure."

"When I got her message on my phone this morning, I just had to rush over here and hand over the paperwork myself," she said.

"Mom called you?"

"Yes, she's decided to take part in the CAVA training session next week," Marcy said. "That's not a commitment or an obligation of any kind, of course. We want all our volunteers to know exactly what they're getting into before they join up with us. We think the training sessions are structured well enough to give them that insight."

"My mom is taking training to volunteer with foster kids?"

Marcy nodded, obviously pleased. "And I know she'll be great at it," she said. "She has a wonderful rapport with young people and a very genuine understanding, not only of the system, but how it feels to be tied up in it."

"Mom doesn't like to remember all that," I said.

"The harder you try to forget something," Marcy said, "the more it stays in your mind. I knew Dawn was one of us the moment I set eyes on her. It's something about that stubborn chin, I think."

When Marcy left, I when went back in the house. Vern was in his study. I could see he was engrossed in something, but I decided to bother him anyway.

"That was the woman from CAVA," I told him.

He glanced up. "She hasn't given up on Dawn yet, huh?"

"Mom's agreed to do the volunteer training," I said.

Vern turned away from the computer at that. He raised his eyebrows and shook his head.

"I'm surprised," he said.

"Me, too."

I walked over and sat down in the leather chair.

Neither of us said anything for a minute or so. I guess we were just trying to take it all in.

"What do you think it means?" I asked.

"I suppose it means your mother is planning to stay awhile," he said. "Although I guess we knew that she'd be here at least until the treatment series is complete."

"Yeah, I guess so."

"And I think it means she's feeling better," Vern said. "This might be an interim stage to getting back into the workforce. She might be testing her stamina."

"Yeah."

We continued to sit there, privately speculating.

"Do you think that school is going to take Sierra?" I asked him.

He looked up at me. "Maybe," he said. "I don't know. They may already have all their vacancies filled. I'm sure they do take on kids whose parents don't pay. But there is probably a qualifying process for that, maybe even a waiting list."

I nodded.

"Just don't get your hopes up," he said.

"It's not my hopes," I told him. "I don't even care if Sierra's disappointed, though I'm sure we'll have to hear about it for eons to come. I just hate for Mom to go out in the world, thinking she can change things and finding out that she can't."

Slowly Vern nodded.

"Some things just can't be changed," he said.

"I know," I told him with a sigh.

There were so many things in my life that I wish could be changed. I felt a momentary sadness that was almost overwhelming. But it was immediately followed by a rush of optimism.

"Maybe it's like fractals," I said hopefully. "If we just alter the equation a little bitty bit, it makes all the difference."

Vern's expression was an unspoken question.

"Mom got cancer so she came back here," I explained. "So we had to meet you and that alters the equation. Maybe the outcome will be different now, it'll look totally different. Isn't that what I learned about chaos theory? You change the equation and it all comes out totally different."

Vern frowned. "That's only half of it," he said.

"Half of what?"

"Half of chaos theory, maybe not even half, it's a portion of the theory. Perhaps not even the most important portion."

"So what's important?" I asked.

He hesitated, thoughtfully gathering his words. "Let me see if I can explain it. Try to get it down to a nutshell," he said. "Chaos theory is really misnamed."

"What do you mean?"

"It's really not about chaos," he said. "It's about order. But when it was discovered, they didn't know that. A meteorologist named Edward Lorenz was working on the problem of weather prediction. He tried to model weather on a computer. It made sense that if you put in the many variables with the correct data that the computer could reasonably be expected to come up with a close assumption on the weather."

"But it didn't work," I said.

"No, it didn't. It wasn't even close," Vern said. "It

was like the fractals. The slightest change in the equation, a degree of temperature or a knot of wind, made a vast difference in the outcome."

"Yeah, you explained all that to me," I told him. "It's the butterfly effect."

"Right, sensitivity to initial conditions is chaos. But that's not the end of it," Vern said. "That's the part that intrigues people, but it's useless without the rest of the theory. What Lorenz eventually realized, along with May and Mandelbrot, Koch and other pioneers of this science, was that this was a new way of looking at order. In all of scientific history we only knew two kinds of change. A steady state, where the variables never change, and periodic behavior where a system goes into a loop repeating itself indefinitely. Chaos variables change and they never loop but, over time, on a graph you can show that the presence of chaos actually produces ordered structures and patterns on a larger scale."

"Huh?"

"Lorenz decided to graph his theory on a chaotic system," Vern said. "He used a water wheel."

"What's a water wheel?"

"It's like that big mill at Pigeon Forge, where the water turns the wheel to grind the corn."

"Oh, yeah," I said, remembering the trip to the Dollywood theme park.

"The water pours into the containers or buckets on the wheel's rim. If the stream of water is too slow, the top buckets never fill fast enough to overcome friction and move the wheel," he said. "But if the stream is faster, the weight starts to turn the wheel."

I nodded, recalling how the big wooden wheel

turned on the side of the building, pouring out water as it went along.

"The rotation might become continuous," Vern said. "That's what you'd want on a water wheel. But if the stream is running too rapidly the buckets might fill too fast. That can make them swing all the way around and up the other side. If it did, the wheel might slow, stop and reverse its rotations, turning first one way and then the other. The uncertainty of the speed of the water makes it a perfect chaotic system."

"Okay."

"Lorenz decided to put the equations for this on a graph to show that it was neither steady nor periodic," Vern said. "He wanted to show that it was a whole new type of change, a change that couldn't be predicted."

"That makes sense," I said.

"It does," Vern agreed. "It made sense to Lorenz, too, but something surprising happened. Let me see if I can get a picture of his graph."

Vern turned to the computer and Googled *Lorenz Attractor*. He quickly sorted through the first citations and clicked on one that brought up a three-dimensional image of a half-folded spiral.

"It didn't matter that all the points on the graph were different, that each shift in the equation resulted in a vastly different outcome; as more and more points were noted down on the graph, a clear pattern emerged. It stayed on the curve, a double spiral. No matter how far away or how close it diverged, this pattern remained. It never repeats, but it definitely shows order."

I looked at the Lorenz Attractor on the screen. It was a beautiful fractal, as pretty as any I'd created. But, I could see what Vern was saying. It really didn't seem random, accidental, easily manipulated or vulnerable at all.

"No matter how arbitrary a system appears to be, if taken in a large enough context, a pattern emerges. It's not the steady change or the periodic change that we're most familiar with, but it is just as definitive."

"I'm not sure I understand," I told him.

Vern nodded. "I'm not sure yet that any of us do," he said. "Mandelbrot looked at coastlines. A map of a coastline will show many bays. Measuring the length of a coastline off a map will miss minor bays that were too small. Or walking along the coastline misses microscopic bays in between grains of sand. No matter how much a coastline is magnified, there will be more bays visible if it's magnified more."

"So the fact that each time you magnify you get more, that's a pattern," I said.

"That's how it seems," he said. "The applications of chaos theory are infinite—seemingly random systems produce quite detectable patterns of irregularity."

"Wow," I said.

Vern nodded. "Wow, indeed. What seems to be emerging in scientific thought is that a universe of disorder is, in its way, ordered. A small change in the equation of a chaotic system can cause a drastically different outcome. But at some level, that outcome is negligible to the overall pattern of the system."

"So what appears to us as chaos, is actually order," I said.

He nodded.

"And there are philosophers and social scientists who take that theory into a real-world example," Vern continued. "They would say that a family is a chaotic system because if you have a tiny problem or a huge problem, either can make dramatic changes in the life of that family. But perhaps, just perhaps, that doesn't really have that much effect in the ultimate destiny of those persons."

I thought about that for a long moment before I spoke.

"So Mom will stay here, or she won't," I said. "And Sierra will either get into the art school, or she won't. But somehow everything will work out like it's supposed to."

"Maybe," he said. "Maybe that's it exactly." Vern sighed heavily and then smiled at me. "Or maybe we could help."

He reached over and started flipping through the phone book. He ran his finger down a page and then picked up the phone and dialed a number. It was a half a minute before anyone answered.

"Hello, this is Vernon Leland," he said. "Does James Palmer still teach there? He's headmaster? Great, could I talk to him, please?"

Vern turned to look at me as he waited. "This has to be our secret," he said.

I nodded mutely.

"Jim, hi, it's Vern Leland," he said and then paused. "Yeah, we're doing fine, fine. How's Rosalee and the boys?"

Vern listened to the other end of the line, smiling nodding.

"Is Clint still thinking of MIT?" he asked and then waited for a response. "Well, tell him when he gets to the point that he needs reference letters, I'd be happy to write one."

The guy on the other end of the line apparently tried to refuse such a generous offer.

"No, really. I'd be delighted," Vern insisted.

There was a lot more talk from the other guy. He was telling some story about his son, I guessed. Vern laughed out loud at one point and philosophized about raising children.

"Actually I'm calling to ask a favor," Vern told him, finally getting to the point. "My little granddaughter, Sonny's oldest girl, has moved back to town with her mother."

That bombshell evoked a certain amount of surprise.

"Yeah, it's great," Vern assured him. "Anyway, she's got her heart set on attending the arts academy."

It seemed like that pleased the guy, as well.

"The problem I have is that her mother won't hear of me paying for her school," he said. "Do you think that I could set up some kind of anonymous donor situation where I could take care of her tuition and supplies and her mother not be aware of where that's coming from?"

The discussion for that seemed to go on forever.

"Yeah, I know it's the last day," Vern said. "Her name is Sierra Leland. She and her mother are down there right now applying for admission."

More listening.

"If you could, I'd really, really appreciate it."

When he hung up the phone, Vern turned to give me a big grin. "It's probably not going to change the world," he said, "but your sister is in."

# SONNY DAYS
## 32

━━►◄━━

Sonny went to work with the Brotherhood of Timber Workers. The national organization had so little hope for widespread unionization that they put very little pressure on him, so Sonny was able to devote his energies to things that were important to him. Mainly he focused on workplace safety issues and he made some headway. The union certainly didn't have the authority to shut a site down and they didn't have enough members to pose any sort of effective work stoppage, but just being there made supervisors less willing to put up with risks and gave them an excuse to be more proactive with company administration.

It was a surprise to Sonny how much he liked the work he did. The job didn't pay that well and didn't utilize much of his education and skills, but he began his workday eager and enthusiastic. That counted for a lot.

It counted for a lot even with Dawn, who found that her days as a stay-at-home mom were behind her. Her wages as a Case Assistant were now required every month for keeping up with the mortgage and paying the bills.

She continued to pursue her education. But her sights were higher now and progress was slow. She'd decided that she wanted to get a master's in social work, qualifying her for top leadership jobs in the department. But the graduate program at the university was a full two years past the B.S. degree. And taking one course a semester was not a lot.

"At this rate, it's going to take me fifteen years," she complained to Sonny.

He nodded. "If you want me to take on more of the responsibilities for the girls," he said, "I will."

She shook her head. "They're growing up so fast," she said. "I want to be there. I want to be with them." Dawn sighed.

"I could take on a second job," Sonny suggested. "Then maybe you could quit work and devote yourself to school full-time."

"No, I like my job," Dawn insisted. "I'd miss it if I quit and I've learned things that they just don't teach in class."

"That's probably true," he admitted.

"I guess I just want everything," she said.

Sonny laughed.

"And you deserve it," he said. "I wish I could give it to you."

She grinned at him. "You've given me everything I ever wanted," Dawn told him. "And you've taught me to want more."

"So it's all my fault, huh?"

"Absolutely," she teased.

Despite their struggles and the constant stress of living paycheck to paycheck, Sonny would have described their life as happy.

The girls were in elementary school. As different as sisters could be. Sierra was a little social butterfly, flitting through the world with a thousand friends and a complete grasp on the personal lives of each and every one of them. Which she generously shared around the dinner table most evenings whether the rest of her family was interested or not.

She'd chatter about whose parents or grandparents were divorcing. Which moms were having babies. Hairdo comparisons of all the female teachers. And which clothes, bags, shoes and school supplies were cool and which were not.

Dakota, on the other hand, was a top student and endlessly curious. Sonny found her grasp of science amazing. They went on rock hound expeditions. Experimented with backyard garden plants. And speculated about mummies and dinosaurs for hours on end. Her love of library visits rivaled his own.

Their differences created a natural amount of sibling stress. There were frequent exchanges of catty remarks. Occasional rows and tantrums. Territorial disputes and accusations of favoritism on both sides. But the two girls cared for each other and had a basic underlying security in their parents' love and respect. That seemed to carry them through the worst of sisterly strife.

Dawn and Sonny were proud of both their children. They applauded their strengths. Helped them make the best of their weaknesses. And managed it all with patience and good humor mixed with parental pride.

As the years progressed, family life got more hectic. There were piano lessons and science club projects. The girls played soccer. Neither were exceptionally good at it. But Sonny coached and they both wanted to be on their daddy's team.

The winters brought basketball games and snowy mountain weekends. The summers were about hiking in Cades Cove and trips to Norris Lake.

The spring that Vern took retirement caught Sonny slightly off guard. He knew that time was passing, that his children were growing, but somehow he'd been lulled into a feeling that his world was stable, that nothing would change. But, of course, change is inevitable.

"It's not like things are perfect," he told his father over a game of chess. "I don't make enough money to really support my family the way I should. Dawn's still trying to eke out a college career one class at a time. Sierra probably won't even be able to go to college if she doesn't start making better grades. Dakota is way too observant and she's sensitive. I worry about how she'll get by if life ever gets tough for her."

Vern nodded.

"But our life is so good," Sonny said. "It's so good, I feel guilty about it. I feel desperate to hang on to it. I don't want anything to affect it."

"I know," his father told him. "I've been there. I've been exactly where you are."

"And?"

"It's a golden time," Vern said. "There are blocks in every life that are that way."

"How can I keep it this way?"

"You can't," Vern told him. "You've got to enjoy it while it's happening. Try not to rush through it or waste it. But you can't cling to it, either. If you cling to it, the gold turns to ashes and you've got nothing to hold on to."

"Are you sure about that?"

"Yes," Vern told him. "When you were here with us, our boy, almost grown, almost a man, you were everything that we wanted in a son. You were our life and we were so proud." He smiled as if just the memory evoked pleasure for him. "Phrona and I were living that golden time. Can you imagine now how she felt when Dawn, an outsider, tried to come and steal it from her?"

Sonny hesitated a moment, thinking, remembering.

"Is that what it was like?" he asked.

"Yes, that was it exactly," Vern said. "I know it looked as if she was a snob about Dawn's background. That she was unwelcoming and unfair. But Phrona was just trying to hang on to her golden time. And that insistence could have easily separated her from you and your family indefinitely."

Sonny nodded thoughtfully.

"So what do we do?" he asked.

"You enjoy life as it comes," Vern said. "You have to recognize that everything is temporary, but have confidence that ultimately it comes around again."

It was good advice.

Shortly after that conversation, Dawn and Sonny had Paul and Tonya over for a backyard barbeque. Paul was still with the company. He'd gotten a couple of great promotions and now had lots of responsibility and was making fabulous money.

Their son was an active toddler and Tonya was pregnant again. She sat in a lawn chair, making jokes about walking blimps and swallowing basketballs. Sierra and Dakota, both feeling like little mothers at age nine and ten, entertained the curly-haired two year old.

The kids were having a great time, fully occupied with each other. The talk among the adults was light-hearted and family oriented. Tonya finally called her husband to task.

"Paul," she said. "Are you going to show Sonny the drawings that you brought or are you planning to chicken out?"

Her husband flushed slightly.

"What drawings?" Sonny asked him.

Paul hesitated for only a moment, glancing at his wife. "You know that accident a few months ago where the guy was killed when the feller buncher tipped over on the steep grade?"

Sonny nodded. "Prescott Ornsby," he said. "The guy was a loudmouth, not always the most popular man at the logging site. But his ex-wife depended on his child support for three kids."

"I was at a site not that far away," Paul said. "As a company administrator, they paged me and had me go over to the accident scene to represent management."

"That's good," Sonny said. "I think it helps everybody if top brass doesn't pretend that nothing is happening."

"Yeah," Paul said. "It was my first experience with anything like that. And I have to say, it affected me."

Sonny nodded.

"I came home that night and I talked to Tonya about it," he said. "And she talked about her father and her family's experience." He paused. "It was good to talk, but I couldn't quite get the memory of it out of my mind. I'm a engineer, really. I can do the corporate thing, but I think about things in terms of mechanisms."

"Yeah."

"I kept thinking about the accident and I came up with an idea for a better stabilizing system for the feller buncher," he said.

Sonny eye's widened and his mouth broadened into a smile. "That's great!"

"I thought so, too," he said. "But I couldn't get anybody at the company interested in it. I thought they could take it, get a team to work on it, maybe present it to the equipment company as something we'd like to have added to our machines."

"I don't think it will go that way," Sonny said.

"It hasn't," Paul admitted. "I couldn't generate even a wisp of interest in anybody."

"They won't want to add more cost to their equipment," Sonny said. "Even if it theoretically would save lives, it wouldn't be proven and it would hurt the bottom line."

"But I think it would work better," Paul said.

"Then you've got to sell it to the equipment company and let them sell it to the users," Sonny said.

"Why would the equipment company want to retool and make their old equipment obsolete?" Paul asked.

"They won't," Sonny told him. "Innovation isn't easy. But if we can show that the technology is safer, we can get affected groups to insist upon implementing it."

"You mean like the union," he said.

Sonny nodded. "The union, the insurers of the company, the insurers of the equipment makers. If you build a better mousetrap and you refuse to use it because of cost concerns, then your culpability, if overrun by mice, goes way up."

The two men spent the next hours with the draft drawing spread out on the dining room table. Tonya and Dawn ended up cooking the hot dogs and burgers. The guys could barely be bothered to eat.

"I knew it was going to be like this," Tonya said as she handed Sonny a juicy burger on a bun. "I knew if you guys started talking about it, Dawn and I would finally get some time to ourselves."

They all laughed at her joke. The guys tried to be a bit more sociable, but were ultimately given permission to talk shop.

By the end of the evening, Sonny had agreed to try to help Paul get some of the connections he'd need to build the new stabilizer and check it out.

"So are you and Paul now in business together?" Dawn asked as they crawled into bed that night.

Sonny's mind was still in a whirl, going in a hundred different directions. Paul's drawings, in their way, presented the newest, most exciting challenge he'd faced since he'd given up his forestry career to work for the union.

"I guess we are," he said. "Don't get your hopes up, Dawn. Things that work on paper don't always work in the real world. And there are lots of hurdles before this thing has even a chance of becoming a staple of logging machinery."

Dawn laughed. "I don't care if it works or doesn't work," she said. "I'm just happy to see you doing something new and exciting. It's good to have you thinking about something that might really make a difference instead of constantly having to plow into paperwork and politics."

She was right about that. It did seem good.

# REAL LIFE
## 33

—▶ ◀—

School started that year as it had every other year. New place, new people, new problems to overcome. I had started so many new schools, faced so many new teachers and classmates, I could hardly even work up a sweat about it anymore. I made a point of joining the Science Club. I knew that's where I'd find any geeky friends I might make. And I tried not to get too comfortable in my classes. I knew as soon as my records from my former schools showed up, I'd probably be moved to a Gifted and Talented curriculum.

Del took Spence and me to school and picked us up. That really was kind of cool. I'd had my mom's boyfriends around before. But I'd never wanted any of them to be mistaken for my dad.

Of course, there were kids who thought that Spence was my little brother. But that wasn't so bad, either. I'd decided that he was really all right for a guy so young. At school there was almost no opportunity to see each other. We had different classes, different lunches, different areas of the building. And after school it was easy for me to hang with him, even if he was a sixth grader.

For one thing, Spence had his own issues. He'd gone to Dogwood Elementary, in his mom's neighborhood. All his school friends were going to middle school over there. But he was at Whittle Springs with me.

"It's not like I'm a problem to Mom and Wiktor," he told me. "I'm really helpful there. And when the baby comes, I could be even more helpful."

I nodded, sure that it was true.

"Your dad is really cool, Spence," I told him. "Why don't you want to stay with him?"

"I do," he said. "I do want to stay with him. But not because I can't stay with my mom."

We were waiting at the curb as the long line of cars took turns parking in the loading zone to pick up kids.

"That sounds like some kind of messed-up control thing," I told him. "Your mom is doing what she thinks is best. Like it or not, it's what's going on in your life. You've just got to deal."

"I know, I know," he said, sighing. "I am being weird, but I can't seem to help it."

"Are you unhappy?"

He shook his head. "Not really, I like being with my dad. I'm glad I'm over here. It's great having a best friend next door."

"Hey, thanks," I told him.

"I just wish I had more say in what happens," Spence said. "It's my life and I don't get much input."

I was sympathetic. "I used to feel the same way about my mom," I told him. "I'd just be getting settled and comfortable and then one day, without so much as a *whaddayathink*, I'd come home to find that we were absolutely out of there and moving on."

"It's crappy being a kid," Spence said.

I shrugged. "I think it's not so different for the adults, either," I told him. "It's not like they're really

in control of anything. Stuff happens to them that
they don't want or expect. My dad got killed. My
mom got cancer. They didn't pick those things."

"My parents picked divorce," Spence said.

"Do you really think so? You said they fought all
the time."

He nodded. "Yeah, they did."

"So maybe they couldn't do anything else," I said.
"Do you wish that the divorce never happened?"

"Of course I wish that," Spence said adamantly
and then backed off. "I also like Wiktor and I see
how happy he and my mom are. And Dad's free to
do the work he likes without having to worry about
buying some huge, expensive house or paying for a
country club membership. I like how things have
turned out, but I can't help wishing it was that other
life, as well."

Del's car pulled up to a stop and we grabbed our
book bags and headed for it.

Spence shook his head and sighed heavily. "I'm
just confused," he told me.

I understood that. I was confused myself.

Mom had started her volunteer training for
CAVA. Her plan was to ride back and forth to the
downtown office on the city bus with Sierra. That
was a good plan. Except Sierra didn't want to do it
quite that way. She wanted to take the bus over to
Seth's neighborhood, so they could ride to school together. That added a full half hour to the trip. And a
half hour was a lot for Mom.

She talked Sierra into sacrificing the morning ride.
Mom was going to do the afternoon on her own.

Vern didn't like Mom traveling on her own so he

picked her up in the afternoons. He really wanted Mom to succeed at this. He thought it was important. I wasn't so sure. What difference did it make if she did a job that nobody paid her for?

Vern and Phrona really encouraged her. So I figured they understood something about it that I didn't.

Anyway, I could see that it was good for Mom having someplace to go every morning. I could also see that she didn't always feel quite up to it, but she went anyway.

She also continued to see Del. He took her out on a date nearly every weekend. And he came over to see her several nights a week. They'd sit on the porch or the patio and talk about nothing. Spence and I put the Nature Sounds Receiver on them several times, but it was never anything worth listening to. He talked about his job and she talked about CAVA and occasionally they said something about one of us kids. But mostly it was more interesting for Spence and me to just talk to each other.

I got home in the afternoons before anyone else. I'd put my books up, change into some jeans and a T-shirt and usually do homework while the house was still quiet. Mostly Phrona was home. Sometimes she'd be puttering around the kitchen. Others she'd be tending her plants. But most usually, she'd be in her office doing genealogy.

After homework I'd sit out in the office and listen to her. She had so many stories. There was not a smidgeon of the American past that her family or the Leland family hadn't had a part in. Her stories really brought my dry, old middle school history book to life. I'd never really been fascinated with history. It just seemed like a lot of reading, but now it was like I knew people who lived back then.

Mostly I just knew Lemuel and Essie. I kept searching for evidence of them, state after state.

It was the first chilly day of fall. Phrona had the heater on in the office. The room was small enough that it didn't take that much to get the chill out of the air.

"I'm going to run into the kitchen a put on a big kettle of stew," she told me. "And I'll stir up some corn bread. Stew isn't much good without corn bread. Do you want to come with me?" she asked.

I shook my head. I still wasn't a great fan of kitchen duty. Phrona was really exacting and she knew how things ought to be done, but she never made me do any of the really boring work.

"I'm almost finished with the census records," I told her. "I might as well get that done and then...well, at least we'll know we were wrong about that."

"Okay, then I'll be back in a half hour," she told me.

I had just turned my attention to looking through North Carolina records when the phone rang.

Phrona hadn't had time to get to the house yet and when she didn't pick it up, I did.

"Hello."

"Oh, hello," the voice said on the other end of the line. "This is Mildred."

"Hi."

"Is this Dakota?"

"Yes, ma'am."

"And how are you doing, sweetie? How is school? Are you making friends?"

"Uh, well, I'm fine," I answered. "School's good. There's lots of kids."

"That's wonderful. That's wonderful. What are you up to this afternoon?"

"I'm looking at some census records online," I said.

"Oh, that is so dear," Mildred said. "Your grandma told me that you were helping with her genealogy work."

"Yeah."

"So how is your mother? Is she still volunteering? How about that chemo? How many more of those treatments is she in for? Is your grandma there? I need to talk to her."

Quickly I sorted through the questions. "My mom is still volunteering. I think she really likes it. She has another two months of chemo, and Phro…and my grandma just went back to the house," I said. "Let me buzz her and she'll pick up."

I hit the little intercom button on the bottom of the phone. A second later, Phrona picked up.

"Hello."

"It's for you, Grandma," I said.

I'd said the word for Mildred, really. It hadn't been for me or for Phrona; it had been for some woman I hardly knew. Yet even after I hung up the phone the sound of my own voice sort of reverberated through my head like some delayed looper of the brain.

Grandma. Grandma. Grandma.

It was a fact of life. That's all it was. Phrona Leland was a line on my family tree. She was my fa-

ther's mother. And whether I was unwilling to give
her that title, filled as it was with all kinds of homey
expectations and mushy cultural baggage, didn't
change it from being so.

I remembered a woman Mom worked with
named Kelly. She had a daughter my age, but she
had her little girl call her by her first name. I'd asked
Mom about it.

"It makes her feel younger."

"I could call you Dawn," I suggested.

She eyed me critically. "Not if you don't want to
spend the rest of your life in time-out," she threatened.

"You don't want to feel younger?"

"Feeling younger can't even compare with how
wonderful it feels to hear the word *mother* and know
that it's meant for me."

I wondered if Phrona, my grandma, might have
felt the same.

I finished North Carolina and was looking
through the records for Kentucky. I was going to do
it.

I was going to start calling her Grandma. All these
people in these genealogy lines, they were all grand-
mas and grandpas, some of them with nine *greats* in
front of that name.

I was going to do it, I decided. I was going to walk
into the kitchen, while she was there cooking. There
would be no one there but just her and me and I'd
call her Grandma. If she didn't like it, I'd know it
right away and it would never happen again.

After a half hour, I marked Kentucky off my list.
I was done. Lemuel and Essie were nowhere. I tried

every state but Tennessee. I should try Tennessee, just to be able to say that I'd looked everywhere.

I pulled up those records, and like every other time, I put in the first of the names. Leland. It yielded hundreds of individuals, many of them I recognized from other parts of the family tree, but not one named Lemuel or Essie. The same with Clafford. Milbanks were even more numerous than the Lelands and Claffords. Finally I put in Medford, Essie's maiden name. It was the last possible choice in the last possible state.

In bright blue letters the citation came up Medford, Lemuel C. Washington County, Jonesborough Township.

It had to be someone else, I quickly reminded myself. Medford was a common family name and Lemuel was typical of the times. There is no way that this could be *my* Essie and Lemuel, living less than a hundred miles from their families. Just two counties over from ruin and scandal.

I pulled up the actual text. The long brown leger pages that had been carried from house to house and from farm to farm had been laid flat and photographed. The families were listed only in the order of their interviews and indexed only to the page. So I had to read down a long list of head-of-household names written in crisp readable letters.

I was more than halfway down the page when I found it. Lemuel C. Medford, head of household. Age forty-two. Occupation: merchant. Beneath his name was Essie, age thirty-nine, a housewife.

"Oh my God, oh my God!" I said aloud.

Below Essie's entry were the couple's two children. A son, Clafford M. Medford, age thirteen and daughter, Sophrona, age eleven.

"Oh my God!" I continued.

I had to show it to Phrona. I couldn't believe it, but I could. I hit the print button. I stood eagerly, impatiently, waiting for the paper to come out of the machine. It took too long.

"Come on! Hurry up!" I yelled at the machine.

Finally I had my paper in hand and went running out of the office and back to the house. I burst into the kitchen.

"Grandma, I found them! I found Lemuel and Essie!"

"You did? Well, good for you!"

She quickly wiped her hands on a dish towel and hurried toward me.

"They were alive, just like you thought," I said. "They were using her maiden name."

I handed her the paper.

"Where were they?" she asked.

"They were right here," I told her.

"Here?"

"He was a merchant in Jonesborough."

"For heaven's sake," my grandmother said, shaking her head. "After all that, they came home."

# REAL LIFE
## 34

—▶ ◀—

It was gray and blustery the day I came from school to find nobody. Both the Dodge and the Saab were gone. I wasn't worried. I figured Vern had gone downtown to pick up Mom, and Phrona had to run to the grocery store or something.

Nobody was home next door, either. Spence's little brother was three days old and had come home from the hospital that morning. He and Del had headed over to his mom's house in Sequoyah Hills to say hi.

I unlocked the door and Rocky came trotting toward me.

"Looks like it's just you and me, guy," I told him.

I went ahead with my normal routine, expecting someone to show up soon. I changed clothes, played with Rocky a few minutes and sat down to do my homework. I was done except for my composition essay. I saved it for last so that I could take my time and not feel rushed. I wanted to say something about the chaos theory and why it was just beginning to be understood, by me and the whole rest of the world. We'd written our thesis statement in class. I thought mine was good.

*As an instrument of exploration, the computer is to*

*chaos theory what the telescope has been to the under-standing of astronomy.*

This probably wasn't going to be the easiest subject to try to explain. The girl who sat next to me was writing on why cheerleaders should be able to letter in their sport like other high school athletes. Her boyfriend, who sat behind her, was postulating that golden retrievers were the best friends among man's best friend. Science was never the easy choice, but it was always interesting to me. And there was the added benefit that the English teacher rarely had a clue of what I was talking about, so I never got graded on what I said, only how I said it.

The front doorbell rang.

My first thought was to ignore it. Then I remembered that I was the only one in the house. Rocky met me in the hall to check it out.

I looked through the peephole and saw an old man standing on the porch. He wasn't anybody that I recognized. But he didn't look like he was selling anything, either. He was a tall guy, pretty muscular to be so old. He was wearing striped overalls and a bright orange cap. I opened the door.

"Hi," I said.

He smiled at me. He had a great big smile that took over his whole face, making his eyes sort of disappear in the creases of it.

"Well, hi there, yourself," he said. "This is the Leland place, right?"

"Yes, it is," I answered.

He looked at me closely. "You're one of Sonny's little girls," he said. "You look just like your daddy."

"Thank you," I said, and then wondered if that was the right response.

"Are you the younger sister or the older?" he asked.

"The younger," I said. "I'm Dakota."

"Ah...then I guess we haven't met. Is your mama around?" he asked.

I shook my head. "She's not here," I told him.

Just then the dog pushed his way past me and rushed up to the man, jumping up and down, tongue hanging out and tail wagging.

"Well, hello, boy," the man said. "You're a happy guy, huh." He let the dog stand up paws at this knees. He rubbed him behind the ears with both hands. "Is this Rocky?"

"Uh...yeah. You know Rocky?"

"I do, but I wouldn't have recognized him," he said. "He looks a lot different from that little puppy your dad picked up at the pound."

"You knew my dad?"

The man was still playing with the dog, but he glanced over at me with a warm smile.

"Sonny and I were friends," he said, simply.

I would never have suspected that. The guy was closer to Vern's age than Sonny Leland's.

Rocky was calmer now, just sitting at the man's feet, wagging his tail.

"I'm really sorry I missed Dawn," he said. "Would you tell her that I came by?"

"You know my mom, too?"

He nodded. "A long time ago. I didn't know she was back in town," the man said. "My daughter works in the courthouse and recognized her name on a volunteer list. I came as soon as I heard."

"We've been here all summer," I told him.

"That's good," he said. "Please tell her that I came by. I'll try to catch her another day."

"Okay."

He started down the steps. Somehow I didn't want to let him go.

"Wait! You didn't tell me your name."

"Oh, yeah, my name's Beale, Lonnie Beale."

"And you were a friend of my dad," I said.

"Yes," he said. "Sonny Leland was the best friend a man could have. He saved my life."

"He what?"

"He saved my life," Lonnie said. "Didn't your mother tell you about how he died?"

I walked out on the porch, shutting the door behind me.

"She said he died in a logging accident."

"And that's all you know?" Lonnie asked.

I shook my head. "I read the report."

"Report?"

"The OSHA report on the accident," I said. "A friend of mine found it on the Internet."

"The Internet?" Lonnie shook his head in disbelief. "Now that's a strange place for a girl to learn about her dad."

I shrugged. "I think it hurts my mom to talk about it," I told him.

He nodded slowly as he thought about that. "I'm sure it does."

"It's not fair, really," I told him. "He's my dad. I need to know what happened."

"I guess that's true," Lonnie said. "But I understand what your mother is thinking. It's easier to talk about the good times, the happy times, when they were alive. My wife died almost twenty years ago now. It's her life I want to share with my children, not her death."

"But you wouldn't mind if somebody else told them," I said.

"No, I guess not."

I sat down in the glider and offered him a seat beside me. "Tell me about my dad," I said. "Tell me how he saved your life."

Lonnie looked at me thoughtfully for a moment and then climbed the porch steps a second time. He sat down. Rocky scooted up close and lay his snout on the cushion beside Lonnie's hand. With a little chuckle the man began to pet him again.

I waited. I didn't even know what question to ask.

"I met Sonny when he came to work on my crew," Lonnie said. "He was a good kid, smart, hardworking. All the things that a boss looks for and a friend admires."

I nodded.

"I knew a bit about what was going on in his life," he said. "He was a happy, optimistic guy, though I knew that he'd had to drop out of college to support a young wife and a baby."

"Did you meet my mom then, too?"

Lonnie nodded.

"Sonny was crazy about her," he said. "And she felt the same about him. They were very different, but I think they brought out the best in each other."

"She loved him," I said.

It wasn't a question but he answered it anyway.

"Yes, I know that she did," Lonnie said. "And he knew that she did."

"How did he save your life?" I asked.

He hesitated for a moment, almost as if he didn't want to remember. Then he laid a hand on the bib front of his overalls like he was touching his heart.

"It was the day he died," he said solemnly. "It was a dark day, not wet, but gray. That's how it all seems in my memory, very gray. We were out near Burke's Ridge cutting some trees on a hillside. We'd been around that area for three weeks or more."

"The report said there was another crew cutting too close."

Lonnie nodded. "Technically the crews weren't breaking any rules," he said. "But all the loggers knew that we were working too close. So we stopped simultaneous cutting."

"What does that mean?"

"It means we let that team fell trees on their side while we waited," he said. "Once they had some of theirs on the ground, then we'd cut while they waited. It makes the day longer, but we thought it was safer."

"But it wasn't."

He shook his head. "Sometimes things just go wrong," he said. "You can't figure out the why, you can't find the mistake. You don't know who to blame."

"What happened?"

"We were just standing around," he said. "A feller from the other crew was topping out a tree. By everything that we know about cutting trees, and we know a lot, it should have fallen straight down, but it didn't."

"Why not?"

Lonnie shook his head. "Some speculated that the

cut was miscalculated. Other people thought there might have been a gust of wind," he said. "But I heard it. It cracked wrong. It was a rogue and there's no way to predict that."

"What's a rogue?"

"It's a tree that's not right, it's not like other trees," he said. "Maybe when it was a sapling or even a seedling, something happened. It made the grain run differently or form a weakness. It's like an invisible defect in a plant that was probably fifty years in the making. Completely undetectable until something happens."

"And that was the day something happened," I said.

"Yes, when the cut was made, it was almost as if the tree threw the top into standing trees," he said. "The speed and the weight broke limbs on a half-dozen trees as it came down. One of those limbs came right where we were standing."

"So the limb landed on my dad," I said.

Lonnie nodded. "It was actually worse than that," he said. "I wouldn't give you the details, except that you can't understand what happened without them."

"Tell me."

"As it came down, the jagged edge of the limb came right at us, like a giant spear," he said. "It landed exactly where I stood."

He stopped talking for a moment and just stared into space as if he were seeing it all once again.

"It should have killed me," he said quietly. "It would have killed me. But at the instant before it landed, not even a second, much less than that, Sonny Leland stepped in front of me."

I was speechless.

"I've gone over that a billion times in my memory," he said. "I've tried to understand if he did it accidentally or instinctively or if it was a deliberate choice to give his life for mine."

"Which is it?"

Lonnie shook his head.

"Did he leave us on purpose?" I asked.

"Sonny had a lot to live for," the man said. "He had a wife who loved and needed him. Two little girls who would never really know their daddy. And his whole young life ahead of him. I don't believe he wanted to die."

"So it was just some quirk of fate?"

"I don't know," he said. "I guess I'll never know. And I've decided that it doesn't matter. It happened the way that it did. What it means for me is that I need to live my life as if it were worth being saved. I've tried to do that. I continue to try every day."

My dad had died for this man. It was hard to get my mind around it.

"I have six children," Lonnie said. "They lost their mother when they were very young. Of course, they all know the story about how Sonny Leland saved my life. They've always empathized with you and your sister. We all know it hasn't been easy for you."

He reached over with a tender gesture and rubbed my head.

"I just wanted to tell you and your mother and sister, that on behalf of myself and my family, we thank you for the sacrifice you've had to make."

I nodded, still not sure exactly how I felt.

"Thanks for coming and telling me," I said.

Lonnie nodded.

We sat there in silence for several moments. He was remembering. I was imagining.

"I have a scar," he said finally.

"A scar?"

"Yes…." He hesitated. "I told you the limb came at us like a spear. It went right through Sonny's body and into my own."

I looked up quickly, his words startled me. I could tell instantly that he regretted being so honest, but it was too late.

"A doctor told me later that it was very quick," he assured me. "So quick, Sonny probably never felt anything."

There was some comfort in that.

"This probably won't make any sense to you," he said. "But when I touch the scar on my chest, I'm aware that it's the place where his body and mine were fused together as he died."

I tried to imagine what it had been like. I tried to imagine a limb falling like a spear. I tried to imagine my father and this man fused together for the last instant of his life. It was hard to imagine.

"May I see it?" I asked him.

I was surprised at my own question.

"The scar? If you want to," he said.

I nodded.

Lonnie unhooked the bib of his overalls and opened his shirt. There on a chest sparsely covered with hair was a jagged road map of healed flesh.

He ran his huge, age-toughened hand along the lines.

Tentatively, I reached out and touched the marks

on Lonnie's chest. It was the closest I'd ever been to my father in my whole life.

There were tears of loss and somehow of joy, as well.

"Thank you," I said finally as I pulled my hand away.

"I'm so sorry, little one," Lonnie said, quietly. "He was a good man. You would have loved him. I know he already loved you."

Those were ordinary, typical words for the comfort of the family. But I knew, somehow, that Lonnie meant them in a way that no one else ever could.

We sat silently together for a long time.

Eventually, we began to converse again. Lonnie told me stories about my dad on the job. His perceptions of the young Sonny and Dawn. The hopes and dreams of a man I would never know. We talked about happier times, things my dad had said. Even words that he'd had for me that morning.

"You were the last thing we talked about," he said. "You were only weeks away and he was anxious to meet you."

"I wish he had," I told him. "All my life, I wish he had."

The man nodded.

I was grateful to Lonnie for talking about everything. For talking to me about my dad. For telling me the truth about the accident. For trying to live his life so that it was worthy of my dad's sacrifice. Which, I guess, was my sacrifice, too.

That was the strangest part. He had stepped in front of Lonnie. That had changed everything for all of us.

I said goodbye.

"I won't be a stranger," he promised in his country way of speech. "I'll be back to check on you, talk with your mother and sister."

"Thanks."

Rocky and I went back inside the house. I returned to my room and my essay, but I couldn't write. I couldn't think about anything but my dad and what had been said and the scar on Lonnie's chest.

This had been my dad's room. This had been my dad's house. Sonny Leland had been my dad. I didn't want to ever forget that.

From beneath my bed, I dragged out my suitcase. Still wrapped in the old T-shirt was the soccer picture. He looked like me. He was smart like me. Or maybe I was smart like him. I looked like him.

Lonnie wasn't the only one who had a reason to make his life count for something.

"Dakota! Dakota!"

My sister was calling out to me as she came through the front door. There was something in her voice, something that had me racing up the hallway.

We met in the dining room.

"What's wrong?"

"Hurry, come quick," she said. "Vern's waiting in the car outside."

"What's happened?"

"Mom's bad, real bad. They've put her in the hospital."

As I followed her out, I realized I was still holding the soccer photo. I set it on the dining room mantel where it had come from in the first place.

# SONNY DAYS
## 35

━━━ ◆ ━━━

The partnership with Paul was a success so surprising that it almost caught the two inexperienced entrepreneurs off guard. They secured the patent and began to approach people about it. Paul reasonably assumed that the equipment designs would be studied and improved upon a dozen times before a prototype was built. The manufacturer would test market it and if they were lucky, someone would show an interest. Sonny fully expected that no one would show any interest, that they would need to find a political solution to force the safety issue onto the industry.

Neither scenario was what happened.

As soon as it became known that Paul had not just allowed the subject of building a safer feller buncher to drop, that he had, in fact, enlisted the help of Union Representative Sonny Leland, rumors were everywhere.

Although Sonny tried to make it very clear that his interest in Safer Logging Equipment Corporation was personal and had nothing whatsoever to do with his official position in the Brotherhood of Timber Workers, the national office called him.

"Really, it's nothing to do with BTW," he assured them. "I just think this is a great safety innovation and

I'm working on my own time to help get it out there to logging sites."

The union was satisfied with his answer, but they were the only ones. All over the region, logging companies were convinced that Sonny was planning to utilize this opportunity, this spotlight, to lure workers into union membership.

All his protestations to the contrary only served to solidify the falsehood that people wanted to believe.

"I can't figure out if I'm hurting or helping," Sonny admitted to Dawn. "If I'm an impediment to this going forward, then I should just drop out of it. Paul knows he can come to me for advice anytime. I don't have to be a part of this for it to work."

"You'll know when it's time to get out," Dawn assured him. "Just continue to do what you think you should be doing."

Ultimately, that turned out to be the best advice.

A coalition of logging firms wanted to make a deal. If the prototype showed potential to be safer, they would be willing to agree to phase in the new equipment at work sites. But they wanted something in return—Sonny would have to break all ties with the Brotherhood of Timber Workers.

The four of them, Sonny, Dawn, Tonya and Paul discussed the deal across the dining table.

"It's not as if safety isn't an issue for logging firms," Paul said. "They want it safe out there, they just don't want it to cost too much and they want to rack up whatever side benefits they can."

"I'm not sure that I understand all this," Dawn said. "You thought they'd want you to give up your interest in the company, but what they want is for you to give up your job?"

Sonny nodded.

"Apparently," Paul said, "Sonny's made more inroads into unionizing than he thought."

"I've made almost no progress at all," Sonny insisted. "I guess any success is too much."

"So the gentleman's agreement is that Sonny gives up the union and heads our little company," Paul said.

"Are you going to do that?" Dawn asked.

Sonny shrugged. "I don't know," he said. "The truth is, I'm tired of my job. I feel frustrated and I'm ready for a new challenge. But I've been in an adversarial position with the logging industry for years now. Bowing to pressure from them to give it up makes me feel like I'm losing."

"But you wouldn't be losing," Tonya said. "You'd be moving on. And it's not as if that's the end of BTW in Tennessee. The union will hire somebody else. And you'll be free to promote safer equipment. That's what it's always been about for you. Safety."

Sonny nodded.

"It seems like a win-win," Dawn said. "I know that's not as satisfying as an I win-you lose. But what you're going to get if you don't agree is a lose-lose. And the industry will be less safe because of it."

She was right and in the end, he agreed to terminate his relationship with the union. They hired a fiery, young environmental radical just out of college. He wasn't as effective as Sonny in signing up members. Nor was he as approachable among the local loggers. But he was technically brilliant. He knew every law and even the most obscure regulations by heart. He kept the companies running scared, safe and legal, every minute.

Sonny focused his full-time effort on their little start-up company. And with the enthusiasm of the manufacturer and the support of the industry, Safer Logging Equipment Corporation flourished.

Within a year, Paul had given up his day job to devote full-time effort to a newly hired creative team of bright young engineers.

He and Sonny remained cochairmen of the company, but it was Sonny who handled the operations. SLEC quickly became lucrative for both of them.

The increased financial security made some immediate and positive changes in the Leland lifestyle. Dawn, who'd finally managed to get her B.S. degree, was able to quit her job and go to graduate school full-time. They were able to do some careful renovation of the old house they loved. They took some lovely vacations and put money aside for the girls' college education. And when Sierra suddenly got the notion that she wanted to attend the Arts Academy, a private high school downtown, they had the money to pay her tuition.

It was early that year, Sierra's last in middle school, that Dawn got what seemed to her a brilliant idea.

"Let's have another baby," she said one cold winter evening.

"What?"

"I'm not going to be working for the next two years," she said. "If there was ever going to be time for us to have another child, this is it."

"Our girls are going to be fifteen and thirteen," Sonny pointed out.

Dawn shrugged. "Our girls are wonderful," she said. "But don't you want a boy, as well?"

"A boy would be nice," he said. "But he's going to be a lot younger than his sisters."

"That doesn't matter," she said. "We're still young, that's what counts. I'm thirty-four. You're thirty-seven. A lot of people are just having their first child about then."

He knew she was right about that. It seemed that there were two groups of parents. Those who had children in their late teens and those who waited until their midthirties. They decided to do both.

Trying to have a baby was something that they'd never done. But neither would have claimed the experience a hardship. Having frequent sex, they discovered that they had, like many other couples, allowed the everyday bustle and stress of life to keep them at a distance in the bedroom. Close and loving, they were enjoying intimacy together as they hadn't in years.

It was an early Wednesday morning in March when Dawn was getting out of the shower. Sonny was standing in front of the mirror, shaving. She grabbed him from behind in a big hug.

"Hey, you should be careful of a guy with a razor in his hand," he said, laughing.

"Careful has never been my part of my nature," she answered. "That's what you've always loved about me."

He turned, pulling her naked body into his arms.

"How's a guy supposed to go to work when he

has this luscious siren luring him to stay home?" he said.

Dawn laughed.

He was running his hands over her body when he suddenly hesitated.

"What's this?" he asked.

Dawn shrugged and shook her head. "It's some kind of weird pimple or something," she said.

Sonny checked it out. "Do you think you ought to have a doctor look at it?"

She nodded. "I'm going to. I thought I'd wait until... Well, I've been feeling sort of... different, you know," she said, grinning. "The sticks aren't turning blue yet, but I think I may be pregnant."

Sonny laughed, delighted. He lifted her off the floor and twirled her around.

When she got her period the next week, they were both a little disappointed.

"I shouldn't have said anything if it wasn't for certain."

Sonny shook his head. "We'll just have to keep trying. That doesn't seem like a bad deal."

By the next week, she was questioning the home pregnancy tests.

"I'm pregnant," she told him. "Period or not, that's all it can be. I crave chocolate like a fiend. I'm eating a half-dozen candy bars a day and I could eat more if I let myself. And do you know what's happened, I've lost five pounds! If you lose weight on an all-candy diet you've got to be PG. Next stop, morning sickness."

The next stop was actually the doctor's office.

"The urine test still says you're not pregnant," he told her. "But let's have a look anyway."

She was already lying on the examination table wearing a blue paper gown, her feet in the stirrups. The doctor flipped on the miner's light on his head and inserted the speculum in her vagina.

"Everything looks pretty normal here," he said. "Normal as in not pregnant."

Dawn hardly had opportunity for disappointment as a sharp stabbing pain took her breath away.

"What's this?"

"It's some kind of sore in my groin," Dawn told him. "It's been there for a month or more. I keep thinking it will go away."

There was a strange expression on the doctor's face.

"He wants to biopsy this thing at the top of my leg," she told Sonny later that night. "They must know we've got good insurance and they're going to get whatever they can out of it."

Sonny couldn't manage such cynicism.

"The doctor is just trying to be thorough," he said. "I'm sure it's a case of better safe than sorry."

"Well," Dawn admitted, "the good news is that they're cutting this awful knot out. It getting so bad it actually hurts just trying to walk upstairs."

Good news was something they didn't get.

The two of them sat across the desk from the doctor as he gave them the results.

"The mass was malignant," he said. "You have a disease called non-Hodgkin's lymphoma. It's a cancer of the lymphatic system. There are treatments. Chemotherapy, radiation. I'm going to transfer your case to an oncologist. She'll be better able to help you understand what is happening and what your options are."

"Chemotherapy?" Dawn said. "I can't have chemotherapy. I'm trying to have a baby. That couldn't be good for it."

"No," the doctor said. "I think you'll have to…to put off any plans of more children."

"For how long?" Dawn asked him. "I'm thirty-four, I can't wait forever."

The doctor looked at Sonny. The expression on his face sent an icy fear through his body. It was the same cold he'd felt as a rough tree sent a broken limb crashing in his direction.

"You'll have to wait," the doctor said. "Your disease, high-grade, large-cell lymphoma—it's very aggressive, very fast."

"It's fast," she said. "You mean it doesn't take long to get over it?"

"No, no, that's not what I mean at all." The doctor folded his hands as if he were praying and set them on the desk. He leaned forward slightly as if shortening the distance between them would somehow make the words easier to say.

"This is a very aggressive cancer. Prognosis for survival is not very good," he said. "About seventy percent live only six months to twelve months beyond diagnosis."

"What?" Sonny's fear solidified into near terror.

"I'm not an oncologist," he continued quickly. "But I think your chances may be better than that. We have caught it early. There are treatments, more treatments, better treatments every day."

Dawn didn't say another word. Sonny thanked the doctor, made arrangements with the receptionist for the appointment with the oncologist. Took the handful of pamphlets the nurse brought out to him. Dawn was completely silent until they got to the car.

"What about my girls?" she asked. "If I die, what will happen with my girls?"

"Don't worry about the girls," Sonny said. "I will take care of the girls. We've got to worry about you. We've got to take care of you."

She broke into tears then. He did, too. They sat in the cold, gray anonymity of the doctor's parking lot and grieved and cried and moaned with fear and anger and disbelief.

"Let's just drive, Sonny."

"Right, right," he said, gathering his composure. "We'll go home."

"No, I mean let's drive away," Dawn said. "We'll pick up the girls at school and then we'll just go. We'll head down the road wherever it takes us. We'll get away. Let's just get away, Sonny."

"Get away? Get away from what?"

"From this?"

"Dawn," he said. "We can't run from this. This comes with us. It's now part of us."

"I don't want to lose my girls, Sonny," she said. "I don't want to lose you."

"I don't want to lose you, either, baby. But we can't run, there is no where to run. We've got to stand here. We've got to fight."

"Fight?"

"We've got to fight for our lives," he said.

"Didn't you hear what he said?" Dawn asked him. "Seventy percent have a year or less."

"That means thirty percent have more," he told her. "Look, the doctor can give all the statistics in the world. But we are not statistics, Dawn, we're people, people with bodies that aren't carbon copies of anyone else's. Minds and experience that are uniquely ours. And life goals that we may not even be aware of. The doctor can give us a prognosis, Dawn, but he can't give us our destiny. It's not up to him or to us. We've just got to play it out. And if we do that together, well that's what life is, isn't it? Living the days we are given."

# REAL LIFE
## 36

———◆——◆———

Vern did his best to reassure us on the way to the hospital.

"It's not some new or terrible thing that's happened," he said. "And it's not something that the doctor's didn't expect. Her white count, the white blood cells in her body, got too low and the medicine she takes to boost it wasn't able to do enough."

"She passed out at the bus stop," Sierra said. "People thought she was a drunk or stoned. Nobody tried to help her. If some passerby hadn't decided to call 911 on her cell phone, I don't know what would have happened to her."

I glanced over at Vern. He was worried, but he seemed equally determined.

"We can't focus on how afraid we are, girls," he told us. "Fear is contagious and it's dangerous. Dawn is in the hospital now and she's doing fine. That's what we have to hang on to, the good that's around us, the successes, the triumphs. If you don't, it will drag you down. It will completely drag you down."

"That's what you told Grandma," I said.

"What?"

"When we first came here last spring," I said. "You told Grandma that she had to hold on to the good things about Sonny's life. And that Sierra and I are some of those good things."

Vern looked at me curiously.

"I don't remember saying that, but it's true," he said. "You girls are the best of Sonny's life. We are so lucky to have you here. To remind us every day of our wonderful son and to learn as much about you as we knew about him. And your mother is the one we have to thank for that. She brought you to Knoxville because even after everything that was said and done, she loves you more than she hated us."

"I don't think she hates you anymore," I said.

Vern nodded. "I don't think she does, either."

The inpatient floor of the hospital was new territory for us. We wove our way around corners and through corridors until we got to her room. It was all boring beige and mauve, wallpaper with stripes, but the sight of Mom's smile brightened it considerably.

Grandma had been sitting in the chair beside her, but she moved out of the way as soon as we walked in. Mom hugged us both.

"Can you believe this place?" she said to Sierra. "We've stayed in flea bag motels that had more style."

"Yeah, but they didn't have this equipment," Sierra said.

She checked Mom's lines, like she knew what she was doing. And asked questions about the blood and the medicines she was getting.

"Vern told you that I'm all right?"

That question was directed at me.

I nodded. "He said that it was just a low white count and that it's not that unusual."

"Right," Mom reassured me. "This last round of

chemo has knocked me back a bit. Look, I'm losing my growth of peach fuzz."

She rubbed her head and a little shower of quarter-inch-long hairs flew around her like a tiny hailstorm.

"My hair, my eyebrows, my toenails, it's bad enough to lose them all once," she said. "To lose them all over again, nobody told me about that. I don't think that part was in the rule book."

"I guess you're just making up your own rules," I said.

Mom laughed. "If I was making up my own, I'd insist on no more cancer, now or ever."

We sat and talked to her for quite a while. She was weak and it showed, but the blood would help and she was trying to act like it already had.

Sierra went with Vern and Phrona to get something to eat in the cafeteria. I stayed with Mom, but I felt more like I was guarding her. Allowing her to not talk, just rest. Not pretend to be well, just try to get that way.

I didn't think to bring a book with me, so I was forced to read one of Sierra's magazines with all the trials and tears of the rich and famous. Why don't we leave them alone, I thought. They're just trying to live their lives. Lives that, except for money and fame, are pretty much as ordinary and happy and uncertain as our own.

"Has your sister converted you? Next time I open my eyes you'll be watching soaps."

I glanced over at Mom.

"I wanted you to rest."

"At the risk of scaring my children, I'd have to say, 'I'll rest when I'm dead.'"

I reached over and took her hand.

"How was your day?"

"Fine."

"That's what you always say. You've got to come up with something more than that."

I smiled.

"Guess who I met today?"

"Who?"

"A man named Lonnie Beale."

"Ah...Lonnie," she said. "He was a nice guy."

"He still is," I told her. "He came by to see you. His daughter works at the courthouse and she told him you were back in town."

"Really? When I knew him, all his kids were still in high school."

"They're all out on their own now," I told her. "And he's retired. Or he's sort of retired. He works for the logger's union now."

"I didn't know the loggers even had a union," Mom said. "It was nice of him to come by."

"Yeah," I said, then hesitated for a moment. "Did you know that my father saved his life?" I asked.

Mom glanced over at me and then nodded.

"Yeah," she said. "He told me the day of the funeral."

"How come you never told me?"

She shrugged. "I don't know," she said. "I guess I thought that when I left this town I left all of that behind me. Sonny. The Lelands. My childhood. I thought I'd left everything here and I'd never have to come back and look at it again."

"But you did."

"I didn't have any choice," she said. "I got cancer. I would have run from that, too, but I was afraid that

I couldn't outrun it. And if I didn't, who would take care of you kids?"

I had known from the beginning that was why we were here. She knew she might die. And if she died, we'd have our grandparents. We wouldn't be just two more unwanted children bouncing around foster care. When it really counted, Sierra and I could count on her.

"Do you think my dad was a hero?" I asked.

"Oh, yes," she answered, without hesitation.

"So why didn't you tell us about how he died saving a man's life?"

Mom thought about that for a minute. "I guess I didn't think it would make any difference," she said. "Sonny was dead. The details weren't that important. Your dad was a wonderful, loving, caring man. He could be selfless when he needed to be. He could be selfish, as well. He wasn't a saint, Dakota. I didn't want you ever thinking he was anything other than a decent ordinary man getting along in the world the best he knew how."

"Do you think he sacrificed his life for Lonnie's?" I asked.

Mom took my hand in her own and looked at me intently. "I don't know," she told me. "But whether he deliberately saved Lonnie's life or stepped in front of him accidentally didn't change any of the truth about Sonny Leland."

"No, I guess it didn't," I agreed. "That's what Lonnie thinks, too. That it doesn't matter how he was saved. Why he was saved is what matters."

"Why he was saved?" Mom looked at me skeptically. "It was some kind of freak accident."

I nodded. "Yeah, but only one man was destined

to die there," I said. "That means there must have been some reason for one man to be destined to live."

She just looked at me. I knew she didn't get it.

"Do you know anything about the chaos theory, Mom?"

"It's that math game you play on the computer," she said. "Where you make all those cool pictures."

"It's actually kind of an idea about the universe," I told her. "I don't really understand it all that much, but it's like things happen sometimes for what seems like no reason."

Mom snorted and shook her head. "You got that right," she said.

"And once something happens, no matter how big it is or how small, it changes everything around it."

"Yeah."

"But ultimately, as the picture gets broader and broader, a pattern emerges."

"A pattern?"

"The pattern that was there all the time," I said.

"I hope this isn't 'things happen for a reason,' because you know I hate that."

"No, it's not that," I said. "It might even be the opposite of that. Some things may happen for no reason. And, big or small, that makes changes. It can make a lot of changes. So what we see in our lives as accident, happenstance, dumb luck, may truly be that. But that is not the end of it. In the long run, the universe and everything in it proceeds exactly as it was meant to all along."

I could tell that Mom wasn't getting it.

"Hydrogen and oxygen had to be present on this planet to create water," I explained. "On other plan-

ets they are either not available or not in the right
quantities or they're overwhelmed by the presence
of other elements. On Earth they both did happen to
be present so there was water and all life was possible because of that. But just because they both happened to be here in exactly the right quantities
doesn't mean that was our good luck and Jupiter's
bad luck."

"Then what does it mean?"

"That maybe the intention was for our planet to
have people and other ones not," I said.

"And that's not probability or fate or just
randomness?"

"There is no real random," I said. "What I'm
thinking is that if the chaos theory is right, once you
get enough perspective, a pattern, an order will be
obvious."

"That would have to be a pretty big perspective,"
Mom said.

"Yeah, when it comes to life, it's maybe an infinite
one," I said quietly.

"You're like talking about the mind of God,"
Mom said.

I shrugged. I thought it would sound too stupid
to say it aloud.

Mom looked at me for a very long time. She
reached out and smoothed my halfway grown-out
bangs out of my eyes and smiled.

"What's this I see?" she said, only a little above a
whisper. "My geeky science caterpillar has turned
into a philosophy butterfly."

"Yeah, one who's flapping her wings like crazy,
trying to change the weather," I said.

"So you think," she said, "that somehow each life has its place in the order of the universe. And that we should fulfill our destiny and trust that God has everything under control."

"I don't think I would have said it like that," I admitted. "But, yeah, Mom. I think that works."

She took my face in her hands and kissed me on the nose.

"How sure are you of that?" she asked.

"Mom, come on," I said. "I'm thirteen now. Don't you remember? Teenagers are sure of everything."

There was a light tap on the door.

"It's open!" Mom called out.

"Delivery for the hot chick on the ward," Del Tegge said as he came into the room carrying a huge bouquet of yellow roses.

He walked over to the side of Mom's bed and leaned over to give her a light kiss on the temple. He did it so casually, it had to have been something he'd done before.

"How are you feeling? I hope you're resting?"

She didn't answer his questions. She was too thrilled by the flowers. "These are beautiful!" Mom said. "How'd you know that yellow roses are my favorite? Did the girls tell you?"

She glanced at me accusingly. I shook my head.

"I didn't know," Del told her. "I was in the flower shop and I saw them and suddenly you just seemed like the yellow roses type."

"The yellow roses type?" she repeated. "Uh-oh." She turned to look at me. "I think Mr. Del Tegge has your mom figured out."

"Well, you've got him figured out, too," I said.

"Oh, yeah?" she asked.

"Do you know what Del's full name is?"

Mom shook her head.

"It's Delbert Spencer Tegge, *Jr.*" I emphasized the last.

Mom looked at me. Her eyes widened and then she laughed. She laughed like she hadn't laughed in months.

She turned to Del.

"Has anybody ever called you Sonny?" she asked.

# REAL LIFE

—▶ ◀—

*Five years later*

"It's amazing how different a church looks for a wedding than for a funeral," Vern said.

We were standing just off to the side in front of the extra congregation seating watching Phrona and Sierra as they made the final run-through of the decor. The flower arrangements were viewed from every angle. The elaborate candelabra on the chancel were cleaned, positioned and ready. The sconces that had been attached to the pews were already lit. Down the center aisle a white linen runner lay ready for a bride and her attendants.

"Don't be sad today, Gramps," I told him. "This is a happy day, a day to celebrate."

"I'm not sad," he assured me. "Memories still get ahold of me, I guess they always will. But I'm not sad. And I am celebrating."

"Good for you."

"I have so much to be grateful for," he said, a teasing smile turning up his lip. "I've got a wonderful wife, who only drives me crazy about forty-five percent of the time. A dog that believes that I retired for the sole purpose of devoting long walks to him. And two lovely granddaughters, the youngest of whom was just accepted to Duke."

"All right!" I said, giving myself a little cheer. "Go Blue Devils."

"Don't say that too loud," Vern cautioned. "We got twenty-eight thousand Vols fans a block away."

"I'm not a traitor," I assured him. "I've just got road trips somewhere in my genetic makeup."

"I'll bet you do," he said.

"Sierra, too," I pointed out. "Now that she's a big fashion mogul, probably planning jaunts to Paris and Rome."

My sister spoke up. "I'd take Atlanta if it was all expenses paid," she said. "Besides, somebody's got to buy clothes for the discount stores. Those people want fashion, too."

Vern and I shared a smile.

"A lucky man," he repeated. "I'm going to have two girls in college and I don't even have to pay for it."

"Thank God for that Brotherhood of Timber Workers Scholarship Fund."

He nodded.

"Of course," I pointed out, "this wedding could easily soak up all those savings."

Vern laughed. "It's the first wedding I ever paid for," he said. "But I'm hoping and praying it won't be my last."

He leaned over and kissed me on the nose.

"I'm telling you," he said. "I am a lucky man."

"You're going to be the man who held up the festivities if you don't get in there and get into your tux," Phrona told him.

She and Sierra had apparently tweaked, tucked and twiddled with everything in the sanctuary. They came up to join us.

"It only takes a minute for me to dress," Vern told us. "And besides, nobody, but nobody will cast an eye in my direction with all you lovely ladies in view."

Sierra giggled. "Gramps, you've got slicker lines than half the men in this town," she told him.

"And Sierra should know," I pointed out. "Since most of them have been used on her."

"That's just jealousy talking."

"Jealousy, along with everyone else," I teased.

"Come on, girls," Phrona said, glancing down at her watch. "We've got to get to the bride's room and get dressed. We haven't even had a crisis yet. And it's a law of nature that you can't have a wedding without a crisis."

"See you soon, Gramps."

We both kissed Vern and then hurried in Phrona's wake.

The bride's room was normally a music hall in the church's education addition. Today it was decorated in bright-yellow bridesmaid dresses and a gown of pure white.

Phrona was already dressed and checked her hair and makeup in the mirror, before helping the bride.

I stripped out of my blue jeans and T-shirt to struggle into panty hose. I didn't normally wear much makeup, but had gone to the trouble in honor of the occasion.

"You need some more blush," Phrona told me.

I glanced at my reflection. "More? Grandma are you sure? I already feel like a painted tart."

"In this yellow, you can't wear too much color," Sierra said.

Phrona nodded in agreement. Dutifully, I added more.

The years in Knoxville had improved my face and figure. I no longer looked like the awkward, unattractive duckling I'd been when we moved here. I would never be as pretty as my sister. But I had the fortunate genetics of two attractive parents. It was no longer a struggle for me to look at myself in the mirror.

The crisis my grandmother predicted did, in fact, occur when inexplicably the heel on Sierra's shoe broke off. At least she managed to catch herself on a chair rather than falling to perhaps break an ankle or leg.

After frantic cell phone calls to Sierra's network of fashionable gal pals, a pair of doable shoes were located and officially on their way. She relaxed a little bit, but didn't actually calm down until the new pair were on her feet.

I waited to put on my dress until the last moment, certain that I'd either wrinkle it, tear it or soil it. When I couldn't put it off a moment longer, I pulled the massively skirted yellow confection, an original Sierra Leland, over my head.

The mirror revealed a young, slightly slimmer version of Mrs. Butterworth.

"Did you forget to change your bra?" Sierra asked.

"Huh?"

"The push-up bra, you don't have on the push-up bra."

"I didn't buy one," I admitted.

"Dakota, what were you thinking?" she asked me. "You hardly have any ta-tas at all."

"I know that, you know that, everybody in Knoxville probably knows that. Wearing a bra to make it look otherwise wouldn't change a thing."

Sierra huffed, annoyed.

"Well, it would make the dress look better on you," she said.

"Nothing, Sierra," I assured her, "would make this dress look any better on me."

"Time to go, time to go," Phrona said. Her voice was high and excited as if she were as nervous as the rest of us.

We walked to the front vestibule. It was rarely used these days, as everyone preferred the convenience of the side entrance.

Vern was waiting, looking very distinguished and handsome in his tux.

"You look great, kid," he told me.

"You too, Gramps."

That was all I had time for. Keli Patrick, who was Jane Wickham's cousin's niece and the wedding coordinator, handed me my bouquet.

"Ouch!" I winced as I glanced down at the little bundle of yellow roses.

"Did you get a thorn?" Keli asked.

"Yes."

She quickly handed me a tissue and I managed to dab my injury before I got any of it on my dress.

"The florist is supposed to shave all those off," she said. "But no matter how careful they are, occasionally there'll be one that got missed."

"I think it's already stopped bleeding," I assured her.

"Well, keep the tissue, you may need it for tears anyway," she said.

The music began.

"Remember, head up, back straight, don't walk too fast. It's not a race," Keli said.

I nodded. But as they opened the door, it was all I could do to keep from running down the aisle.

"Go, go," Keli said. "And smile."

I began to walk forward. One step, another, another. The church was full and every eye was on me. Knox Villains my mom had once called them. Now they were our friends, our neighbors, even our family.

Smile, I remembered. This was a wonderful day. A fabulous day. A day I'd hoped for and prayed for and maybe never truly believed would happen.

Up ahead I caught sight of a very familiar face. Spence stood as tall as his dad now, but still had all the skinny awkwardness that was the definition of *age sixteen.* His tux was a perfect match for his father's but his hair was gel-spiked into the current style.

I reached the end of the linen runner, stepped up to the same level as Spence, but turned my back to him heading for the far left, where I stopped and stood facing the crowd.

Sierra was only half a church behind me. Her smile didn't look at all nervous or forced. She was bright, vivacious and oh so pretty. It shone from the inside out. And unlike me, she looked smashing in the thousand yards of yellow tulle skirt. She took her place at my side.

There was a moment of hesitation. A pause that

said everything about excitement and expectation and solemnity.

Then the organist began the wedding march.

There was Mom, on Vern's arm. Her natural brown curls flirted around her collarbone and were adorned only by the pin that held her pillbox hat in place. Her dress was straight cut, almost masculine, emphasizing the slim curves of her very feminine body.

I hadn't forgotten the years of sickness, the fear of death. Remission. Recurrence. More chemo. New chemo. Radiation. Bone marrow. The uncertainty was for Mom an ominous cloud that hangs over all of those who know it can happen to them. But today all of that was very far away. There was nothing inside Church Street Methodist but health and hope and future.

Mom still volunteered with CAVA, though she was hard-pressed for time these days. With the help of my grandparents, Mom had started college the year I started high school. With the ups and downs of her disease, she still had a way to go before graduation, but we all knew she was going to get there. It was just going to take time. And we thought, we hoped, we prayed, that she would have plenty of that.

But the groom hadn't wanted to wait any longer, he'd told her. There was never going to be a magic day when they knew for sure that all their worries would be over. They must grab for their future, worries and all, and refuse to let life be lost in the anticipation of it.

Mom had agreed. Sierra and I did, too.

"Who gives this woman to be married?" the minister asked.

"All of us who are her family," Vern answered.

Mom reached out and put her hand in Del's. It was a very small act. It altered the equation. Yet somehow I had the confidence now that things work out as they are meant to be.

**MIRA®**

From the bestselling author of *Her Mother's Shadow* and *Kiss River* comes a haunting tale of dangerous passions and dark family secrets....

# DIANE CHAMBERLAIN

Her family's cottage on the New Jersey shore was a place of freedom and innocence for Julie Bauer—until tragedy struck when her seventeen-year-old sister, Isabel, was murdered. It's been more than forty years since that August night, but Julie's memories of her sister's death still color her world, causing turmoil in all of her relationships.

Now an unexpected phone call from someone in her past raises questions about what really happened that night. Questions about Julie's own complicity. Questions about the man who went to prison for Isabel's murder—and about the man who didn't. Julie must harness the courage to revisit her past and untangle the shattering emotions that led to one unspeakable act of violence on the bay at midnight.

"Chamberlain adeptly unfolds layers of rage, guilt, longing, repression and rebellion, while gently preaching a message of trust and forgiveness. Complex, credible characterization..."
—*Publishers Weekly*
on *Her Mother's Shadow*

*Available the first week of February 2005, wherever books are sold!*

## The Bay At Midnight

**www.MIRABooks.com**

MDC2146

NEW YORK TIMES BESTSELLING AUTHOR

# HEATHER GRAHAM

## CHOREOGRAPHS A SEXY THRILLER OF PASSION AND MURDER....

Private investigator Quinn O'Casey thinks Lara Trudeau's overdose is a simple case of death by misadventure—until he goes undercover and learns that everyone who knew the accomplished dancer had good reason to want her dead. A drama of broken hearts, shattered dreams and tangled motives unfolds as fatal events begin to multiply—and only Quinn can stop the killing.

# DEAD ON THE DANCE FLOOR

## GRAHAM "WILL KEEP FANS TURNING THE PAGES."
### —PUBLISHERS WEEKLY ON PICTURE ME DEAD

*Available the first week of February 2005, wherever paperbacks are sold!*

**www.MIRABooks.com**

MHG2137

Emotions have reached
the boiling point....

# MARY LYNN
# BAXTER

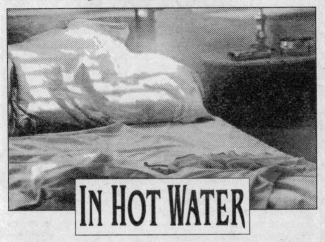

## IN HOT WATER

Married with a young son, Maci Malone Ramsey has a stable
and secure life…until her husband, a prominent physician, is
arrested in connection with the death of one of his patients. The
case against Dr. Seymour Ramsey appears rock solid—especially
when Maci learns of her husband's prescription drug habit. In
desperation, the couple calls in Seymour's estranged son, Holt,
a brilliant attorney. And Maci's world explodes. Two years ago,
Maci and Holt shared a night of unforgettable passion, never
learning each other's real names, never planning to see each
other again. Now they walk a tightrope of dizzying emotion and
divided loyalties—with Maci's future on the line.

"Taut and suspenseful, Baxter's contemporary tale is gripping."
—*Booklist* on *Pulse Points*

*Available the first week of February 2005, wherever paperbacks are sold!*

www.MIRABooks.com                                    MMLB2142

If you enjoyed what you just read,
then we've got an offer you can't resist!

# Take 2 bestselling novels FREE!
# Plus get a FREE surprise gift!

**Clip this page and mail it to MIRA®**

**IN U.S.A.**
3010 Walden Ave.
P.O. Box 1867
Buffalo, N.Y. 14240-1867

**IN CANADA**
P.O. Box 609
Fort Erie, Ontario
L2A 5X3

**YES!** Please send me 2 free MIRA® novels and my free surprise gift. After receiving them, if I don't wish to receive anymore, I can return the shipping statement marked cancel. If I don't cancel, I will receive 4 brand-new novels every month, before they're available in stores! In the U.S.A., bill me at the bargain price of $4.99 plus 25¢ shipping and handling per book and applicable sales tax, if any*. In Canada, bill me at the bargain price of $5.49 plus 25¢ shipping and handling per book and applicable taxes**. That's the complete price and a savings of over 20% off the cover prices—what a great deal! I understand that accepting the 2 free books and gift places me under no obligation ever to buy any books. I can always return a shipment and cancel at any time. Even if I never buy another The Best of the Best™ book, the 2 free books and gift are mine to keep forever.

185 MDN DZ7J
385 MDN DZ7K

| | |
|---|---|
| Name | (PLEASE PRINT) |
| Address | Apt.# |
| City | State/Prov.     Zip/Postal Code |

*Not valid to current The Best of the Best™, Mira®, suspense and romance subscribers.*

*Want to try two free books from another series?*
*Call 1-800-873-8635 or visit www.morefreebooks.com.*

\* Terms and prices subject to change without notice. Sales tax applicable in N.Y.
\*\* Canadian residents will be charged applicable provincial taxes and GST.
  All orders subject to approval. Offer limited to one per household.
® and ™are registered trademarks owned and used by the trademark owner and or its licensee.

BOB04R            ©2004 Harlequin Enterprises Limited

# MIRABooks.com

## We've got the lowdown on your favorite author!

☆ Read an excerpt of your favorite author's newest book

☆ Check out her bio

☆ Talk to her in our Discussion Forums

☆ Read interviews, diaries, and more

☆ Find her current bestseller, and even her backlist titles

### All this and more available at

# www.MiraBooks.com

MEAUT1R3

# PAMELA
# MORSI

| | | |
|---|---|---|
| 32011 SUBURBAN RENEWAL | ___ $5.99 U.S. | ___ $6.99 CAN. |
| 66656 LETTING GO | ___ $6.99 U.S. | ___ $8.50 CAN. |
| 66884 DOING GOOD | ___ $6.99 U.S. | ___ $8.50 CAN. |

*(limited quantities available)*

| | |
|---|---|
| TOTAL AMOUNT | $ _____ |
| POSTAGE & HANDLING | $ _____ |
| ($1.00 FOR 1 BOOK, 50¢ for each additional) | |
| APPLICABLE TAXES* | $ _____ |
| TOTAL PAYABLE | $ _____ |

*(check or money order—please do not send cash)*

To order, complete this form and send it, along with a check or money order for the total above, payable to MIRA Books, to: **In the U.S.:** 3010 Walden Avenue, P.O. Box 9077, Buffalo, NY 14269-9077; **In Canada:** P.O. Box 636, Fort Erie, Ontario, L2A 5X3.

Name: _____
Address: _____ City: _____
State/Prov.: _____ Zip/Postal Code: _____
Account Number (if applicable): _____
075 CSAS

*New York residents remit applicable sales taxes.
*Canadian residents remit applicable GST and provincial taxes.

**MIRA®**

www.MIRABooks.com

MPM0205BL